MURDER BY ANY OTHER NAME

MURDER BY ANY OTHER NAME

JANET G. BRANTLEY

MURDER BY ANY OTHER NAME
Janet G. Brantley
ISBN – 13: 978-1502537-41-6
ISBN – 10: 1-502537-419
Copyright ©2014 by Janet G. Brantley

This is a work of fiction. Names, characters, and incidents are all products of the author's imagination or are used for fictional purposes.

For my husband, Bill, who has been at my side for the past 47 years. But who's counting?

ACKNOWLEDGMENTS

I am deeply indebted to the friends and family who encouraged me to pursue my dream of writing – and a special thank you to my cousin, Shawn Elizabeth Nelson, who read my first (very) rough draft and ordered: "Finish this book, refine it, and sell it for a million dollars." Two out of three isn't bad.

Many thanks to those who helped me with the technical aspects of writing about a real place and actual law enforcement agencies. It's not so simple, I found, to corral characters who choose to work for the Mississippi Department of Public Safety, the Harrison County Sheriff's Department, the Jackson County Sheriff's Department, the Ocean Springs Police Department, and the Biloxi Police Department – all with overlapping or back-to-back jurisdictions.

Thanks especially to Captain Drew Balius, Watch Commander for the Biloxi Police Department's Patrol Division, for his insights into law enforcement protocols on the Mississippi Gulf Coast. I would also like to thank Debbie Quinn, former dispatcher for Harrison County. Over dinner at Wasabi one night, Debbie shared information that helped me avoid numerous mistakes, thereby strengthening the story. And thank you to staff of the Harrison County Sheriff's Department who answered a number of questions I'd be willing to bet they had never been asked before.

My beta readers proved to be more than up to the job of taking me to task over unclear areas in my plot. Thank you Shawn E. Nelson, Erica Williams, and Willa Brantley. Thanks to my husband Bill, who found several typos everyone else had missed! I am grateful to my grandson, Keaton Brantley, who listened intently to my "pitch" and then asked perceptive questions that steered me in the right direction more than once.

I also want to thank some very special online writers' groups to which I belong: Jeff Goins's My 500 Words group, which kept me on task as I finished my first draft; The Originals (a spinoff of the early My 500 Words group); and Janie Sullivan at the Center for Writing Excellence. I offer a heartfelt thank you to my writing sisters at The Cloisters (excellent writers all). An extra-large "Thank You!" to Laura Scott, Willa Brantley, and Roslynn Pryor for their excellent technical suggestions.

MURDER BY ANY OTHER NAME

Chapter 1

SOMETHING WAS COMING, but I didn't know what, and that not knowing had sent me here this evening after work – to the beach in Ocean Springs, where I could watch the balloon of golden sun setting over toward Texas. I had parked Bernice, my little red Beetle, in one of the pull-offs, taken off my sandals, grabbed a quilt, and set out to find the perfect spot to watch another of our glorious sunsets.

On this Thursday afternoon, I needed solitude, though I wasn't sure why. My day at work at the Mississippi Emergency Management Agency had been easy and without controversy. This didn't feel like it had anything to do with work, anyway. The person on my mind, the one who'd been on my mind all day, was Richie.

I stepped out onto the toasty sand, enjoying the feel of it squishing between my toes, and headed west down Front Beach, our relatively quiet little piece of sand across the Bay Bridge from Biloxi. Reaching an empty spot, I dropped my quilt in a heap and strolled down to the water's edge, where I could step off into the cool sand, damp from the incoming surf. The waves were gentle this afternoon, so gentle dozens of fiddler crabs were skittering in and out of the water as the tide moved ever closer to their temporary homes.

These tiny, almost translucent creatures with one giant claw always amazed and amused me. I bent over to watch one industrious denizen of the beach racing up the sand to burrow out a new home – only to have the next wave crash on top of him. His home was swept out from over him, and he scurried a bit farther inland, burrowing in again, acting for all the world as if he believed the previous wave had surely been the last one.

"You poor little devil," I said. "You just never learn the lesson, do you? Sometimes we humans don't learn our lessons, either."

At the sound of my voice, a noisy flock of seagulls swooped down, circling about my head demanding sustenance. "Feed me!" they all shouted in unison, reminding me of the carnivorous plant in "The Little Shop of Horrors." I waved an arm, trying to shoo the pesky birds away so I could have the peace and quiet I craved this afternoon.

When the flock finally decided they'd probably do better elsewhere, I meandered back to my quilt, shook it out in the evening breeze, and laid it back onto the warm sand, settling myself on top of it. I was glad my work clothes were casual – brown capris, a beige Henley shirt with our agency's name, and a cap with matching logo. As usual, my longish, straight black hair was caught up in a high ponytail I'd pulled through the opening at the rear of the cap. For all of my twenty-eight years, I admit I still looked more like a teenager than a twenty-eight year old.

I had felt progressively more anxious as the afternoon wore on, and now, sitting quietly, my mind raced with possible reasons for my unease. The women in my mother's family were known for their premonitions. Aunt Bess had a vision of Uncle Joe lying on a sidewalk, not moving – just a few hours before she got a call from his work place telling her he'd been taken to the hospital with an apparent heart attack. By the time she got there, he was already dead. That's just one instance; there have been more.

Sometimes we just get a "feeling" something weird is on the way. And it doesn't even have to be something bad. We might have a thought out of the blue that someone we haven't seen in a long while is nearby, and then the phone or doorbell will ring and there they'll be. This can be a worrisome experience, this seeming glimpse into the near future. My brother Richie just makes fun of Mom and me when we talk about things like that.

"You women are really something, you know that?" he said to us last year after we compared notes and found we'd both had dreams about my cousin Glynnis up in Oklahoma. But we had the last laugh, because Glynnis phoned the next day to tell me she was coming down for a visit the next week.

I guess what was causing me so much uneasiness this afternoon was that I kept thinking of Richie, which made me worry that he was in greater danger than usual. I didn't think I'd be able to stand it if something happened to him. He's my big brother, and he's always looked out for me, despite his penchant for laughing at my many hang-ups.

And I have lots of those. I have occasional anxiety attacks that've been known to put me on the phone at two in the morning calling Richie, just so he can talk to me while I wait for my "two beer pill" to take effect. That's what I call my anti-anxiety medication. Richie never ever laughs at me when I call in a panic, heart racing, hardly able to control my tears enough to let him know what has set me off this time. Last time I called about three in the morning. Richie took the phone downstairs and started chatting about the last movie he'd seen, and describing the antics of his four-year-old son, Owen, at his T-ball practice. God, I love my brother.

I stretched out my legs and leaned back on my elbows, breathing deeply of the salty air, so tangy, so sea-weedy, so heavenly. I couldn't imagine having been born and raised in some place like Arizona, with its wide open skies and stark landscape. I'd traveled through the southwest several times and I always felt like I was in some magical, otherworldly place – but I sure wouldn't want to live there. Too dry. Too hot. Too... Well, just too. That's all.

I really did appreciate the colors of the sunsets in the desert, the purples, pinks, blues, and grays that painted streaks across the sky from horizon to horizon. I thought of them now, as the sun began to slide toward the horizon and we had a few of our own multi-hued streaks above. The orb itself was a burnished gold, but just before it disappeared, it glowed a red almost the hue of blood, and that old Tanya Tucker song drifted into my mind: "That Georgia Sun Was Blood Red and Going Down."

Now what had made me think of that? I reached into my pocket and pulled out my cell phone. Tapping on the picture of a smiling Richie – he was always smiling – in his deputy's uniform, I put the phone to my ear and waited for him to answer. When I heard his deep, soft voice, I swallowed the lump I hadn't even realized had formed in my throat.

"Hey, how's my favorite brother?" I asked, struggling to keep the husky sound from my voice. The question was an old joke between us.

"Your *only* brother is just fine, hon. And how's my favorite sis?" I could feel the smile in his voice.

"Well, your *only* sister is doing well this beautiful afternoon."

"Is that gulls squawking in the background? You hangin' out at the beach again?"

"Best way I know of to end a day. The only things that would make it any better would be a big pitcher of margaritas and a handsome guy to pour them for me."

"You're incorrigible, Becca," he chuckled. But when you decide you mean it, I have a buddy just getting settled here in town and he doesn't know many people. Just say the word…"

"Whoa! I just want someone to *pour margaritas*," I protested, "not someone to spend the rest of my life with. And don't even say you didn't have that in mind." This, as I cut him off before he could protest I had the wrong idea. We'd been down this road before. A few times.

"Okay, okay. But I'm serious. I really need you to help me out, help me get him situated and introduced to some nice ladies."

"I don't know any nice ladies," I said, giggling. "How about if I just introduce him to Valerie at work?" I waited for the explosion, which wasn't long in coming.

"Hell, no!" Richie sputtered. "You told me yourself she's a dingy bitch. Why would you want to inflict someone like her on one of my best friends?"

"You didn't say he was one of your best friends," I pointed out. "When you say 'buddy,' I just assume you're talking about an acquaintance, not someone you're really close to."

"No, he's a great guy. Damian and I go back a long way. We went through the police academy together, and we got our first job together up in Jackson. We even got to work as partners for a while before I left to move back home."

"Oh, Damian! You should have said who it was. I remember you talking about him. He does sound like a really good guy. I'm sorry I suggested we introduce him to Valerie. Surely we can do better than that."

Richie laughed, and I heard relief in his voice. "Seriously, sis, I do want to help him get settled. He's coming off a bad break-up, and I'm not trying to set him up with anybody. But I also don't want him to just sit in his apartment watching ESPN every night. Surely there can be something in between."

"Maybe so," I said uncertainly. In my experience relationships between the sexes are seldom "in between."

"So, what's really up with you? You don't usually call me this time of day. Sure you're okay?"

"Absolutely," I answered, perhaps a bit too quickly. "I'm just sitting here watching the sunset and thought I'd give you a call, just to say hello. That's okay, isn't it? Am I interrupting anything? You and Justine getting frisky?"

"Not hardly. Owen and I just got back from T-ball practice, and he's passed out in front of the TV. Man, he's doing great at practice. You'd think he was born knowing how to play baseball. He's gonna be so ready for Fall Ball this year."

"Spoken like a proud dad," I said, thinking what a *good* dad Richie was. He was working the night shift for the next three months, just so he could pick Owen up from daycare and get him to ball practice and see all his games. Richie also helped to coach Owen's team, the Panthers. Owen was a miniature version of his daddy – sturdy and serious, sandy-haired and tanned, always smiling, always giving. Thank goodness he doesn't seem to take after his mother.

"Give him a hug for me, okay? I'd better go so I can get my stuff packed up before bedtime. I need to get home and fix myself something to eat."

"You be careful, Becca. Watch out for the panhandlers." We did have occasional panhandlers, what with all the casinos scattered up and down our coast.

"I will. You be careful tonight, too, okay Richie?" I tried my best to keep the worry out of my voice.

"You betcha. Love you, Sis."

"Love you too, big guy." I closed my phone and stood, picking up my quilt and shaking as much sand out of it as I could. "Please be extra careful tonight, Richie," I whispered. "Please don't let this premonition come true."

I drove home with a sense of dread, not sure why but sure it was there, and the hours crept by. Finally about ten I decided to turn in…but my mind wouldn't shut down, and I was soon roaming the house again. I went downstairs to the kitchen for a glass of water and then made myself get back in bed. I finally dropped off into a restless sleep about midnight.

***

The sound of Joe Walsh's intricate guitar work on "Hotel California" jarred me awake and I grabbed for my cell phone before I even got my eyes open. What time was it anyway? The phone read 1:38 in the morning. I hit the green button reluctantly, realizing too late I didn't recognize the number. Just habit to always answer.

"Hello?" I said, my voice still thick with sleep.

"Rebecca? Is this Rebecca McCallum?" a gravelly voice asked.

"Yes. Who is this?"

"This is Police Chief James Sikes. I'm a friend of your folks, and we've talked a few times at the law enforcement picnics."

My heart jumped into my throat and I had to swallow before I could speak again. Only one reason he would be calling me now. My throat tightened convulsively, my voice coming out in a croak. "What is it, Chief? What's happened to Richie?" Part of me didn't want to hear his response, but another part wanted to know so I could get to my brother and help him.

"Rebecca, I'm sorry to have to tell you this, but Richard was involved in an accident tonight. He's been taken to County General Hospital, and I need to come and get you right away."

"No need, Chief. I'll be ready in five minutes and I can get there faster on my own." No way would I wait around for the man to drive across town to get me.

"I don't think that would be such a good idea," he responded. "You don't need to be driving when you're upset. And don't worry, I won't slow you down." He paused. "In fact, I'm sitting in your driveway right now."

I sprang out of bed and pulled back the linen curtain to peer outside. Dark as it was, I could see the police chief's car. A fluttering began in my stomach. This must really be serious.

"I'll be right out, Chief. Thanks." What was wrong with me? I prided myself on being strong and independent. But I was neither of those things where my brother was concerned.

I turned on a lamp and grabbed the first clothes I saw. That's how I came to be seen on the local news wearing my MEMA work clothes I had just stepped out of a few hours ago. I grabbed my purse and keys and flew down the stairs to the front door. Sikes stood there as if about to knock. The light from the hallway illuminated the haggard lines on his face. When our eyes met, I felt my knees buckle. "Is he…?" I couldn't form the word.

"He's alive – just barely. They were taking him into surgery when I left to come over here. He's hurt pretty bad, Rebecca. He took a gunshot wound to the head. That's about all I know," he sighed.

I sucked in my breath and the tears came, hard as I tried to keep them back. I blinked a few times, fast. *Not his gorgeous face.* I pulled the door shut behind me, making sure it was locked. "Let's go," I ordered. "You can tell me more on the way."

I ran around to the passenger's side of the hulking black Crown Victoria and jerked the door open before Sikes had made it to the end of the walkway. Sliding into the seat I threw my purse on the floor and strapped on the seat belt, then sat there fidgeting as he made the same methodical preparations for driving I'm sure he makes each time he gets into the car. *C'mon, c'mon.* As Chief of Police, he didn't often have to use his warning devices, but now he slammed them into place. I managed not to ask any more questions until he had backed out of the drive, turned on the siren and lights, and we were speeding off into the night.

The sedan's combined scents of Old Spice and leather polish reminded me of my dad, and I swallowed a few times trying not to cry again. I wondered if I should call my parents. They couldn't get here from Key West quickly, whatever happened, and it was the middle of the night. No, best to wait. *Hold on, Richie.* I kept mouthing the words, making no sound. Finally I could take the silence no longer. I stole a look at Chief Sikes, his craggy face in profile, muscles working in his jaw, as he concentrated on his driving – he was just about my dad's age. Traffic was light. With luck we'd be at the hospital in ten minutes.

The rising moon cast its light over the Sound, and as we crossed the long, curving bridge from Ocean Springs into Biloxi, I stared at the bits of moonlight bright as diamonds sparkling on the waves. My eyes watered, whether from the glitter or from tears, or both, I wasn't sure.

"Chief, what happened? You said Richie was shot? How did it happen? Where was he?"

"They say it got pretty crazy out there tonight. There's still a lot we don't know. But I'll give it my best shot." He winced. "I'm sorry. I didn't mean to say that."

"Doesn't matter. Just tell me. Where did it happen? And *what* happened? Was it a robbery or drugs?"

"Slow down, girl. I will tell you what I know. Most important, they got the guy who did it. He didn't get away."

"What? They caught him?"

The chief swung into the left lane to pass a couple of cars and we sped on our way.

"Guess you could say that. He's dead."

"Good!" Anybody who tried to take my big brother out deserved to be dead. "What else?"

"Well, Richard was on patrol up at the north end of the county tonight, up near Saucier. The Sheriff's office had a call come in about midnight from a person who reported someone trying to break into their house. Dispatcher put out a call, and Richard was in the area and took the call. Apparently he followed a suspicious vehicle, found it stopped, and called it in. The truck was stolen, so he said he would wait for another officer to arrive.

"After that point, things get a little murky," he continued. "The next call that came in just gave the location, the officer down code, the request for certain equipment."

"So, who made that call, if Richie had already been…?"

"Another deputy, Paul Simmons."

"Oh! I know Paul. Was he hurt?"

"He's okay. He reported shots fired *after* Richard was hit, but as far as we know the only person hit in that exchange was the suspect who'd been driving the suspicious truck."

"What do you know about the guy who shot Richie?"

In his gravelly drawl, the Chief said, "Now Rebecca, it is just way too early for us to go speculating about what went on out there, away from everything like it was. The place is really isolated. At this point you really know all I know. So let's just hold off on the questions, okay? There are at least two teams of investigators out there working the scene."

"All right, but it's hard – I just want to know everything."

"There is one more thing." He paused. "It appears Richard was shot with his own gun."

That brought me up short. How on earth could that have happened? I asked as much.

"I can't tell you that yet," the Chief replied.

I looked up as he turned into the hospital parking lot.

"Oh, thank God. Here's the hospital!" I said. Other questions could wait.

Sikes pulled into a police parking spot near the emergency exit and we opened our car doors at the same time. That's when I remembered – Richie had worked under Sikes when he first came back to Biloxi and joined the police force, after working in Jackson for five years and before he moved to the Sheriff's Department a couple of years ago. Sikes was the commander Richie had respected most.

"Chief Sikes, this has got to be hell for you, too, since you know Richie so well."

"Yes, and that's why I insisted on being the one to tell you – that's what your dad would want me to do."

I nodded once and got out of the car. I hesitated for just a second before slamming the car door. *Please, God, don't take him away from me.*

Chapter 2

CHIEF SIKES TURNED TOWARD ME as we neared the entrance. "Now Rebecca, I know you're not prepared for this, but remember there are lots of other people who care about Richard, too. It's pretty crowded in there."

I hadn't thought of that, but I nodded. "It's okay."

We walked into a scene from a movie: a sea of blue and black uniforms, with people huddled in small groups. I thought I must know many of these people, but to me that's what they were – just people, no faces, because I couldn't make myself look at anyone. I didn't want their pity; I just wanted my brother.

I turned to Sikes. "Where do I go?"

He led me over to the receptionist, and I finally had to look up. I felt my skin prickling, and the hairs on my arms stood at attention. It was Sandy, younger sister of my ex-boyfriend, Mark Barrington. I hadn't seen Sandy since Mark broke up with me more than a year before.

"Becca, I'm so sorry about this," she said, her puppy dog brown eyes glistening with unshed tears. "If there's anything at all I can do, let me know."

I gave a brief nod to acknowledge her words of support. Then I thought about what she'd said and how she'd said it. She made it sound as if Richie was already dead. But that just couldn't be.

"Thanks, Sandy. I just want to see my brother. Is he still in surgery, or have they moved him to recovery?"

"Honey, I think I'd better take you back to the family room. Justine's already there, and the doctor will speak with you soon." I didn't like the sound of her voice, too quiet and soothing.

A chill shot through my body then, beginning as a crawling in my scalp, vibrating down my neck and shoulders to my spine, weakening my legs, then my ankles...at which point I felt myself melt toward the floor. I landed with my back against the desk, knees drawn up protectively. Chief Sikes and Sandy dropped down to the floor with me immediately, one on each side. I shook my head from side to side, willing all of this to go away.

"No, no, no," I murmured. I kept repeating that one word, using my voice to stave off what I was afraid I'd hear if I ever stopped. I wanted to be anywhere but here, here with all these cops who were even now leaning into each other's arms, tears flowing down their faces like rain on a windowpane during a coastal thunderstorm.

"C'mon, Becca. Let's get you up," Sikes said, and I heard the pain softening his usually gruff voice. "Sandy, where's this family room?"

"This way, Chief." She led us down the hall, made a right turn, and opened a door. I felt like I'd been kicked in the stomach, but I made myself hold my head up as we walked in, knowing my sister-in-law was waiting. Justine had her back to the room, staring out the window into the blackness. Her friend Clarissa had her arm around Justine's shoulders, but Justine drew away from her and turned to face us. To face me.

Justine's complexion, always fair, had no color at all. Her usually sparkling brown eyes were swollen from crying and she clutched a wad of tissues in one hand. "Oh, Rebecca," she said, rushing across the room toward me. "Please tell me it can't be true. He can't be gone."

"I don't *know*, Justine. I just got here. Nobody's told me anything. Where is he? Have you seen him? How did this happen?" It seemed I couldn't stop asking questions; then all of a sudden I did stop. I stared at her...waited...held my breath...finally heard the words she'd said.

"The door was open a few minutes ago, and I heard some nurses talking. They said Richard didn't make it – through the surgery, I mean – but I just can't believe it. There must be some mistake. Tell them, Rebecca! Go find out!"

We'd been left alone in the room, except for Clarissa, and I looked around helplessly. The door creaked as Sandy held the door for someone in green scrubs. He hesitated, then nodded to us. "Which of you is Mrs. McCallum?" he asked as he hurried in.

Justine stepped forward. "I am. Are you Richard's doctor?"

"I'm Robert Chessman," he said, nodding and reaching to shake her hand. I looked at his long, slim fingers, wondering absently if they had just been on my brother. "I'm a surgeon here at County General. Do you have other family here?"

"I'm his sister," I said, joining them.

He nodded. "Mrs. McCallum, please. Why don't the two of you come over here and have a seat?" He gestured toward a seating area where a green sofa with sagging cushions, a large overstuffed chair, and several waiting room-type chairs huddled, giving off an air of sadness. I wondered how many families had been led to these seats before us.

"Dr. Chessman," I said, dropping into one of the hard chairs, "please tell us what's going on."

The doctor sat down across from me after he motioned Justine to the cushy chair. "Mrs. McCallum, I'm sorry to have to tell you, but we lost your husband. We took Captain McCallum into surgery just over an hour ago, but we barely got started with exploratory when his vitals shut down. He didn't make it. I'm very sorry."

I stared at him. How do doctors get through things like this? I stood and retreated to the other side of the room. When I turned back I saw it in his eyes – the hurt, the sense of failure, the anger, even. *So it's still tough on him, too.*

"Your husband's injuries were so severe that we had little hope of being able to save him, but we tried. We really tried," he said to Justine. "I know it's hard for you to accept that. Head wounds are always tricky, and his was in an unusual location. You're likely to have questions for me, and my door will be open whenever you want to come by. I don't know how much help I can be, but I'll do what I can." He stood and placed a hand lightly on Justine's shoulder, which was vibrating from her sobs. She had not said one word.

At his touch, the shaking stopped and she looked up at him. Then she patted his hand before letting her pale one drop listlessly back into her lap. "Thank you, Doctor," she whispered.

I added my thanks to hers, wondering why I found it necessary to thank the man who had just taken my brother away from me. The rational part of my brain recognized the unfairness of that thought, but my heart wasn't ready to accept any of it. A war raged inside me, and I had a fleeting thought there might be nothing left of me when the war was over.

The doctor opened the door, paused for a moment, and said, "You can see him in a little while, after we move him to a private area for you." Then he hung his head and walked out. Sandy and Chief Sikes came in as he left. I couldn't help myself. I launched myself at the Chief, startling him. I threw my arms around his waist. "I want my daddy," I said against his chest. He gathered me awkwardly into a huge bear hug, and we stood there for a minute, swaying and sobbing together.

"I'll go call your parents myself," he said, wiping the wetness from his face with the back of his hand. Then he reached into a back pocket, pulled out a handkerchief, and handed it to me. "Do you have their number in Key West?" I fumbled in my purse for my phone, scrolled to the right spot and handed it to him. He released me and I was swamped with a feeling of being more alone than I'd ever been. He gave Justine a hug as well, dabbed at his eyes once more, and walked out of the room, shoulders drooping dejectedly.

***

By 3:30 a.m., we were almost ready to leave the hospital. Justine and I were ushered into the room where Richie's body lay covered in a white sheet. We both insisted on seeing him one last time. I knew Justine must be like me; I had to see for myself what had been done to him. I wish to God I hadn't. He had been cleaned up a bit, and most of his sweet face looked as it always had, but his skin was already gray and cold and dry. When I came closer, I saw not much of the rear of his head was left. I sucked in my breath, vowing not to be sick. I heard Justine retching behind me and turned to try to comfort her.

"I can't do this!" I could hear the trembling in her voice even though she was whispering. "I can't do this, Richard. I can't let you go."

I laid my hand on his left cheek. "Oh, Richie," I whispered, "how could you let this happen? You're supposed to be invincible. That's what I always thought. Why'd you have to prove me wrong?"

I turned back to Justine. She and I had our differences, but this was no time to think of that. Right now neither of us had anyone else but each other, not family at least. We held each other and cried until it seemed we must surely have used up all our tears. Heads together, we looked over at Richie's body, so stiff and unyielding, so unlike the man we'd known and loved.

"How am I going to tell Owen?" she asked. "How do I tell him his daddy's never coming home again?"

"I don't know, but you won't have to tell him by yourself. It's up to us to give him the love his daddy can't give him now," I said. "You ready? I have to get out of here."

She nodded, her dark curls falling across her face. At five foot two, she was half a head shorter than I, and I felt like an Amazon next to her. I used to tease Richie about his "little woman." "What you want with a skinny dame like her?" I asked once. "You do know I could take her out with one sharp blow, don't you?" That was perhaps an exaggeration, but both Richie and I were exercise nuts, and I knew I had lots more muscles than Justine. Right now I was wishing she had a little more of my toughness. Who was I kidding? I wasn't feeling so tough just now. Justine, Owen, and I – all our worlds had just spun out of orbit, and I didn't know if any of us would survive.

***

Sitting in the consultation room alone, waiting for Justine to go through mandatory paperwork, I thought back to yesterday afternoon at the beach. This chain of events had been set in motion for me when I'd found myself headed there rather than home after work. I went back over my thoughts and actions. *Could I have done anything to stop this from happening? Should I have told Richie I was freaked out, and why? Would he perhaps still be alive if I had? Or would he simply have laughed at me again?*

Now my premonition had been made manifest. I laid my arms on the table, put my forehead against them, and let my tears fall. *Sit up Becca. You can't let them see you like this. You need to be strong for Justine.* Was that my voice, or was it Richie's? I sat up and reached for a tissue, blotted my eyes, blew my nose. It seemed I could hear Richie's little-boy voice saying, "Officer Richard McCallum reporting in, Sheriff," and Mom's serious reply: "Yes, sir, duly noted sir! Be at ease, Deputy." *Oh, Mom...how are you going to take this news? And Dad, can you be strong enough for the both of you? I need you here. I need you to get back home.*

What was I supposed to tell them? It seemed nobody knew what had happened to my brother. But "I don't know" wasn't going to be good enough. I still knew little about how this had all transpired, but I vowed to myself I would find out the truth no matter what.

Justine came into the room followed by Chief Sikes and I hoped he might have more information by now. Justine and I sat down on the ratty sofa and the Chief chose a chair facing us. He sighed. "This is one of the hardest days of my career," he began. Over the next few minutes, he laid out all he knew so far about what had happened, which wasn't much.

He'd already told me some of this, but I was listening closely now, trying to glean a few more details. He said Richie had been on his routine patrol up near Saucier in northern Harrison County when Dispatch relayed a call about a prowler. Two deputies were out on patrol, but Richie was much closer so he responded. He radioed in a few minutes later to say he'd seen a suspicious truck and was in pursuit. He called again about two minutes after that to say he had found the truck abandoned and would wait for the second officer to respond. That was Richie's last communication.

When the second deputy, Paul Simmons, arrived, he found Richie in his patrol car. Dispatch had just sent word the truck was stolen. They discussed the situation: The truck sat near an old barn and they thought the suspect might be inside. They split up and Richie went around back while Paul covered the front. Paul then heard a shout and a shot, ran around to the back of the barn, and found Richie lying in a pool of blood, his service revolver near his head. It was splattered with blood.

He ran to his car and called for assistance, and then saw the suspect jump into the truck and try to start it. The guy stuck a pistol out the window and fired but missed Paul, who then returned fire and killed the suspect.

"Who was it who killed my husband?" Justine asked, her face pinched and her eyes dull. "Just tell me that."

"I can't give you a name yet, Justine. I'm sorry. We still have to locate and identify his next of kin. And it's Sheriff Bixby's place to make any kind of announcement."

"I don't give a damn about his next of kin. I want to know his name."

"What does that matter?" I asked, finally pushed beyond the point of staying quiet. "He killed my brother and now he's dead. That's all I care about. It's hard enough, losing Richie. Can you imagine how much harder it would be if his killer were still out there on the loose?"

She shuddered, then seemed to collect herself, giving the Chief a forced smile. "You're right, I'm sure."

"Now, I think y'all should think about going home." He handed Justine a sheet of paper. Here's a list of Richard's things – you can get them later, after the investigation is complete." Justine took the paper and stared at it for a long moment. "Can we go now? Clarissa is going to drive me home."

"I'm more than ready," I said. "But you realize the hospital is full of Richie's friends and people he worked with? We have to acknowledge them in some way."

She shuddered again, and I figured she was almost in a state of shock. "I don't want to see them," she spat. "They're like a bunch of vultures."

"Justine!" I protested. "These people love Richie – loved him," I corrected myself. "You know the officers and emergency response people are all like family. They just want to help."

Her smile was lifeless, her eyes empty. "You're right," she said. "I don't know what I'm saying."

"Well, of course you don't." I put my arm around her. "Come on. We can do this together." We walked out of the family room and down the hall, ready to face Richie's colleagues.

Chapter 3

EXCEPT WE WEREN'T READY. The grief coming from the waiting room was palpable. Sadness and misery hung over the place like an early morning fog lying just off the coast, thick and cloying and inescapable, waiting to envelop anything that moved.

For the next half hour we were hugged and cried over, and cried with, by dozen of officers and staff members. It seemed as if half the town must be there, seemed they must be coming in one door and going out another, shoved through by others wanting, needing to take their places.

I was standing near Chief Sikes and the Assistant Chief of Police when I felt a sudden stillness envelop the room. What now, I thought. I looked up to see people beginning to follow each other's gazes toward the outside door. I stepped past the Chief to see what was going on: Paul Simmons had just entered the hospital. My guts clenched; so did my fists. *What's he doing here? Should he even be here? Has he already been released by the investigators?*

He stood still for a long moment, taking in the room full of people now staring at him. I studied his appearance – he wore jeans and a white t-shirt instead of his uniform. *Of course, his uniform is probably soaked in Richie's blood.* He was of slight build, about five ten and wiry, with the shaved head so popular among his peers. He had a slightly receding chin that made him appear weak, but I doubted he was. His expression had been very much hang-dog when he arrived, but as he began to get a true feel for the animosity being trained on him, he seemed to reach a decision. He stood straighter, squared his shoulders, and let his eyes travel around the room until they lighted on Justine and me. He strode across the room. Face to face with us, however, he seemed once again unsure of himself. Justine didn't help matters.

"Paul, what happened out there tonight?" she asked, stepping forward until she was less than a foot from him, making her have to tilt her head back to look up at him. The room was quiet, as it seemed all those gathered held their breaths. "What happened to my husband? Why was he shot? Why weren't you there to cover him? Or did you cover him but just not well enough? Is that it? Should Richard still be alive now?" She looked ready to scratch his eyes out.

"Justine, here, come and sit down with me," the Chief said, putting an arm around her shoulders and trying to lead her away.

"No! I don't want to sit down! I want this man to answer me. Right now." She shook off Sikes's arm and stamped her tiny foot like a child throwing a tantrum because she'd been refused the lollipop she so badly wanted. The comparison might not be far off the mark, I thought, and felt a hysterical giggle threatening to escape from my throat.

I had to do something. We were going to be the talk of the town already. For Richie's sake I had to get a handle on this situation. I stepped forward, determined to put on a composed and friendly face.

"Thanks for coming, Paul." I held out my hand. "I know this is hard for you, too."

He grasped my hand in a death grip, his gaze telegraphing his thanks to me. "Hey, Rebecca. Justine." He nodded his head to her. He didn't let go of my hand, and I gave a gentle squeeze. "I can't believe this happened. I mean, I was there and I still can't believe it. I don't understand it at all."

"*You* don't understand it?" Justine spat at him. "*You* don't understand? What about me? What about our little boy? Tell me how *he's* supposed to understand it."

I laid my free hand on her arm and wrapped my fingers around her tiny wrist. I squeezed a bit, trying to get her to meet my gaze. I felt like a boxing referee. "Justine, don't," I said in a whisper. "Richie wouldn't want us to do this, especially not here, not now." She gave me a cold stare but I made my gaze hold hers, and after a long-held breath she sighed and stepped back.

"You're right, Rebecca." She acquiesced easily and, surprised, I let her go. Turning her back on Paul she sauntered across the room to where Clarissa stood watching with a frown on her face.

"Paul, I'm sorry…"

He gave his head a sharp shake. "No, Rebecca. Don't apologize to me, not for Justine, not for anything. I deserve everything she wants to throw at me. But I'll tell you one thing: She can't make me feel any worse than I already do. I'll never forget this night as long as I live, no matter how hard I try." He swallowed audibly and wiped at a tear rolling down his cheek.

"None of us will," I agreed. "Chief Sikes told me what you did to try to help Richie out there. Thank you for that."

"But I couldn't do anything. I tried to keep him warm since he was in shock, but I couldn't take a chance on touching his… his…" But at this point he broke down and so did I. He threw his arms around me sobbing fiercely, and though I didn't know him well at all, I clung to him too, willing myself not to cry aloud.

"You're one of the last people on earth to see my sweet brother alive," I managed to say around the tears in my throat. I hardly recognized my voice. "We are going to have a long talk someday soon…but not now. Now I just want to go home, and you should probably do the same thing."

Paul stepped back from me and nodded. As he walked back across the waiting room toward the door, it touched me to see several of the cops reach out and shake his hand.

At long last the ER waiting room began to empty. Only then did I notice the two other families who huddled in different corners of the space. I was stricken when I realized we had just taken the place over as if nobody in the world mattered except Richie – which, for me, was true. I wondered if one of the families belonged to the suspect – but then again, I didn't really want to know.

***

"I should find Chief Sikes," I said, wondering if Sandy would know where he'd gone. I headed for her desk and stopped in my tracks. I must be seeing things. Surely he was not here, not now, after all this time. He walked toward me, stopping about two feet away and waiting. Mark Barrington, the man I had been in love with a year ago – perhaps was still in love with.

He looked the same, his thick, golden-brown hair looking as if he'd been running his hands through it, which he probably had. The other features I'd so loved looked different in this room, his green eyes dulled at the moment by a strong emotion, his coarse brows drawn into a frown, his full lips pulled tight now and his jaw muscles working, as if in anger. But he wasn't angry – I could tell. I knew his expressions as well as I knew my own. He was hurting, too.

I froze; I certainly hadn't expected to see Mark here. We hadn't parted the best of friends, and I hadn't seen him in more than six months. He'd talked about moving to Atlanta, and I'd supposed he was already gone.

His quiet stare was full of concern and he held out his hand tentatively. "Becca, I'm so sorry. I…"

What possessed me next I'm still not sure, but before I realized what I was doing I had flown into his arms as if I had no place else in the world to go. He folded his arms round me and hugged me close, as I let loose a torrent of tears I wouldn't have believed I still possessed. Mark didn't say a word, didn't try to shush me – he just held me. After what seemed a lifetime I drew back and wiped my hands across my cheeks.

"Mark, what are you doing here?"

"Sandy called me right after they brought Richard in. I wanted to come over as soon as she called, but she told me I should wait until she called back. It was hell sitting there waiting, imagining what you – what all of you – were going through."

I felt tears welling in my eyes again. Life without Richie – impossible to even imagine. And what about Mom and Dad? Richie was their only son. As if in direct response to my thoughts, Chief Sikes appeared and laid a hand on my shoulder, holding out my cell phone.

"Rebecca, I spoke with your father and told him what happened. He wants you to call him as soon as you get home."

"Thanks, Chief." I gave him a quick hug. "I think I'm ready to go now."

Mark stepped up beside me and shook hands with the chief. "Mark Barrington, sir," he said, and the chief nodded to him. "I'd be glad to take Becca home. I know you've been here all night."

The chief looked from Mark to me, his brow furrowed and his jaw set. I looked at him closely for the first time the entire night. He had a full day's growth of stubble and dark circles under his watery blue eyes. My heart went out to him. Richie had been like family to him, and I understood the control required for him to stay with me through the ordeal, always there with a shoulder to lean on, keeping reporters at bay, doing whatever a father would do. He was about fifty but right now looked like he should be on Medicare. I had to let him get home.

"Chief, I think that would be a good idea. You've been here for so many hours, and I hope you'll go on home and try to get a bit of rest before your day gets *really* busy. Okay?" I gave him a small smile. "I'll be fine. I'll talk with you later today. Now go home." I patted his shoulder.

Suddenly, more than anything, home was what I wanted: the home Richie and I grew up in, the rambling two-story house just outside the city limits of Ocean Springs. The house where Mom spent hours after work cooking up good wholesome food for us and all our friends. Ours was the most popular house in the community, at least with the hungry teenagers. But the house was mine now, and so empty with just me rattling around in it. Mom and Dad were in Key West, living an idyllic retirement filled with reading, fishing, and traveling.

"Rebecca, they want to know when we can get together to make arrangements for the funeral," Justine said, breaking into my thoughts. I heard no inflection in her voice at all; she might have been reciting the alphabet. "Do you want to be involved, or do you want me to take care of it?"

I cringed at how callous she sounded, but I tried to tell myself she, too, was in a state of shock. "Justine, I think we should wait for Mom and Dad," I said, careful to keep any hint of disapproval out of my voice. "I'm supposed to call them back as soon as I get home. Can we get with the funeral home people sometime later?"

"Oh, yes, I'm sure they'll understand. There are lots of things to think about, after all, what with Richard's position working in the community. You just let me know when you know something. I'm going home now myself. I have got to get some rest before I start receiving visitors," she said. She might have been discussing a formal tea or a party, but I knew she was right. As his wife, she knew everyone would gravitate to their house.

"Do you need any help getting things ready?" I asked, hoping she'd say no, which she did. Clarissa offered to clear things away in the house while Justine slept.

"If I can sleep at all. I just don't know. . ." Justine murmured as Clarissa steered her toward the outer doors. I wondered about that myself. Would I ever sleep soundly again?

I turned my back on my departing sister-in-law. "Mark, can I go home now?" He nodded and took my hand, I gave the Chief a final hug. Then I walked out and left my brother there all alone.

Chapter 4

I'VE HEARD PEOPLE SAY before that certain events were "just a blur" for them – now I can attest to that being possible. For me, the four days following Richie's death were a blur of people, words, and tears. Only a few moments stand out to me.

Mom and Dad arrived midday on Friday. I still hadn't seen Owen, since after sleeping a few hours I had to drive to Gulfport to the airport. With my car being so small, Mark had insisted on driving me over in his Escape. The new-looking SUV was a step up from the 1996 Camaro he drove when we were together.

He was being his old self, nice and sweet, but not romantic; I wasn't surprised – he'd made his feelings clear when we parted. Like I said, he was just being a friend when I really needed one. I promised myself I'd never forget how supportive he was being.

The meeting with my parents was difficult, especially since we were in the middle of the airport lobby. Mom cried, I cried, and Dad's face became so red I feared he was about to have a stroke in his effort *not* to cry. All the way back to Biloxi, they plied me with questions, most of which I couldn't answer – questions also plaguing me, questions about how – and why – such a thing could have happened. Richie was strong, capable, calm, a good shot, smart, how could he not have realized the danger? How could he not have prevented it?

And the question plaguing *me* most of all, but which I had not mentioned to Mom and Dad: How could Richie have been shot across the back of his head when he was armed? And *had* he been shot with his own gun? After all, it was covered with his blood. It sounded like an execution to me. But that was a crazy thought. Wasn't it?

***

Justine's and Richie's house became our headquarters until time for the funeral. A few of Mom and Dad's old friends dropped by my house to visit with them away from the hubbub, but for the most part we pulled together and stayed close. My first priority right now was Owen, whose four-year-old's curiosity we had no way to truly satisfy. We answered the few questions we could about his daddy. We told him Daddy was in Heaven now with Jesus, and we would all be with him again someday. But not for a long time. We told him yes, Daddy did "get the bad guy," and yes, Daddy was a hero.

Owen reminded me of pictures I'd seen from President Kennedy's funeral, especially the one where little John-John, at about Owen's age, stood and saluted his father's casket as it went by on the caisson. A neighbor from down the street came by and picked him up about three, taking him home with her for a sleepover with his friend Danny.

By Friday night the house was bursting at the seams. People were spilling into the backyard, where they wandered in groups of two or three, talking quietly. The June night held no hint of the steaminess that would soon be our constant companion on the coast. Occasional sheet lightning lit the sky off to the south, but it was such a common occurrence in the summer no one paid attention. For the most part, people were being thoughtful, I was thinking, as I went to answer another knock at the door. But what did I really want? For everyone to just go away and leave us alone. Leave me alone, at least.

I opened the door to one of the most gorgeous guys I'd ever seen in my life. A bit over six feet tall, slim but muscular, wavy dark hair that refused to lie neatly despite being on the short side, though you could tell he'd tried – and blue eyes that at least equaled the Mississippi late afternoon sky. What was the matter with me? I shouldn't be thinking this way. My brother was being buried in a few days.

"Hello," the stranger said, "you must be Rebecca. I think I would know you anywhere."

What a strange thing to say. "That's right," I said, stepping back from the door to invite him in. "I don't believe we've met before." I tried to put a casual question into my voice.

"No, we haven't. My name's Damian Wentworth. I'm an old friend of Richard's."

"Damian...Oh, yes, Damian. Richie told me you'd just moved to Biloxi."

"Yeah. He's been after me for the last couple of years to come down here. Said I'd like it much better than Jackson." He smiled, but his brow furrowed and there was sadness in his eyes. "I wish I'd made the move sooner. Seems like as soon as I came, all hell broke loose. Sorry. Shouldn't have said that."

"No, that's okay," I said. "That's how I feel about things."

"I'm so very sorry..." he broke off as if unable to continue.

I nodded. "Thank you. Come on in. I'm sure my folks would like to meet you." I turned at the sound of Justine's laughter and cringed, seeing her holding a glass of wine. "And Richie's widow, as well. Or have you already met Justine?"

"Once. I met the lady last year." Something in his voice caught my attention. Perhaps this was one guy who would be able to see through Justine's façade. If so, he was most unusual.

I was so sick of small talk. I took Damian to meet my folks, then headed for the kitchen, planning to slip out the back door and around the side of the house to my car. *I hope you understand, Richie, but I have to get away from this place.*

As I came through the house, though, the front door opened and another stranger walked in. He didn't have nearly the panache that Damian had – wasn't nearly as good looking, either.

He had one of those three-day carefully trimmed beards so popular among certain celebrities, one copied around the world by ordinary men who *wish* they were celebrities, or at least wish they had as many women as celebrities did, but that didn't appeal to me at all.

His hair was dark and curly, cropped close to his head, giving him the look of a Greek statue – I didn't think he'd chosen the style by accident. About five foot ten, he wore the muscled torso of someone who works out regularly and stringently. *Thinks he's God's gift to women.*

Probably one of the deputies Richie worked with – I was sure there were a few I hadn't met. I was so tired, but I began to make my way to the door where the newcomer was still standing, looking a bit lost, like I'd felt a few times in college when I'd been invited to some swanky soiree hosted by some Southern belle who hadn't outgrown her debutante days.

Before I reached him, however, Justine swooped in out of nowhere and stepped in front of him with her back to me. He bent down to hear what she said, uttered a few words in reply and nodded. Okay, that encounter looked a bit weird; still, maybe it was innocent. He could be a colleague of Richie's, and their little tête-a-tête might be nothing. Surely it was nothing. My Lord, her husband lay in a funeral home and he would be buried on Monday. She surely wouldn't bring – wouldn't allow – someone she was involved with, here – would she? *Maybe I should check this out.*

Justine must have felt me coming, because she took the guy by the arm and steered him into the living room and began to introduce him to the police officers present. *Hmm, not one of them, then.*

"Hello," I said, circling around to face him on the other side from Justine. "Thanks so much for coming. I'm Rebecca McCallum, Richie's sister."

When he turned to face me, I felt something akin to an electric shock. His eyes were like black holes that could devour anything in his line of sight. The thought hung there in my mind, and then, just as suddenly, it vanished. I wondered where the thought had come from, because when he said hello, he sounded and looked normal.

"I'm sorry about your brother," he said, shaking my hand. "I'm a friend of Justine's. I never got to meet Richard, but Justine's told me lots of good things about him."

"Thank you, Mr. … I didn't catch your name."

"Jake, Jake Coffee."

"Hi, Jake. Come in and make yourself comfortable. We have coffee and other drinks in the kitchen, and the food's beginning to pile up. Somebody's going to have to eat with us."

"Thanks. I'll pass on the food, but I might take an iced tea."

"Jake is such a health nut," Justine said. "Coffee and tea are just about his only vices, as far as I know."

He hadn't taken his eyes off her yet. "Well, help yourself. I'm just on my way out. Justine, I'm going to try to get Mom and Dad to go home now. They're exhausted and so am I. Will you be okay? The crowd will probably start to clear out about eight or eight-thirty. Do you have someone staying with you?"

"Yes, Clarissa's staying. I understand about your folks. I saw Irene a little earlier and she did look really tired. This is so hard for her. I cannot imagine how hard it is for her as a mother. If anything ever happened to Owen…" Her voice trailed off as she seemed to stare at nothing.

"Nothing's going to happen to Owen," I reassured her. "Here, give me a hug. We'll see you tomorrow. I'll call you, okay? Call us if you need anything at all."

"I will, thanks. I think I'll be fine. You just take care of Mom and Dad. The next few days are going to be really hard."

"Nice to have met you, Jake." *I'll find out more about you later.*

***

Ten o'clock Saturday morning found the four of us – Mom and Dad, Justine and myself – at the funeral home sitting at one end of a long mahogany table with the owner of Hinton's Mortuary. The table could easily accommodate a dozen people, and I wondered idly what it would be like, trying to satisfy that many clients at once on one of the worst days of their lives.

No way could I be a mortician, for that reason and for many others. All the morticians I'd seen here were so *solemn*. I wouldn't make it through the first day, if laughing out loud was a no-no, as it seemed to be.

I brought my thoughts back to the present. The first thing we were told was that the funeral home would take care of all expenses for Richie's funeral, something the original owners had vowed to do for any public safety officer killed in the line of duty within Biloxi's three coastal counties. I knew when word of this act of generosity got out – and it would – the place would gain priceless publicity for the business, but I still deeply appreciated the gesture and said so.

Someone tapped on the door, and Mr. Hinton introduced us to Sgt. Ralph Thomas, a liaison with the law enforcement agencies. He said any of several standard things could be done, only if we were agreeable, so we listened to the litany of details that seemed to go on forever.

There would be an honor guard with Richie's body until his interment, if we wished it; we did. The funeral would follow the procedure used for other military funerals, if that was okay with us; it was. Several people would speak at the services, including the mayor, the president of the police union, Sheriff Bixby as Richie's commander, and Chief Sikes in his position as chief of police, if we agreed; but here they found us less accommodating.

"I don't want strangers up there talking about Richard like they knew him, and knew what kind of man he was," Justine protested. "I don't think Richard would want that, either."

We were all in agreement, and the liaison officer gave in with grace.

Dad spoke up then, for the first time. "If it's okay with the rest of you, I *would* like to have James Sikes be a part of the services. He's been a good friend over the years, and he was Richard's chief when he first moved back to Biloxi. I know Richard thought a lot of him." Justine nodded, but her thoughts seemed to be elsewhere. We also knew Sheriff Bixby had a role to play.

Justine had a few specific requests, but the rest of us mainly wanted the process completed, and since the things on her list were both appropriate and dignified, we acquiesced. Mom and Dad went with Justine back to her house, and to prepare myself for what would surely be an arduous day, I stopped by our church to have a few quiet moments alone in the chapel.

Sunlight streamed through the beautiful stained glass windows at the front of the church.

Hurricane Katrina had damaged the building but it had finally been completely restored by early 2008; the process only took about two and a half years. It was now better than before, in fact, since the church dated to about 1950. It had been due for a remodel.

Alone in the sanctuary, with no music, no candles, nothing but the Celtic cross of stained glass directly in front of me, I drank in the stillness. It lulled my aching heart, and I dreaded returning to the scene I knew would be playing out at Justine's. But I thought of Owen, who would be back home today after spending the night with his buddy. Sighing, I left the sanctuary and headed across town.

My little Beetle Bernice and I arrived at Justine's at the same time as Chief Sikes and Sheriff Bixby. As they walked down the street from their car, I observed the sheriff. Bixby was tall and lanky, with a face reminiscent of a bloodhound. I couldn't help smiling as I thought of the cartoon character Huckleberry Hound. His skin seemed to hang limply from his bones. With mixed feelings I waited for them on the walkway and we went into the house together.

Chapter 5

I FOUND MOM AND DAD in the kitchen visiting with a couple they used to play golf with, and we took the two men up to Justine's guest bedroom so we could talk privately. I wondered if they would have anything to tell us that warranted secrecy. I caught Justine's eye as we started upstairs and she followed us shortly. The men stood there looking uncomfortable, Bixby holding a small package.

Justine sat down on the side of the bed and pulled Mom down next to her, putting a protective arm around her. The sheriff handed her the bundle he held, saying, "Here are most of Richard's personal effects. We still have his service revolver and holster."

"I don't want to see those, not ever again," Justine said flatly. "Thank you for bringing these things." She laid the package aside, I supposed waiting for a time when only the family would be there. "Thank you, Chief, Sheriff. I'm sure this is not ever an easy job for the two of you, but it must be much harder when you knew Richard so well."

"Yes, ma'am, you're right about that," Bixby said. "It just about breaks my heart to see you folks here under these circumstances."

Dad went over and shook their hands, thanking them for their concern. Sikes said it would probably be several days before they had any more information for us. Bixby said all indications were the suspect had simply overpowered Richie, taken his gun, and shot him. The investigation was far from over, but he didn't expect it to show anything different. One thing remained certain: Richie *had* been killed with his own gun.

After they left, Justine said, "If y'all don't mind, I'd like to be by myself for a little while." She laid her hand on the package, and I realized she didn't plan to open it while we were there.

"But Justine…" I began, before Mom took my hand and herded me out of the room. In the hall I whirled on Mom and Dad.

"I don't think it's right for her to be going through Richie's things without us," I hissed. I was angry, fuming, but I didn't want to make a scene. He was my brother, and I desperately needed to touch the things he'd touched last, hoping they'd help me hold on to the connection with him I could feel fading a bit already. I didn't want to tell Mom and Dad this, though, so I took a step or two away from them, intending to head back downstairs and straight out the door.

"Becca, I know how you feel," Mom said, and I knew she did. I was only his sister – she had given birth to him. I sighed as I leaned against the railing. The house had an open stairwell, and as much as I didn't want to make a scene with Justine, I also didn't want to draw attention to the three of us from anyone downstairs.

"I know, Mom," I said. "It's all right. No big deal. I have Richie right here," I laid a hand over my heart, "and I know you both do, too." I gave her and Dad a hug. "I love you both. But I really have to get out of here." I started down the stairs.

"Becca…" Mom called after me, but I kept going.

"Let her go, Irene," I heard Dad say, bless him.

***

I rounded the stairs, planning a quick escape, and ran smack into a male somebody, my nose bumping into the guy's chest. "Ow!" I said, recoiling to see who'd made me see stars.

"Sorry," said Damian Wentworth, catching me by the arms to keep me from falling. *Stars indeed.* "You okay?"

I was holding my nose, tears had sprung from my eyes, and I'm sure my face blazed as red as a tomato. "Yeah, I'm okay. I'm sorry, too. I just about ran around the stairs and I sure wasn't looking where I was going."

"Well, you're not used to having people prowling all around the house," he said, flashing a grin that showed perfect white teeth. I noticed something else about him – I hadn't noticed it before – he had dimples. I adore dimples. Dimples on guys, on babies, on old ladies, on anyone at all. I've always been a sucker for a guy with dimples. It had led me down the wrong path a couple of times…and I had vowed never to let that happen again.

"Actually, I'm looking for Owen," I said, striving for an air of friendly aloofness. *Is that an oxymoron? Like ugly dimples?*

"Owen?"

"Yes, Richie and Justine's little boy. I thought he'd be back from his friend's but I haven't seen him yet."

"I see." He looked around. The house felt quiet still, with many people not stopping by on bereavement visits before three or four in the afternoon, these days. Time was, Mom had once told me, when as a sign of respect a house of mourning was never allowed to be left with only family members there after a death in the family.

In those days the body of the deceased (*Lord, I hate thinking of Richie in those terms*) was prepared for burial, placed in the casket, and brought home to lie in state in the living room of the home until time for the funeral. I was enormously thankful those days were past. I'd hate for little Owen to forever have memories of his dead father lying in a big box right next to the television.

Unable to hide my smile, I thought of some of the outrageous things Richie would no doubt have said had he been there.

"I'm glad to see you're able to smile a bit today."

"Just thinking about Richie's weird sense of humor. I know he'd have had a few choice things to say about this whole bereavement thing."

He smiled, too. "You're right there. Don't get me wrong; when we were on duty with a funeral procession, nobody showed more respect than Rich. But I sure did enjoy his unique take on the world over-all – and some of our 'clients' in particular." He laid his hand on my arm. "Rebecca, I was hoping I'd have a chance to talk to you today…it's kind of important." It must be, I thought, for him to change topics so suddenly.

"Well, okay. Let's go out to the backyard. The neighbors have brought over lawn chairs, so we should be able to find a place to sit out there."

Five minutes later we were settled into a couple of well-padded lounge chairs under a curly willow tree. Its feathery branches gave us just a bit of shade, where we could sip our drinks in comfort, and even privacy. Damian had a cup of coffee. I didn't understand how he could be drinking something hot and told him so. He just laughed.

"Coffee drinkers the world over have been drinking hot coffee in hot weather for centuries," he stated pompously, then laughed.

"Yeah...I've heard that before. In fact, Richie used to say the same thing, back when he first started drinking coffee, years ago."

Damian ducked his head. "He's the only person I ever heard say it. I guess I picked it up from him without realizing it."

"So what did you want to talk to me about?" I asked, fidgeting in my chair. I couldn't believe I was so eager to get away from this guy. Any other time I might have been hanging on every word he said, but not now.

"Well, you know I just moved here from Jackson," he said, and I nodded. "I found something of Richard's when I was packing to move, so I brought it along with me. But then I forgot about it, so I still have it. I wanted to give it to somebody in the family. But now I'm wondering if this is the right time." He frowned. "I'm so sorry, I keep causing you problems." He rose suddenly and turned to go.

I stood, too, and laid a hand on his arm. "Wait, Damian, please. Sit down." He hesitated, but then sat, his elbows on the arms of the chair, staring at the ground. He looked so like Owen when he strikes out in T-ball I couldn't help smiling. "Come on, Damian, nobody knows how to act in situations like this."

"I know that's true, but it doesn't make me feel any better about it. It seems everything I've done today is a screw-up."

"Don't worry about it. Now what's this thing of Richie's you were talking about?"

He tilted his head back and looked over at me. His awkward position caused his forehead to furrow and those seawater blue eyes to open even wider. *Oh my, a girl could get lost in those eyes and never find her way out.* I blushed, and he straightened up suddenly.

"What? What'd I do now?" he asked, trying to look angry but failing miserably by letting those dimples show again.

"Nothing. It's just been such a weird few days. I don't think I've done one really rational thing since Thursday afternoon."

"Oh, yeah? What did you do then?"

My mind drifted back to that day at the beach, when I tried to relax but couldn't, not without calling my big brother just to know he was okay. "I called Richie," I said quietly, and felt a tear run down my cheek, then another.

He reached into his pocket and drew out a handkerchief. *A handsome man with a clean handkerchief for the damsel in distress.* Damian was certainly full of surprises. I dabbed at my eyes. "Let's change the subject," he said. "What kind of work do you do?"

"I work for MEMA. I'm an assistant to the coordinator of emergency services for the three coastal counties."

"Do you live here in Biloxi?"

"No, I live just outside Ocean Springs."

"I've heard a lot about Ocean Springs. Sounds like a cool town. I hear it's full of art and artists." He smiled.

"Yep, that's our claim to fame. But I'm not one of them." I shrugged.

"So…how's the hurricane season looking this year? It'll be my first year on the coast, you know."

I knew he was just talking off the top of his head, trying to make up for making me uncomfortable earlier. But I found it comforting to talk to someone who was at least trying to carry on a normal conversation.

"We do have other kinds of emergencies, but this time of year hurricanes are our biggest threat – hurricanes, tornadoes, storm surges, and flooding. The Atlantic is quiet so far. Now stop asking me questions, and tell me what you have."

He sat back in his chair and crossed his arms. "It's a small cedar box," he said, "and it contains a leather journal."

That surprised me. I would've expected maybe a baseball glove or a pair of cufflinks, perhaps an old CD. But a journal? Richie? I was intrigued.

"Richard and I were roommates for a while when I first moved to Jackson."

"I never made it up there to visit. Usually he'd head home for a weekend, swing by USM and pick me up, and we'd do our catching up during the trip."

"Yeah, I know you didn't come to visit...I never would have forgotten it if you had." I let his last remark pass. ""Too bad I couldn't make it down for the wedding – I could have met you long ago."

When I blushed, he added, "I'm talking your ear off. I should go."

He stood and stretched, and I felt a flutter, looking up at his sturdy frame. I stood too.

"So, what should I do with the box? Do you think I should give it to his wife?"

"No!" The word came out so suddenly it startled both of us. "No, I mean if he wrote in this journal, it was years before he even met Justine. He may have written about old girlfriends or something. Unless... have you read it?"

"Absolutely not!" he protested. "I just found it stuck back in a corner of the hall closet when I moved, so I brought it with me. You may not even want to see it yourself."

"Oh, yeah," I smiled. "I do. Not right now, but in a few days, or a week, or two..." My voice trailed off.

"Got it," he said. "And now I really am going. If I don't see you before the funeral, Rebecca, take care of yourself." He gave me a quick brotherly hug and left me standing alone in the late morning sunshine, with birds singing and squirrels chirping in the yard next door, as if scolding me for having the kind of thoughts I shouldn't be having right now.

I heard the screen door slam and saw Justine striding purposefully across the yard – a woman on a mission, I thought. Lord, what now?

Chapter 6

I DIDN'T GET ANY ALONE TIME on Saturday. By the time I had finished calming Justine down – she wasn't happy with the florist we were using – Mom and Dad were looking for me, too, saying they needed to rest.

They'd eaten at Justine's, from the many dishes covering every square inch of the kitchen – chicken and spaghetti, pot roast and vegetables, salads of all kinds, fried chicken, pecan pie, two coconut cakes and plenty of others, too many other things to name – but I wasn't hungry so we planned to say our goodbyes and go straight home.

Once again I was thwarted, though. Leaving my folks in the kitchen I made another sweep through the house. Justine was in the living room. She wasn't alone. Jake Coffee was with her again. I found them seated on the sofa talking quietly. Justine had her shoes off, feet curled up under her, her elbow propped up on the back of the sofa. She stroked her thick black hair, absently twisting its curls in her slim fingers. Jake's eyes were fixated on her hand, completely mesmerized. The two might not be intimately involved, but if so it clearly wasn't because Jake wasn't interested.

Anyone who walked into the room right now would get the same idea I just had – and I didn't want that to happen. My brother deserved better than to have such gossip tarnishing his memory. I didn't want either of our parents to see this. I had to do something.

"Justine, there you are. And Jake, hello." Justine gave me a frosty look, but to his credit, Jake seemed a bit embarrassed. He got to his feet and, after the briefest of greetings, left.

As Jake was leaving, I saw him nod to Paul Simmons, who was on his way in. Paul wore civilian clothes – gray slacks and a black shirt open at the collar, black loafers and a thick ring he kept twisting round and round his finger. He was probably upset at the thought of facing Richie's family. I had to give the guy credit for showing up.

"Hi, Paul," I said. "Why don't you come out to the kitchen? I'd like you to meet my folks." Justine had risen to her feet, but behind his back I mouthed for her to stay back. I didn't want another scene like the one at the hospital. Reluctantly she sat down again, glaring daggers at Paul.

"Justine doesn't want me here," Paul said as we walked down the hall.

"Paul, wait a minute." I stopped and faced him. "I'm sorry for what Justine said to you, and I'm sorry for the way she said it. I'm sure you did all you could to save my brother. From what the doctors told us, nothing anyone could have done would have kept Richie alive."

"Maybe so, but I still feel responsible for what happened."

"Why should you? Richie was the one who responded, the one who followed that truck, the one who thought it his place to take the lead in going to investigate – and he was right."

He hung his head. "I just feel like everybody in town is blaming me," he said softly. "Like they wish it had been me instead of Richard."

"Don't be ridiculous. Nobody blames you for what happened," I said, trying to convince myself as much as him. "Just wait out the investigation. I'm sure when it's over your name will be cleared and you can get on with your life."

"Thank you, Rebecca, for saying so. I hope you're right..." His voice trailed off. "You know, I think I'm going to go now and wait about seeing your parents. I'm afraid I'll just upset them more. I can see myself out."

"If you're sure... I'll tell Mom and Dad you stopped by. And next time you're not getting away without us having a long talk."

"Sure, but I'm sorry we have to have that conversation at all."

Me, too, Paul. Me, too.

***

I caught a glimpse of Chief Sikes as I started back down the hall. He was headed out the front door with Paul. I hesitated for only a moment, then turned back toward the two men. "Chief!" I called, and both of them turned toward me. "I'm sorry to bother you – I see you're trying to leave, and I'm sure you have lots to do, but..."

"Rebecca, if I can do anything at all for you I will. What do you need?" Bless his heart, his gruff voice seemed about an octave lower today; dark circles under his eyes said he hadn't slept much, either.

I glanced at Paul, still standing in the open door. "It's a bit personal..."

Paul held up a hand. "Say no more. I'm out of here. Rebecca, I'll see you at the service. You take care now." I closed the door behind him and turned to the Chief. "Can we sit in the back yard for a few minutes? I'd like to talk privately."

"Why, sure, Rebecca. Lead the way."

Soon I was sitting in the same chair I'd sat in with Damian, but with Chief Sikes sitting across from me. He still held his well-worn Western hat in his hands and turned it slowly in circles. Men and their foibles. If they have a hat in their hand, they're fiddling with it. Same thing with change in their pockets.

"I haven't had a chance to thank you for taking care of me last night," I said, leaning forward to lay my hand over his calloused one. "I'm so glad you took me to the hospital. On my own, I'd have fallen completely apart."

"I'm glad I could help you. I was going to be there anyway, and I couldn't stand the idea of you getting a call and having to get out by yourself. But it's nothing to thank me for, Rebecca. I know your dad would do the same for my daughter."

"You and dad go back a long way, don't you? I remember you coming by the house a few times when I was a little girl."

"Yes, we do – a good thirty years, maybe more. I guess it *has* been more than thirty – I remember when Richard was born. My wife and I had just gotten married, and seeing your brother as a baby really put us in the mood to have one of our own. He was sure a pretty little thing," he said gruffly. He added quickly, afraid he'd hurt my feelings, "Now, you were a beautiful baby, too, from the first time I laid eyes on you. Bald as a golf ball, but with those huge eyes just seeming to look right into a person's soul."

I have to do this, so get on with it. I looked Chief Sikes straight in the eye, and he stared back, our gazes locked. "What is it Rebecca? Something's obviously worrying you. Besides losing your brother, I mean. I'll try to help if you're wanting to talk about it."

"Chief, I had a few questions I didn't want to ask in front of Mom and Dad – or Paul. I could just wait until everything is over and they go back home, but I feel like the longer I wait the worse the outcome may be."

"Sounds serious. Go ahead, ask whatever you want to."

"Well, the thing is, I really don't even know what questions to ask you. This is all so far out of my comfort zone...but I'll try. I'm still a bit confused about how all this happened."

"We all are, I suppose. I've learned one thing I didn't know before – it *was* Richard's service revolver that was used to kill him."

"You're sure?" I think I had not wanted that to be true. It seemed to make the whole situation so much worse, more bizarre. I shook my head to try and clear my thoughts. "I simply don't understand *how* that could have happened to *Richie*. Some other officer, maybe. But Richie was smart, careful, and strong. I can't see him letting himself be taken so completely off guard that somebody could take his gun away from him and shoot him with it."

"I hear what you're saying, girl. And you're right, as far as it goes. But it has been my experience through the years that just about anything can and will take place when an officer goes to confront a suspect."

"I understand that. But if things happened the way Paul said they did – and I'm not doubting what he said – then it seems the shooter was really lucky he avoided Paul. Could he have gone into the barn at the rear? Is that how they managed to not run into each other?"

"Well, I haven't been out to the scene yet, but I have read the reports. Bascom Bixby says there are two doors to the barn, wide one in front and one single door in the rear. So I guess that would explain it. The IA teams will have to figure it all out. I know they've talked with Paul several times, and I'm sure they'll talk to him several more. But so far, his story has been consistent. I really have no reason to believe he's being less than completely truthful."

"I'm sure you're right. I guess my real question, Chief, is this: Could there have been anyone else involved, somebody we don't know anything about? Seems it would have taken more than one person to get to Richie like they did." There, I'd said it, this thing that was eating me up inside. Even as I played the proper role here at Justine's and made sure my folks were taken care of, I had this thing gnawing at me, this feeling, stronger by the hour, of something being in play here none of us really understood.

Chief Sikes stared at me for a long minute, and I began to think he wasn't going to answer me. Understandable, I guess; I'd probably shocked him into silence. Finally he leaned forward and rested his elbows on his knees. *Is this a universal man thing? It seems to have innumerable meanings. Or maybe it means nothing at all.*

"Are you saying you think there was somebody else with the boy, somebody who got away?" He shook his head. "I don't think so. The facts seem cut and dried. There were only his fingerprints on the truck, and no other footprints other than those of the officers and the boy who was killed."

"I don't know – but I've certainly been thinking about it. Paul seems absolutely sure it was the guy from the truck at the back of the barn with Richard – though Paul never saw him until they were both back at the front of the barn…That is what he said, isn't it?"

Sikes nodded. "There was only that small door at the rear. Looked like only one person's footprints inside and also out back, and none anywhere else. I don't see how somebody else could have been there and not have left any trace of himself. Especially if he had about the same amount of smarts as the kid who pulled a gun on Paul."

"Yeah, that makes sense." I gave the chief what I hoped was a convincing smile. "I'm sure I'm clutching at straws, trying to make it into something it's not."

"You're allowed, girl. I know how close you and that brother of yours were. He would be the same way if something had happened to you. It will just take time for you to even start to think clearly. You're not being any different than most relatives of victims I've dealt with over the years. So just try to relax, get some rest, and get through these next few days. I think you'll feel a lot different by this time next week."

"I sure hope so," I sighed. "Well, thanks for the talk, Chief. I do feel better now." He donned his big Stetson and gave me a nod.

"Guess I'll be going now, if that's all…"

I nodded. "I just needed to ask those questions. I think in time I can let it all go."

He excused himself and I sat there, dreading going in to round up my folks. I didn't know how long I could put up a brave front for all the friends and neighbors milling through the house.

Especially now… since I was more convinced than ever the authorities did not have a clue what had happened out at that barn Thursday night.

I knew I couldn't come to grips with Richie's death until I'd determined to my satisfaction if someone besides the dead suspect had been involved. It was scary to think someone might have tried to set up a situation where Richie would be targeted, and it was impossible for me to figure out a way such a thing could have been done. Lord knows I'd tried, lying in bed last night unable to get to sleep for wondering – wondering if a killer was walking around free, wondering who he – or she – was, wondering why, if that were so, Richie had been the target in the first place. Who could have had it in for my brother? Had he known his killer?

***

Back at my house with my parents, we went in through the kitchen, the same way we had done the whole time I was growing up. I stooped to pick up a potted plant sitting on the back porch that hadn't been there when we left.

"It's from my neighbor across the street, Mrs. Goodson," I said, reading the attached note and passing it over to Mom. "She says she's bringing food over later."

"I appreciate people showing us how much Richard meant to them," Mom said, looking at the plant. "But I can't eat anything else right now."

"I know, Mom. But she's such a sweet lady. I hope she doesn't bring too much. Right now I need a nap." I kicked off my sandals and carried them upstairs. Just as I got to the last step the doorbell rang. "I don't think I can face one more person," I groaned.

"You go on to your room, baby. I can handle this." Have I said before that my mom is the best? Well, my mom is the best. I slipped into my bedroom and shut the door quietly, hearing voices in the hall downstairs.

I'd just changed into shorts and a slouchy USM t-shirt and had fallen across the bed, almost in a stupor, when I heard a tentative knocking on the door. *What now?*

"Becca, it's Mom."

"C'mon in, Mom. Door's open."

She stuck her head in. "I hated to disturb you. I know you said you didn't want to see anybody, but...well, Mark is here. What do you want me to tell him?"

I dragged myself off the bed. "Tell him I'll be down in a minute, Mom." He'd been too kind to me – I couldn't ignore him now.

We sat in the back porch swing, not talking much. The evening was warm and sticky, but Mark had picked the spot. In his jeans and navy polo, he looked about twenty, instead of his actual thirty. I was exhausted and could barely keep my eyes open.

He put his arm around my shoulder. "C'mon, hon, put your head on my shoulder and rest." The invitation was too great to resist. He began to hum a nameless tune and I relaxed against him. Within minutes I fell asleep.

***

Richie's wake was set for Saturday evening, so I only had an hour or so to relax before getting dressed again. I saw Mark out and then went upstairs to search through my closet for something appropriate to wear. I only owned one black dress, and it was for nights on the town. *Guess I'll have to shop sometime tomorrow.* I finally picked a navy blue dress I'd had since I interviewed for my job.

Mom, Dad, and I left a couple of hours early, since the first viewing was supposed to be for family only. Yet we had to pull to the rear of the funeral home and go in a side door to get past the crowd milling around out front.

A hundred or so people craned their necks to see what they could see, and reporters were scattered across the lawn, some filming news reports, others interviewing people in the crowd.

"What the hell is going on? Nobody should be here," I muttered.

"Now, Becca," Dad said, "they just want to show respect for your brother, so be nice."

I couldn't believe he said that to me. I didn't understand this whole thing about us having to be nice to them.

"I lost my brother. These people didn't lose anybody, Dad. Give me a break." Mom reached across the console and patted my arm. "Sorry," I muttered, but I wasn't, not really.

One of the somber morticians ushered us into the chapel where Richie lay. The honor guard saluted and moved a discreet distance away as we were led forward. An American flag lay folded atop the shiny walnut casket, ready to cover it after we said goodbye to him. Justine sat in the front row alone. She turned when she saw us.

"I'm so glad you're here. I could not handle this wake alone."

Two morticians came to open the casket for us. Ready or not, it was time.

I'd only attended a couple of wakes, and had never stayed long, so I wasn't sure what to expect. My parents, though, knew the ropes and helped Justine and me through it. I was thankful she'd had the sense not to bring Owen. The funeral would be hard enough for him.

For two hours we stood beside Richie's casket and received words of sympathy from friends and acquaintances. After the first hour, I was struggling not to wince when someone reached for my hand. When I glanced at Justine, I read the same thoughts in her eyes. We'd both have sore hands for the next few days.

I just kept trying to remember these people were here because they loved and respected Richie. Most of the time it worked.

Chapter 7

I STOOD ON THE BACK PORCH looking out across the yard to the old tree house. What I would give to be able to climb that ladder, go inside, and never come back out again. I didn't understand how someone could be completely surrounded by people yet still feel so alone.

"Becca, it's time." Dad's voice pulled me back to the present. "C'mon, honey." Putting his arm round my shoulder, he tugged me inside. The funeral was upon us, and a reel kept playing in my mind about how we'd gotten here.

I'd woken just after dawn – early for me – after a restless night that had found me migrating from my bed to my chair to the kitchen, over and over. I sat up in bed, hugging my knees and thinking again about everything that had been running through my mind. Something was wrong with the scenario we'd been given.

I didn't think the authorities were intentionally misleading us. But I knew my brother better than anyone else, and the idea that he'd been overpowered by a punk kid? No. That I couldn't accept.

What had emerged from my long night was this conviction: Something was wrong with the whole picture of how Richie died. I couldn't convince myself a lone suspect could overpower him, take his gun from him, and shoot him in the side of the head. Nor could I believe all of it happened in the few moments after Richie left Paul and headed to the rear of the barn.

In other words, something else had been in play. And before morning had come, I'd made up my mind to figure it out. The guy couldn't have acted alone, and that suggested premeditation. I meant to start investigating as soon as things settled down and Mom and Dad were back in Florida. But right now I had a funeral to attend.

***

The service was as brief as it could have been, considering words were spoken by Sheriff Bixby and Tom Fowler, an old high school buddy of Richie's, with Chief Sikes giving a brief eulogy. I don't remember much of what they said, only the love and sense of loss with which they said it.

Four hundred or so police officers from across Mississippi and surrounding states made the trek to Biloxi to pay their respects to Richie. Even with several people riding in each vehicle, it made for a terribly long procession. With firefighters driving their trucks of red or white, EMTs in a brightly colored mini-caravan of their own, and a DPS vehicle from every county in the state, I could imagine what it looked like from above – a monstrous serpent wending its way between Richie's church in Biloxi and the cemetery outside Ocean Springs.

Riding in the back of the somber black family car, we followed the pallbearers' cars and the hearse carrying my sweet brother's body across the two-and-a-half mile long post-Katrina bridge over Biloxi Bay at just about three-thirty. Sparkling shards of sunlight flickered on the gentle waves moving slowly out with the tide. All traffic stopped as our procession advanced: cars, delivery trucks, and a stretch limo from the Hard Rock. Even a Greyhound bus. Many drivers stood outside their vehicles, hands over hearts in a silent tribute. To our right, every single walker and jogger on the bridge's footpath was either in a similar pose or simply standing, hands at their sides, taking the time to show respect for a fallen officer.

Silence filled the car, except when one of us would reply to Owen's few questions. Dad had his arm around Mom, and his other hand clung to hers. Justine held Owen close to her side between us. I felt miles away from them all. I leaned my forehead against the darkened window and stared across the bay. I'd never felt so alone among family in my life.

Justine was a beautiful grieving widow, dressed in black from her simple pumps to the black netting covering her head. Her face was ghostly white, her eyes red and swollen. Her chin quivered, but her crying was silent, just as mine was. Richie wouldn't have been happy with an overt show of our grief. Owen, bless him, held his mommy's hand and patted her arm. He seemed overwhelmed with all the flowers, the flag atop the casket, the mournful music, and his eyes grew round and bright when the rifles fired. I don't think any of us had thought to prepare him for that.

Richie received full military honors, and Justine received the flag from the casket. I'd attended similar funerals but had never paid much attention to the precision with which the presentation of the flag is carried out. As two of Richie's fellow officers, in their dark blue uniforms, wearing white dress gloves, slowly and methodically removed the flag and made thirteen precise folds, tears streamed down my face. Don made the final fold and tucked the last bit of flag inside, creating a tidy triangular bundle to present to Richie's wife. When she turned to Owen and handed him the flag, he looked up at her with his solemn blue eyes, so like his daddy's, and said, "I'll take care of you, Mommy." It was the only time Justine sobbed aloud.

My own moment came when, after the moving skirl of bagpipes had drifted over the cemetery with the plaintive sounds of "Amazing Grace," and after silence had fallen following the twenty-one gun salute, I heard Dispatch call over a nearby police car's radio from Headquarters: "Dispatch to Unit eight-two-five, come in eight-two-five... This is the last call for radio number eight-two-five. No response from Captain Richard McCallum. Radio number eight-two-five is out of service. Rest in peace, our friend. The time is 4:17 p.m., June 8, 2013." This was just about more than I could bear. I buried my head in Daddy's shoulder and sobbed quietly into his scratchy tweed jacket, as a single bugler off to the side played "Taps."

***

Keeping to the southern tradition, we all went back to Justine's, where ladies from her church had prepared supper. Before we could get away, we had to stop for several hugs, handshakes, expressions of sympathy, offers of unspecified help, and introductions here and there.

As Mark and I walked away from the gravesite, me holding a red rose from the family spray even though I detested the way people held on to such things, we met Damian.

He wore his dress uniform, cap held under his left arm. He held out his right hand as if to shake mine, but I just shook my head and put my arm around his waist, feeling his arm come clumsily around me in a gentle hug. Mark stiffened beside me.

"How're you doing?" Damian asked quietly. "Could you stand a bit of company later?"

I stepped back, smiling up at him through a sweep of fresh tears. "I'm okay. You know how things work here, Damian. We will be at Justine's for the next few hours greeting people, but then I'll try to get Mom and Dad home to rest."

"How are they holding up?"

"Better than I'd expected. Dad's trying to keep a stiff upper lip for Mom and me, and Mom's trying to keep her grieving inside. We know that's what Richie would want, for Owen's sake. We'll do our grieving in private later. And yes, I would like for you to stop by. Probably sometime after seven would be best."

"Okay, I'll see you then. Mark," he nodded, acknowledging Mark's presence. Turning, he settled his cap into place and walked away.

"What was that about?" Mark asked when we were alone. "Why does he want to come by again? You don't even know him."

"I know him a bit," I said, linking arms with him and giving him a tug. "Let's go before someone else catches up with us. I need to get out of here."

"Sure thing, hon."

"To answer your question.. I think he's just grieving for Richie, like we are – only he's pretty much alone here in town and doesn't have anybody but us to share his grief with."

"He has all his sheriff's department buddies," Mark groused, but I could tell it was mostly posturing. *Jealous? Surely not.*

***

The evening was pleasantly warm, with sunset having brought a respite from the humidity-laden low nineties we'd suffered through at the cemetery earlier today. Mark and I had escaped to the back porch for a little fresh air, while Mom and Dad sat in the living room going through sympathy cards that had started to arrive this morning. I couldn't sit there another minute with Mom reading all those loving words from friends and distant family members. With each one, she had to stop and bring up something about the sender, and she and Dad would be off down memory lane.

We'd just gotten settled in the swing to enjoy the evening breeze when Dad stuck his head out the kitchen door. "Becca, that young man we met the other day is here to see you. Damian, he said."

"Oh, I'd forgotten he was coming by. I'll be right there." I stood, smoothing my dress. Why, I wasn't sure. I didn't plan to wear it ever again. What I'd really like to do would be to burn it, but I supposed I'd send it to Goodwill instead.

"Y'all go on and visit. I'm gonna run and check on things at the Paradise. Want me to come back later?"

I nodded. "Thanks again for being there for me. You've made things much easier."

He gave me a quick hug. "I hope so. Becca, I know this is hard. But I want you to remember you can count on me, whenever, for whatever. I still care about you, and I want to help any way I can."

I laughed shakily. "Just keep a box of tissues handy, I guess." He smiled and reached down to a small side table and plucked two out of a box, touching them to my eyes.

"You got it. I guess you'd better go and see to your guest."

I nodded. "See you later." I went to meet with Damian as Mark jumped off the porch and headed around the side of the house.

Damian stayed about half an hour. We sat in the living room and visited with Mom and Dad, but they excused themselves after just a few minutes and went up to bed.

"Your parents are wonderful people," Damian said after they'd left. "Even after going through all of this, and being so exhausted, they treated me with more kindness than I deserve. Y'all don't even really know me."

"Not true. You were Richie's friend. That means we know you, but I hope we get to know each other better now that the hardest part is over."

"I hope so, too, Rebecca," he said. I heard someone asking you about your running the other day. Do you do races?"

48

I laughed. "No, nothing like that. I just run on the beach and the bridge. Richie and I ran together a lot."

"So you might be in need of a running partner? I try to run three times a week besides my regular workouts."

So that explains all the muscles.

"Could be. Not sure when I'll get back into it, but yeah, it'd be nice not to be alone."

"Maybe I'll see you one day." I nodded. "I'll go now and let you rest. You look like you need it."

Gee, thanks," I scowled at him in mock irritation. He colored, but then the dimples showed up. "Yeah, I'm teasing," I said. "Don't be a stranger."

"No danger of that," he said huskily. "Take care of yourself."

When he'd gone I hurried upstairs to change clothes. I unzipped my dress and tossed it into a corner, where the shoes soon joined it. Then I put on denim capris and a sleeveless knit top, slipped my feet into leather flip flops, and went downstairs to fix a glass of iced tea and wait for Mark.

Chapter 8

MARK CAME BACK VERY LATE. He'd had to deal with a problem at work and had been delayed. He had called to let me know – I wasn't sure why. He didn't owe me an explanation.

We were back in the swing now, night sounds all around us, darkness forming a cocoon that enveloped us and made me feel safe and protected.

"This is my favorite spot in this house," I laughed, "and it isn't even *in* the house. What do you think makes it so special to me?"

"Might have something to do with you growing up here. Maybe a childhood memory, or remnant of it, that speaks to your heart, your soul, or both."

"Mark Barrington, pure poetry. Where'd you learn to talk like that?" I sure didn't remember him ever having waxed poetic when we'd been together.

"Ahh, I don't know. All I know is my tastes in reading have changed. I've been reading a bit of poetry and history, a few political thrillers thrown in for good measure. I've even picked up books by authors I never heard of. I've sort of wished I had somebody to talk with about my reading."

"There are several reading clubs in the area..."

"No, no way," he said, shushing me with his hand. "I don't want to sit around in someone's living room drinking coffee and deciding who's gonna bring dessert next month. And I don't want to be doing required reading from some list like Oprah's."

I laughed at the picture his words brought to mind. "Oh, Mark," I said, "you would be the most popular member of the group if you joined an

Oprah Book Club!" He grunted, not impressed. "But then I bet you'd learn more about women than you'd care to know."

"Well, it's just not happening." He twitched his shoulders. "This reading stuff is personal, you know?"

"Yeah, I do. Oh, if Richie were only here to hear this conversation!" A sob swallowed my next giggle, and I felt Mark's arm come round my shoulders, pulling me close. It seemed so natural, and I regretted anew my actions that had split us apart. And now I was also without my big brother.

"It's just not right!" I said, pounding my fist against the arm of the swing. "Not right, and not fair. Richie was a good man, and a wonderful father. Why couldn't it have been just the car thief who died? He deserved to die – Richie didn't!"

"I know, hon, I know. You're right. But I'm not going to try to tell you it's all a part of God's plan, someday we'll understand why it happened, all that stuff. I don't believe God causes bad things to happen so someone will learn a lesson from it, or be made stronger by going through something terrible."

"You don't know how hard it has been over the past few days, listening to all the people who think they have something profound to say. I'd much rather they hadn't said anything at all. Sometimes silence really is golden, and this has been one of those times."

Rocking his foot back and forth, Mark pushed the swing gently, all the while keeping me close. I laid my head back against his arm, straining my eyes in the darkness for something, but I couldn't put my finger on it. I sucked in my breath and blew it toward the ceiling.

"Thinking about Richard?" Mark's voice was low and velvety, not much more than a whisper.

"I'm thinking about Owen, about what his life will be like with no daddy, and with Justine for a mother."

"Think she'll be a bad mother?"

"No, Justine's a good mother. I'd never want to take that away from her. But she also likes going out on the town – she was always trying to get Richie to take her out someplace. He wasn't much of a party animal, so Justine couldn't really be one either. Now, though, I guess there won't be anyone stopping her from going out whenever she feels like it." I couldn't keep the spite out of my voice.

"And Aunt Becca will be there to babysit Owen when she does want to go out?"

"You'd better believe Aunt Becca would be *willing* to be there. But I doubt she'll let me."

"Why not? Who would she ever find to care for Owen as well as you would? Why spend money to have a stranger take care of him? That doesn't make sense."

"It does if you think the way Justine thinks. For one thing, she's not going to have money worries from here on out. She's getting a huge payout from Richie's law officer's policy, and I'm sure she's already busy making plans for how to spend it."

Mark whistled and said, "Huge payout? I hope she finds someone good to help handle it okay."

"She'll handle it, don't worry. I'm sure she'll do so well there won't be a dime left by the time Owen turns eighteen."

"Seriously? But she's a young woman. I'm sure she'll find someone else someday. Don't you think she would want to get a job, do something productive with her life?"

"I don't want to talk about Justine anymore," I spat, jerking away from Mark and going to stand at the porch rail. "I'm sick of even thinking about her. I wouldn't put it past her to have had Richie killed so she could have her freedom and his money."

Even the crickets seemed to be holding their collective breaths. *Where did that come from? Is that what I really believe?*

After a long, uncomfortable silence, Mark stirred in the swing. "You don't really believe that, do you?"

"I guess not," I groused. "She probably doesn't have the brains to pull off something like that, anyway. I mean, it would take a huge amount of planning to not only make sure Richie died but also to be sure someone else was framed for his murder. I don't think she's capable of doing all that. I'm not so sure about Paul, though. We only have his word for the way things happened."

"But they worked together!"

"Yeah, and it could have been accidental, even if I can't see how. Maybe he's afraid to tell the truth."

"You've seriously thought about this, haven't you?" he asked, stepping up close behind me. If he only knew how much. Last night, during those restless hours, I'd even come down here to the swing once, where I'd done much of my heavy thinking in my early years. That's when I'd become convicted that I had to do something – but I wasn't ready to share that yet.

"The past few days have made it impossible to think straight about anything," I hedged. "But when I close my eyes, it all runs through my mind, over and over, until I can hardly stand to stay in my skin. I almost wish I'd gone with him."

He grabbed my arm and whirled me around to face him. "Don't ever say anything like that again!" he growled. "Don't even think it."

I almost fell when he let me go. "I'm sorry," he whispered.

"I don't know where that came from. I really don't mean it," I said.

"Damn straight you don't mean it. I don't even want to think about what losing you would do to your folks. They're heartbroken right now. If something happened to you..." I heard a catch in his voice, and when he'd cleared his throat he went on. "I think it might finish them off. Then there's Owen. The way you talk about Justine, I know one thing: Richard's little boy is really going to need you as he grows up."

I sat in the swing for a long time after Mark left, feeling like my head was stuffed with cotton fluff and Richie was trying to tell me something I couldn't quite make out.

Chapter 9

MOM AND DAD STAYED for several days. I took the entire week off after the funeral on Monday. We huddled close to home, all of us having responded to condolences about as long as we were able. I know I, for one, felt like I was at the breaking point, ready to snap somebody's head off at the slightest provocation, or with no provocation at all.

Dad spent most of his time puttering around my house, taking care of little projects I'd been putting off: changing air filters, putting new handles I'd bought months ago on my bathroom cabinets, fixing the leaky faucet in the kitchen.

I drove over and picked Owen up from Justine a couple of afternoons. Mom plied him with her chocolate chip cookies, and he followed us wherever we went. I'd escaped to the swing on the back porch one afternoon, having had about as many questions from him as I thought I could stand. I loved the little guy, but it was really hard dealing with him. He looked so like his daddy my heart ached each time he walked into the room, and I knew I needed to pull myself together for his sake.

That thought went through my head when I heard his sweet little voice calling me. I didn't answer, hoping Mom would waylay him. No such luck.

"There you are, Aunt Becca!" he said, literally leaping through the doorway from the kitchen and landing right in front of me. "Guess who I am!" I looked up at him and burst out laughing for the first time in days. The laugh morphed into semi-hysterical giggling, but it felt so good I didn't even try to make myself stop. I laughed so hard I felt a stitch of pain in my side, and still I couldn't stop.

"Mom!" I yelled. "Where are you? You've got to come out here." I lapsed into wild giggling again. Owen stood, hands on his hips, frowning at me. His bottom lip stuck out in a pout like I'd never seen on him, and that only made me laugh harder.

"Honey, I'd take a guess you're Superman," I finally managed to say, and he beamed at me, irritation forgotten.

"You guessed! How could you tell?"

"My first hint was the blue towel around your shoulders. Are those clothespins holding it together? Very smart, Superman. The second hint was Grandma's pantyhose you've managed to put on." Giggles took over again, just as Mom stepped out onto the porch, wiping her hands on a dishtowel.

"Becca, whatever is going on out here?" Then she spied Owen. "Superman, when did you get here? And what have you done with my grandson?" she asked dramatically, holding her head in both hands. "Becca, where's Owen? And what's Superman doing here?"

"No, Grandma, it's me! It's Owen!" he said, tossing the towel away. "I'm right here. See?" He was struggling with all the might of a four-year-old to get out of the clingy pantyhose. When he'd done so he flung out his arms, fingers splayed. "See? It's only me!"

"Oh, thank heavens!" Mom cried, scooping him up in her arms. "I'm so glad it's you. I mean Superman is nice and all, but nobody can compare to you, sweet boy!"

He flung his arms around her neck. "So can I have another cookie?" he asked, leaning back in her arms to flash his best smile. "And can Aunt Becca have one too?" He whispered conspiratorially into her ear, "I think I scared her."

After they went inside I gradually began to recover from my hysterics – for that was what my mad laughter had been, I realized. My face was hot and my side still ached...but oh, I felt better. Better than I had felt since, well, since the last time I saw Richie.

***

Mom and I went down to Front Beach several times, walking the edge of the sand until sunset. June sunsets along the coast can be spectacular, but

I don't think either of us really noticed. We just strolled arm in arm, not talking much. She told me stories I hadn't heard before about Richie and me as small children, and we laughed and cried together. One afternoon I turned to her and said, "Mommy, my life will never be full again, not without his smile, his hugs, his teasing. What am I going to do?"

"You're going to do what your dad and I are going to do," she said, setting her chin. "You're going to put one foot in front of the other, day after day, week after week, until one day, maybe, it won't hurt so much. That's what I'm praying for – for that 'peace which passeth all understanding.'"

***

Mark came by and called daily. He and Dad sat in the back yard sipping iced tea and nibbling on Mom's chocolate chip cookies. I wondered what they found to talk about for hours. On Thursday Mark drove me out to the cemetery, parking near Richie's grave. He waited in the car as I got out and strolled over to the mound of flowers, already shriveled in the early summer sun.

A pair of scissors in hand, I stooped and began to cut pieces of ribbon that held written sentiments: "Beloved Son," "Comrades in Arms," "District 23," "Love of My Life," "Best Daddy in the World." I paused when I reached these last two, streamers from the family spray…Justine's doing. Apparently she felt she had to keep up the pretense of being the loving wife. I knew she had really loved my brother once, but that time was long past, and the hypocrisy of her message made me want to puke.

Nevertheless, I collected that streamer along with all the others, knowing Mom had plans for them. It was an old southern tradition – one I didn't adhere to – to save such ribbons in a scrapbook. Mom had already been collecting news clippings and gathering photos from our family collection. This was going to be one sad scrapbook.

"Hey, Richie," I whispered. "I miss you so much. I can't stand the thought of you not being in my life. What am I going to do? I feel so lost without you."

Behind me, Mark cleared his throat softly. He walked up to stand beside me. He reached for my hand and intertwined our fingers. "You're not alone, Becca. I promise to be here – no strings," he added quickly, hearing my intake of breath. "I'm your friend, and you can always lean on me."

So I did. Lean on him, I mean. He *had* been a good friend, and Lord knew I needed one now. I'd never had many close friends, and except for my bestie, Lorelei Steggemann, those who had come by the house seemed so distant. I guess I was the one being distant, but I didn't know how to change that. I kept thinking, "*You* haven't lost a brother. *You* don't know." I'm not sure why it was different with Mark, except maybe I could see the pain in his eyes that told me how much my brother had meant to him, too.

I whirled around and hurried back to the car, Mark following more slowly. "Can we go home now?" I said. "I don't have time to stand around talking about friendships." I realized I was being too abrupt, but I couldn't seem to help myself these days.

"C'mon, I'll take you home." He started the car. "Think we both need some space for a bit. I'm going to the Paradise to catch up on work I've been neglecting."

"Will you come back later?"

He lifted his eyebrows and shrugged. "Sure, Becca, whatever you want."

***

A familiar Crown Vic was parked in the driveway when we got back home. "What would bring Chief Sikes back out to the house? "Do you think he has news? Maybe they finished the investigation." In my haste I left Mark far behind, slamming the door shut behind me on my way in. I got all the way into the living room before I remembered him. Sheepishly, I went back and opened the door. His face loomed like a thundercloud, and rightfully so.

"Sorry." I winced at the hurt look in his eyes. He shrugged and pushed past me into the room.

"I can now tell you a little bit more about what happened last week," Chief Sikes was saying as he folded his six foot two frame into an easy chair. "It's not much, but..." I squeezed in between Mom and Dad on the sofa. Mark stood near the window, carefully not looking at me. "You already know the other officer responding was Paul Simmons. He's been pretty broken up over all of this. He was put on paid administrative leave, but I feel sure he'll be cleared by the Internal Affairs team."

"That's good," Dad said. "I know he and Richard were friends. I'm sure he did what he could for our boy."

The Chief nodded. "The dead suspect is Tommy Hollingshead, a twenty-five-year-old who lived in East Biloxi. He worked at a local body shop – a place called Bert's. He had a few scrapes with the law several years ago, nothing lately."

Something nagged at me, something I should remember. I frowned, lost in thought.

"Becca, something wrong?" Mark asked.

"I'm not sure. There's something about that name. I feel like I should know it." I sat trying to remember as they continued to discuss the case. Then, with a jolt, it came to me. Oh, my God.

"Chief!" I broke in. "That's a boy Richie tried to help a few years ago – at least I'm almost sure that was his name. He was about eighteen at the time. I don't remember what kind of trouble he'd been in, but I remember Richie talking about him. I think I even remember meeting him once."

Sikes turned toward me. "Are you sure? When was this?"

"One afternoon sometime last year. I'd had a fender bender and Richie went with me to get insurance estimates on my car. We stopped at a body shop and Richie met up with this Tommy guy there. Afterward Richie told me a bit about him. He was convinced the guy had gotten a raw deal, and I think he'd sort of taken him under his wing, tried to help him find a job, you know, and followed up with him for a while. But then he lost track of him. He said Tommy didn't seem happy to see him that day."

"Yeah, we found something about Richie and the suspect in the files. Well. At any rate, that's about all the information I have. I just wanted to get it to you before the media gets hold of it." He got up to leave. "Sorry I couldn't tell you more."

"Thanks, James," Dad said. "Let me walk you out." Mark gave me a wave and left with them. I watched him drive away while Dad stood leaning against the Chief's car, arms folded, still talking even though Sikes seemed anxious to get away.

"Your dad is still at it," Mom said beside me. "He never knows when to stop talking and let people leave." She was chuckling as she headed toward the kitchen.

Dad walked in while I was still giggling over her remark; he came and grabbed me up in a huge bear hug. "It's really good to hear that laugh again, Becca. I just about forgot what it sounded like." He laid his cheek next to mine and started us swaying from side to side.

"Your laughter has always reminded me of so many beautiful things – cool mountain water splashing over rocks shining in the sun, mockingbird parents out teaching their babies to fly, wind whistling through the pines, your mother's smile."

"Daddy! Where did that come from?" His words were like poetry being whispered in my ear. I turned to look at him. "You've never said things like that to me. You've said you loved me. But this feels different."

He shook his head sadly, his shoulders drooping now that they weren't encircling me. "I don't know, baby. I guess I've just realized nobody is guaranteed any time on this earth. In spite of his job, I'm sure Richie thought he had worlds of time…"

"You're right," I said, taking his large, square hands in mine and giving them a squeeze. "We have no promises at all. Thank you for giving me the gift of those special words – I'll always remember them and think of you. Love you, Dad."

I gave him a swift peck on the cheek and ran upstairs to get my journal. I *would* always remember those words …but not without a bit of help. When I got to the top of the stairs, I thought of Mark's troubled look; I hoped I hadn't run him off like last time.

Chapter 10

IT WAS LATE WHEN I HEARD Mark's car in the driveway. I'd been sitting in the dark living room, thinking – and napping. Flicking on a lamp I trudged to the door and opened it, waiting for him.

"Hey, how's it going?" he asked. I stepped back and he came in, reaching around me to flip on the hall light. "Not so good?" I knew I looked terrible. I'd fallen asleep on the sofa, and looking in the hall mirror I could see my hair in shambles.

"Oh, my gosh," I said. "You should turn right around and go on home. I'm a mess."

"Un-huh, not going anywhere." He placed his hands on my shoulders and spun me around. "Except maybe to the back porch. Did you feel what it's like outside? It's a beautiful night."

He set his glass of tea on the porch rail and joined me when I sat down in the padded swing and patted the seat.

"I've missed your mom's sweet tea," he laughed, settling into the swing next to me. He gave a deep sigh of contentment. "Now this is much more enjoyable than running scans on our system and printing out reports."

"I don't know…"

"What don't you know?"

"Oh. Sorry, thinking out loud, I guess."

When I didn't say anything more he nudged me in the side with his elbow. I grinned, remembering. "You haven't done that in a long time," I said. "You could always get me out of a bad mood."

"Sometimes," he corrected me. "Not always. So?"

"Oh, you were just talking about how you'd prefer to be here than at work. And I was thinking as bad as I dread going back to MEMA, I really need to. I need to get back into a routine, get some structure back into my life."

We swung quietly for a few minutes. The only sounds were the crickets singing in the live oaks, the rusty creaking of the swing, the buzzing of one or two mosquitoes. We had no breeze to speak of, but the air was cool for June, making for an enjoyable atmosphere.

Mark's arm lay across the back of the swing, and each time I shifted I became more aware of it. "Ahh, it feels great out here," he sighed. "The company isn't so bad, either."

"Barrington, I think you only wanted to come back tonight so you could share my swing and my backyard."

He laughed. "I admit it. I have really missed this swing." Now it was my turn to poke him in the ribs. His arm came down around my shoulder and he squeezed. I felt a delicious shiver where his arm touched me, and I didn't resist when he laid his hand on the side of my face, pulled my head over onto his shoulder, and began stroking my hair.

It felt so nice, so right, I could hardly bear it. Too soon my folks would be going home, I'd be going back to work, and Mark would be going back to whatever was a part of his life these days. *Or whoever*, a little voice inside nudged me.

I'd been wanting to have a chance to talk with him – to hold an actual conversation – for the past few days. But it seemed whenever I got up my courage, something or someone interrupted us. *No time like the present.*

"Mark, I…"

"Becca, I…"

We'd both started talking at the same time, and we laughed together. I felt like I was in one of those old romantic comedies from the 1940s. I love those movies – the sets, the songs, the stars, the happy endings.

"You first," he said.

"Okay." I raised my head from his shoulder and shifted around in the swing to face him. Light from the kitchen window spilled onto the porch and I could just make out his face. Lit from one side, I could see the planes and creases of his face, that face my hands had touched so many times. My fingers itched from wanting to touch him again. But I didn't have that right anymore. I laced my fingers together in my lap.

"When we broke up, you said you thought you were moving to Atlanta. But you're still here. Why did you change your mind?"

He shifted a bit too, and now the light fell on his soft, golden-brown hair. I wanted to twirl my fingers through it.

"I *was* making plans to move. Then I ran into Bob Steggemann – at a Saints game in New Orleans, of all places," he chuckled. "We got to talking, one thing led to another, and next thing I knew he'd offered to put me in charge of all the electrical equipment at the casino. Said he needed someone he could trust to take charge at the Paradise, get things back in shape."

"Take charge? You make it sound like he wanted you to go in and take names and kick some butt."

"That's just what he wanted. He said he'd been having problems with theft by his employees. He'd finally gotten a handle on that situation but needed someone who could come in and hit the ground running to reorganize things, and with my combination of business and electrical experience, he thought I was the man for the job."

"Lorelei never said a word about you working for Bob." That puzzled me. She knew I was broken up over our split, yet she didn't let me know Mark was still within reach. *I might have kept trying.*

"Well, now, that's my fault, if it's anybody's," he said, a note of embarrassment in his voice. He stood suddenly and walked over to lean against the porch rail. The light no longer touched his face, and when he spoke, his voice was low. "I was hurt and upset. I didn't think I could handle seeing you again. It wasn't a nice thing to do, asking her to keep something from her best friend. She argued with me about it but finally agreed. I hope this won't cause problems in y'all's friendship."

"Lorelei and I have been through so much...one more little stab-in-the-back won't make any difference. I'll find a way to make her pay." He grew still, as still as the night had become. Somewhere away to the north an owl hooted. Such a lonely sound. I giggled. "I'm kidding, Mark. Just kidding."

He flung himself back down in the swing beside me. "You're a mean woman, Ms. McCallum," he grumbled.

"Yeah, I've been told that before," I said. "Honestly...there's nothing in the world that would make me not love Lorelei like a sister. I'm sure she'd say the same thing about me."

"She did, in fact. I mean, when she finally agreed not to tell you, she said you'd forgive her when you found out, because you'd forgive her anything, just like she'd forgive you anything."

"Damn straight," I said, and this time I wasn't giggling.

"That's one of the things I loved most about you, Becca. You love so easily – lots of people don't have that ability. I don't think I do, that's for sure." He reached for my hand, turning it so our palms touched. I felt that tingle in the pit of my stomach again. How could this man still get to me so easily after all this time?

"The job at the Paradise has been good for me," he went on almost absently, twining my fingers with his. "Bob's a great guy, and a great boss. He leaves me to take care of things without much oversight at all. He says he likes my ability to 'be effective in work and succinct in reporting.'" I could hear a lilt in his voice. "I'd never have had an opportunity like this if I'd gone to Atlanta. I'd have had to start over, up there. I've already done that a time or two, and...well, I'm just getting too old to keep on reinventing myself." I sensed a note of shyness in his voice I didn't remember. It didn't keep him from kneading my fingers with his two hands, though, and I began to feel a bit shy myself.

I slowly eased my hand from his grasp. My fingers were almost numb from his vigorous manipulation. The man didn't even realize what he'd been doing to my poor metatarsals. Not wanting him to think I was rejecting him, I laid my hand on his leg just above his knee, and squeezed gently. I heard the intake of his breath, and he groaned softly.

"Lady, I've missed you something awful – and you're killing me," he said, and my hand stilled. "God, Becca, I'm sorry. I didn't mean to say that. I don't know what I..." I touched my once again tingling fingers against his lips.

"Don't," I said. "It's okay." I leaned forward and touched my lips to the spot where my fingers had just been, touched his soft, sweet mouth, the one I'd longed for on many lonely nights. He responded immediately, bringing his hand up to cradle the back of my neck and hold us there together, suspended in time, his mouth sweetly insistent on mine. It was almost too much, realizing I'd had to lose Richie to bring Mark back into my life. Just one kiss, but with the promise of more. I vowed not to mess things up this time if I got another chance.

"I've missed you so much," I said, leaning back to look at him.

"I missed you, too, sweet thing."

Sweet thing. He remembers. But how long will he be here with me? How long before I do something to drive him away again?

***

Dinner on Friday night was one I knew I'd remember for a long time. Mom and I decided to pull out all the stops at least once before they flew back home, and tonight was the night. I stopped by Rouse's, our wonderful local supermarket, and picked up everything from apples to zucchini, adding several varieties of cheeses. At the seafood department I had them steam five pounds of fresh Gulf shrimp – my dad does love his shrimp.

I told Mom we could get excellent rolls at Rouse's and she could avoid a hot kitchen...but she insisted on spending most of the day making her prize yeast rolls. The house smelled heavenly, and I think it served as therapy for her.

By the time I got back from shopping she'd found and ironed an aqua tablecloth and sunshine yellow napkins, and she was putting the finishing touches on an arrangement of candles and a few of the pots of ivy which had been sent to us at the house.

"It's beautiful, Mom," I said, giving her a hug.

"Thanks." She touched one of the plants. "I wanted to have a small piece of Richard here with us tonight."

Later, as I sliced and arranged fruits, veggies, and cheeses, Mom came into the kitchen and stood watching me work. "You have beautiful hands,

Becca," she said. I couldn't help laughing, which I don't think was the response she was expecting.

"Did I say something wrong?" She looked close to tears.

"No, of course not," I said, laying down my knife and wiping my hands to go and give her a hug. "It's just that Dad was sounding sentimental earlier about my beautiful laughter, and... and... oh, I don't know. It's just kind of weird."

"I suppose we're both feeling a bit fragile right now," she said, sinking into a chair. "We're probably smothering you, wanting to hold on to the one child we have left, wanting you to know how much you mean to us."

"To tell the truth," I sighed, "I am feeling just a bit short of breath from time to time." I batted my eyelashes at her. She made a face at me and we both laughed.

I went back to work and we chatted for a few minutes, but I kept feeling she had something specific she wanted to say. Finally I said, without stopping my chopping, "C'mon, Mom, let's have it."

"Have what?"

"You know what, I don't. You've wanted to say something ever since we finished talking about my 'beautiful hands.'"

I looked over my shoulder at her. "What is it?"

"Well, since you mention it... Well, I've been wanting to talk to you about Mark."

Uh-oh. I should have seen this one coming. He had, after all, been at my beck and call, and theirs, ever since they arrived. She probably did have questions.

"Okay, I don't know what I can tell you, but go ahead."

"Well, we've been here for a week now...and Mark has been here every single day. I'm not complaining; on the contrary, I don't know what we all would have done without him."

"First things first, Mom. Could you please try to stop beginning every sentence with 'well'?" I grinned at her, and she made a pooh-pooh gesture, waving her hand in front of her face. "Yes, he's been like a rock for me, and for you and Dad, too."

"We never really talked last year about what happened between the two of you."

"No, Mom, *I* never talked to *you* about it. I remember you asked me about it several times, and I closed off from you every time you asked."

"Well...Oh, sorry," she giggled.

"I give up," I teased her. "Talk however you want to. I'm really not trying to avoid this conversation."

She arched her perfectly-groomed eyebrows and said, "Oh, really? Okay then, let's talk about it."

She surprised me again. I'd thought she would have at least beat around the bush about it. Directness was not one of the woman's strong suits.

I laid my paring knife aside, dried my hands again, and went to join Mom at the table. Might as well get comfortable. This could take a while.

"We never had a big blow-up or anything major at all. I realize now it was mostly my fault...maybe *all* my fault."

She laid a hand on my arm. "No, Rebecca, nothing is *ever* all anyone's fault. If two people are involved, both are to blame when something goes wrong." It crossed my mind to wonder if she would still say the same thing if we were discussing Richie and Justine. Mom had always found it hard to blame her fair-haired boy for anything at all.

"That's probably true. I just know I feel responsible for our break-up, and I don't blame Mark."

"That's nice to hear. At least my judgment of his character wasn't wrong. I don't know what your dad would do if he ever thought Mark had been to blame for making his little girl miserable. And don't try to tell me you weren't miserable! When you visited us last summer you moped around the house like a little lost puppy."

"I'm sorry, Mom," I said, feeling myself redden. "I never wanted you and Dad to worry about me. I thought I hid my feelings really well."

"A mother always knows, Missy. So what did you do?"

"What did I *do*?" I repeated "Oh, Mom, so many things. So many little things. I can sum it all up fairly simply, though. I was stubborn, and selfish, and I never put Mark first in anything. But you of all people know what I've been like."

"So you're saying you were just being yourself?"

I felt my cheeks flush. She sure wasn't cutting me any slack.

She sat back in her chair, waiting.

"After Mark broke up with me," I grimaced at her surprise. *So she thought I broke up with him.* "I tried to get him back. I called, wrote, texted. He wouldn't have anything to do with me. I went through a rough period, and if it hadn't been for Lorelei I don't know if I'd have made it."

I got up and put the kettle on to heat water for tea. After setting out two mugs and the tea canister I sat back down and looked her straight in the eye. "Lorelei tried to get me to see a therapist, but I refused. I kept trying to lay the blame all on Mark, saying he was the one who needed to see the therapist. She finally gave up."

"But she didn't give up on you."

"No, Mom, she didn't. She never would. But the thing is, after all that's happened, I'm thinking I might take Lorelei up on her offer to set me up with a friend of hers. She swears by the woman, and she told me if I ever changed my mind she could get me in to see the doctor in a matter of days."

Mom nodded. "I think that would be a good idea. You've been so strong this week, when, I confess, I feared what your father and I would find when we got here. You loved your brother so much. I was afraid you couldn't handle all of this without falling apart, but you seem to be doing okay – as okay as any of us."

I gave a bitter laugh. "Oh, believe me, I've fallen apart inside. But I've tried to be strong, for you and Dad – and for Owen, too. After y'all leave, I suppose I'll be just about the most stable person in his little world. Isn't that scary?"

"No, Becca, it isn't. And you want to know why?" She got up and poured the now boiling water in our cups and brought them to the table, then went back and brought the tea packets with her when she sat back down. I waited expectantly. Truly I had expected her to agree with me. "It isn't scary at all, because I can see just how much little Owen loves you and looks up to you. I know I can count on you to be there for him. Now, back to this therapist."

I was silent for another minute as we both worked on our tea. Then I began to talk, really talk, to my mom for the first time in years. For the next half hour I talked from my heart, telling her the stupid things I'd done and said to Mark. I told her how patient he'd been with me, how he only ever tried to tease me out of behaving badly, which I admitted I had done often. To her credit, Mom just let me talk.

I watched the expressions move across her face during that time, and I saw what I needed to see: how much she loved me. When I finally ran out of things to say, she said, "Well, Rebecca, you have well and truly surprised me this time. I don't think you've ever talked this much, or shared this much of yourself with me, during your entire life."

"I know, Mom. I don't understand why I shut myself off from people so much, especially family. I don't want to be that way, and I've been trying to get better. And I think I was – until last week."

"I know, baby, I'm feeling kind of fragile myself. But we're going to make it. We Brighton women come from strong stock. Agreed?"

"Yep, I agree." We toasted each other with our mugs of tea.

I got up to finish laying out the vegetables. "So tell me," Mom said, "what do you plan to do about Mark?"

"You're impossible," I said, flinging drops of water from the faucet at her.

"Oh, Becca, don't!" she squealed. "Don't make me come over there and get you."

Suddenly I remembered a similar water fight when I was about fifteen. "Mom, do you remember the water hose incident?"

"How could I ever forget it?" she shook her head, smiling at the memory.

I had been washing dishes under protest that day, complaining the whole time. Mom had come into the kitchen and heard a few of my choice words and decided, naturally, I needed to clean out my mouth. She didn't try to wash it out with soap, but she did think just a squirt or two from the kitchen hose might not be a bad idea.

The hose was an old one, though, and we had hardly ever used it anymore. Nobody had realized how brittle the old spray attachment had become – but we soon found out. When she jerked on the spray head the hose broke and she tumbled backward. I tried to catch her but my hands were too soapy and she slipped right through my fingers. So I lunged for her – and that's how we both ended up on the floor, rolling around and giggling like two first graders.

That's the way Dad had found us that day, having been alerted by our screams of laughter. And that's the way Dad and Mark found us today – standing in the middle of the kitchen, arms wrapped round each other, tears running down our faces, shrieking with laughter.

They gave each other similarly disgusted looks, then turned and left us there.

Chapter 11

IN A WAY I DREADED going back to work that next Monday. I'd had it "up to here" with sympathy, hugs, and tears. But my job with MEMA needed all hands on deck during hurricane season. And in some ways, I was looking forward to the distractions of preparing for whatever might be brewing off the coast of Africa. Now if I could only get myself out the door in the mornings.

Mark helped me get Mom and Dad to the Gulfport airport on Sunday afternoon. We'd all held each other and cried together one last time. I could feel the tension was a bit less, as if somehow we were managing to come to grips with the reality of Richie's death. I knew they needed to get back home, get back into their routines, see the friends they'd made after their move. And I needed the house to myself again, lonely as it would be.

For I, too, needed a routine. With these open and empty days, I had too much time to think – even with them around. I had decided entirely too much credit was given to the benefits of thinking. Me…I just wanted to forget. That being impossible, I'd take the next best thing: I was ready to get back to work.

On Monday morning, I parked Bernice in our usual spot, underneath a massive live oak draped in Spanish moss, locked the doors, and reluctantly headed inside. Our offices were on the fourth floor and, as always, I took the stairs, running the whole way. I stopped to catch my breath before I entered our complex.

When I checked in at the office, Susan showed me the current map. She pointed to her computer screen. "The Cape Verdes are getting busy now.

And the Gulf Stream pattern suggests we may have movement our way for the next few developing storms."

"I'd better get to my office then," I said, "and do a rundown of our preparations. I for one am not up to another Katrina situation."

"You and me both!" Susan said. "Rebecca – it's good to have you back. If I can do anything…"

"Thanks, SuSu." I smiled. "I'm okay. It's going to be okay." I hurried away before any tears could fall.

I spent the rest of that day reviewing printouts, making calls, and trying to get back up to speed. We had many issues to deal with during hurricane season: the hurricanes themselves, popup tornadoes spawned by the unstable atmosphere; evacuation for those in low-lying coastal areas and those along our many canals and bayous; shelters for those who couldn't or wouldn't evacuate. We had few problems with hard-liners who refused to leave now, after the debacle that was Katrina in 2005.

I'd had my baptism by fire with Katrina. I was attending USM, working on an environmental science degree, when Katrina hit. I'd been home for the summer doing an internship in Biloxi and was due to return to Hattiesburg the first week of September. Because of the emergency, though, classes were postponed for two weeks and I was able to stay with Mom and Dad and help out a bit.

August 29, 2005 – the date is forever imprinted on the hearts and minds of people along the Mississippi Gulf Coast. People here didn't wait around to see who might come to their assistance – they picked up their tools and got to work. Even before the National Guard arrived with supplies, people were working their way back to their houses and starting the arduous process of ripping out carpet, drywall, and cabinets, fighting alone to save their homes. As I had driven the rubble-filled streets in my state-issued truck, I'd felt my heart swell with pride at the courage, strength, and determination of my neighbors.

Now, almost eight years later, the Mississippi Coast had made a remarkable recovery. When hurricane season arrived each year, we all prayed, "Please, just not another Katrina." So far we'd been lucky, but that luck, we all knew, wouldn't last forever.

We had been blessed at our home. Mom and Dad had built their house in 1980 with the 1969 destruction wrought by Camille in mind. They had pored over topographical maps of the entire area and settled at last on a small piece of property that lay about half a mile inland from the Gulf and about thirty-eight feet above sea level. When Katrina's near thirty foot storm surge slammed into the coast, the debris field came within five hundred feet of our house.

Richie still lived in Jackson then, but spent most of his free time in New Orleans, dating Justine. They married a year later. They had a beautiful wedding, and anyone could see they were deeply in love. I wondered again what had gone wrong for them.

Several months ago, Richie confided in me he thought Justine was cheating on him, but he dreaded a confrontation. During one of their arguments, she threatened to move to New Orleans, where her sister lived. She told Richie no judge would give custody to a man with his job, where he put his life in danger daily, and where he changed shifts often. That was no life for a little boy, Justine insisted, and Richie and I tended to agree.

So things had rocked along between them. At times they still seemed happy together. They had occasional date nights and had friends in, and they even talked about having another child. I admit I discouraged Richie when he asked what I thought about that. He hoped another baby might make Justine settle down. She was a good mother to Owen, most of the time, and Richie said two kids might keep her busy so she'd stop her running around.

"What if she doesn't stop?" I'd asked, staring into his eyes. "Then what happens? To the new baby, to Owen? To all of you?"

"Okay, Sis," he'd agreed. "I'll give it some more thought. For now, we'll keep playing it safe." That conversation had taken place about two months ago. I felt ashamed at being so grateful Justine only had Owen now.

***

A knock on my open door brought me back to the present. I was surprised to see Paul Simmons standing there.

"Do you have a minute?" he asked. "I won't stay long."

"Sure, come on in." *Why are you here?* He'd been at the funeral and had stopped to pay his respects to the family. Maybe he was ready to talk about that night.

"What brings you by, Paul?"

He smiled shyly. "Just wanted to see how you're doing."

"I'm good, better now that I'm back to work."

"Yeah, it helps to keep busy…at least I suppose it would." I realized he must be grieving too, for Richie, and for his role in the events of that night.

He'd brought it up, so I asked: "How's the investigation going? Any decisions yet?" I probably sounded like I was accusing him, but after all, he was the one who was in my office, not vice versa.

He shook his head glumly. "No, it'll be some time before the teams reach a consensus."

"Really? Why? Have they discovered something new?"

He shrugged. "They aren't telling me." A sour note of sarcasm tinged his voice. "They won't even discuss it with me."

"Isn't that standard operating procedure? I'm sure they're doing things this way for your sake as well as for that of the investigation."

"I guess so. Well, I just wanted to stop by and say hello." He unfolded himself from the chair and eased toward the door. "I'll let you get back to work."

"Paul," I called as he stepped into the hall. He stuck his head back around the doorframe. "I'm sure it will all turn out all right." He gave a weak smile, and with a wave of his hand he was gone.

I'm really not so sure at all. He still could be involved.

The ringing telephone interrupted my musings. The MEMA director had a whole host of questions about our evacuation plans, and I spent the rest of the day tracking down answers for her. No more time for fretting about Justine or Paul, at least not at the office.

***

The next day was hectic at work: Quarterly reports were almost due, public disaster drills had to be scheduled, and we had to stay on top of the many details of keeping three counties ready for virtually anything man or

Mother Nature could throw at us. As I left work I realized I hadn't once had time to think about Richie and the events of the last couple of weeks. I guess it's true what they say, that keeping busy is sometimes the best medicine.

Yet when I pulled into my driveway half an hour later, I just sat in the car, unable to muster the energy to open the door, get out, and go into the house. It was the heat, finally, that drove me out of the car; I'd killed the motor when I first got home, and Mississippi in June is no time to be sitting in a car any longer than necessary.

I waved to Mrs. Goodson, my neighbor across the street, and started up the walk.

"Rebecca! Honey, do you have a minute?" Mrs. G. stood at her mailbox with an armload of catalogs – the woman was an intrepid online shopper.

"Sure, Mrs. G. What's up?" I had no desire to stop for a heart to heart, or for a "How're you doing?" even, but she was a sweet lady. I ordered myself not to take out my bad mood on her as I walked out to the street where she waited.

"I just wanted to let you know there was a young man at your place earlier today, just about lunchtime. I was sitting by the window reading when I heard a door slam over your way. I looked out and saw this beautiful man headed up your walk."

"Now, Mrs. G., you'd better watch it. Mr. Goodson might not like hearing you talk that way," I said, dropping the lid on my mailbox and scowling at the stack of mail inside.

"Hon, we've been married for forty-five years. If he gets jealous over a few words at this late date, he can just go jump in the Pascagoula River." I saw the pink flush in her cheeks and couldn't help grinning.

"So tell me about this beautiful man," I laughed, giving her shoulders a squeeze.

"Well, he was about as tall as Mr. Goodson," she began, "but a bit leaner, if you get my drift." I did. The Goodsons enjoyed the cheap buffets at the local casinos, where they met friends for lunch a few times a week. "He had short, dark hair, and he was wearing black slacks and a white shirt. He was too far away for me to see what color his eyes were... I sure would

74

have liked to get a look at them. He had a good tan. He knocked on your door and waited for a minute, then got in his car and left."

"What kind of car did he drive?"

"I'm not very good with cars, especially these newer ones. But it was black and it had a good wax job. It looked like he cared a lot about that car."

I shook my head, laughing. "Oh, I bet he does."

"Oh, so you know this young man?"

"I think so. It was probably Damian, a friend of Richie's who moved here not long before…"

"Oh, my dear. I'm so sorry you're having to go through this – and all alone. I *have* seen that nice young man you were seeing last year… He's been stopping by fairly often since Richard died, hasn't he?" I knew what she wanted to ask but wouldn't dare bring up, at least not directly.

"Yes, Mark's been a big help. But that's all, Mrs. G., he's just being a friend."

"Well now, two young men coming around – and both of them very handsome."

I refused to be baited further, so I excused myself and started back across the street. As I stepped onto the grass, I turned back. "Oh, Mrs. G.!" I called, as I watched her walking slowly back toward her house, "His eyes are drop dead gorgeous blue!"

She waved, and I heard her giggling all the way to her front door.

Chapter 12

I CHANGED INTO SHORTS and a tank top, thinking I might go out for a run a bit later when the temperature dropped a few degrees. Rummaging in the fridge I found the makings for a salad and threw it all into a bowl, then carried it into the darkened living room, the coolest room in the house. Collapsing onto the sofa, I forked a tomato and chewed on it as I thought about how much I missed Richie – and Owen. I picked up the phone and called Justine.

*****

An hour later I sat in the floor of my nephew's room playing Old Maid with him. I tried hard to keep a straight face as he decided which card to take from my hand. He clapped his hands with glee when he took my firefighter, leaving me the "Old Maid."

"Can we go watch cartoons now, Aunt Becca?"

"If that's what you want, and if it's okay with your mommy."

"Sure," Justine said from the doorway. "I wanted to talk to Aunt Becca anyway. Let me get you set up – Becca, you stay right there." *What did I do now?*

A couple of minutes later she came in and shut the door. "Rebecca, I don't mind you coming by to visit with Owen. He needs to spend time with you, especially now. But I don't want you to get the idea that it's okay to just drop by anytime you're feeling lonely. We do have our own lives to live, and I'd appreciate it if you'd give us a bit more notice next time."

"Well, sure, Justine. I'm sorry I sort of barged in today – but this is hard for me, too, and seeing Owen helps a bit, you know?"

"Yes, I do know. I just don't want you to start using Owen as a crutch the way you did his daddy. He's just a little boy, and he's hurting too, and he doesn't need that kind of pressure from you."

"I would never put pressure on Owen!" I felt my face heat up at her words. I wasn't sure whether I was more hurt or angry. "Why would you even think something like that?"

"Rebecca, I'm only going by how you always clung so to Richard." Obviously she resented the hell out of me. But I knew Richie would be happy I was here with his son. "Now that Richard's gone, you won't need to come by as often."

"No, I suppose not," I replied. "But I do want to see Owen regularly – I don't mean specific days, but I want to be a part of his life, and I sure want him to be a part of mine."

"He can be a *part* of your life, but don't expect Owen to be at your beck and call, available to come over and keep you company whenever you start missing your dear brother."

I stared at her, not believing what she'd said. Justine sounded so very bitter. It was hard to believe we'd been friends at one time. "I'd never dream of doing any such thing," I protested. "I just love Owen, and he loves me, and I'd like to know you're going to be okay with me seeing him frequently."

"You can see Owen – you just can't own him. He's mine, not yours. If you want a child, find yourself a husband and get your own."

"Justine! Why are you saying such things? Remember when you and Richard first moved here, when you were expecting Owen? Remember all the fun we had, shopping, fixing up Owen's nursery, taking long walks so you could exercise, shopping in all the little shops downtown? Whatever happened to us? What'd I do to make you resent me so much?"

"You really don't know." I heard the sneer in her voice, and the skepticism.

"No, I really don't. Why don't you tell me?" I had to find out, had to try to fix things with her so she wouldn't spoil my relationship with Owen. I couldn't stand it if I lost him, too.

"Okay, let me see…Where to start? How about the phone calls at anywhere from one to four in the morning, all those desperate times when you just had to talk to Richard, or more to the point, have him talk to you? He'd leave my bed and go downstairs, and after a while I'd give up and go back to sleep. Sometimes I didn't even know when he came back to bed, but when I did know, it was always after at least an hour."

I knew Richie hadn't minded me calling him – I only called when I was having an especially rough time with my anxiety. I'd wake in a panic, certain this time it really was a heart attack – the weakness, shortness of breath, palpitations, sweating – but then I'd take my meds and pick up the phone, and Richie would patiently sit up and talk with me until my meds began to make me sleepy. Some of our most heartfelt talks took place in the wee hours of the morning. But clearly Justine had disliked my taking Richie's attention like that.

"Then there were all the afternoons you just 'dropped by' and ended up staying for dinner, offering to put Owen to bed and read to him, then sitting around talking with Richard about all of y'all's old friends, people I don't know, hanging around until almost bedtime or time for Richard to go to work." I flushed, knowing there was truth in what she said.

"But you know we never meant to exclude you, Justine."

"And you know most of the time when y'all were together, you talked about things I didn't know about, couldn't talk about with you. How was I supposed to feel, other than left out?"

"I'm truly sorry you feel that way, sorry if I contributed to the problems between you and Richie. I never thought …"

"Who said anything about problems?" she snapped. "I'll have you know your brother loved me very much, and we were very happy together. I just wish we'd had more time…"

Okay, that was enough of that. Before she could get deeply into her melodramatic act, I cut her off. "Don't bother trying to convince me all was moonlight and roses over here. I know more than you think I do about the problems in your marriage to my brother."

"How dare you! Where do you get off, coming into my house and suggesting Richard was not happy with me? He loved me, and we were together until the day he died."

"I know he loved you, Justine. What I can't figure out is why. You were what I'd call high maintenance, after all. Always wanting to go out partying, needing new clothes for some event or other…"

"Get out. Just get out of my house right now. I don't have to listen to this from you. You don't know what you're talking about."

But I just couldn't let it go. I was like a dog worrying at a bone that isn't all that appetizing but that he isn't quite ready to give up, not knowing when or if another bone might come along. I knew I was only antagonizing her more, and she was mad enough already. I might as well see what kind of reaction I'd get from her if I brought up what was really bothering me.

"I know you're already throwing money around like there's no tomorrow. I know you had threatened to leave Richie and take Owen, said you'd go to San Antonio or to New Orleans, and that would have broken his heart."

"And what about my heart?" she said, the anguish thick in her throat, her eyes shimmering with unshed tears. "This hasn't been easy for me, you know – moving here to a strange place, watching my husband leave for work every day and wondering if he'd make it back home at night, sitting around day after day, night after night, never going out and having any fun."

"Well, you don't have to worry about Richie cramping your style now, do you? You can do what you want, and you have plenty of money to do it with. I would think you're well satisfied with the situation. You know, I didn't really think you were responsible for Richie's murder," I saw her eyes widen at my use of the word, "but hey, maybe I'm wrong." I was furious, with her and with myself. I shouldn't have let her get to me this way, and I shouldn't have made that last comment.

"Just what are you implying? Surely you're not suggesting I *wanted* to see Richard dead. Rebecca, that's a low blow, even for you. If you want suspects, I'd suggest you take a closer look at Paul Simmons." I stared at her. "Well. He *was* there after all!"

She resumed her pacing of the room, wheeling suddenly when she reached the window. "I think I already told you to leave. I won't tell you again. It wouldn't be very fitting for the fallen hero's widow to have to call for help in getting her sister-in-law out of her house."

I jumped to my feet. "No need. I'm going." I opened the door, then turned to face her again. "I'm warning you, Justine. Don't try to keep me away from Owen. If you do, it'll backfire. There'll come a day when he's old enough to stand the truth, and I'll be sure to see he gets it. For now, maybe it's best for us to agree to disagree." I yanked open the door and almost ran to the car.

I backed out of the drive, frustrated with Justine, and with myself for meeting her on her level. Disgusted, I gunned the motor and sped away. But less than two blocks from her house, I was already second-guessing my part of the argument. And I hadn't even said goodbye to Owen.

I sighed heavily and swept Bernice into a U-turn, then raced back toward my sister-in-law's house to try to make amends. As I neared her driveway, though, I noticed a man stepping out of a pickup in front of Justine's house. Athletic build, dark curls – Jake Coffee had wasted no time getting to Justine's after I left. He ran up the walkway, whistling, carrying a vulgarly large bouquet of red roses. I saw the door open, saw him go inside and shut the door behind him. Furious with myself for coming back to try to make up, I circled the block and headed home.

***

I was so angry I didn't notice Mark pulling into the drive right behind me. I slammed the car door and stormed toward the house.

Hey, where's the fire?"

Whirling around to face him, I couldn't keep the venom out of my voice. "My sister-in-law is a slut," I said unceremoniously. "Hi, Mark. C'mon in, if you can take my bad mood."

He shrugged and followed me inside, where I flopped down on the couch.

"What'd Justine do now?" He sat down and patted my knee.

I spat out details of our argument and told him about Jake's romantic visit.

He whistled. "Not wasting time, is he?"

"Neither is she," I grumbled.

"So, how's Owen taking all of this?"

I cringed. "I don't even know! I left without saying goodbye. I can't believe myself."

Mark put a comforting arm around me, pulling me close, and I laid my forehead against his shoulder and let the tears fall.

The doorbell rang.

"Expecting company?"

"No…could you please get that? I'll be right back." I hurried toward the guest bath to blot my face.

"I stopped by earlier, but nobody was home," I heard Damian saying when I came back into the room. "Oh, hey, Rebecca. I was telling Mark…I brought Richard's journal."

He reached toward me with a cedar box.

"Thanks, Damian." I took the box and set it on a side table. "Can you stay awhile?"

Before he could answer, Mark's cell phone rang. "It's work," he said. "I'll take it in the kitchen."

"My neighbor said somebody was here about noon. Was that you?"

"Yeah. Don't know why I thought you'd be here at lunchtime," he laughed. "But I was hoping I could take you to dinner."

"I was hoping that, too," Mark said behind me. "But I've got to go back in – probably for a few hours."

"I'm sorry," I said, hugging him.

"Why don't you two go on? I'll call you later, okay?"

At the door he murmured, "Don't have *too* much fun." I swatted him on the arm and grinned.

"Get going, Barrington. See ya soon. Thanks for the shoulder."

I turned back to face Damian. "So, how do you feel about Italian?" I asked.

Chapter 13

I WOKE FROM THE DREAM in a cold sweat, my eyes darting around my bedroom looking for Richie. It seemed I could still hear his voice, more faintly each time: "Find out the truth, Becca. I need the truth."

I threw back the sheet and strode across the hall to sit in the guest room's window seat overlooking the backyard, the yard where Richie and I grew up. In the back corner, our treehouse stood nestled snug against the live oak, the three-quarter moon illuminating the Spanish moss swaying in the breeze from the Gulf. Far enough away to be safe, close enough to feel and smell the salt air.

Ours was the only treehouse in the neighborhood. Dad had gone all out when he built it for Richie and me the year I turned six. At eight by twelve feet, it snuggled up to the ancient oak for protection. He laid a solid floor, saying if we broke our legs or arms it would be from a fall outside, *not* from falling through his flooring. Throughout the whole first summer after he finished it, we'd wheedled Mom for old furniture she had in the attic. Finally she gave us an old bean bag chair, a wicker rocker, a small rug, some discarded plastic glasses.

Lugging Richie's boom box, a Tupperware container full of Mom's chocolate chip cookies, and a jug of lemonade, we'd disappear for the afternoon. Before long we would be joined by one or more of Richie's friends. After a while they accepted my presence or forgot I was there – easy to do, since I usually curled up on the rug and read from the stash of books I kept in the corner.

When I hit my teen years, a time when you'd have thought I'd want to spend more time with Richie's friends, just the opposite happened. When I became interested in boys, I realized all the guys from the treehouse were boring. I knew too much about them. I'd been there when they belched, told gross jokes and blew Dr. Pepper out their noses while giggling over them, farted even. No thanks. I wanted a man of mystery. My treehouse gang days were over. After that realization, I only climbed up when I knew Richie wouldn't be there. Then I was free to read and daydream in solitude.

My big brother and I remained close, however. We'd take long walks in the late afternoon, down to the beach and along the sand. We'd find a quiet place to watch the sunset and talk – about life, about our hopes and dreams. He knew from the time he was twelve he wanted to be a police officer. I don't remember what made him choose that career, but he never talked about anything else. Unlike my brother, I went through several careers before settling on one. First I wanted to be a flight attendant so I could travel the world. Later I decided on medicine, but I didn't like blood and couldn't see how to handle that situation. Then came the model phase, the teacher phase (our mom was a teacher), the architect phase.

But somewhere along the way I decided to go the environmental science route so I could get a job that would let me work outdoors at least part-time. I found what I wanted at the Mississippi Emergency Management Agency. MEMA was statewide – a huge organization – all I had to do was jump in, do a great job, work my way up in seniority, and wait for the right opening. Then I could come home and do the job I loved here on the coast. I was still amazed that my first job offer had come from Harrison County.

The squall of a feral cat cut into my thoughts and brought me back to the present. I tried to recapture my dream. I'd been walking along the beach on a hot afternoon. The sand was scalding my bare feet, but I kept walking, looking first far up the beach, then far out into the Gulf, shading my eyes with my hand. Suddenly on the breeze I could hear Richie's voice, pleading: "Becca, help me. Help. Becca." I shook as if from a chill, remembering how plaintive his voice had sounded. I'd continued along the beach, not sure what I was seeking. Richie's voice waxed and waned in concert with the wind, and I kept feeling him just out of my reach.

"What is it, Richie?" I scanned the empty sand ahead of me. "What do you want?"

"*The truth,*" he said. "*I want you to find out the truth.*"

"What truth?" I felt lost and confused.

"*Find out the truth, Becca.. The truth about my murder.*"

Murder! That word again. I paced the room before returning to the window seat. What did the dream mean? I hadn't dreamed about Richie except for the night after his funeral, when I'd seen myself dropping rose petals on top of his coffin as it was lowered into the ground. That night I'd awakened petrified, tears having already wet my pillow.

Now, weeks later, to have such a dream was unnerving, to say the least. We Brighton women did have a sort of sixth sense – I thought of my mom, Aunt Hester, Grandma Brighton. I wondered just how far back in my lineage this ability went, and I wondered, not for the first time, if it was real.

Could I actually be getting a message from Richie? I'd never believed the dead came back to speak to us, even in dreams. Much more likely those thoughts had been rattling around in my brain, I'd been ignoring them, and they were finally demanding to be heard.

Find out the truth. The truth about my murder. Did I truly believe Richie's murder was still unexplained? If I did, how could I go about finding the truth? I was an emergency responder, not a detective. I had no idea where to start investigating something, especially in a case which had been so quickly deemed an open and shut case. Nobody had even hinted Richie might have been killed in some way other than what appeared to be the case. Yes, I had vowed to find the truth right after he was killed…that first week had been rough. And I *had* tossed out the veiled accusation to Justine when we fought, but did I really still believe that?

I sat in the window seat for hours that night gazing out at our treehouse. Finally sometime after four, I fell into an exhausted sleep curled in the cramped quarters, still hearing Richie's voice.

***

I couldn't face going in to work the next morning. Things were still calm in the tropics, so I figured it would be a quiet day in the office and maybe nobody would miss me. As it turned out, I was wrong about that.

About mid-morning I made a cup of tea and carried it out to the treehouse. I carefully held my mug in one hand while I gripped the ladder with the other and hoisted myself up and inside. The place looked much the same. I walked over to the rocker, picked up the cushion and beat it against the chair arm to get rid of the biggest part of the dust, replaced it, and sat down, breathing in the musty smell of a space too long unused. Closing my eyes, I thought back to good times here with Richie when we were young...

My cellphone vibrated in the pocket of my khaki capris, stilling my troubled thoughts. I looked at the caller ID: Lorelei Steggemann. I hadn't seen my best friend since the funeral. We had talked by phone, but I was really missing our times together. Lorelei had been busy lately with a charity benefit she chaired each year.

"Hey lady, you okay?" she asked right off. "I called your office and they said you didn't come in today. What's going on?"

I smiled at her brusque way of getting to the point. "I'm fine. Just a restless night. Too tired to concentrate today."

"Where are you? You sound like you're in an echo chamber."

"I'm in the treehouse." I waited for the scolding to begin.

"Oh, sweetie, by yourself? We can't have that. I'm coming over."

"No, Lorelei!" I said more sharply than I intended. I went on quietly, "I'm really okay. I needed to check the place out for Owen."

"How is the little guy? And how's his mommy?" Lorelei had never made a secret of the fact that she neither liked nor trusted Justine. My friend was happily married, yet I think she'd held on to a bit of the crush she'd had on Richie since ninth grade. "Never mind. You can tell me at lunch. I want you to come down to the Paradise so we can have a good long visit. How about one o'clock?"

Lorelei's husband, Bob, managed the Paradise, one of the eleven casinos here on the Mississippi coast. I wasn't a big fan of the casinos, knowing the problems caused by gambling addictions. But Bob Steggemann was one of the nicest men I knew, and I felt more comfortable in his casino than any other on the coast. I sighed, then gave in. It would be great to have a good heart to heart with Lorelei. Besides…that's where Mark worked.

***

Just before one I pulled into the parking garage at the Paradise, rode the elevator down to casino level, made my way through the promenade of specialty shops too expensive to even look into, and zeroed in on the steak house, the Gilded Lily. Lorelei preferred the steak house here and never willingly ate anywhere else. She liked her privacy as much as she did her food, and I had a feeling today we'd have the most private table.

"There you are!" Lorelei called, motioning to me from the restaurant entrance. I wove through the always present crowds moving through the casino. I laughed when I got a good look at her. The two of us had grown up one street away from each other, we were the same age, and we went off to USM together. But there the resemblance ended.

At five seven, I usually felt able to hold my own in a crowd – until I stood next to Lorelei, a willowy five ten in her bare feet. Lorelei seemed to glory in her height. Today she wore strappy silver sandals with four inch heels to complement a black silk blouse and grey silk pencil skirt that skimmed the top of her knees. A heavy platinum chain sparkled in the casino's fancy lighting but couldn't compete with the rocks on her left hand. She looked like a million dollars and knew it. More than one passing male glanced her way.

"It's a good thing I love you," I said, giving her a quick hug. "Otherwise I wouldn't put up with this inferiority complex that threatens to overwhelm me every time I'm around you."

Lorelei gave a ladylike snort. "Give me a break. You'd rather be dressed the way you are than like I am, and we both know it."

She was right. I was comfortable in my white sundress and espadrilles, and my only jewelry was the set of delicate gold chains Richie gave me on my last birthday. When I reached for jewelry, I always wanted something he'd given me. I had plenty to choose from – I'd received jewelry on every occasion since I turned sixteen. That was the year he turned eighteen and got his first paying job.

Linking her arm in mine, she steered me through the restaurant to a booth in the back corner. The staff eyed us warily, and I knew we wouldn't be overlooked, even in our secluded spot. Lorelei had already organized lunch, but I had little appetite, even for the endive salad, steamed veggies, crusty bread, steamed Gulf shrimp bought off the ship this morning, and lemon gelato for dessert. I couldn't really do justice to the food, but I gave it my best shot, for her sake.

We talked throughout the meal, just catching up. By dessert, though, I was so fidgety that Lorelei laid down her spoon and said, "Okay, friend. Something's on your mind, and it isn't Richie and this whole mess. No, this has something to do with me – what gives?"

She had me...like always. The two of us had been through way too much together. It was impossible for me to hide my discomfort.

"How long have you known Mark was still in town and working here?" I already knew the answer.

Lorelei drew back a bit at my brusqueness. "Since he first started. Why are you asking?"

"You know he's been my rock for the past few weeks."

She smiled like a cat that has just been served a three course meal: canary, catnip, and cream. "Yeah, I had noticed that."

"What's that look for? He's been helping me out – as a friend."

"Yeah, okay, if you say so."

"I *do* say so. And I was really surprised to find out he'd been working here over a year."

"And your point?" I could have wrung her neck. She didn't make this easy.

"Why didn't you tell me, Loree?"

She sipped her wine. "Because he asked me not to." She set down the glass and looked at me with a *back in your court* stare.

Chapter 14

WELL. *THAT* STUNG. I'd expected her to give me some drivel about "doing it for your own good," or "I didn't think you'd want to know." *Because he asked her not to?*

"Why do you think he did that?" When Mark and I talked about this, he never really told me why. Maybe he wanted to forget me, to make our separation complete.

"Well, I don't know, Becca," she snorted. "Why do *you* think he didn't want you to know?"

"I don't know, Lorelei," I tossed right back at her. "Maybe he was afraid if I knew I'd start hangin' around here tryin' to get him back."

"Maybe so. I don't know. But he asked me, as a favor, so I said okay, as a favor. Why does it matter to you anyway? You're over him...aren't you?"

I opened my mouth to give her a quick reply, but no words came out.

"Well?"

"Well...oh, heck, I don't know!"

She laid her hand over mine. "Are you sure you don't know, Becca? You've been through an awful time lately. Maybe it's caused you to re-think some things." She smiled at me knowingly.

"Maybe you're right. God knows all I've done for the past few weeks is think." I felt my face flush, realizing that wasn't completely true. I hadn't only been thinking when I'd been with Damian – there had been a little acting out, too.

"Wait. You don't blush easily, girl. What brought this on?" She arched her brows. "Have you and Mark…"

"No, nothing like that. God, Lorelei!"

"Well, something's going on. The only thing that's ever made you blush is guys." Her gaze sharpened, and I couldn't help it…I blushed harder. How do you blush "harder" exactly? Well, for me it involves rapid eye blinking and my already reddened face turning blotchy. Which was happening now.

"Have you found another guy?"

"Not exactly."

"What does 'not exactly' mean?"

"I did meet someone." *But I don't really want to talk about him.* Didn't matter…I was about to do just that. "He's an old friend of Richie's from Jackson. They worked together for a while, but I never met him back then."

"We were still in school then, and usually busy. I suppose that's understandable."

She had been busier than I, having met her future husband there. By marrying Bob she'd fulfilled that old put-down about southern girls who only went to college to "major in husband hunting." But it wasn't that way with Lorelei and Bob. They truly loved each other.

I tried to decide what to tell her about Damian, not sure how much of him I wanted to share yet.

"Start talking," she ordered.

"There's not much to tell. His name is Damian Wentworth, and he'd just moved to Biloxi when Richie got shot. Richie had helped him get a job with the Sheriff's Department. They'd worked together in Jackson."

"Are you okay talking about this?"

"Believe me, this is the easy part." She looked sharply at me.

"What are you talking about, Becca?"

"Nothing. What d'you want to know about him?"

"Everything, of course," she giggled.

"I don't know *everything* about him, far from it. He has secrets in his past, and I don't really want to get involved with someone who isn't an open book, not after witnessing Richie's experience with Justine."

"Speaking of whom…" she began, then waved her hand for me to continue. "Don't stop now. We can talk about her majesty later." I giggled. Lorelei and Justine had never been friends. "Go on," she ordered.

"Damian came by Justine's the day after Richie died, when the situation was so crazy. You remember, people wandered around all over the house. The rest of the family was busy, so I answered the door, and there stood this gorgeous guy."

Lorelei shivered. "Delicious."

"You probably won't believe this, but I didn't even notice his dimples the first time I saw him."

"What!" she cried in mock horror. "That should be a headline: 'Becca Misses Dimples, Falls for Guy Anyway.'" She threw her head back and laughed with abandon, and several diners turned to look in our direction.

'Shh, Lorelei. I suppose it's impossible for them to throw you out of here, but still… And remember, my brother had just died."

She sank back into her seat. "Sorry, Becca. I wasn't thinking." She patted my arm. "I'm sure you didn't notice them."

"It's okay, Loree, I know you didn't mean anything by it." I paused, then said, "He *is* really good looking, though."

"I can see that, because you're still blushing." She grinned. "Keep talking. Blonde? Dark? What color eyes?"

"Dark hair, and these magnetic blue eyes that just drag you in."

"Sounds yummy."

"He came by the house a few days later to return something of Richie's. He brought me a journal – I didn't know Richie ever kept a journal. I haven't read it yet. Anyway, while he was there, he asked me to dinner. We went to the Italian place downtown."

"Not here?" she asked, in mock horror. "Never mind. Did you have a good time?"

"Yes, we did," I admitted. "We sat and talked for hours. I still don't know that much about him, but I do feel more comfortable with him now. Lorelei, his eyes are the most incredible blue." I couldn't help smiling.

"He's made an impression, I see. When do I get to meet him? You have to bring him to dinner one night soon."

"Okay, *if* I see him again. Now, can we change the subject?" She sighed, but recognized I'd told her all I was going to for now.

It was time to go, but I caught her up on Mom and Dad, and Owen and Justine.

"You see them often? Owen and Justine, I mean?"

"I don't see Owen as often as I would like," I shrugged. "But I understand they need to learn to get on with their lives. Justine and I had one big argument. I was afraid she wouldn't let me see him at all after that. We both made some harsh accusations. I was surprised when she let me keep him overnight one weekend."

"I'll just bet she did," Lorelei muttered. I drew my eyebrows together, frowning.

"What do you mean?"

"Nothing, really. She's just been here several times lately."

This surprised me. But then I knew Justine hadn't been happy with her quiet lifestyle. What Lorelei said next gave me pause.

"She's here a couple of times a week, and always on the weekend." Her tone made clear what she thought about that. "She's mostly at the craps tables, but sometimes blackjack."

"The little bitch. She's spending Richie's life insurance money."

"Did he have enough for her to be spending like this? Most young couples don't worry about things like insurance."

"I don't think they had much insurance, either, but police officers are covered by a million dollar policy. *I* sure don't have coverage like that – but then, I don't have dependents, either." I shook my head, unsettled by what I'd heard. "She's gonna spend that kid's money before he's old enough to do anything about it. Thank goodness the system puts aside money for college for kids of fallen officers. I guarantee his mom won't be saving any of that money for him."

"Like most people, she has good nights and bad nights. So far she's staying fairly even," Lorelei said. I knew she wanted to ease my concerns – it wasn't working.

"She already bought a new Porsche SUV. That's a good chunk of change right there." We were both quiet for a moment, until I finally got up the nerve to ask: "She coming in with any men friends yet?" I felt sure she hadn't been alone, but I didn't want even Lorelei to know I'd suspected Justine of affairs while Richie was alive.

"A few times. I'm not here all the time, but…"

"But Bob tells you all about the Merry Widow," I said, curling my lip. "I'm glad he does, and I'm glad you told me. I'm trying to help Owen through this rough time, but she makes it hard sometimes, you know?" I felt tears of frustration about to escape from my eyes. "Lorelei, you have no idea how many times I've cussed that woman, in my mind, during the last six months." *Uh-oh.*

"Six months?" I knew she wouldn't miss that slip-up. "What's been going on for six months?"

I sipped my water before saying, "I think…Richie thought…well, *we* thought Justine might be cheating on him. I don't know for sure," I said quickly. "There were just some suspicious things she did."

Lorelei sighed, and I did, too.

"So y'all thought Justine was cheating on Richie, and now he's dead, and she's out throwing money around all over the place, and bringing guys like Jake Coffee in…"

"Jake! That over-muscled under-brained…" Lorelei raised her brows. I felt my chest tighten, and the hair on my arms stood on end. "I should go over to her house and…"

"No, Becca. That is the one thing you must not do." Lorelei grabbed my wrist and held on tightly. "Listen to me. You have to think about Owen. You're all he's got right now. You're the only stability in his little life."

"I *know.*" I clenched and unclenched my fists. Finally Lorelei released my arm. "It's not only Owen," I said. "There's also Mom and Dad. This has been so hard on them already. I don't know if they'd survive finding out Justine might've had something to do with what happened to Richie."

Lorelei went still, and I sat there hardly breathing. She always did this to me. A casual conversation with her could turn so easily into Rebecca-tells-all confession time. I searched for a way to undo what I'd let slip but could think of nothing. Trouble was, I was *thinking* that, *suspecting* that, and now Lorelei knew how I felt.

"You probably think I've gone crazy," I whispered, as if by whispering I could make it all go away – or at least make it not be real. I leaned my head back against the cool leather of our booth. "Promise you won't say anything to Bob about this. If Justine ever heard I'd been saying such things about her...I'd probably never get to see Owen again. She'd move to California or New York, and then she'd probably find a way to disappear."

"Becca, tell me. How many secrets have you and I shared over the years? Yeah," she answered her own question, "way too many to count. My lips are sealed."

Chapter 15

Paul Simmons sat across from me at the weathered picnic table, plates of The Shed's famous pulled pork barbecue sandwiches between us. We were at a weathered outdoor table far away from the restaurant, next to the pond where a little duck family swam, the babies still covered with yellow fuzz.

I'd seen Paul three times now since that night at the hospital; this time I was determined he would give me a complete rundown about what had happened that night.

I knew Paul was nervous. I hadn't explained to him what I wanted when I asked him to meet me at The Shed. I took another bite of my sandwich. Questions could wait a bit.

After a few minutes of companionable munching, I tore off another paper towel and carefully wiped my hands. I laid The Shed's "napkin" aside and faced Paul squarely.

"So. I'm sure you know why I asked you to dinner." I made it a statement rather than a question.

"Yeah, I have a good idea. I guess you have a few questions about…that night."

"Not so many questions. What I need is to hear, in your words, what happened. Every single thing."

Paul stiffened, tossing his napkin aside. His always lean face had become even thinner over the past few weeks. His cheekbones were sunken, and he had dark shadows underneath his brown eyes, which now flashed with sudden anger.

"Guess you think I had something to do with Richard's death, too, don't you?" he spat out. "You and everybody else in town."

Surprised by his vehemence, I drank my iced tea and considered him for a minute before answering. "Paul, I lost my only brother three weeks ago, and the fact is, you were there. Don't you think it's a reasonable request for me to hear from you what happened? Dry reports don't give me the clarity I need." Our eyes locked for a long moment, then he dropped his gaze and blinked a few times. I watched his Adam's apple working before he spoke.

"Sorry, Rebecca. But it's been rough, you know, answering questions like that over and over and over. I feel like they're not gonna stop asking questions until I change my answers. And that's not gonna happen, because I've been telling them the truth."

"Okay, I understand that," I said softly. "But could you please tell *me* what you've been telling *them*, just one more time? I will believe you." *Probably.* "I need to hear it firsthand rather than once or twice removed."

I couldn't understand his reticence. After all, I was a victim here, too, not one of the examiners who'd been raking him over the coals for weeks. Was he being *too* defensive? *Did* he have something to hide? Despite my concerns, I had to make him feel comfortable so he would talk, so I could hear about it from him directly.

Shoving his plate to the side, he rested his arms on the rough wood of the bare table. I did the same. We must have looked like two adversaries preparing for the final bout of an arm-wrestling competition. I gave him a tentative smile of encouragement.

"All right. I do get what you're saying. I'll do the best I can. But some of it won't be easy for you to hear."

"Won't be as hard as hearing Richie was dead. I can handle it."

And so he began. For the next twenty minutes I sat back and let him talk, telling his story in whatever way he wanted, sitting in the late, sticky-hot Mississippi afternoon, hearing the faint drone of bumblebees in a patch of nearby wildflowers, my eyes never leaving his face except when drawn to his restless hands. In the distance I heard the first twangs of a banjo as the bluegrass band began its warm-up.

I didn't interrupt until he got to the point where he'd begun to tell me about the decision to check out the barn. "Whose suggestion was it for Richie to go to the rear of the barn while you stayed out front?"

"His, of course," he said defensively. "He was the officer in charge, and I was backup. If he'd told me to go around to the rear, I would have obeyed. He chose to do that himself."

I didn't respond, but waited until he was ready to continue. The next part was the most difficult for me to hear. To his credit, Paul didn't shy away from giving me the details he knew I craved. But when he began to describe the stillness of Richie's body, the pallor of his face, and the circle of blood already beginning to pool around him, it was as if I were right there with him in the dirt, gazing down on my brother, waiting for him to die all over again.

"I shone my light all around the area," Paul said. "Richard lay in a clearing that extended out in all directions probably twenty feet or so. I knew the shooter could be just about anywhere, and with woods surrounding us, I knew I'd need help to find him. I was also praying help would get there in time for Richard. So I ran back to my patrol car and radioed in the situation, then grabbed a blanket from my trunk to take back and cover him. I'd felt a faint pulse and I knew he'd be in shock. But I couldn't make it back to him right then, because that's when I heard the sound from the truck."

I shivered in spite of the heat of the evening, as I pictured him there alone, a mortally wounded brother-in-arms and a dangerous suspect nearby.

"Right when I shut the trunk I heard the sound. I dropped the blanket and began to creep around my car and up toward Richard's, for a better viewpoint, you know? There was a guy in the driver's seat of the pickup, hunched over the steering wheel, cranking the ignition."

His eyes held a faraway look, and I knew he was back there again, standing with a gun pointed on the suspect. "So I gave the command for him to get out of the truck. But rather than doing that, he turned toward me, placed an arm along the ledge of the open window, and laid a handgun across his arm like he was trying to hold it steady."

This was the first I'd heard of the suspect's actual movements; I was shaken anew.

"I gave the order for him to drop the gun. But instead, he fired and I returned fire. He missed me, but I hit him three times and he slumped in the truck seat. After I ascertained the suspect was dead, I radioed it in, grabbed the blanket, and ran back to Richard. I tucked the blanket around him and kept talking to him, hoping for a response...any kind of sound or movement from him, but he never moved at all."

Paul's voice broke on these words, and his head came forward to rest in his hands, his elbows on the table. His tears dropped onto the faded-out wood where they disappeared almost as soon as they touched down, and I felt more tears sliding down my own face.

After a while he leaned back and reached to tear a paper towel off the roll sitting beside our plates. "Sorry," he said, his voice husky with more unshed tears. "For all the times I've talked about this, today's the first time I have cried. I never cried during any of the interrogations."

I laid a hand on his arm. "Maybe you should have."

He gave a short, bitter laugh. "Maybe you're right. Just telling them the truth hasn't been working so well."

He blew his nose into the towel, wadded it into a ball, and tossed it into a nearby trash can, where it made a quiet "thunk" as it dropped in.

I sat back and looked at the grieving man across from me. I believed him, believed he was telling me the truth about that night. So if Paul wasn't involved, what *did* happen at that barn? How would I ever be able to find out who was responsible? Because I *would* find out.

"Thank you, Paul. You can't know how much you telling me this today has helped."

"I'll do anything to help, Rebecca. I feel so responsible for what happened to Richard."

"I don't believe you're at all responsible," I assured him. "But Paul..." I hesitated, waiting until his eyes had met mine. "I do believe someone besides Hollingshead may be responsible." I saw the shock of what I said register in his eyes.

"What are you saying, Rebecca?"

"I'm saying I don't think that kid acted alone that night. I think somebody else was involved, and together they set up this elaborate scheme designed to get Richie out there alone."

"But how could that be? I mean, how could anybody know who would respond to that call? That doesn't make sense. I could have been the one to respond instead."

"And if you had, I think nothing would have happened…that night. I think they would have re-worked their plan and waited for a better time."

"Are you saying you think somebody *murdered* Richard, and they had it planned ahead of time?"

"I know how crazy this sounds. Way too many variables were involved that night for something like that to work…but I think it *did* work. I don't know if those who planned it were too dumb to know all the ways their plan could go wrong, or if they didn't care, wanted to take the chance. I won't know that until I find out who wanted my brother dead bad enough to try to pull off something like that."

"But the suspect, Hollingshead… He shot at me, and I shot back. How could someone else be involved?"

"*Did* he shoot at you, Paul?"

"What? Sure he did. I heard the shot! I did not shoot an innocent man." His eyes bored into mine.

"That's not what I asked. I asked you if *he* shot at you. Do you remember seeing the muzzle flash?"

He stared at me. "Yes, Rebecca, I saw it."

"Could somebody else have been somewhere around the place?"

"We didn't find any sign of anybody else."

"That's not what I asked. The authorities just 'assumed' things happened a certain way. But I think they're wrong."

"But what's made you question things this way?"

"You want to know the first thing that made me suspicious that they – you all – might not really have the facts straight?" I leaned forward and clenched my hands on the table. "It was when I found out Richie had been shot in the back of the head, from the left side, *with his own gun*." I leaned back. "That makes no sense to me whatsoever, Paul. Does it make sense to you? Honestly?"

"No, I admit it doesn't. I could hardly believe it even though I was there and saw it for myself."

"But what precisely did you see? What if someone else was there who got away?"

"Oh, my God, Rebecca. How are we gonna find out?"

"*We* aren't gonna do anything, yet. I want to talk to a few more people, but you can't get involved, not with this investigation hanging over your head. You have enough on your plate."

"But we can't let this go," he protested.

"We aren't going to," I promised him, this old partner of my brother's, this man who'd tried to save him and now had his career on the line. "But if I'm right, then the person, or persons, responsible aren't going anywhere. They'll be right here, and the more time that passes, the greater the chances they'll slip up and I'll be able to tie them directly to Richie's murder."

"Hey, you can't tackle this alone. You need the authorities. Have you talked to anybody at headquarters about what you think happened?"

"I've tried, but they see me as an overwrought sister grieving the loss of her brother and clutching at straws to find a way to make somebody pay when the person responsible is already dead."

"What if I talk to somebody?"

"No! No, you can't do that. I've already said this, Paul. You can't afford to get involved with anything that muddies the waters. Just keep answering their questions, wait it out, and I believe in time the truth will come out."

He shook his head. "I don't feel good about this at all."

"I don't either, but it's the only choice, as far as I can see. So promise you won't say a word about this to anybody, not until I say so."

"I'm afraid you're heading toward something dangerous, and you don't even know what it is, or who's behind it. But yeah, I promise. I won't say anything…for now." He looked across the pond toward woods that looked similar to those behind the barn where this all started.

Suddenly he turned to me, eyes dancing. "I just don't see how this could have played out logistically. If another shooter was there, where was he? How did he get there? How did he get away? I mean, I didn't hear anything at all until I heard the first sirens coming in."

"What if the shooter managed to sneak away under cover of the sirens?"

He nodded thoughtfully. "That's surely possible. As soon as the EMTs arrived I began shouting for them to come around back to get Richard. Radios were squawking, people were yelling, sirens were still blaring – the place was nothing but a mass of confusion for a few minutes."

"Did anyone ever mention the possibility of other suspects?"

"No, but then, the other officers just checked out the guy in the truck, and he was dead. And then they asked me what happened. I told them, at least what I thought at the time had happened." He swallowed visibly. "God, what if I got it wrong? What if I allowed Richard's real killer to get away because I thought I knew what had happened?"

"If you did, it was because somebody planned it well enough for you to think that way. I know our brains tend to latch onto the most obvious choice unless something specific intervenes, and nothing did, that night."

"You're right." He shook his head as if to clear his thinking. "I still can't believe it happened the way you're thinking. Or maybe I don't want to believe it. After all, it sure wouldn't make me look at all competent, would it?"

"Listen, Paul," I said, shifting to get more comfortable on the wooden bench where I'd been sitting for a while now, "if it *did* happen that way, it was because somebody planned it to the last detail. I still can't quite wrap my head around how it could have been done. But I'm convinced it was. And Paul, there's no way they could have known it would be you responding along with Richie. They planned for it to fool just about anybody."

"I suppose," he said in a barely audible voice, "it could have all been part of some grand scheme. Someone may have been hiding in the woods, watching, waiting for the right opportunity."

"Yes, and I doubt Tommy knew the whole plan. If you hadn't shot him, I think someone else would have."

"So, when I drove up, he panicked and shot, but if I hadn't gotten him, you think he'd have died anyway."

"Yes. I think the *real* killer planned for Tommy not to survive the night."

After Paul left, I sat staring at the mama duck and her ducklings wading ashore to get settled down for the night, thinking about all he'd said. I hoped I'd done the right thing, trusting him with my suspicions. *I do believe his version of what happened, don't I? But what if I'm wrong? What then?*

Chapter 16

O N FRIDAY I DROVE OUT to the cemetery after work, something I'd begun to do a couple of times a week. I'd sit beside Richie's headstone and try to recapture the feeling of completeness which hadn't really been there since he died.

Today I'd brought something I hoped would help. I sat down and folded my feet under me, opening the brown leather journal for the first time. On the inside cover Richie had scrawled his name and the date: "Richard Allan McCallum, March 1, 2004." I opened to the first entry and began to read:

"I've never kept a journal in my life – not sure why I'm starting now. I just feel like I'm jumping off into a brand new life and want to document it. I probably won't write very much very often, but I'd like to know I have a place to come to if I'm ever needing to de-stress.

"Today was the first day of the rest of my life. I know people say that all the time, but I mean it. I had my first day as a police officer today. Just started work for the Jackson P.D. Went on the street with Brent Meldon, a veteran of fifteen years on the force.. Glad they paired us up like that. It'll be good to learn the ropes from someone who knows what he's doing. I will soon enough though. This is my dream come true."

Oh, Richie, I'm sorry you only had a few years as an officer, but I'm so thankful you did have those years. I miss you so much, and I need your help.

That dream, did it come from you or from inside my head? Am I right in thinking there's more to your death than anyone knows right now? Richie?

But I felt no connection, none at all. I was on my own. I trudged back across the lawn, found Bernice, and said, "Come on girl, let's go home."

Great. Now I was talking to my dead brother *and* my car. What next…lampposts?

***

The next morning, though it was Saturday, I was up at dawn, exhausted from all the tossing and turning. I stumbled into the bathroom and looked at myself in the mirror. "You look like you've had a way better time than I know to be true," I said, sticking my tongue out at my reflection in the mirror. "You'd better get yourself together if you're going to go get Owen later."

I'd texted Justine last night and asked if he could come over today and stay the night, and she'd agreed, more excited than I'd expected, in fact. I brushed aside that thought, since I was learning to accept lots more from her just so I could see Owen regularly. Lord only knew what she'd do if she ever really got it in for me for any other reason besides her jealousy.

After brushing my teeth and putting on a pair of denim shorts and a yellow tank top, I fixed a bowl of cereal and sat down with a pad and pen, planning to make out a grocery list that would include a few of a certain little boy's special favorite foods, such as hot dogs, ice cream, and chocolate cake. Okay, so those were the three things he *always* wanted when he came over. I figured both he and I could use a bit of comfort food today.

My cell phone began to vibrate on the table, "Morning, Mark," I said, feeling a bit more chipper already. "What's up?"

I could feel his hesitation through the phone. Finally, "Good morning, Becca. I take it from your perky voice you haven't yet looked at Saturday's paper."

My heart leapt into my throat, then plummeted to my stomach. He sounded positively somber. "No, I just woke up," I said. "What's happened?" Even as I was saying this I was on my way to the front door. I opened the door and stepped outside, then ran down the driveway to scoop up my paper and dart back into the house. I slammed the door behind me.

"Well, guess you'll see for yourself by the time I can tell you," he said. "Why don't I just wait for the explosion?"

I hit the speaker button and dropped the phone on the sofa, flopping down beside it. I snatched the rubber band off the paper and unrolled it. "Slain Officer's Widow Suggests Law Enforcement Cover-up!"

"Oh, my Lord," I wailed. "Justine, what have you done now?"

Quickly I scanned the top-of-the-fold article. "It's Paul," I said. "She's done everything but accuse him of murdering Richie."

"Where would she ever get such a crazy idea?" Mark asked in a perplexed voice. "She say anything about this to you?"

I hesitated, trying to decide how to answer. "Well...it did come up one day last week when I'd gone over to the house to pick up Owen."

"What do you mean it came up?" he spat out. "You haven't said anything to me about that."

Suddenly I was seeing red. "I don't think I like the tone of your voice," I said. "You sound like I *owe* it to you to tell you – like I should be sharing every single thing with you. You don't have a claim on me, Mark."

Silence. "No, I guess you're right," he said, finally. "No claim at all. Well, I thought you might want to know before you started to get inquiring phone calls. Gotta go now."

"Mark, wait. I'm sorry. It's just that...well, I had a bad night, didn't sleep much, and then I'm trying to make plans for spending the day with Owen, and..." My voice trailed off. My excuses sounded flimsy even to me.

"It's okay," he said stiffly. "But I need to get off the phone. I'm at work. See you soon."

"Mark?" But he'd hung up. Why could I not learn to curb my sharp tongue? Chewing on a thumbnail, I sat and finished the article. *What are you up to, Justine?* Well, I'd find out in time, one way or another.

***

I saw Owen's little face pressed up against the window when I drove up, so I wasn't surprised when he threw open the door seconds later. He waited on the porch. He wasn't supposed to go outside without Mommy, and he was twisting his body and stepping from one foot to another, trying to be patient while I got out of the car.

"Hey, little guy!" I ran around the car, crossed the short space of lawn, and bounded up the steps, sweeping him up in a joyous hug. His squeals and giggles brought Justine into the hallway, and I set him down to close the door.

"Do the two of you do this all the time when you go to your Aunt Rebecca's?" Justine asked, frowning. "I don't like the idea of too much roughhousing."

One of those days, is it?

"Justine, do you have a minute so we could talk?"

"Only a minute. I'm very busy in the office right now, working on our financial things. I swear, Richard left them in quite a mess."

I swallowed a retort that I knew wouldn't set well with her and said to Owen, "How about you go and play in your room for a few minutes, hmm? I need to talk to your mommy about something."

When he had gone upstairs to his room, Justine and I moved into the living room.

"What is it, Rebecca? Make it fast, okay?"

"It's about the article in today's paper," I began. "I was a bit surprised you've decided to go after Paul Simmons that way."

"Why are you surprised? I've said all along I thought there was more to his story than what we heard. I do believe it's possible that he shot Richard. Maybe not intentionally, but in the heat of the chase, things just happen."

"You can't believe that! How would Paul have gotten Richie's gun away from him? And what would be his reason?"

"Well, I don't know, Rebecca. As I said, things just happen. I just want someone to keep after him, that's all."

"I believe Paul's story, Justine. And I think you should think more carefully before you go shooting off your mouth to a reporter."

"Excuse me? Is Richard's little sister trying to tell me how to run my life? *My life?*"

"Once in a while someone needs to try, and it seems I'm the only one who will disagree with you. But I guess I don't count."

She stood staring at me for a long, silent moment, and said, "You're right. You don't count. And you never will." I don't know why I'd expected any other kind of response from her.

"Oh, Justine, I thought we'd made a bit of progress lately in our relationship."

"We don't have a relationship," she spat. "And as for Owen, I don't think today would be a good day for him to go with you. He needs to stay with me."

Now she was pulling out the big guns – my love for Owen would make me accept just about anything she wanted to dish out.

"Justine, please. Don't punish him because you're angry at me," I said, fighting hard to hold back the tears that were threatening to spill. *Don't let her see you cry.* "Take it out on me some other way, but let him come with me. He's been so excited."

"Too excited." I stared at her in disbelief.

"How could a four-year-old possibly *be* too excited?" I asked impatiently. I lowered my voice to a whisper. "He just lost his daddy, Justine. I would think you'd be happy to see him excited about something."

"What-*ev*-er. The bottom line is that Owen's not going with you today. I'm not sure when we might be able to reschedule. Maybe next weekend." With that, she walked back to the front door and flung it open. "Give me a call later next week and we'll see."

I opened my mouth to say something but couldn't think of anything. I squared my shoulders and brushed past her. She slammed the door as soon as I was outside. I stood there for a minute, trying to calm myself before I got behind the wheel. As I slipped into the car, I felt it begin.

First came the feeling of ice running through every vein in my body. Then came the weakness and the chest pains. *You've been through these before. You can get through this one, too.* But I had always had Richie to talk me through these anxiety attacks. *Well, you're a big girl now, with no big brother. It's up to you to hold yourself together.*

I dug into my purse and found my medicine, popped two into my mouth, chewed, and swallowed. I shuddered at the bitter taste, knowing it would linger a while until I could get something liquid to wash it down with. So I backed Bernice from the drive, made a few turns as I drove, and reached Hwy. 90, where I turned west toward home. I stopped at the first drive-in I saw and ordered a Sprite. After swishing a few gulps around in my mouth, I lost the bitter aftertaste.

I feared, however, I'd never lose the bitter aftertaste from the scene with Justine. I leaned my forehead on the steering wheel and let the tears fall. *I didn't even get to see Owen to say goodbye.*

But moments later, I sat up, wiped away the tears with a napkin, and blew my nose. I began deep breathing exercises, counting in four, holding four, exhaling on four. I closed my eyes and tried to call to mind a laughing Richie to help me through. But he wasn't there. Thirty minutes later, I had finally calmed down enough to drive the rest of the way home.

She is not going to turn Owen away from me," I vowed. "I love him too much. He and I share the same blood. He's tied to me as much as I am to him. In the end, surely, she will relent, for his sake."

My heart didn't believe it for a minute.

Chapter 17

A S THE STIFLING, SULTRY, spongy days dragged us on toward July, I continued to be haunted by Richie's words from my dream. *Find the truth about my murder*. Why had I dreamed that? Was there something in my subconscious trying to worm its way out? One day I finally hunted up a notebook, went outside to the treehouse, and started writing things down. At first I wrote in a sort of journal form – letting thoughts meander onto the page and go where they would.

But then I found myself turning to a new page and labeling it "Possible Suspects." I struggled with that page for over two hours. What was it they were always harping about in the police shows? Means. Motive. Opportunity. So who had motive? I listed Justine, Jake, Paul, and Damian with a question. I also listed Justine and Jake jointly.

As to opportunity, well, nobody and everybody had a possible opportunity. Except for Paul, who definitely had opportunity – he was there, and alone, for a short amount of time, and admitted to being within about twenty yards of Richie when he was shot.

Was Damian working that night, or would he have been free? I should find out. Did he know enough about the local area to plan something to the degree this would have had to be planned? I put Justine at the bottom of the list as far as opportunity went. She was too feminine to seek out that sort of scenario.

On to means. Well, Richie was shot with his own gun, so no weapon needed there. I didn't think he could have been surprised by anyone he didn't know – he was too careful about having complete control of his weapon.

But someone he knew might have caught him off guard enough to get close to his gun and grab it from his holster. No, he'd have had his gun drawn going into the situation he faced that night. Maybe Paul and Richie both went around the barn and Paul pointed his gun at Richie and took his gun from him. Richie was stronger than Paul, I knew, but it could have happened.

If Justine had been involved I'd guess she'd have hired a hit man who would've had access to weapons and been able to set up such a situation. Jake could have guns. Even if he planned and executed everything, Justine could still have helped. What about Damian? I didn't have enough information, but my tendency was to discount him. I'd have to put Paul at the top of my list as far as method was concerned, with Justine a close second *if* she hired a hit man.

Last, motive. Jake and Justine both had clear motives – I viewed them as tied for first in that category.

I turned to a new page and listed what I'd concluded. As of this moment, I'd put Paul at the top of the list concerning Opportunity, Paul tied with Justine for Means, and Justine and Jake tied on Motive.

Obviously I needed to know lots more, because I had no clear winner. Okay, then. The next few weeks could be crucial to finding out the truth about that night. I took in a deep breath and blew it out.

Hot and thirsty after a couple of hours in the old treehouse, I left my notebook, climbed down, and went to the kitchen for a glass of cold water. I'd taken a few sweet gulps, leaning against the kitchen counter, when I heard a knock on the front door.

***

"Damian, what a surprise. Come on in." He followed me to the kitchen and we sat at the kitchen table. He had dropped by a couple of times before, each time when he was on his way to work. I had the feeling he wanted to check up on me yet didn't want any attachments.

Damian Wentworth was a puzzle to me. He was good looking, smart, funny. We'd had a really good time the one time we went out, and he always made me feel better when he came by. He had an infectious laugh, and he was always telling little stories about work. And then there were the dimples.

He'd been subjected to a mild initiation from his fellow officers. On his first day on the job, as he struggled to get the lay of the land, Dispatch sent him on half a dozen calls into the boondocks – always in broad daylight, always with another car shadowing his. Nobody wanted anything serious to happen to him. He took it all in stride, and within a few weeks he had become an integral member of the team of deputies serving the county.

"I wish Richie could be here to work with you," I said. "I know he had really looked forward to that. He talked about you often, during those last few weeks."

Damian jerked his head up, locking eyes with me. "Really? What did he say about me?" I felt a chill, so out of sync with this sweltering day. What was wrong with him? He acted as if Richie had been spilling secrets about him.

"Oh, nothing much," I said quickly, not sure why I felt so keen to reassure him. "He said you two had become good friends in Jackson, and he'd been trying to get you to move down here for a couple of years."

He nodded. "That's true. I don't know why I took so long to decide," he said, his voice husky. "If I'd been here sooner, I might have been able to, well, you know, maybe things wouldn't have worked out the way they did." *What does he mean by that?*

"We'll never know that, but I do know in my heart Richie wouldn't want us dwelling on might-have-been's." I shook off the nagging thought that this man had a background filled with secrets.

"That's true for you, too, Rebecca," he said softly, twirling his glass on the tabletop. I couldn't seem to look away from those mesmerizing blue eyes.

At last I smiled. "My friends call me Becca," I said softly.

Damian leaned forward, placing his hand on my shoulder. "Well, hello, Becca, my new friend," he said, and kissed me lightly. His lips were soft and warm against my mouth, and I felt a spark shooting between us, startling me in its strength.

He drew back first. "Hey, I didn't come by to hit on you. But it's my first Saturday off and I'm hoping I can take you to dinner." He gave me a dimply grin. I surprised myself by saying yes. When he asked for the best place in Ocean Springs for fresh seafood, I knew right where to take him.

I thought briefly of my promise to Lorelei to take him to the Paradise, but if he wanted seafood, that wasn't the way to go.

Doc's was a hole-in-the-wall sort of place compared to our more glitzy restaurants, but it served the most mouth-watering seafood I'd ever had. With little turnover in the kitchen staff, the food was always good. Doc and his wife Nancy did most of the cooking and they closely supervised anyone they hired. I worked for them from the time I turned sixteen until I left for college, and I knew firsthand how important cooking was to them. They were good people, and I had grown to love them.

I hadn't been out to Doc's since I lost my brother, and Nancy wrapped me in a huge hug when we walked in. I saw Damian trying to hide a smile.

"Doc! Doc, come out here!" Nancy called, causing the handful of customers to look around. I knew most of the people there and waved to a few. "Look who's come to visit!"

Doc came out of the kitchen, wiping his hands on his apron. He beamed when he saw me. "Hello, pretty lady!" he said, wrapping me in a hug as big as that of his wife. "About time you paid us a visit, right, Nancy?"

She nodded, wiping the corner of her eye with a dishtowel.

I introduced them to Damian and Nancy escorted us to my favorite spot – outside on the veranda, overlooking the marshes adjoining Biloxi Bay. I felt a whole bunch of eyes on us as we left the main dining area.

"That wasn't so bad," I said under my breath. Damian raised his eyebrows. "I haven't been here since I lost Richie." After we were seated, I decided to try to get an answer to at least one of my questions. "I've wondered…were you on duty the night Richie died? How did you find out?"

"Yeah, I had patrol duty over around Gulfport that night. I heard calls on the radio, but I didn't know who was involved. I couldn't believe it when I heard it was Rich. I finally used my phone to call in about two-thirty, and

Dispatch told me. By the time I got off at seven, you'd all gone from the hospital."

His story was interrupted when Nancy came out with the food. She bustled around, bringing out dish after dish for Damian to try. She seemed eager to please him. We nibbled on shrimp prepared three different ways, oysters both fried and on the half-shell, and crab cakes that made my mouth water just looking at them. The seafood was accompanied by fried green tomatoes bursting with flavors both sweet and sour, baked sweet potatoes oozing with melting butter, coleslaw, and hush puppies.

"Not the most nutritious meal," I whispered conspiratorially, "but you won't find anything that tastes better."

"Always room for comfort food," Damian laughed. I really did like this man.

For two hours we ate and talked, and finally Damian relaxed enough to tell me a bit about himself. The oldest of four children, he was originally from Atlanta, Georgia, and the rest of his family still lived there. He'd moved to Jackson in 2003, shortly after graduating from Ole Miss, and had then enrolled in the state police training academy. He and Richie had been hired by the Jackson P. D. about the same time.

As roommates and brother officers, they'd become fast friends. But Richie had moved back home after about a year. They'd stayed in touch and managed to meet up for lunch fairly often – up until about a year ago. At this point Damian paused and sat back, folding his arms. I felt we'd run up against a concrete barrier.

But I needed to know more. Richie had mentioned more than once that Damian had "gone through a rough time" during the past few years. Remembering our last conversation, when he had once again urged me to give his old buddy a chance, I plowed ahead.

"Damian, can I ask you something?" He didn't unfold his arms, but he gave a slight nod. "Richie thought the world of you," I said, by way of beginning. "He told me more than once what a great guy you were, and I think he had hopes that we, that you and I…"

"Would get together?" he grinned and reached out to take my hand in his tanned ones. Nancy picked that moment to come outside, but she quickly whirled and went back in, chuckling. Catching her movement out of the corner of his eye, he smiled out one side of his mouth. I felt the pink creeping up my neck.

"You're very appealing when you blush," he said, leaning in to give me a kiss. I couldn't help responding, opening my lips to his. "Umm, delicious," he said lightly, but I could see those blue eyes turning darker, looking more like a storm-tossed Gulf than the magical blue of Florida's panhandle.

When he smiled, and those dimples appeared, I about melted. "Now, what did you want to ask me? No, I know Richard told you I'd had some troubles. You're wondering what that was all about."

"Yeah, I guess so," I confessed.

"Well, it all started with a woman," he grimaced.

Now I felt like a voyeur. I opened my mouth to apologize, but he shook his head. "It's okay, really it is. I don't think good friends should have secrets from each other. Secrets ruin relationships." He shifted in his seat.

"It isn't really any of my business…"

"I want to tell you."

I shrugged. "If you're sure…" He nodded.

"I met Olivia Martin when I'd been on the Jackson P.D. for just under four years. I was three years older than her. She was beautiful…long blonde hair – natural – brown eyes, tall and willowy. She said she worked as an insurance claims adjuster. I thought that explained her erratic schedule. I fell hard for her, so I probably overlooked signs I shouldn't have."

"She was married."

"No. God, I wish that had been it. She had a drug problem. She wasn't a user…she was a dealer."

"Oh, Damian!"

"Yeah, I know, right? I'm a police officer involved with a drug dealer." He shook his head. "Don't know how I could have been so stupid. Anyway, one afternoon I drive by this convenience store and see Olivia's car parked out back. She's talking to a guy. My first thought was, she was cheating on me, but then I realized they were acting suspicious, like lots of suspects do. If it hadn't been her, I'd have stopped right then and investigated. God, I wish I had."

"This was her contact?"

He nodded. "It took a while, but after surveilling her on my off-hours I had enough evidence to confront her. First she got mad, then she started apologizing, saying she'd been wanting to get out but the money was just too good. I gave her an ultimatum…get out of the business or I'd turn her in."

"What a horrible position for you!"

He snorted. "I don't know why I was ever crazy enough to think she'd give up that life for me."

"So she didn't."

"Nah, she called my bluff. Only it wasn't a bluff." So I went to the head of our drug task force and told him the whole story. Damn, but that was embarrassing. Not only did I have to give details about everything, including my sex life with Olivia, but I also had to face his disappointment in me and my judgment. That was the hardest thing I ever did, Becca!"

"But you loved her!"

"Doesn't matter. Should've known better."

"Did Richie know about all this while it was going on?"

"Nah. Not at first. You know what a straight arrow he was. He'd have never let it go on as long as I did." He grinned lazily, one corner of his mouth turning up. "It took several weeks, but the task force finally got enough evidence to move. That's when my hell really began."

"What do you mean?"

"When they brought her in, she set out to cut herself a deal. She told them I'd been in it with her all along, that *she* worked for *me*, and that when she walked out on me I turned her in, told her nobody would believe I was involved."

"Surely nobody would take her word for it!"

"You would think not. Didn't work out that way, though. They put me on paid leave while they investigated. Started dissecting my background. Talking to all my friends, asking if they'd seen any 'odd behavior' or 'illegal activities.'"

"Oh, Damian…"

"Yeah. By the time they finished with me and *finally* decided I was clean, my rep was shot. I couldn't walk in anywhere for a cup of coffee without someone staring. My fellow officers had all judged me and found me guilty, and you know how cops are when they think there's a dirty cop among them."

I nodded. I felt sick for him.

"I think I'd have lost it completely if it hadn't been for Rich."

I looked at him in surprise. "Richie? But he was here."

"Yeah, and he was a better friend to me from here than my old buddies were in Jackson. When it all started going south, about three years ago, and I'd had it up to here, I got in the car one night and started driving No idea where I was going. When I made the loop around Hattiesburg and pulled back onto Highway 49, I realized I was headed to the one cop I knew wouldn't turn his back on me."

I smiled, even as I felt my eyes begin to fill with tears. Damian's story reminded me of myself, needing to call Richie during my anxiety attacks.

"I finally got up the nerve to call him about half an hour before I hit town. But then I saw it was 3:30 in the morning, and I decided to wait for a decent hour. When I got in, I pulled into one of the casinos and went in and hung out for a few hours, had a bite of breakfast. When I finally called Rich, he chewed my ass out for not calling him as soon as I got into town."

I laughed at this, for I knew that was a perfect example of Richie's personality.

"He thought a lot of you, Damian," I said, reaching out to put my hand on his arm.

"The feeling was mutual, Becca. Your brother was something special." He was quiet for a moment.

"So what did you guys do?"

He grinned, his eyes holding a faraway look.

"Rich drove by his house and picked up a couple of rods and some baits and such, and we drove out on the new fishing pier down by the Palace. Nobody was around, and I told him the whole ugly story."

"Did he have any advice for you?"

"Just to hang in there. But it was okay – all that was important was that he believed me. No hesitation, no questions. Just complete faith. I can't tell you how important that time with him turned out to be. I went back to Jackson with a completely different attitude."

He reached for my hand and gave it a squeeze. "Your brother saved my life, Becca."

With his touch, I recognized anew how much I had loved that brother.

"What happened to Olivia?"

"She was sentenced to three years, served just over two, and I have no idea what she's doing now. Probably the same thing but somewhere else."

My insides were churning. *Does Damian's past have anything to do with Richie's murder? How could it? But what if it does? And how in the world am I supposed to find out?*

"I can't believe you went through all that and you're not bitter."

He snorted. "Oh, I'm bitter, all right. But I swore I wouldn't let her ruin my life, and that I'd put it behind me. Especially when I got the chance to move down here and start fresh." His thick brows drew together as he asked, "Do you think that's really possible? Will it make a difference in the way *you* feel about me? I hope we can still be friends."

"Hey, you didn't do anything except fall in love and try to help the woman you loved. Why would that make a difference to me?" *I hope I'm telling him the truth.*

***

As time passed, it seemed my life was getting more, rather than less, complicated. On one hand, there was Mark, this decent man I'd loved for years and who I was now being given another chance with, perhaps. I couldn't have asked for more support than he had given me over the past few weeks. But I still couldn't decide how I felt about him working with Bob and asking Lorelei not to tell me he was still in town. I wondered if he'd told me the true reason.

And now there was Damian.

Chapter 18

I SPENT SEVERAL MISERABLE, sleepless nights, wandering from one room to another, thinking, trying to figure out what Richie would do if *he* were here and there were any question about why *I* were dead.

After one such night, about four in the morning it came to me: He would go out and visit the scene of the crime. I'd given that some thought already, but I didn't think Mom and Dad would approve. Now that they'd flown back home, though, nobody was standing in my way.

I didn't want to go alone. For one thing, I didn't know exactly how to get to the locations involved. For another, I did not trust myself not to go to pieces once I got there, and figured I had less chance of that happening if I had someone with me.

Lorelei was my first choice, but I knew she couldn't spare the time, with her benefit coming up soon. She'd chaired the benefit last year for the first time, and I'd watched in amusement as she got deeper into the plans and our weekly lunch dates tapered off and then stopped altogether. I remember the first time we managed to get together after the benefit. She didn't even want food – she insisted we spend my lunch hour in the Paradise spa. No, I didn't need to bother her.

Damian? I knew he was interested in me, but I'd only known him a few weeks. I wanted somebody I trusted implicitly.

Mark, of course. He'd been so helpful, so supportive. And he'd made me promise to call if I needed anything at all. Well, I did need something. And I figured he might be the only person in town who wouldn't try to dissuade me. My decision made, I finally curled up in my bed and got a couple of hours of much needed sleep.

Once again I ditched work, and way too early I called Mark, whose mumbled "Hullo?" told me he'd still been sleeping.

"Morning. Sorry I woke you."

"No problem." He yawned in my ear. "Had a late night at work, that's all. We had a generator break down and it took a while to get enough workers called in. Didn't get home 'til about three."

"Oh, Mark, I'm sorry. I wanted to ask you a favor, but I don't need it now. I'll call later. Go back to sleep."

"Don't talk crazy, woman. I'm awake now. Ask me your favor and *then* I'll go back to sleep." The smile in his voice warmed my heart.

I cut to the chase. "Okay. I'd like to go out and visit the place where Richie died."

He sighed, a sound magnified by the phone. "You sure you're ready for that?"

"It doesn't matter if I am or not…I have to go. This is just something I have to do, and I have to do it today. So…can you go with me?"

"Yeah, course I can. What time you want to go?"

We made our plans and Mark promised me he'd go back to sleep. I got dressed in nice cool clothes – walking shorts, sleeveless white blouse, and sandals – and set out to take care of a bit of business I hoped would make our trip this afternoon at least a bit easier. I was determined to get help from Sheriff Bixby.

***

The lanky sheriff met me at his office door. "Miss McCallum. How are you? And what can I do for you?" He led me to a visitor's chair across from his leather one, which creaked when he sat in it. He looked across the broad mahogany desk with its neat stacks of files I knew he'd rather be working on than dealing with me.

When I told him about my plans to go out to the scene, he tried to change my mind, as I'd expected. "You know I want to help you any way I can, but I don't think it's a good idea for you to go off out there in the boonies poking around." I frowned at him and he added, "Your situation isn't unique. I'd tell anybody else the same thing. In fact, I have told people that very thing, when they want to go visit the place where they lost their loved one."

"I understand, Sheriff, but I really need to do this." If he could be stubborn, I could be more stubborn.

"I know you think you do. But I can tell you from experience, doing this won't give you the closure I suspect you're looking for."

"I'm sure it won't," I said wryly. "In fact, it will probably have the opposite effect. But I'm going, and I need your help."

His eyes narrowed and his forehead wrinkled. "Well, if you think you'll feel worse afterward, then why put yourself through it?"

I drew in a deep breath and let it out slowly. "Because I don't believe things happened the way the experts think they did, and I have to find out if I'm right or wrong."

"What do you mean?" he asked with a puzzled frown. "There's only one way things could have happened, and I've explained that to you and your family. There's nothing else to see there. All the signs of what happened that night are gone."

"I know all that," I said irritably. "I still want to see for myself. So will you help me or not?"

"I don't have the manpower or resources to take you," he said flatly. "Besides, just what do you hope to find?"

"I'm not sure," I admitted. "But I just have this feeling there's something that I'm meant to figure out. Sheriff, I don't believe this Tommy guy overpowered Richie and took his gun away from him."

His face flushed; I didn't know if he felt embarrassed or angry – or both. "Are you accusing Paul Simmons of killing your brother? Rebecca, that's absurb. It's also insulting to a good law enforcement officer and to the department. Simmons tried to help Richard. He watched over him, did the best he could for him. Besides, why would he want to hurt Richard? The two of them were friends, for goodness sake."

Sparks flew from his eyes, and I tried to defuse the situation. "I'm not accusing Paul of doing anything wrong. It's just that...oh, I don't know. I don't know how to explain it, but I have this strong feeling I'm supposed to go out there to see for myself."

"So long as you promise to leave Simmons out of this." He paused, looked away out the north facing window, which gave him a perfect view of the incessant traffic out on I-10, and suddenly seemed to come to a decision about something. "I shouldn't be telling you this, and if I do, I have to have your word you'll keep it in the strictest confidence. If I hear you've breathed one word of this to the press, or anybody else, and word gets out before it's released publicly, I won't help you ever again, no matter how much you say you 'need' me to."

"Sheriff Bixby, all you have to do is tell me not to say anything and I won't." I knew I sounded huffy. By way of apology, I said, "Richie told me things I never said a word about, even *after* it became public knowledge." I stared into his eyes.

"All right, then. About a week ago Paul Simmons walked into the DPS Crime Scene office and demanded they give him a polygraph test." *Well, this is a surprise.*

"He did? Why? People don't usually volunteer for those things."

"You're right, but Paul said he was tired of being looked at like a liar and a murderer, and he wanted to prove he was neither one."

"Well? Did he prove it?" I asked impatiently.

"Yes, ma'am, he did. At least as well as anyone can do on a test like that. You and I both know there is always the possibility someone can cheat the test and fool the testers, but it rarely happens. I personally have never known it to happen."

"So, what did Paul say?"

"The examiners went over the story with him, and it appeared to have happened just like he said it did. Then when asked if he had anything to do with Richard's death... he said no, absolutely not, except he couldn't save him."

An overwhelming sense of relief washed over me. It hadn't been his fellow police officer and friend that had killed my brother.

"Thank you for telling me, Sheriff," I said, wiping my eyes. "Now, about that favor..."

***

The scent of Mom's gardenias drifted up to greet me as my leg brushed past them on the sidewalk, and I marveled anew at the feeling of serenity I always felt when I smelled their perfume, all sweet and delicious, recalling memories from my childhood when Mom's newly-planted flowers first began to bloom abundantly. Like the crape myrtles in the back yard that had proved to be a weekly distraction to Dad as he mowed the lawn, ducking and muttering when he had to wrestle with the branches on each of his passes around the yard.

I smiled, remembering, and Mark, leaning against his car, arms folded, followed me with those brilliant green eyes and broke into a lazy smile as I came near. "I don't know what's put you in this kind of mood today, but I'm glad you're feeling better." He waggled his thick eyebrows at me. I'd missed that. He had always reminded me of Groucho Marx.

He opened the door for me – something he apparently would never stop doing, so I didn't bother to protest, just offered a quiet "thank you" – and came around the front of the car and got in. He started the engine and turned to face me.

"Where to first? Do you know where we're going?"

"I think so," I said. "I went to see Sheriff Bixby and he marked places on a map for me. I've been up in that area several times since I went to work for MEMA, but we go so many places I usually depend on GPS to get me somewhere and forget about the location after I leave."

I pulled the map from my pocket and unfolded it. "I think you know which direction we're going, right?"

"Yep. I read details in the paper, but they didn't give too much specific information."

"I couldn't bring myself to read anything right then. I'd sort of like to now, but I don't really want to go down to the newspaper office to ask for old copies. I'm tired of getting all these pitying looks everywhere I go. Makes me not want to go anywhere at all."

"I'm sure it does. You don't have to make that trip, though." He looked aside from driving long enough to say, "I had a feeling that might be the case. I gathered up your papers for you."

"Mark! You did that?" I was surprised, impressed, and infinitely grateful and told him so.

He shrugged. "It's what I'd have wanted you to do if it had been me in your situation."

"I hope and pray nothing similar will ever happen. But if you ever need *anything*, I'll do my best to be there for you like you've been there for me."

"Now that that's behind us –where are we going?"

I laughed, a bit surprised at how close to normal my laugh sounded. For a few days I'd thought I'd never laugh again, at least for real. I gazed out the window at the area we were passing through. Fields of cattle, stands of Southern pines, some of them forming permanent arches towards the west from their battle with Katrina almost eight years ago.

For the next few minutes I concentrated on giving directions. "Looks like the road we want sort of Y's off to the right. It's CR 986. About a mile more."

Once we'd turned onto the road leading to the farmhouse where the intruder had set things in motion, it grew quiet in the car.

I'd been checking my map as we talked, and now I tapped Mark on the arm. "Here, I think this is the place, up here on the right. But drive slow – I don't want to stop yet."

"Yes, ma'am." He slowed the Escape to about twenty miles an hour and I looked the place over as well as I could without stopping. The name on the mailbox read "Ledbetter." The letters were neat – someone had painted them recently, and the miniature black and white cow perched atop the flip-down box looked, well, contented.

Lining the driveway, which ran back about thirty yards to the well-tended farmhouse with its white clapboard siding and black trim, were white crape myrtles spaced among mounds of orange daylilies. Near one corner of the wide front porch I spied a Satsuma tree, its fruits still green. I didn't see any signs of activity, but a small blue sedan sat under the carport, and an older model pickup rested in the shade of an ancient live oak nearby.

That much I saw before we were past, and before I was ready for it, we had reached the narrow dirt road that turned off to the left. Mark pulled off and parked, and we sat in silence for what seemed like an eternity but must have been no more than three or four minutes. He kept the car running, probably because he wasn't sure what I'd want to do, but also because we needed the air conditioning.

Finally I sighed. "You know, I don't think I'm ready to travel down this road just yet, Mark." I wrinkled my brow and felt myself tensing up so that my face must have looked about like one of those dried apple doll faces so popular in the South for a while there. I wanted so much not to cry right now, and I struggled to keep the tears buried and unshed.

"That's okay. Whatever you want, sweet thing." He cleared his throat and shifted in the seat. "We can come back later – maybe a few more days will help."

"No! No, I didn't mean that. I only meant I'm not ready to see the spot today *yet*. But I *do* want to come back," I assured him. "I think I'd like to go check out the farmhouse first, though."

He nodded, putting the car into reverse and turning around to go back the way we had come.

"Do you have any idea how grateful I am to you for being so supportive?"

"Don't know, don't need to know, don't care. Just doin' what I know is right." He gave me a quick glance. "Ready to go meet the Ledbetters?" I nodded.

Chapter 19

A FEROCIOUS-LOOKING BORDER COLLIE came to meet us halfway up the driveway. I could tell he was ferocious by the energetic waving of his bushy tail and the way he skipped alongside the car as Mark navigated the drive, intent on avoiding both the dog and the flowerbeds.

"Okay," Mark said when he'd parked, "I'm gonna let you do all the talking. If you get ready for me to jump in, give me a nod."

"C'mon. Let's get this done."

"Yes, ma'am."

"And stop with the 'yes ma'am's' already."

"Yes, ma'am."

I scowled at him. "Are you trying to upset me? Because it's not working."

"Nope...trying to help you relax. This'll be a lot easier for you if you do."

I gave him a brief smile of thanks as I reached to open the door, and he nodded.

The dog was waiting when I opened the car door, sitting as I'm sure he'd been trained to do, but with his tail thumping the ground impatiently, his wet, golden brown eyes staring into my face. "Friend or foe? Dog person or cat person?" I could almost hear his voice. He'd probably sound a lot like Chief Sikes.

I held out the back of my hand for him to sniff, and he did so delicately; then I slowly reached up to scratch behind his ears, and he leaned his head against my hand, urging me not to stop.

"Sorry, boy," I said. "We have business with your masters." I straightened and walked toward the farmhouse with Mark, the dog following on my heels.

As we climbed the set of three wooden steps to the porch, the door creaked open and a small woman who looked to be in her mid-seventies said with a broad smile, "I see you've met Chester, our fierce guard dog." I liked her immediately.

"Mrs. Ledbetter?" I asked, and she nodded. "I'm Rebecca McCallum, and this is my friend, Mark Barrington. We wondered if you might have a few minutes to talk with us. It's about an incident that happened near here a few weeks ago."

"You must mean when that deputy got shot. That's the only thing going on out here I know about."

"Yes, ma'am," I said, turning to scowl at a smiling Mark.

"Are you people reporters? I don't like the idea of talking to reporters."

"No, we have a personal interest in what happened."

"Well, I guess it would be all right," she said slowly. "But I don't really know much about it."

"That's okay," I assured her.

"Come on in, then." She ushered us into a small, neat living room. A television sat in one corner of the room, a fireplace with a plain brick hearth nestled in the next corner. Between the two hung a large picture of two little boys in overalls, hands in their pockets. A caption read, "So, how long you been farming?" I smiled at it and Mrs. Ledbetter noticed.

"One of Martin's nieces gave him that picture on his seventy-fifth birthday," she said. "That's where he hung it five years ago, and I expect it'll still be there when we're both gone." She turned to look me square in the face. "But that's not what you came here to talk about."

She motioned us toward the faded green sofa in front of the windows and settled herself in a bentwood rocker near the fireplace, looking at me expectantly.

"To tell the truth, I'm not sure why I'm here," I confessed. "I don't know what I'm looking for, really, but...Mrs. Ledbetter, the deputy killed near here was my brother, Richard McCallum."

125

"That's it!" she said. "I knew your name sounded familiar, but I felt sure we'd never met. Oh, my dear, I am so sorry."

"Thank you." When would I stop having to say those words?

"I was hoping you could tell me something about the..."

I broke off at the sound of someone slamming the back door. "Oh, good, that'll be Martin. He may be better able to help you, anyway." She leaned toward us and whispered, "I don't remember some things so good these days."

"Martin, we have visitors!" she called, a lilt in her voice.

A tall, slim man dressed in overalls and a plaid short-sleeved shirt came into the room and gave us a nod. He had a warm smile, one he seemed to have used often, judging by the crinkles around his eyes. For his age, he had remarkably few lines on his face otherwise. "I'll bet these two have had a wonderful life together," I thought, looking from one to the other. He walked over to the recliner that sat at a perfect viewing angle from the television but remained standing. *An old school gentleman.*

"Martin, this is Rebecca McCallum." I saw the immediate recognition in his eyes, and he ducked his head slightly. "And her friend, Mark. I'm sorry, Mark. I don't remember your last name."

Barrington, sir," Mark said, rising to shake hands with Mr. Ledbetter. "Pleased to meet you."

"Welcome. McCallum, is it? The deputy killed out near here, he was...?" He waited for me to finish.

I nodded. "My brother. Richie was three years older than me."

"I'm really sorry." He shook his head. "That was a bad business. Just no sense in it."

He said it so simply. The truth in a nutshell.

"I was about to ask your wife what she could tell me about the intruder, and she said I should probably ask you, anyway." I smiled at her and looked back at him expectantly. They looked at each other in confusion, brows wrinkling.

"What intruder would that be, Miss?" he asked.

"Please call me Rebecca. I'm talking about the intruder you called the police about that night."

He shook his head. "I'm sorry, Rebecca. We told the officers that night we didn't know anything about that."

I wrinkled my forehead, somewhat puzzled. Could they *both* have problems remembering things? "Sheriff Bixby told me a 911 call came in from this house that night close to midnight, with a report of someone who seemed to be trying to find a way into your home." When they continued to give me confused looks, I asked, "Are you telling me you *didn't* make a 911 call that night?"

I glanced at Mark and he lifted his shoulders slightly, a questioning look in his eyes which I'm sure matched the one in mine.

"Why, no, Miss McCallum. We didn't. Thank the Lord, we've never had a need to use 911," Mr. Ledbetter said. "We had a couple of officers stop by that night. They woke me and my nephew up to see if we were okay, but we didn't know what they were looking for. They didn't say much. We heard lots of traffic on the road then."

I could tell the two elderly people were both puzzled. I shook my head and gave a small forced laugh. "Oh, I must have gotten the information wrong. I guess they got it straightened out but didn't tell me. Police, you know." I shrugged. Gazing into Mrs. Ledbetter's eyes, I said, "The past few weeks have been hard on me, as you might imagine."

"Oh, honey," she said, rising slowly from her rocker and coming over to put her arm around my shoulders, "I'm sure they have. It's not right, losing good young people like your brother. I don't know what the world is coming to."

"Sometimes I wonder that myself," I said, placing a hand over hers. "Thank you both for being so sweet about this. I'm sorry for the mix-up."

I looked at Mark and nodded. "Well, folks," he said, "I think it's about time for us to be going. I'm sure y'all have plenty of things to do other than sit and visit."

We both rose and I gave Mrs. Ledbetter a hug while Mark shook hands with her husband. I didn't understand it, but somehow this lady, with her quiet compassion and sympathetic hug, had done more for me in the last twenty minutes than most of my friends or family, what was left of them, had been able to do.

We all stepped out onto the porch, and Mr. Ledbetter said, "No need to rush off. We don't get much company anymore. Kind of nice to hear young people's voices in the house."

"Yes," his wife added, "we have a nephew who lives with us – my sister's son – but he just eats and sleeps here. He never brings his friends to the house." Her soft voice held a wistful tone, and I wondered if the couple had children of their own.

We walked down the steps and headed toward the car, with the black and white dog following close behind.

"Now, Chester, don't you bother these folks," Mr. Ledbetter said.

Suddenly I stopped and spun around. "Mrs. Ledbetter, I wonder…would it be all right if I came by to visit again sometime? It's so peaceful here, and you've been so nice." I left off talking, embarrassed.

"Why, Rebecca, you come and see me whenever you want to. I'd love to sit and visit more, maybe under happier circumstances," she said, smiling broadly. "And if you will let me know ahead of time, I'll bake a batch of my lemon cookies."

"Sounds great. But I don't want you to go to any trouble."

"My missus loves baking, Rebecca. And this diabetes keeps me from enjoying much of the sweet stuff anymore. So you come on back. She'll feed you good and send some home with you – and if I'm lucky, I might get one or two."

We all laughed, and I waved back as they both saw us off from the porch. I had a lump in my throat as we backed down the drive. They were still standing there when we got out to the main road.

***

"Sweet, sweet people," I said.

"Yep. What my dad would call the 'salt of the earth.'"

"I really meant it. I do want to come back and see her."

"I know you do. I could see some kind of special connection being forged between the two of you." He looked both ways before backing onto the road. "Which way should I go? You ready to give it up for today?"

I shook my head. "Not yet. I think I'd like to try again to go down to the barn."

Mark stared into my face for several seconds, as if trying to gauge whether I was ready. He must have decided I was, because he backed out without a word and drove toward the lane leading to the barn.

Chapter 20

THE BARN SAT BACK FROM the main road about three hundred yards. On the left side were woods, mostly pine with some oak and elm mixed in. Growing along the right side of the single lane road were a mixture of weeds, vines, and grasses.

A dilapidated barbed-wire fence half covered in wild dewberry vines and wild roses ran alongside the road. Cedar trees, both young sprouts and older, well-established trees, grew next to, and in places through, the fence, having taken root where seeds had been dropped by birds alighting to devour their tasty meals.

The road was simply two ruts of gravel with grass growing up the middle.

I had the feeling this had once been an old homestead. If I'd found this place on my own, and it weren't tied to my losing Richie, I would have found it charming

But now I wanted to do what I came for and get away as quickly as possible.

"Looks like the land was clear-cut sometime in the last few years," Mark said. "Probably took out the pines after Katrina, since most timber was in such bad shape already."

"Um-hmm. There was a lot of that going around."

Here we were, almost on top of the scene where my brother had died, and we were making small talk. But that's what we do, I thought. We have all kinds of defenses against hurt, against the kind of pain I felt trying to break through.

Mark stopped the car about thirty yards back from the barn, and I sat gazing at it for a minute or two. Could have been much longer, might have been only a few seconds. I lost all sense of time, staring as if I could bring the whole terrible scene back to life, if I tried hard enough. Well, sitting would get us nowhere. I jerked the handle of the door and stepped out.

"So this is where Richie spent his last minutes."

Mark came around the car and took my hand. In his other hand he held the folder I had picked up from Sheriff Bixby. He wasn't about to come with us, but he did make copies of the investigators' reports, which included detailed drawings of the crime scene. He had left out the crime scene photos.

We consulted the file now, and I squinted into the afternoon sun as I tried to visualize what it must have looked like that night, with only a sliver of a moon. The afternoon had been hot, the humidity smothering, but the evening had been pleasant after I'd returned from my reverie at the beach, the afternoon I talked to Richie the last time.

I still cringed when I thought of how I had chosen not to say "Be extra careful tonight," even as something inside me had yelled those words over and over until they echoed through my brain. *What if I had? Would he have thought twice about driving down this road and confronting a threat he didn't have a handle on, without waiting for backup?*

"Bixby laid the situation out clearly," Mark said, trying to get me back on track. He was worried about me, I could see that – but somehow now I knew I could get through the next hour. Because finally I was going to make sense of these unknowns. Well, at least some things. At least I was going to try.

We stood in front of his car and compared the scene before us to the drawings in the folder. Mark dropped my hand and began to make sweeping gestures to explain what he was seeing on paper. I followed his movements. As he talked, he began to move into the scene slowly, and I continued to stand by the car so I could see the entire area.

"The pickup sat about ten feet out from the barn, near the right front corner. I guess it would have been about here." He turned and looked back to where I stood, and I nodded.

"Looks about right."

"And Richard's patrol car was about thirty feet from the barn, parked facing the barn, and still on the dirt road." He moved back toward me and stepped off the distance. "That about right?"

"I think so. And Paul told me he parked his car about two car lengths behind Richie's and pulled off into the grass. I think his headlights were shining on the scene around the barn. Does that agree with what's in the report?"

He consulted the sheaf of papers. "Yep. Guess he was trying to get in position so his headlights wouldn't be hindered by Richard's patrol car, but would add more light to the scene." He turned in a slow circle, coming to a stop facing the barn. "How should we do this? Want me to read the report word for word, or paraphrase most of it and only read Richard's communications with dispatch?"

Anxious to get into the scene, I said, "Put it in your words. I've read it, so I'll be able to keep up with you. But I need to hear Richie's words, here in this place."

"Okay. Well, here goes. He had responded to Dispatch's request for someone to take the 911 call that came in at 12:26 a.m. A male caller had reported someone suspicious lurking around his house, disturbing his dog, and walking on his back porch. Dispatch put out a call to see who was available to go to the Ledbetter residence at 1721 County Road 986. Two deputies were in the general area, but Richard was several minutes closer, so he took the call. Then Paul Simmons reported he was in route to the scene as well."

"But then Richie must have seen the pickup leave the Ledbetter's place. You know, I believe them when they say they never made the call, but I also believe Dispatch got the address right. We can sort that out later, though. So then Richie called Dispatch again, and said…"

"Harrison, this is Unit eight-two-five. My 10-20 is eastbound on 986, just past 1721. 10-94, dark late model pickup….Can't see license yet. Suspect has turned north on dirt road, I'm following.'" As Mark read off some of the final words spoken by my big brother, I closed my eyes and envisioned the scene. *Oh, if he'd only waited.*

"When he parked he called in the license number on the pickup, right?" I asked. "And then he must have approached the truck and found it empty, because he went back to his car and told Dispatch it was unoccupied and the driver could possibly be inside the barn."

"Yeah, and then he asked if Paul was coming, and when the Dispatcher said yes, Richard said he would wait for him before investigating further."

"Was that when they told him the truck had been stolen?"

"Yes, stolen two days before."

I walked to the spot where I thought Paul's car would have been. "Does this look about right for the second patrol car?"

"A bit further back, I think." I took a few steps backward and stopped. "That's it. Right about there."

I tried to see the scene through Paul's eyes as he tried to absorb it that night. He had an officer directly in front of him, and it was Richie, his old mentor. He had said as he walked up to the car Richie got out, explained what he knew about the situation, and they discussed what they should do next. I moved to stand beside Mark where Richie's car had been that night.

Mark took over again, consulting the sheriff's notes from time to time.

"According to Paul, they decided to check out the barn, and Richard went around the right side, headed to the back to look for a rear entrance. He told Paul to cover the front, and Paul stayed with his gun trained on the large sliding doors. The next thing he knew a gunshot rang out from the rear of the barn, and he traced Richard's footsteps to the rear right corner.

"Looking around the corner, he saw Richard lying about ten feet from the corner of the barn. After shining his light around the area, he ran to Richard and saw he had taken a shot to the back of the head. He checked for vitals, and found a pulse, so he ran back around the barn to his patrol car and called in a request for emergency vehicles and assistance. Then he grabbed a blanket from the trunk of his car to take it back to Richard."

As he talked, Mark and I had made our way to the rear of the barn, following the trail laid out in the reports. I shivered, realizing I stood on hallowed ground, for me at least. "There's the back door."

"Paul planned to stay with Richard until help arrived," Mark said.

"He just wanted to keep him comfortable, keep him alive."

"But right after he slammed his trunk shut he heard a noise near the barn. He moved forward until he was situated at the rear of Richard's car. He saw someone in the pickup who appeared to be trying to get it started. Paul called out an order for the suspect to halt and put his hands in the air. Suspect looked up but refused to comply. He didn't say anything, but when Paul gave the order the second time, the suspect raised a gun and pointed it at him, Paul. Paul ordered him to drop his gun and raise his hands in the air, but instead the guy shook his head as if to refuse.

"The guy fired and Simmons returned fire, striking the gunman on the back of his right hand, in his left shoulder, and in his head, the shot that killed him."

"The investigation showed the guy's gun had been fired, right?"

Mark leafed through several pages, a puzzled look on his face. "Yeah, here it is. Don't know why they had it in a different place. Yep, one bullet missing, and the gun had been fired recently."

"C'mon, let's get back up front. We have to get in Paul's shoes and those of the suspect." I left Mark shuffling the pages and made a beeline back to the front of the barn. I stood staring at nothing, trying to figure out what *had* happened here that night.

I balled my hands into fists and slammed them onto my hips in frustration when Mark caught up with me. He looked about as confused as I felt.

"What does the report say next? Let me see." I grabbed the papers from his hand and strode back to the car, where I planned to spread them out on the hood. But I hadn't accounted for the slope of the Escape's hood, so I stomped around to the passenger door and jerked it open. I climbed in and began to sift through the papers.

After a minute, Mark got in on the driver's side and sat there not saying anything. In fact, he was so quiet that finally I began to feel uncomfortable. I could feel his eyes on me but I didn't want to look at him. I was behaving like a spoiled brat, just like old times. What was wrong with me? He'd been nothing but kind to me since the night he came to the hospital. He'd supported me, helped me however he could. Finally I put down the papers and made myself turn and face him.

***

The look in his eyes devastated me. They were so filled with revulsion I could hardly stand it. The day we broke up came back to me clear as day, except that I can't remember what had upset me so…nothing much, I'm sure. I got upset all the time in those days, and when I did I lashed out, like I had a moment ago. Mark had finally had enough, and he had turned and walked out the door. I ran after him, tried to get him to stop, tried to apologize. He got to his car and turned to look at me, with much the same look on his face then as now.

"I'm tired, Becca," he had said. "I'm tired of having to walk on eggshells around you, tired of taking the brunt of your outbursts over the littlest of things. I'm just tired. I'm going home."

That's the way it had ended between us. I'd tried to call him, had gone by his house, but he wouldn't see me or talk to me. A few days later I got a letter from him – a real, honest to goodness letter – and when I read it I knew we were through.

He had laid out the reasons why he was ending our relationship, and they all had to do with my juvenile behavior. He'd said at twenty-seven I still acted like a child. I thought about that a lot, after I knew it was really over.

I'd talked to Lorelei about it regularly, until she finally said, "Becca, give it a rest. You're saying the same things over and over, but I don't hear you saying anything about changing. And if you don't want the next guy walking away because of your little girl behavior, then you'd better grow up soon, before Mr. Right comes along and you're not ready for him."

"But, Loree, he already did come along," I had cried. Lorelei loved me unconditionally and believed that gave her the right and duty to make me help myself. The next time she came by the house her arms were loaded with books – relationships, Peter Pan syndrome (I'd never heard of it), *How to Win Friends and Influence People, Law of Attraction, Men are from Mars*, birth order in families – you name it, I had a book about it.

One long, lonely night late last fall I finally picked up the smallest, thinnest book in the stack and started reading. By the time I fell asleep about five the next morning, I had a nice little pile of books I'd studied. Changing a behavior isn't easy when you don't have someone to practice on. So I kept reading and studying and journaling my responses, and praying.

"Mark, I'm sorry," I said now. Hesitantly, I reached out and laid a hand on his arm. He didn't pull away, didn't react at all, only looked at me. My tears began to fall, but I made no sound at all. Remembering the papers in my lap, I scooped them up with one hand and dropped them, folder and all, into the floorboard.

"I *am* sorry. I've tried hard to do better. When you walked away from me that day I knew I couldn't go on like I was. I'd ruined friendships before with that behavior, but when I lost you – well, that's what made me listen to Lorelei, made me read all the self-help books she brought me. You didn't know that, but I do want you to know I try not to do things or say things the way I used to."

"Becca, I…"

"Let me finish," I said, giving his arm a little squeeze. "After I lost Richie, I think I would have fallen apart if it hadn't been for you. You'll never know how much seeing you in the ER that morning meant to me, what it means to me now. You didn't have to come to me, and you certainly didn't have to do all the things you've done for me since then. You don't have to be here *now*." He lifted an eyebrow and gave a little shrug.

"But for whatever reason, you are here. I'll always be grateful to you for that, and for every single thing you've done for me. I don't know why you're still here supporting me, I really don't. I know I don't deserve it. This is one of the few times I've lashed out since Richie died, and I don't know why it had to be with you."

He cleared his throat.

"All I can do is apologize." I watched the emotions play across his sweet face, saw the pain and the loving kindness seemingly at war in his expressive eyes, and prayed he would forgive me. I realized how much I needed him, how much I would hate to have him walk away again. "Mark, please. Say something."

Suddenly his left hand came up to grab my hand from his arm, and his other hand closed over it as well. He didn't take his eyes away from mine as he slowly brought my hand to his lips, kissed my knuckles tenderly, and held on. When he finally lowered our hands, he opened his and placed our open palms together with my hand covered by his two large capable ones.

I knew then – somehow it was going to be all right.

"I've changed a lot in the last year, too. I'm sure both of us needed to grow up some. I hate you've had to go through all of this. I know, probably as well as anybody and more than most, how close the two of you were. I know you feel like a part of you died that night, too. What kind of man would I be if I let one little temper tantrum cause me to walk out...again?"

He reached into the console and handed me two tissues. "I know one won't be enough," he said, and I laughed. The tension between us disappeared like the streaks of color in a summer sunset when the sun has dropped far below the horizon. All was well between us again...for now. I asked myself, "Am I good enough for this man? Do I deserve him?" If I were honest, I guess I'd say no. But from that moment, I resolved to try to do right by him.

"Now, are we going to try to make sense out of all this," he motioned to the pile of papers by my feet, "or are we gonna sit here feeling sorry for ourselves for the rest of the day?" I felt shivers on my spine, and I gulped. He'd used the words "we" and "ourselves," placing himself firmly in my corner. For the first time I let myself dream about what it could be like if we got back together, but then I pushed such thoughts away and returned to the problem at hand.

"We're going to do our best," I said, wiping my eyes and bashfully blowing my nose, "to find out who killed my big brother."

If I'd hurt him before, now I had startled him.

"Killed him? Well, we know that, don't we?" Mark drew his breath in, held it several seconds, and let it flow out between his lips, as slow as molasses on a cold winter morning. "Becca, what are you thinking? I don't see how I can help you if I don't know what's going on in that pretty head of yours."

Chapter 21

MARK SAT STILL, LISTENING intently, as I laid out my reasons for distrusting the official report about Richie's death. When I'd finished, he shook his head slowly.

"That's quite a stretch to go from the findings of the official report to believing someone else, someone nobody knows about, was involved —that somebody else killed your brother – and the whole thing was planned. Premeditated, I guess would be the term. Whew! That's a serious accusation, Becca."

"I know," I said, slowly flexing my fingers, trying to relieve the tension. "Believe me, I know. I didn't come to this point lightly."

"Well, I can see how you might begin to question the reports, now that we've read through them. This is the first time you've seen the reports for yourself, right?"

I nodded.

"Well, what do *you* think happened?"

"I would say I have no idea, but I'm afraid I might, after all."

He blinked and stared at me. "Going to share it with me?" he asked, after I sat staring at the barn, not saying anything else.

"You know, Mark, at this point you're one of the few people *not* on my list of suspects!" I gave a sarcastic laugh. "I've talked to Chief Sikes and Sheriff Bixby, and I trust them, I guess, but they say there's no reason for me to think anything happened other than what's in here." I picked up a couple of papers, then with a frustrated snort I dropped them in my lap.

"Why *do* you think there's more to this than meets the eye?"

"You mean what made me begin to question things before I saw the report, right?"

"Yeah, pretty much." He gave me a sly grin. "You haven't had one of your dreams or premonitions, have you?" I looked at him, trying to give off an innocent air, but he knew me too well. "Aw, Becca. You did, didn't you?"

"You'll think this is crazy. I didn't even mention it to the Chief, because I knew he'd tell me I need a shrink. I don't know, maybe I do. Anyway, I'm hoping you don't feel the same way."

"I know you pretty well," he grinned. "So I'm not making any promises."

"I appreciate your honesty," I said with a twist of my mouth. "Okay, here goes. A few days ago I woke from a dream about Richie. I was on the beach and I kept hearing his voice but couldn't see him. Finally his words became clear." I paused, took a deep breath, and continued. "He said, 'Find out the truth, Becca. Find out the truth about my murder.' When I woke up, I kept hearing his voice repeating those words."

I waited, trying to give Mark time to process what I'd said. He gave a small tilt of his head, almost like a sideways nod. Was that an "I believe you," or "You're crazy" look?

"I said I know you pretty well. And I really do. I remember more than once while we were together when your dreams, or premonitions, whatever they are, did come true."

I nodded. "I remember the time your cousin called and came to visit after you and your mom both dreamed about her."

"Yeah, I was thinking about that at the beach the afternoon before..." I stopped suddenly.

"What?" he asked, after a few heartbeats during which I felt my face flush and my eyes begin to swim in tears. "Aw, Becca. Don't tell me. You had a premonition about Richard before he died." It was a statement, not a question. He tilted his head back and laid it against the headrest, staring at the ceiling.

"Yes," I whispered. I was afraid he might turn away from me. But he didn't. He just sat for what seemed like minutes, but surely must have been only a few seconds. The swarm of bees in the vines of the fence row sounded loud in the silence. With a shake of his shoulders, he sat forward in his seat and shifted so he could face me almost squarely.

"Okay, tell me what you have, or at least what you think you have." That's one thing I always liked about Mark. He would tease me and kid around, but when he saw I was really serious he always buckled down to try to help me. Yet I was amazed that after all we had been through he was apparently still ready to help me with no hesitation.

"I don't *have* anything. But here's what I've put together. For one thing, it doesn't make sense to me that Richie let some punk take his gun away from him and shoot him in the back of the head with it. Does it make sense to you?" I locked eyes with him.

"No, I have to admit that's bothered me, too. But you know how crazy things can get around crime scenes. Anything is possible."

"Possible, yes. Probable? That's another story altogether."

"Knowing Richard, I guess I would have to agree with you there. The guy was smart, strong, tough as nails when he had to be. When I first heard what they said had happened out here, I couldn't believe it. But then, you know how the media is. They always get things wrong, and you can't trust much of what they say. I figured the authorities refused to respond and clarify the information for a couple of reasons. They don't respond to the media that way, and they probably figured the more the whole thing was kept on the front burner, the more miserable all of you in the family would be."

"I don't think our personal comfort entered their minds at all, to tell you the truth. I think they have so many questions themselves they're not about to let the reporters near them, at least until and unless they get things figured out. Then again, nobody seems to be investigating at all now." I shrugged. "Maybe we just don't hear about it."

"But I still don't get how you can seem so sure things didn't happen the way we were told they did. I mean, what made you start to think all of this," he gestured at our surroundings, "was hiding something that seems unbelievable?"

"Mark, how long had it been since you'd seen Richie, at least to really talk with him? Do you have any idea what was going in his life? I mean his life with Justine, with their marriage?"

"Don't have a clue, only what you've mentioned. I hadn't seen Richard in months. Last time I saw him he was playing ball at the park with Owen, probably six months ago or more."

Surprised, I asked, "What on earth were you doing at the park?"

"Oh, I, uh…I took my nephew Sam – Sandy's kid, he's nine now – out one Saturday afternoon so he could practice at the batting cages. But that's beside the point. Let's get back to this issue."

Did I imagine it, or was there hesitation in his response to my question? Mark was the one person I had felt sure had nothing at all to hide. Now I wasn't so sure.

For the time being, at least, I would give him the benefit of the doubt. So I shared with him my conversations with Richie about Justine, and about their marital problems. "He really was convinced she was having an affair, ya know?" I wanted Mark to understand where I was coming from. "This isn't just something from my imagination. I'd never dreamed she would cheat on him. They were so in love when they got married."

"Most people are in love when they get married, but about half the marriages today end in divorce. That should tell you something about how durable love really is." Stung by the pain in his voice, I hung my head, unable to meet his gaze. I didn't want him to see the effect his words had on me.

"I know, but I guess I couldn't believe anything could change them. Clearly something did change, because I'm now convinced Justine was cheating on Richie right up until the day he died, and I'm not so sure she wasn't relieved that he did die." I did look at Mark then, daring him to tell me I was wrong. "Would you like to know why I'm so sure? Because the guy she's having an affair with had the nerve to come to her house – to *Richie's* house – the day after he died, and the way he felt about Justine was written all over his face." I spat out the last sentence, reliving the disgusting scenes I'd witnessed between Justine and Jake during those days.

"You're joking! Becca, people just don't do things like that. I'd think the guy would stay as far away from her as possible right then, especially if he really cared about her."

"Oh, I think he cares about her, all right. That may be part of the problem. I don't think Jake can stay away from her."

"Jake... Wait, didn't I meet someone named Jake? Yeah, sure I did. He was the guy you introduced me and your folks to, the guy with all the muscles, right?"

"That's him. I walked in on them a few times when he didn't see me coming, and Mark, I promise you, he reminded me of a lovesick little boy. Justine sure knows how to bring that out in him!"

I told him about the things I'd heard from Lorelei, and other things I'd witnessed myself. Then I dropped the bigger bomb.

"So you see, that's one reason why I wouldn't be surprised to find out Justine or Jake, or both of them, were involved in Richie's murder." There – I'd called it murder out loud, again...but in a different way this time.

"Becca, this is starting to sound like one of those one-hour television murder mysteries where the scheming, lying, cheating spouse *plans* to kill their partner so they can start over."

"I guess that's because I'm suspicious that may be the case."

We were both quiet on the way back into town, and I was grateful when Mark just walked me to the door and said he needed to go to work for a while. I needed time by myself after all that talking. I needed to think instead.

I didn't spend the next few hours thinking about Richie...I was too caught up in trying to decipher my emotional responses lately. I *knew* I was still in love with Mark. Yet when Damian was around I felt a surge of attraction that matched what I felt with Mark. For a long-term relationship, that couldn't be good.

And what if I was reading more into Mark's actions toward me than I should? Was he just being a really good friend? When he used the word love, in what way did he mean it?

Damian had come on to me a time or two, and my body had responded. What did that mean? I wanted Damian, but I also wanted Mark. What did that make me? *Can you say the word 'slut'?* I had to get my feelings sorted out soon. But I needed to set them aside for now and concentrate on what we'd learned, and hadn't learned, at the Ledbetter's and the barn.

Chapter 22

J UST OVER A WEEK LATER, I managed to get back out of town to visit Mrs. Ledbetter. Before I left I ducked into the pet store and picked up a small bag of treats for Chester, then walked next door to a kitchen shop, where I bought Mrs. Ledbetter a set of seashell cookie cutters. The manager fancied them up in a cute little bag with ribbons. *What a life some people lead.*

The summer afternoon was clear and bright, and sweet music played on my radio as I headed north out of town. I really looked forward to seeing Mrs. Ledbetter again. When I'd phoned this morning to make sure it would be okay to visit, she'd sounded pleased. Thinking of her, I realized I missed Mom in a bad way. We'd been speaking by phone most days, texting too, but it wasn't the same as having her with me.

So long as I'd had Richie, I hadn't missed Mom and Dad so much, no more than most women my age would. But with him gone, and my folks back in Key West, I'd come to realize I'd been living a much too lonely life. My best friend was married and had social responsibilities I wasn't a part of, nor did I want to be. Lorelei was a great friend and I loved her, but I couldn't see myself hanging out with the mayor and our state senator, a regular occurrence with her.

For almost three years – until just over a year ago – I'd spent most of my free time with Mark, anything but lonely. Besides, I'd had Richie and Owen. I still had Owen, in a way, but Justine was making my visits with him more and more difficult, and who knew what next week or next month would bring?

I slowed Bernice and began to watch for the road number to the Ledbetter farm. This really was pretty country. Cattle grazing in the lush green fields, horses here and there – some thoroughbreds but most ordinary looking animals. The few scattered farmhouses looked much as they probably had when they were first built in the 1970s. I saw the sign up ahead and turned onto County Road 986. Not long now and I'd be visiting with my new friend.

I hoped this visit would help me get my mind off the events of the past few days. I needed a break…and time to think. I'd seriously thought about taking a sleeping bag and a cooler to the tree house and telling everybody I was going away for the weekend, sans cell phone. I felt if I had the time…and the space…I could get this all figured out.

Mrs. Ledbetter greeted me at the door looking lovely in her soft pink dress. She invited me into the kitchen, spotless despite the aroma of freshly baked cookies layered on a platter on the farm-style table beside a frosty pitcher of iced tea and two matching glasses. Her preparations said this meeting meant a lot to her, too.

For the next couple of hours, we got acquainted in between bites of her luscious lemon cookies. Her husband was right – they were the best I'd ever had. She told me the story of how she met Mr. Ledbetter, and I told her about my college years and my job. She explained how the farm worked, what crops they grew, and I told her about how hurricane preparation plans had changed since Katrina.

She asked me to call her Lucy…and I asked her to call me Becca.

At last I felt comfortable enough to talk about Richie for a bit, and she sat listening intently, smiling occasionally at my tales of our childhood pranks. I found myself telling her about incidents I didn't even know I remembered. She had that effect on me. When I looked at my watch I was surprised to see more than two hours had passed.

"Lucy, I hate to leave – I'm having a wonderful time," I said. "I'd love to come back sometime."

"I'd love that, Becca. You're welcome any time." We stepped onto the front porch just as a large, black truck with dually wheels came up the drive. I didn't understand the attraction of those things.

"Oh, good. Here's my nephew – I'm glad you'll get to meet him."

***

When the man stepped from the truck, I sucked in my breath sharply. *No, this can't be.* He could not be here, not with this sweet lady. Could I have been right about him after all? Had he been pulling the rug over his aunt and uncle's eyes? The grin on his face faded when he realized who I was.

"Becca, I'd like you to meet my nephew, Jake Coffee. Jake, this is Rebecca McCallum."

"Actually, we've already met," I said, trying to make my voice sound natural. I didn't want to mention Justine. "We have some mutual friends. Hello, Jake. How are you?"

I could see he, too, was making an effort at normalcy. "Hi, Rebecca, I'm good. You?"

"Fine. I was just leaving. I've been here most of the afternoon, and I need to be getting back to town."

"I guess Aunt Lucy's been filling you with stories and cookies," he said, laughing.

A shrill ring came from inside the house. "Oh, there's the telephone," she said. "I'll be right back, Becca. Don't leave before I get back." She hurried into the house.

Jake leaned against the porch rail and crossed his arms, appraising me through slitted dark eyes. The muscles in his neck were tensing and relaxing, giving me the impression he held himself in check.

"Becca," he stressed my shortened name, "I'm surprised you've met my Aunt Lucy so soon after you and I met for the first time." He tilted his head and gave me a questioning look. My stomach tensed as I felt his animosity, only lightly covered over.

"I know," I said, trying for an attitude of nonchalance. "Isn't it crazy? Mr. and Mrs. Ledbetter mentioned when I first met them that they had a nephew, but I had no idea it would turn out to be someone I knew."

"How did you happen to meet them?" *I'd better play this close to the vest.*

"Well, I didn't just 'happen' to meet them," I said, playing for time, trying to think. "I'd talked with the sheriff a couple of weeks ago and he told me the barn where Richie was killed was somewhere in this area so I drove out one afternoon. I wasn't sure I was still on the right road, so I stopped here to see if they knew anything about where it had happened. I told them who I was and why I was looking for the barn." I stopped speaking, feeling like I was rattling on and making him suspicious.

I was suspicious enough of him. Why had he not mentioned to any of us that he lived this close to the place where Richie was killed? Or maybe he had – who knew what he'd told Justine? But if he had, she hadn't shared anything with us. Why would she keep something like that to herself? This case was getting weirder and weirder. *Case? When did this become a "case?"*

"And so, did you? See the barn area, I mean."

"Yeah, finally. I ended up staying and visiting with them for a while. I think once I was this close I realized I was still unprepared, but I also wasn't ready to turn around and go home. After we talked here for a while, I decided to give it a try, and it turned out okay."

"I'm glad for you. Must have been hard going out there all alone." He paused, then added, "Not to mention – it could have been dangerous."

I looked at him sharply. "Dangerous? Why? If the suspect – the Hollingshead boy – was the one who killed Richie, and he's dead, what would have made it dangerous?"

I saw a fraction of a second's hesitation in his dark eyes, then he said, "Oh, I didn't mean that kind of dangerous. I only meant there are lots of animals on the prowl out here, some with rabies, and I'll bet you didn't have any protection with you."

"Oh, I wasn't alone. Mark Barrington was with me."

"Mark. Really? Justine told me y'all had dated for a while, but I'd understood you weren't together now. I knew he was with you all during the funeral, but she said he was just a friend."

"Yeah, Mark's a really nice guy." I left it at that. My personal life was none of his business, and I was in no mood to be railroaded into divulging anything I didn't want to. Especially since I had nothing to divulge.

The screen door creaked and Lucy came back out. "I'm sorry about that, Becca," she said, shaking her head. "That was one of our little church ladies. Her brother was having knee surgery today and she'd said she would call and give us an update. Seems the surgery went very well."

"That's good, Lucy," I said, giving her a hug. I was thinking of her calling the other woman "one of our little church ladies." I smiled, wondering what the congregation called *her*. "Now I'd better be getting back home." I shook my head when she started to protest. "No, I really do have to go. Thank you again for these spectacular lemon cookies. I promise I'll come back again."

"Try to make it soon, my dear. I get a bit lonely sometimes, when Martin has work to do out on the farm."

I shot Jake a look, but he seemed oblivious, lost in thought.

"And I'd love for you to visit me one day. I'm not really much of a cook – and I'm *sure* no baker – but I know this little place where they make the best potato donuts you've ever put in your mouth, and I drive right by there on my way home from work."

"I'd be happy to take you in to visit Becca sometime, Aunt Lucy," Jake volunteered. "You name the day." I cringed at his use of the familiar form of my name, but smiled brightly anyway.

"That'd be great, Jake," I said. "Bye now, Lucy. Take care of yourself. See you soon, either here or there."

She said goodbye and went back into the house. She lifted her handkerchief to her eyes before she shut the door behind her.

"Your aunt's a special woman," I said to Jake, making my way down the steps. "Oh, hey Chester! Where'd you come from?" I bent to scratch him behind his cute black ears and on the white ruff encircling his neck. "Chester's special, too." I glanced around at Jake. "You're really lucky to have a home with them."

"What do you mean?" he asked, his dark eyes clouding over suddenly. "What did she tell you about me?"

"Nothing, really," I said quickly. "But she did tell me you'd lived with them for several years, ever since your parents died."

"Yeah, they've been really good to me. I'd do almost anything for them."

"I'm sure they appreciate you. I really do have to be on my way. I don't like to be out on unfamiliar roads at night."

"Understood. I'll be here a while, so if you run into any trouble give us a call. And Becca?"

"Yes?"

"I appreciate you taking an interest in my aunt. She seems really happy today."

I smiled, blushing at the compliment, even if it had come from Jake. "Bye, Jake. I'm sure I'll be seeing you around."

"You can bet on it...Becca."

I got in Bernice and turned around in the drive. I could see him in my rearview mirror, leaning against the front porch post, arms folded, staring after me until I'd pulled out onto the road and the house disappeared from view.

My mind spun with thoughts and questions. Would Jake be satisfied with my explanation for my first visit? Or would he question Lucy and Martin, in which case they'd probably mention the questions I'd asked about the 911 call?

Before I knew Jake was their nephew, we'd all been thinking maybe the nephew was the person who'd called in the intruder report. Now that I knew Jake's relationship to them, I suspected him even more.

Why would he have made the call if, as they'd all said, there was no intruder? If there was an intruder, why didn't he mention anything about it to the Ledbetters? Shouldn't they know if someone was prowling around their house?

The thing that had shaken me the most, however, had been the sewn-on embroidered name tag on Jake's work shirt. He'd been wearing a shirt printed with Bert's Auto Body Shop – the same place Tommy had worked. The realization stunned me. This meant something – I knew it did.

I shook my head to clear it. "Bernice," I said, "this has gotten me really suspicious. But what should my next move be? How can I find out more about this whole situation?" She didn't answer me, and not for the first time I wished she could.

I turned the radio up loud, trying to drown out my thoughts so I could pay attention to my driving. Serious thinking would have to wait until I got home. According to Jimmy Buffett's radio station, Margaritaville, it *was* five o'clock somewhere. I considered stopping by to pick up the makings for a pitcher of margaritas for myself, but I didn't have the energy.

Chapter 23

PAUL SIMMONS WAS SITTING on my front steps when I pulled into my driveway. *Now what? What does* he *want with me?* I parked and went to meet him, carrying my bag of cookies Lucy had packed for me. "Hey, Paul," I said, "what brings you by?"

"Rebecca," he nodded. "Sorry to drop by without calling, but I was in the neighborhood and…"

"Don't worry about it, Paul. What's going on?"

He stood aside and waited for me to get the door unlocked. I stepped in, set the cookies on the hall table, and motioned him in. "Do you have a few minutes to talk?" he asked.

I supposed he wanted to discuss the latest media reports about a couple of charges of police brutality someone had made against him. I'd read about them but didn't want to hear anything more. But he looked so serious I couldn't help myself. I invited him into the kitchen, where I grabbed a couple of bottles of water from the fridge. "Come on into the living room," I invited. I set out a couple of coasters. When we were settled on the sofa I tucked one foot under me and turned to face him. "Now, what's this about?" I thought I knew, but we'd see.

"I suppose you've heard about those charges that've been made against me," he said, a question in his voice, his brow furrowed.

"Well, you don't mind getting right to the point, do you?" And I'd been wondering how I might bring the subject up with him. "Yes, I've heard a few things. Saw a couple of headlines in the paper. What about them?"

"I'd like a chance to tell you my side of the story."

"Paul, you don't owe me any explanations. Whatever happened is your business. I'm sorry it's been put out there for the public to speculate on and gossip about. But I guess that's part of living in a small town." I shrugged as I said this last bit.

"You're right, but the things that happened involved Richard to an extent, so I wanted you to know in case that becomes public knowledge."

I frowned as I set down my water. "I don't understand. How was Richie involved?"

"It's a long story, but I'll try to give you the brief version. First, I want you to know – some of the things they hinted at in the paper did happen."

"You don't have to tell me this. I really don't want to get caught up in something this public. And I sure don't want to have to testify about anything you've said."

He gave a sarcastic laugh. I couldn't blame him. "I've already told all of this to the IA team. They probably wouldn't be too happy if they find out I told you about it before the investigation is finished, but frankly, right now I don't much give a damn."

Okay, he had my interest now. He took a long pull from his water bottle, set it down, and turned to face me full on. "I thought after we had our talk at The Shed this might all blow over, but…" He shrugged. "Guess that ain't happenin.'"

"This what?"

He waved a hand at me impatiently. "Rebecca, this isn't easy for me. I need to tell it my way." I frowned in frustration but nodded.

"I've known your brother since he was sixteen and I was two years younger. He volunteered at an after-school program where I hung out. I thought he was the coolest guy I'd ever met. He already knew exactly what he wanted to do with his life. He was going to college, then to the law enforcement academy, then he planned to work his way up to being a state trooper."

I smiled, remembering how an even younger Richie had often turned our laundry room into his jail. I was always his first arrest – sometimes for bank robbery, maybe for car theft, once in a while for murder. Mom would sneak one of her cookies to me in a piece of bread during my incarceration.

And when he got on a real tear, Trooper Richard would round up half the kids in the neighborhood, and Mom sometimes had to bake an extra batch of cookies for the detainees. Those were good times.

"He got me and some of the other guys in the program out of a bad situation, and made sure we had fun while he was around," Paul was saying. "I never was one of the 'cool' kids, but with Richard around it didn't matter. After he went off to college, he'd stop by from time to time to check on us, and I remember how proud I felt the day he came by and found me working as a counselor." He paused and turned to gaze out the front window.

"I didn't have a nice childhood like you and Richard did," he said, completely without rancor, just matter of fact. "My mom got sick with Parkinson's when I was young, and my old man ran off when I was about ten – said he couldn't take her and her problems anymore. After that I took care of her. She died a couple of years ago."

I laid a hand on his arm, but he didn't seem to notice. "It's because of Richard I went into law enforcement. He was so good to me, and I wanted to be just like him. So I got a couple of years of classes out at MGCCC and then, with his support, got in at the academy. I guess you could say I've followed in his footsteps, only a bit behind him because of our age difference."

"I'm sure Richie was happy he could help you."

"Oh, I know. He was there the day I graduated, sitting down front wearing a smile as big as Texas." Paul smiled too, but I could hear unshed tears in his voice. He cleared his throat.

"Well. My first position was in Vicksburg, and I hated it, but figured I had to pay my dues. I was discouraged, and lonely, when out of the blue I got a call from Richard telling me Jackson was about to hire half a dozen officers. I applied, and I got the job. I'll always think he pulled a few strings for me, or at least put in a good word. A few years later he made the move back here to Biloxi, and I followed him again, about six months later.

"It was great working with him, seeing him both on the job and off. He kept telling me it was time for us to try to get a job with DPS. I felt nervous, but when Richard got something in his head you usually had to go along with it."

"Don't I know it."

"So that was in both our plans – to move up to state trooper." Paul stopped talking and blinked several times. "A while after I became a deputy, my mother died. It was…was a rough time for me. I was feeling guilty that I hadn't been able to help her more. Under other circumstances, she might have lived years longer."

"And she might not have."

"We'll never know. I do know I wasn't myself for a while there. Going out drinking after work – didn't want to go home to that empty house. Got in a few fights with some of my friends – guys I know now were only trying to help me. And then one night on patrol a few miles outside the city limits I saw this car weaving all over the road, so I pulled it over."

He flopped back down on the sofa and knotted his hands together, holding them between his thighs as if they were about to take charge of him. I'd never seen anyone more animated than him, yet he struggled mightily to remain where he was.

He gave a bitter laugh. "Wouldn't you know it? I'd stopped one of the old gang – not *my* gang, but the 'cool' one – and I smelled the pot as soon as he rolled his window down. I got him out of the car and a joint fell out when he slid out of the seat. With probable cause, I searched the car. He had meth and a bunch of prescription drugs packaged up, plus about an ounce of pot – I figured for his personal use. Well the s.o.b. offered to split it with me if I'd let him off.

"This was about a month after Mom died. He was strung out, but I was strung awfully tight myself. I saw red, and I guess I roughed him up a bit. Bad thing, or good, depending on your viewpoint, Richard came along just then. He stopped, dragged me off the guy, and I still wonder if I would have stopped if he hadn't showed up."

I wasn't comfortable listening to this "true confessions" stuff, but Paul was on a roll now. I probably couldn't stop him if I tried – and it might be something I really needed to hear.

"Couple of weeks after that, similar situation. Only, this time it was my old man. I tell you, my luck was running really bad about then. He'd been drinking, and when he asked me how the 'old lady' was doing, I lost it.

Started calling him names, pounding on him with both fists. I wanted to kill him, Rebecca, I really did. He was talking bad about my mom. But once again, your brother came to my rescue. He got me off my old man and put him into his patrol car and took him in for me. Explained the bruises by saying the guy had gone berserk when he tried to get him in the car. I'm still surprised my old man kept quiet.

"He was so drunk nobody would listen to him. I paid his bail the next day, hoping that would keep him quiet about me, and I guess it did…for a while."

Now there were tears in Paul's eyes and in his voice. *Why don't I feel like crying now? I've cried at everything else.* "Your brother saved me both times, Rebecca. He was real upset with me, but he didn't rat on me. He started in on me to see a counselor. But I was afraid my superiors would find out and I'd lose my job. Thing is, I probably have no business being in law enforcement at all. But it's all I know how to do, and it's the only thing I want to do."

Poor guy. I could see how much he was hurting – tears falling onto his hands, his shoulders shuddering, as if he could cry all his misery away. *Why the tears now? Real or fake? But why would he do that?* He'd have to have a very good reason to come to me and do such a thing. *Like what?* I don't know, like maybe to draw suspicion away from himself after these public allegations. *So what does he expect me to do?* Maybe he hopes I'll come out and support him publicly, to counteract Justine's comments, at the least.

"Paul, I don't see what I can do to help you in this situation," I said, getting up and moving so the coffee table was between us.

"No, I'm not asking you to do anything, Rebecca. I'd never do that. You have been through hell already. I hope maybe you can understand how much Richard's friendship meant to me. I could never have done anything to hurt him. Never!"

He moved to stand facing me, his hands hanging limp at his sides. I backed up a step before I realized I'd done so, then folded my arms across my chest and stared at him, my gaze moving slowly across his face and settling on his soft brown eyes that reminded me so much of a deer's open stare. I held that gaze for a long, slow moment, and then said, "I think I believe you."

He expelled a breath I hadn't been aware he was holding. "Thank God," he said. His hands met in front of him as if in prayer. "Thank you, God," he repeated. "And thank you, Rebecca."

Suddenly I was so very tired. Tired of dealing with a psychotic sister-in-law. Tired of thinking about the night Richie died. Tired of trying to figure out what happened to him out there at that barn. Tired of walking the floor at night unable to settle down to sleep. And right now I was tired of listening to Paul. I know I sound selfish and hard-hearted, but dammit, *I* was the one who lost her brother. *I* was the one who had loved him unconditionally. *I* was the one grieving.

"You should go, Paul. I don't think I can listen to anything more." I paused and looked up at him. "There *isn't* anything more – is there?"

He shook his head, then slowly made his way to the door. He opened it but then turned back to give me one final look. "Thanks for listening to me, Rebecca." He smiled, straightened his shoulders, and closed the door softly behind him.

***

I curled up in the corner of the sofa, drew the shades to put the room in semi-darkness, and cried myself to sleep. I don't know how long I slept before my cell phone jarred me awake. Groggily I fumbled around until I found my purse on the floor and dug it out.

"Hello?" I said, my voice still thick with leftover tears and sleep. "Damian, what do you want?" I heard the snippiness in my voice but couldn't help it.

I heard nothing for a few seconds, then Damian said, "Rebecca? What's wrong with you?"

"Why are you calling, Damian?"

"Sometimes I don't understand you at all. You don't sound so good. I'm gonna come over." *Well, Damian, sometimes I don't understand myself at all, either.*

"No, Damian, I'm okay; you don't have to do that." But I was talking to a dead phone. I reached around to turn on a lamp.

It must have been longer, but it seemed that he arrived in no more than five minutes. I invited him into the living room and plopped down on the sofa. "Okay, you're here. Now what?"

He cocked his head and drew his brows together. "Hey, lady, I was worried about you. Is that all right? I don't mean to butt in…"

"You don't mean to, yet here you are." I couldn't seem to control the bitchiness I heard in my voice. "I *told* you not to bother coming over."

He stood in the middle of the room, rubbing the back of his neck and staring down at me, not saying anything. After several moments of uncomfortable silence, I peeked at him through my damp lashes. He sported dark circles under his eyes, and his usually bright blue eyes had a dull sheen. His hair was messier than usual. In a word, he looked exhausted.

My attitude toward him began to gnaw at me. The guy didn't deserve this. I motioned for him to sit beside me, then laid a hand on one of his. "Hey. You seem really tired. Been working hard?"

"Pulled a double shift overnight. Was just about to hit the sheets when I decided to give you a call. After I heard your voice, I knew I couldn't get to sleep without checking on you."

Talk about knowing how to give a girl a guilt trip. "I'm okay, really. This has just been a very long day for me, too, and I'm also overly tired. Sorry I was short with you on the phone." I squeezed his hand, and he squeezed back. "You should go home and get to bed, and I'll do the same thing. I'm all talked out for today."

"Sounds like a plan. Call you tomorrow?"

"Yeah, tomorrow. 'Nite."

I let him out, locked up, and went upstairs and straight to bed. I felt like Scarlett O'Hara. *But it's true…tomorrow really* is *a new day.*

***

After I fixed my toast and coffee, I sat down at the table and opened Richie's journal. I hadn't been reading it from the beginning, just letting it fall open wherever it would. Today I opened to one of the last few entries:

Things are going great at work, but I have to admit I'm having a hard time keeping my mind on the job. I just met one of the cutest little ladies ever, and I think I'm in love. Her name is Justine Rodgers. She's a New Orleans beauty, so tiny and dark, and sexy as hell. We met one night at a club in NOLA, and now I see her every chance I get. It's never often enough.

I'm gonna marry that girl one of these days.

I'm kind of worried about Damian. He's seeing this woman I think is trouble, but I can't say anything. Not when I don't really know anything. Just a feeling. Maybe this is what Mom and Becca experience. Makes me uneasy.

Hmm. Richie did know Damian's girlfriend. Too bad he didn't warn Damian about her. Wait, what am I saying? *I* didn't warn Richie when I was worried about *him*. What a mixed up mess.

Chapter 24

I HUMMED ALONG TO THE RADIO as I drove over to pick up Owen to spend the night. I slowed for two kids, about seven or eight, riding skateboards in the middle of the street. I stopped the car and rolled down my window.

"Where are your parents?" I barked. "Don't you know *anything* could happen to you out here alone?"

They gazed at me for a moment, openmouthed, then grabbed their boards and ran for the house, not looking back until they reached their front door.

I chuckled to myself. *Maybe I gave them enough of a scare that they'll think twice before venturing out like that again.*

That's when I saw them: Justine and Jake. Her front door was open and she leaned against the jamb. Stopped only a few houses away from hers, I had a clear view of them, but they obviously hadn't noticed me. Not that they'd notice anyone.

Jake had one hand on the jamb over her head and was leaning into Justine; her hands were on his hips. As I watched, he bent to kiss her and she flowed forward into him, pulling him tighter into her. The kiss went on and on, until finally Jake stepped back and stared down into her upturned face. I could see his lips moving. I couldn't see his expression from here, but she looked like a schoolgirl mooning over the good looking quarterback. Jake chucked her under that cute little chin, laughed, and bounded down the steps and out to his car. Justine watched him until he drove out of sight, then she stepped inside and closed the door.

I put Bernice back into gear. But rather than going on down the street to pick up Owen, I made a quick U-turn and drove away before I could do something I'd regret. Because what I really wanted to do was barge into that house and beat the crap out of her.

And then I was pushing Bernice, weaving in and out of rush hour traffic, heading south toward the beach – my haven – swinging west onto Hwy. 90, squinting into the afternoon sun glaring off surfaces in front of me, barely missing a battered old pickup pulling out at St. Peters Avenue. I jerked the wheel to the left, crossed in front of an oncoming tour bus, and whipped into the public beach pull off.

I lost track of time as I sat there shaking, feeling the onset of an anxiety attack. Digging through my purse, I sighed when my hand grasped my two-beer meds. I popped a couple into my mouth and grabbed the bottle of water I'd started keeping in the car. I grimaced as the warm water hit my tongue. *Better than nothing, I guess.*

Closing my eyes, I leaned my head against the headrest, struggling to get a handle on my breathing. *Count of four in, hold four, count of four out. Repeat.*

I jerked and my eyes flew open at the sound of a thumping on my window. Damian! *My God, I can't get away from him.*

He was scowling when I rolled down the window.

"What's the matter? What are you doing here?" I asked, irritated at having been caught in such a condition.

"I could ask you the same thing. Are you okay?"

"Why wouldn't I be?" I asked, swallowing the lump in my throat and loosening my death grip on the steering wheel.

"Oh, I don't know. Maybe something about the way you tore through that intersection back there." He jerked his thumb back toward town.

"What? You're following me now?"

"I wasn't at first, but I decided maybe I'd better. Now how about letting me inside?"

I tilted my head, motioning him toward the passenger side. He opened the door and eased inside, struggling to fold his six foot two frame into my little car.

I said nothing, just stared toward the water.

"Are you going to tell me what's the matter, Becca? You and Mark have a fight?"

You wish.

I kept struggling with that huge lump in my throat. I figured I should *try* to explain it to him. He did seem concerned.

All at once the tears came. *I'm so sick of crying. I don't like being this weak.*

Sighing, I turned to look at him. His brows were drawn into a scowl, his jaw muscles flexing.

"Just a bit of an anxiety attack," I said, shivering. "I miss Richie so much at times like this. He could always help me through them."

Damian laid a hand on my wrist and eased my hand off the steering wheel. "Maybe I can help. What do you need? What would Rich do?"

I smiled in spite of myself. "Talk to me 'til my meds kicked in."

"Well, hell, I can handle *that*. What do you say we get out and walk a while near the water?"

I looked him up and down, noticing his white dress shirt, black slacks, and expensive looking loafers.

"You're not exactly dressed for the beach," I protested.

"Just give me a minute," he said, beginning to unfasten his belt.

"What are you *doing*?"

"Getting comfortable." He slipped off his belt and tugged his shirttail loose, giving me a brief glimpse of his toned stomach. He kicked off his shoes, stripped off his socks, and gathered all his discarded clothing.

"Shall we?"

"I guess so," I said, opening my door. Clearly he wasn't taking no for an answer. By the time I'd locked up and pocketed my keys, Damian had tossed everything into his car and was busily rolling up his pants legs.

"Ready when you are," he grinned. "Beat you to the water!" And he sprinted off.

I followed slowly, watching as he waded into the surf and looked back at me.

"Hey, you're not even trying," he groused. But as I drew near him, his teasing look disappeared. He took my hand and began to pull me along beside the surf, the outgoing tide acting for all the world as if it were trying to flee from us.

"Now, tell me what's going on," he dimpled, hands on his hips. "I'm really a good listener."

"You must think I've totally lost it, Damian."

"What I *think*," he said, stopping and turning me to face him, "is that something has you more upset than you've been since we met. I hate to see you suffering this way."

I shrugged, in a move meant to suggest, "So, Becca's upset; what else is new?" I looked away from his sharp gaze, concentrating instead on the fine black hairs on the back of his darkly tanned hands as they massaged my forearms, his thumbs making small circular motions over the pulse beating at my wrists – the pulse that had been racing so recently but that was now backing off its frantic pace to a more steady rhythm.

I lifted my chin and forced myself to look into his eyes, dark with concern. The longing I saw in their depths shook me to my core – and Damian knew it. His thumbs stopped their gyrations, and abruptly he pulled away.

He walked a few feet up the beach and flopped down into the dry, burning-hot sand.

"Shit!" he winced.

I couldn't help laughing.

I walked up to where he sat and, bending over, dug my hand deep into the sand and shoved the top layer aside, repeating the motion until I had a cool spot to sit. Then I joined him.

He scowled as he watched me. "I suppose growing up on the coast taught you that. You could have warned me, McCallum."

"You didn't give me a chance, Wentworth."

We didn't speak for a few minutes, content to breathe in the salt air and watch the gentle waves continuously receding from us.

Finally I began to talk, starting not with this afternoon's events but with the first time I met Jake Coffee. As I told him of Richie's suspicions about

Justine, thunderclouds began to build behind his eyes. I stopped short of mentioning my suspicions about Richie's murder, since technically Damian was still among my list of possible suspects. I honestly doubted his involvement, especially after I'd found out he was on duty that night. Nevertheless, I kept close to the facts of what I had seen happening between Justine and Jake, only hinting at a long-standing relationship between the two.

"They have to have been involved with each other since before Richie died," he said, when I paused to catch my breath and collect my thoughts. "This sounds too complicated to have started only after his death – I knew there was a reason I didn't like her." He gave a snort as of disgust.

"I'm sure you're right. I used to think I knew Justine…they moved here when she was pregnant with Owen, and she didn't know a soul in town. I tried, I really tried, to be supportive of her, tried to make friends. And I thought for a long time we *were* friends. We used to go shopping, and we'd explore the area sometimes. We found all sorts of nature trails where we could walk. She was trying hard to keep in shape while she was pregnant.

"We'd walk and talk for hours, sharing stories about our pasts. I told her all sorts of things about Richie as a little boy, and she would laugh until she cried. After they found out they were having a boy, she seemed even more curious about 'Little Richard,' as she called him." I smiled in spite of myself, remembering.

"She couldn't wait for him to get home at night. She only wanted to be with him, and he was the same with her. They had fallen in love in New Orleans, and that romance seemed to carry over with them for years."

"What do you think went wrong between them?" Damian asked, when my voice trailed off.

"I don't know, I really don't. I knew they were having some problems, but the only thing Richie ever talked to me about was Justine wanting to go out partying and him wanting to stay at home and take it easy, especially since he had so little time with her and Owen. I know he resented her for wanting to take him away from his little boy, when she had all her time to spend with Owen." He nodded, as if considering what I was saying.

"Looking at it from her perspective, full-time motherhood was most likely what she resented – being the one responsible for taking care of Owen's basic needs," he said. From what I've heard from my sisters, it's not uncommon for mothers to feel like they're carrying too much of the load when it comes to raising babies."

"I wouldn't know about that, not having kids of my own."

He smiled a slow smile. "You are going to make a great mother someday, Becca. I know it."

"You think so? Maybe not, if I can't gain control over these anxiety attacks."

"But you didn't seem too bad to me today. Was this one typical?"

I shot him a quick look of surprise, then shook my head.

"No, not so much. In fact, I was already getting past the worst when you showed up." I blinked, realizing my meds hadn't had time to work by then. I'd pretty much taken control of things myself.

I smiled at the realization, then frowned at what that implied.

"Hey, your expression changed completely just then. Why?"

I jumped to my feet.

"Can we head back to the cars? I've got a little boy to pick up."

Damian stood and slapped sand from his slacks.

"So, are you going to tell me what you were thinking just now?" He reached for my hand as we walked.

"I realized that I handled this attack without Richie's support – *and* without my meds having time to work."

"That's great...isn't it?"

"Well, yeah..." I stared off at a caravan of pelicans riding a current of air along the beach beside us. "But then I realized I'd been relying on Richie all these years when I should have been handling it myself. I depended on him to fix it, like I depended on him to fix *everything*."

He pulled me toward him and leaned forward to touch his forehead to mine.

"Isn't that what big brothers are for?"

"I always thought so," I sighed. "But now I'm seeing there's more truth than I've been willing to admit, to what Justine said about my monopolizing Richie's time."

We walked in silence then, with only the sounds of the gentle waves, the squawking gulls, and the afternoon traffic on nearby Highway 90. At last we made it back to where I'd parked Bernice. Damian's sleek black Camaro snuggled up next to her, the two of them looking for all the world like lovers.

For the first time, I felt the gritty sand making its way into all of my pores and crevices, and I had to resist the urge to scratch several parts of my body. I couldn't get into a shower soon enough, but first I had to get Owen squared away. My comfort had to wait.

"Damian, thank you. Seriously, I think talking it out with you helped a lot."

His fingers brushed across my cheek, flicking away a few clinging grains of sand. "Are you okay to drive?"

I sucked in a deep, if still somewhat shaky, breath and nodded. "Gotta go get my boy."

He stared down at me for a long moment, and I felt something shift between us. "I don't mean to take advantage of your being upset, but..." His voice trailed off as he leaned in and brushed his lips softly against mine, and my body responded, leaning into his. Just as suddenly, he pulled back from me, his gaze traveling over my face. "God, woman, you have the most irresistible lips...full, warm, inviting, sweet-tasting...they beg to be kissed." He leaned in for another kiss. I didn't pull away.

Against my mouth, he said, "I see that mouth when I close my eyes at night, I think about you first thing in the morning. I don't know why I couldn't have met you when Richard and I were living in Jackson."

"Oh, Damian," I sighed, backing away from him slightly. "There are way too many might-have-beens in my life right now. I don't think I can handle pressure of any kind." I reached into the pocket of my shorts and drew out my car keys. "I've gotta run. Owen's probably fit to be tied about now."

He ran a hand through his spiky hair and laughed, the sound tinged with bitterness. "What about me? I'm about fit to be tied, too. Sorry…forget I said that. I have no right to be imposing my feelings on you, especially not today."

I couldn't walk away from him as if nothing at all had changed between us. I didn't know just what *was* going on, but I had to admit something was there. *Time to find out what it is? Not now, but soon.*

"Hey, why don't you come over for dinner one night next week? Are you free Monday?"

His eyes lit up. "I'd love to, thank you." His speech sounded formal all of a sudden. "Tell me what time."

"About seven? Casual dress," I said. Looking down at his bare feet, I added impishly, "Shoes and socks optional. Now, I'd better go have it out with the wicked witch." Damian opened his mouth to protest, but I waved him away. "Just kidding. I'm okay. This is one of those times when it's better to laugh. Otherwise I may start bawling and never stop."

I gave him a quick hug and jumped into the car. Backing up and pulling out of the parking spot, I waved and left him standing, staring after me.

Chapter 25

OWEN RAN OUT THE FRONT DOOR as soon as I got out of the car. "Aunt Becca, where were you? I was worried about you!" he said, throwing his arms around my knees. "I didn't think you were ever coming back." His little face was red, his eyes swollen.

"You should have your butt kicked, Rebecca McCallum," I chided myself, realizing what my being late had done to him. I wondered how long it might be before he would stop worrying about losing more of the people he loved, wondered if he would ever stop worrying. I vowed then and there to stop thinking of myself and my loss first, and to put Owen first instead. Lord knew he needed to be first in somebody's life. Every child deserved that.

"I'm so sorry, sweetie," I said, reaching down to hug him tightly to me. "Something came up I had to take care of right away. I'm sorry I didn't let you know. But everything's okay now, and I'm ready to get our weekend started. How about you?"

"Owen, come pick up your toys from the living room floor. We'll be inside in a minute," Justine said. When he reached the porch, she almost shoved him through the front door, shutting it behind her.

"Just where *have* you been, Rebecca? You're over an hour late. Have a hot date?" She arched her perfectly chiseled eyebrows.

I had to battle the urge to scratch her eyes out right here in front of God and everybody. But I thought of Owen, the innocent little boy I loved so much, and I made myself look her in the eye and force a tiny, if tight, smile.

"I'm sorry, Justine. Hope I didn't mess up your plans too much. You didn't have tickets to something, did you?" My voice honey-sweet, I tried to sound sufficiently worried and concerned.

She flounced ahead of me into the house and snatched her cell phone from the hall table.

"Sorry about that. Owen's aunt is here now, so I should be able to leave in about ten minutes. Yes, me, too."

She flipped the phone closed and gave me a scathing look. "Next time you're going to be late, let me know. Or Owen won't be going anywhere with you when you do get here."

I bit my tongue, not wanting Owen to hear us arguing. I hated it had come to this. Once drawn together by our love for my brother, clearly our friendship had been dead far longer than Richie had been.

***

I closed the book and sat without talking, giving Owen time to process the ending to the story. While I waited, I gazed around the room, realizing I had some serious redecorating to do. The room wasn't overly feminine, but I'd left it alone after I moved in. Mom and Dad stayed in their old room whenever they visited, and hardly anyone else stayed overnight.

But now I could see it wouldn't work as a room for a little boy. The soft cream walls needed to be replaced – maybe with a clean white that would be a suitable background for a room filled with primary reds, blues, and yellows. Maybe a few sea creatures for company – and maybe a Velveteen Rabbit.

"How did you like the story?" I asked finally.

"I liked it a lot. It was sad they were just gonna burn the little vel-ve-teen rabbit. I'm glad the fairy made him real."

"Yes, I'm glad she came along. Do you remember what I said velveteen was?"

"Yeah. You can make clothes out of it and it's really soft."

"That's right. Way too hot to wear in Mississippi. I can't show you. But I do have this."

I rose from the bed where I had been sitting beside him and crossed to the cedar chest in the corner. The guest bedroom had twin beds, and Owen had already dressed for bed, but in the way of children, begged me to keep reading, since he badly wanted to stave off sleep. I looked down at the chest and tried to prepare myself to look inside. *I almost wish I hadn't said anything to him about it. I don't know if I can do this.*

I hadn't opened the chest full of childhood treasures since we lost Richie. Now I realized I was about to be bombarded by a slew of memories of my big brother. Quickly I took in a breath and popped the fastener underneath the lid. A whiff of cedar assailed my nostrils, taking me back to my childhood when Mom had first shown me the baby things she'd saved up to that point in our lives.

The bracelet I wore home from the hospital, with my name spelled out in tiny white beads. The baby book of Richie's filled from front to back with photos, hair clippings, and other things long forgotten, alongside *my* baby book with its scarcely opened pages. The second child never gets as much attention, I thought for perhaps the hundredth time.

"What'cha doin', Aunt Becca?" The curious voice brought me back to the present, and I moved aside a few things to get to what I wanted. My hand touched the downy fur of a stuffed toy. Closing the chest, I went over to sit on the side of Owen's bed.

"Owen, meet my old friend, Buddy." I handed him the stuffed rabbit I'd toted for about three years before I got too old for such baby things. All of seven years old at the time, I gave him up to Mom's cedar chest. Buddy had clearly seen better days. He was about ten inches long, gray and white, with pink bead eyes that still glistened. One of his ears, lined with pink, flopped to the side, while the other fell forward over his right eye. He had a tear under his right arm, from my having dragged him up and down the stairs too many times. Mom had sewn him up at least three times, but once I got my hands on him, it didn't take long for the stitches to come undone. My toys took a beating.

"He's neat!" Owen said, and looking into his sparkling blue eyes I could see he meant it. "He looks like the Velveteen Rabbit."

"Nice job! Your vocabulary is improving every day."

"What's that mean?"

I laughed. "Well, it means the words you know. When you were a baby, you couldn't talk at all. Now look at you – you're not even five yet, and you know thousands of words!"

"Did you like the story of the Velveteen Rabbit?" he asked me.

"I loved the story. I know it's a sad story in a way, but it's a good story, too, don't you think?"

He nodded vigorously. "I hope the Velveteen Rabbit gets to stay with the other rabbits forever. I hope they don't leave him, like my daddy left me."

The sadness in his voice, and in the way his little head drooped on his shoulders, tugged at my heart; I felt as if it were being ripped from my chest. "That's one of the wonderful things about stories," I said. "When a story ends, that's really the end. Everything can stay the same as it is on the final page. In the real world, sometimes things change for the better, sometimes for the worse. Losing your daddy was a very much 'worse' thing for all of us. It's bad when we have to lose the people we love, but…"

I stopped, unsure how to go on from there.

"But sometimes we just have to," he finished for me. "That's what Grandma Irene said. I nodded, blinking back tears, and he sighed. "I sure hope Uncle Jake doesn't have to go away and not come back, the way Daddy did. I'd be sad if he went away."

"Oh, sweetie, I don't think you have to worry about that. Uncle Jake is crazy about your mother – I mean, he likes her a lot – and he doesn't plan to go anywhere."

"But I'm still sorta scared," he whispered.

"Scared? Why would you be scared?"

"Well Mommy and Uncle Jake have been yelling at each other, like Mommy and Daddy used to do, and Daddy went away…"

"But your daddy died while doing his job. A very bad man hurt him. Jake doesn't work around guns. I think he'll be safe." I tried for a teasing tone in my voice, hoping to get the little guy out of his worried state. It didn't seem to be working.

"When did you hear them yelling?"

He cuddled Buddy beneath his neck and didn't answer at first.

"Owen?"

"I was in bed. I think I was asleep, but I woke up and heard Mommy yelling. She sounded like when she used to yell at Daddy."

"That's all you heard, your mom yelling? Maybe she was just talking loud, really excited about something?"

"No, it wasn't like that. If I tell you, promise you won't tell her what I did? I don't want her to get mad at me, too."

"Sweetie, you're my buddy! Promise I won't tell."

"Umm...I got out of bed and went out into the hall so I could hear better. They were in the living room, so I tiptoed over to the top of the stairs and sat there. I could hear real good then."

I bet you could. I couldn't help smiling at his description of his clandestine efforts to sneak around and listen where he shouldn't be. Seems the boy did get something from Aunt Becca.

"Was your mommy really upset?"

"Yes. She yelled loud. Uncle Jake kept telling her to be quiet. She asked him something like, how could he do somethin' like that."

"Did she say what he'd done, why she was so angry?"

"No, she just asked him that. He said he thought she'd be happy about it. She said, "Well, I'm not. What if somebody finds out?" and he said they wouldn't if she kept her mouth shut."

"Oh!"

"That's not a nice way to talk to somebody. And I don't want him mad at her, cause I don't want him to leave!" I shifted around on the bed to face him. His little mouth quivered and his eyes spilled tears down his sweet face. Suddenly he launched himself at me, wrapping both arms around my neck and sobbing wildly. I felt like a lowlife, pumping him for information.

I rocked back and forth making shushing noises and humming tunelessly, rubbing his small back and holding him close. Gradually his sobs diminished, until finally I could ease out of his clutches. I grabbed a box of tissues and wiped his face, then helped him blow his runny nose.

"Honey, listen to me. Can you do that?" He nodded. "Good, because this is important. You know your mommy loves you very much, don't you?"

He nodded again. "Well, I'm sure Jake loves both your mommy and you. That's why he wants you to call him Uncle Jake, so you'll know he wants you all to be happy together. But sometimes grownups don't act all that grownup, you know?"

He giggled a bit at that. "You mean you act like little kids?"

I laughed, too. "Yeah, sometimes we do. We don't always set a good example for you kiddos. We try, but..." I let my voice trail off, thinking not so much of Justine and Jake as of myself and Mark, and me with Damian. Well. I'd have to think on that later.

"What do you say to some milk and a chocolate chip cookie?"

"Yum! Did Grandma make the cookies?"

"Yes, she did. She baked lots and put them up in the freezer in little bags and said to give you one when you came over to visit, so you wouldn't forget her."

"I won't ever forget her," he protested. "She's my daddy's mommy." Oh, out of the mouths of babes for sure. I tweaked his nose.

"That's my boy. Come down with me and we'll get that snack."

***

Back upstairs after our snack, I turned out the lamp, leaving only the small pink rose nightlight. *It has to go, too.* I sat at the foot of Owen's bed until his blonde lashes fluttered closed at last against his chubby cheeks, then climbed into the other bed – where I sat staring into the gloom for the next two hours, not even coming close to falling asleep. Sleep doesn't come easy, I've found, when your life involves a small precious boy who's feeling lost, two gorgeous guys who've both professed to care about you, an unknown someone of your acquaintance who may be a killer, and, oh yes, a job that has you waiting on pins and needles for the next disaster to strike.

How was I supposed to handle this latest twist? Sure, I'd had my suspicions about Jake, and about Justine, but as the pieces of "evidence" began to come together, I grew more worried about what the outcome would be.

I looked over at Owen, my sweet nephew who had just lost his daddy. Now he was afraid of losing the only male figure in his life, and what was I doing? Picking and prying, hoping to find evidence that the man he looked up to was a murderer, and what's more, that he'd murdered the little boy's dad.

Would I ever find the information to lead me to Richie's killer? And if I did so, would I have the courage to confront them? And if it turned out to be either Jake or Justine, or both of them, what would that do to Owen, who loved them both so much? Would it be better to let sleeping dogs lie? But I couldn't do that.

For one thing, I expected Richie would continue to haunt my dreams if I tried to drop the matter. He'd always been the really persistent sort. Well, so was I, but I had a feeling I'd need more than persistence to figure out this puzzle. I'd just have to wait and see.

Before I finally slept, I'd made one major decision. I was ready to get Lorelei to hook me up with her therapist.

***

When I opened the door to Justine the next day, Owen burst past me. "Hey Mommy! Can we go to the treehouse right now?"

Justine followed behind him more slowly, looking like she'd rather be anywhere else. We gave each other noncommittal "hellos." This would be Owen's first time in the treehouse and no way would she allow Owen up there without her.

"Not so fast, hotshot." I raced after him and scooped him up in my arms, causing him to squeal in delight. "We have to lay down a few ground rules first." I planted him on the sofa next to me, and Justine sank into a chair with a grimace. I couldn't tell if she was hurting or unhappy. Maybe both. I rubbed my knuckles over the top of Owen's head like I'd seen Richie do so many times. Justine had been watching us, but at that movement she turned her head and stared out the window at the street.

"I'm going to tell you the same thing Grandpa Ken told your daddy and me when he built the treehouse for us. He said once we were inside the treehouse we were safe, but climbing up and down the ladder was a dangerous thing, so we had to be extra careful then. He said if one of us broke an arm or a leg, he didn't want anybody blaming him."

"Did you?"

"Break any bones? No. We were always careful. We were afraid he'd take it down if we ever got hurt." He nodded solemnly, his blue eyes round and unblinking.

Cautioning him to wait and let me help him up the ladder the first time, I snatched up the picnic basket as we went through the kitchen. At the ladder Owen stood looking up, chubby hands clasped in front of him. I demonstrated how to grip a higher rung and take one step at a time, then backed down and said, "You ready?"

He nodded but made no move toward the ladder. "I'll have to help you for a while, until your legs get a bit longer, okay?"

Justine stood close by but she didn't speak or try to help. I helped Owen snag the first board with his foot, grabbed his ankle with one hand, and gripped him beneath his left armpit. He grabbed hold of the sides of the ladder and I helped him swing his second foot up. That was all it took. After that I only had to keep a hand underneath his bottom as he climbed. At the top I moved up close behind him so I could support him with one knee as I grabbed even higher and boosted him onto the porch.

"I did it! I did it, Mommy!" Justine clapped and waved up at him, her brown eyes alight with feeling.

"I see you, little man. You did great!"

I hoisted myself onto the porch and reached for the picnic basket. Justine handed it up and then climbed up herself. I pushed back the flap of the black tarpaper nailed over the opening to the house and Owen ducked inside, with me right behind.

He popped up and looked around the eight by ten foot room. "Wow, this is giant!" he said, and I smiled, thinking back to the first time I'd climbed up here many years ago.

I heard Justine muttering as she climbed onto the porch: "I still don't see what's so neat about a dirty old treehouse. You'd think he'd rather go play at the beach than come out here." But when she pushed the tarpaper aside and joined us, she sat up and looked around. "Oh, Owen, isn't this neat? I don't know what I expected, but it wasn't this." She was so petite that she fit up here much better than I did, looking almost like a kid herself.

She stayed with us for about half an hour, watching Owen explore every corner and looking at her watch often. Finally, tired of her distraction, I said, "Justine, if you have errands to run, why don't you go on and take care of them? We'll be fine here."

"If you're sure... Do you want me to pick him up later, or would you like to bring him home?"

"Okay if I just text you?" She nodded and scooted across the floor to give Owen a hug.

Owen poked his head out the doorway and waved to his mom as she crossed the yard. Then he turned back to me, eyes sparkling. "Time for our picnic now?"

Chapter 26

G ROWING UP DOWN SOUTH, the Fourth of July was my favorite holiday – next to Christmas. Dad's company always threw a big picnic for all the workers' families. I loved the carnival rides and games, and I always begged Dad and Richie to win me a bear or some other stuffed toy. Dad didn't have much time, though, because he helped with the cooking. The menu was always the same: barbecue chicken and brisket, potato salad, baked beans, corn on the cob. And for dessert, pies and ice cream. Mom never made cherry pies, so I looked forward to having that, and Dad always made sure I got an extra big slice.

Times have sure changed. Most companies can't afford, or don't bother, to hold picnics like that anymore. The main businesses here now are the casinos, and they are all business. One thing we can usually count on from them, though, is that at least one will put on a nice fireworks display. This year that privilege fell to the Paradise.

"You and Mark have to come up to Cloud Nine tonight to watch the show with us," Lorelei had begged. Cloud Nine was the swanky rooftop restaurant I never went to because it was too expensive and exclusive. "It'll be like old times, celebrating the Fourth together."

What did she mean – like when Richie was still alive? It wasn't as if we'd ever celebrated in the restaurant. I loved Lorelei like a sister, but I wasn't about to spend the Fourth with all of Biloxi's glitterati.

***

I thought about tonight as I finished getting dressed. Mark would be here at ten – he'd promised me a fun day today but gave no hints beyond telling me I'd need a swimsuit, shorts, and a dinner dress. Given the lack of information, I decided to pack a small makeup bag and a few things for my hair as well.

I'd just brought my bag downstairs when the doorbell rang. "You're early!" I sang out as I swung the door open. But it wasn't Mark.

Damian's gaze traveled over me and he put his hands on his hips and whistled. "Wow, lady, you look fantastic!" The way he was looking at me made me almost have second thoughts about my plans for the day. I blushed.

"Damian, what are you doing here?" He was wearing khaki cargo shorts and a fitted blue t-shirt that enhanced his eyes. Shades perched atop his black hair. I stole a look at his tanned legs.

"Looks like I got here too late to take you out for breakfast."

I wrinkled my nose, trying to look disappointed – but not too much so. "Yeah, sorry…I promised to spend the day with Mark."

"I see. So what do you two have planned?"

I shrugged. "Not sure. He wouldn't tell me."

"Surprise, hmm? Sounds like fun." He stepped back from the door. "Guess I'll let you finish getting ready. Have a good time, okay?"

"Hey…thanks for the invitation."

"No problem. I should have asked you when I was here for dinner the other night. You're better off with him today anyway – I'm working the evening shift."

"Be careful out there. Watch out for the crazies."

He flashed his dimples. "Will do." With a wave he was gone. I closed the door and leaned against it with a sigh. *Why does he have to be so good looking?*

Next time the doorbell rang I waited to be sure it was Mark. He grinned when he saw me. "You look good enough to eat."

"Not so bad yourself, Barrington." He wore olive green shorts and a Hawaiian print shirt, boat shoes, no socks. A visor sat jauntily on his head, giving him the look of an island surfer.

"Got your surfboard on top of the Escape?" I teased.

"How did you know?" He waggled his Groucho eyebrows. "Ready?"

"As ever." I grabbed my bag.

"Looks like you're planning to be away for the weekend." The eyebrows again.

"You wouldn't tell me what to expect."

He rubbed his palms together. "Let's go. Time's a-wasting." He grabbed my bag and hopped off the porch. I shut the door and skipped down the steps to join him.

***

"I don't get what we're doing at the Paradise, Mark. You know I don't gamble."

"C'mon, get a move on. You won't find out at this rate." He shoved open the door under the Exit sign and motioned me through. I gasped when I stepped out onto a sort of veranda. Down below us the sparkling waters of the Gulf beckoned. Between us and the Gulf were arrayed a bevy of watercraft ranging from dinghies to yachts.

"Move it!" Mark tugged me by the hand, almost running down the steps to the dock. He stopped next to a sleek cabin cruiser, grinning. "Like her?" I looked from the beautiful boat to him and back again.

"What is this?"

"It's a boat, doofus," he laughed.

I hit him in the ribs. "Don't play dumb. I mean…"

"I know what you mean. She belongs to a friend of mine, and they're visiting relatives in Virginia, so he told me I could take her out while they were gone. We go fishing about once a month, and I've gotten reasonably good at handling her."

"She's beautiful." The boat was probably a thirty-footer, a cabin cruiser; it looked brand new. An American flag and another with the name Creighton flew proudly from the mast. "Those the owners?" I gestured to the flag.

He nodded and held out his hand. "Let me help you aboard so I can introduce you to *Destiny*."

Soon we had our gear stowed away and were making our way out of the harbor and into the Gulf, navigating among several other pleasure boats bound on the same journey. I stood with Mark on the flybridge so I wouldn't miss a single thing, but he'd suggested the foredeck as a good place for sunning later. I was learning lots of new boating terms today. I was also learning how skillful this man was on the water.

When we were out in the open water, he pushed the throttle forward and we surged ahead. After weeks of having felt like I was stagnating, I suddenly felt completely alive again. I know my smile was wider than usual, and when he saw it, he pulled me into him for a boisterous kiss, and my heart sang.

"I've missed that smile," he said and put his arm around me. "Think I'll keep you close for a while."

I leaned against him and savored the sweetness of the day.

***

Mark cut the motor so that we were hardly moving at all, planning to circumnavigate Horn Island. I lay sunbathing on the foredeck where I could talk with him as he drove.

We found a place where water plants grew thickly and nobody was around – a perfect place to stop and have our late lunch. Mark had packed ham and cheese sandwiches, chips, and a bowl of cut fruit. Perfect for a day on the water.

The afternoon was still, with white and gray fluffy clouds scattered round the horizon and a few mare's tails, wispy and almost transparent against the faded blue sky. After we ate, we continued around the island. We waved at a few picnickers but just kept moving. Birds in abundance – raucous seagulls, inquisitive egrets, statuesque herons – frolicked along the shore.

As I lay watching their intermingled carryings-on, Mark said, "Becca, look up!" His velvety voice sounded excited, almost shaky. I tilted my head back and looked in the direction he pointed. I drew in my breath.

The bird was almost unbelievably large, its wing span about seven feet. Its feathers were golden brown, almost glowing as the afternoon sun shone through them. It had a large, white head. *An eagle!* The eagle soared and swooped, and I found I was holding my breath.

"I knew they were here," Mark said, "but this is the first one I've seen in years."

"Me, too. Isn't it beautiful? No, it's majestic."

Then the eagle was joined by another, and an aerial dance began – a dance of love. They dived and swooped, soared and swept by each other. Their shrill cries were the only sounds we could hear.

We must have watched them for fifteen minutes, although time seemed to be standing still. I hadn't realized that Mark had cut the engine completely until I felt him slide onto the seat behind me. He wrapped his arms around me, sliding his hands down my arms to grasp my hands, and I nestled against his chest. I could feel his heart pounding, and I knew mine beat as strong.

"Did you know that bald eagles have about seven thousand feathers?" Mark whispered. "And their crying out to each other is building the mating bond between them." I shivered as his breath caressed my neck.

We stayed like that until the pair of eagles made one last wide circle overhead and then headed inland, perhaps bound for a nest in a tall pine tree. We still didn't speak for a minute. Then Mark said, "You know, I doubt we'll see anything neater than that today. You about ready to head back?"

I nodded. "Almost." I turned toward him and pulled him in for a kiss. He growled and pulled me close to him. Butterflies were swarming in my stomach. "Now I'm ready," I grinned at him.

His green eyes sparked and I wondered if I'd pushed too far. "Not nice, woman." He slapped each of my thighs lightly and nuzzled my neck, then sighed. "I do love you, Becca."

"Love you too, baby. You still okay with waiting?"

"Um-hmm. But days like this make it hard – more ways than one." He shifted and adjusted his shorts. I giggled. "Okay, I better get up on the bridge. Want to come with me?"

"Sure thing." I fumbled around in my bag, pulled out my white cover-up, and slipped it on. Then I climbed up behind him.

Half an hour later we were easing off the throttle to begin making our way into the harbor. On our way back the sun had set, and Mark said, "It's probably more than an hour 'til time for the fireworks to begin. Would you rather stay out here 'til then, or go on and get dressed so we can get a seat with a view at the restaurant?"

It took me all of twenty seconds to choose dinner. Mark grinned. "That's my girl."

Chapter 27

A N HOUR LATER I MET MARK in the lobby of the Paradise. Lorelei had given us keys to two rooms where we could shower and cool off. I'd donned a halter dress, USA blue. Almost backless, with a vee-neckline, the hem was one of those high-low things, and I liked that the dress showed off my tanned legs and arms.

Mark had changed into khakis and a forest green button-down shirt with sleeves rolled up almost to his elbows. His brilliant green eyes lit up and he gave me a lazy smile as he held out his hand.

"C'mon, beautiful. Let's get you fed." He led me toward double doors that opened onto an outdoor restaurant I hadn't been to before. A few tiki torches were scattered around, and there were candles on each table, but the lighting was still romantic. And dim enough so we'd be better able to see the fireworks later.

We followed the hostess to a table at the outer edge of the patio. The evening air was balmy, especially coming in off the Gulf. The breeze ruffled Mark's wavy hair, and I felt a few tendrils fluttering around my face. My skin glowed pink from the day's sun, and the air sent chill bumps up my arms.

The fireworks started just as we were finishing dinner but before dessert came. Mark and I walked out to the railing around the patio where it was a bit darker. Just as we got there, the lights all along the waterfront began to dim, and the color bursts sparkling over the dark waters of the Gulf seemed multiplied. I'd seen the moon shining on the water plenty of times and it always mesmerized me, and I'd seen fireworks many times – but this was different. Something about being here with the guy I loved, his arms holding me close, and all these bursts of color seeming to fall right toward us made me feel I could just reach out and touch them. I felt a bit scared and at the same time excited, even more so after Mark stepped behind me and hugged me close, his mouth against my hair.

"They never last long enough," I complained. "I could watch for hours…except my neck wouldn't take it."

"Aww, does your neck hurt? Here, let me make it better." Mark leaned down and kissed me just under my earlobe, and I shivered. "Cold?" he laughed huskily, his warm fingers massaging my neck.

"Your hands are amazing. Oh, good. They've turned the lights back up. Let's go get dessert so we can get out of here." We made our way back to our table and signaled for the server.

"Have a good time today?"

I grinned as I met his smoky gaze. "You know I did. And do you know what else? I didn't think about anything besides us all afternoon." I reached for his hand. "This is the best, most carefree day I've had in weeks."

The crinkles around his eyes deepened, and I saw the muscles in his jaw working before he said, "You don't know how happy that makes me. I've been waiting for a day like this."

"Me, too," I said softly. "Thank you…for everything."

"I hope you know I'm doing all I can to make you happy. I won't really be happy until that smile is back on your face for good."

We ordered a huge ice cream concoction to share. I had no idea how large it would be, but the waiter assured us we wouldn't be sorry. When we saw it, we agreed.

We were about halfway through dessert, and Mark had just told me a story about work that had me giggling, when I got the feeling we were being watched. I looked around and my eyes met a set of eyes as green as Mark's – but these belonged to a woman. She was staring across the patio at us, or at one of us. I knew I didn't know her, so I thought Mark must.

"That woman keeps looking at us. Know her?"

He turned to look and gave a small grunt of acknowledgment. The blonde smiled and lifted her glass in a salute, and Mark nodded his head slightly. "So who is she, Mark?" Before he had time to answer, she rose from her seat and sauntered across toward us, her walk sexy as hell. I didn't like the look on her face at all.

"Hi, Mark," she said when she got to our table. She put a hand on his shoulder, her touch looking for all the world like a caress. "It's been a while. How've you been?"

"Savannah," he said, getting to his feet. "Been fine. You?" It wasn't like him to be so reticent.

"Oh, just peachy." She looked down at me. "Well, are you going to introduce me to your friend, or do I have to do the deed myself?" I felt like a ten-year-old. I didn't think I liked this woman.

He seemed to have forgotten I was there. "Yes, I'm sorry. Savannah Greene, Rebecca McCallum." He reached for my hand and grasped it tightly. His palm was sweating. What was up with that?

"My date got an important business call and I have been abandoned...temporarily," she said, smiling at Mark and ignoring me. "So when I saw you over here I decided to come and say hello." He nodded. "I also wanted to ask you: Have you had a chance to do anything with that property yet? I know you were excited about getting the cabin fixed up, and I'm sure it'll be really special when you're finished with it."

"Uhh, no, I haven't done anything with it at all yet. I've been busy lately. Besides, I'm not so sure that I want to fix it up like I'd thought. I'm going to wait awhile, make sure I know what I want to do."

"Well, whatever you do, I hope you'll let me see the 'after', since I've already seen the 'before.'" She finally turned to me. "I'm sure you've seen it, Rebecca. Isn't it a special place? So secluded, but so near the water. I just love it."

I smiled noncommittally, not prepared to let her know I was clueless. Mark sat back down and I casually laid my hand on his knee. The movement wasn't lost on her, and sparks flew from those green eyes, so like Mark's yet at the same time so unlike his.

She glanced over her shoulder. "Well, I see my fella's back, so I'll run along now. Good to meet you, Rebecca. And really nice to see you again, Mark." She leaned down and gave him a peck on the cheek that was anything but sisterly, and the red imprint on his face wasn't that much brighter than the flush that crept up from his neck.

It was quiet at our table after Savannah left. So quiet I could hear our breathing. Or was that just the blood pounding in my head?

"Who is she, Mark? She seemed awfully familiar with you. And don't tell me her name again. I got that."

He sucked in his breath and blew it out in a rush. "Savannah works for an attorney. I met her when I had to go in to take care of some family business last year."

"And you dated?"

He shifted uncomfortably. Good, I was uncomfortable myself. "Yeah, we dated for a few months."

"When did you meet?"

"Last summer, July, I think."

"Were you two serious?"

"Becca, I don't know how to answer that question." My heart dropped into my stomach. "I mean, we dated steadily for several months, but I realized I wasn't serious about her and finally broke it off with her."

"I see."

"I'm not so sure you do."

"What about this land she mentioned? And a cabin? You've not said anything about that to me before this." I knew my voice was sounding accusatory, but I couldn't seem to help it.

"Okay, I guess I should start at the beginning." He sighed again and leaned back in his chair, dessert forgotten. I sat back, too. "Last June my Uncle Thurman passed away. He was my mother's brother. He lived here during the years I was growing up. Guess you'd say I was his favorite nephew. He never married, and he had moved to Miami years ago, but he had a piece of land here he decided to hold on to."

"Oh. I get it. Your uncle left that land to you when he died."

He nodded. "It's over toward Pascagoula, off one of the county roads. There's almost five acres that fronts on Rawlings Canal. He built a cabin there in the early seventies, a small one, just a couple of rooms. It's primitive, but it could be fixed up into something special. I'd been wanting to show it to you, but there's been so much going on, I never seemed to find a good time. I kept hoping things would get settled down…"

"Doesn't seem like that's happening any time soon, does it?"

"Becca, don't. I just wanted to wait to show it to you after you were more relaxed and could enjoy it with me."

"I'm sorry I've been a drag on you," I said. "I'm sure Savannah wouldn't have a problem helping you decide what to do with it."

He gave an exasperated snort. "Give me a break. You know I'm right where I want to be and doing what I want to do. Don't you?" He put his finger under my chin (which made me angry by trembling) and tilted my face to his. "This cabin and land mean nothing to me, compared to how I feel about you. That can wait. I want to help you get to a comfortable place. I want to help you find the answers you need. The land will be there later."

"That's sweet, Mark. But you don't have to feel responsible for me."

"Dammit, don't do this." He reached for my hand and squeezed it tightly. "Don't make this into something it's not."

"I'm just realizing how much I've brought upset into your life. Just a bit over a month ago you were going your merry way, and then you put your life on hold to come and take care of me. You've been with me ever since. But if Richie hadn't died, you'd still be doing what made you happy. Or whoever." *But it wouldn't be me.*

"I swear I was never serious about Savannah. I've never been serious about anyone, not since I first met you. You're the love of my life, Becca. The only love. Please don't let a chance meeting like this mess up what we've been rediscovering." He leaned forward to lock eyes with me, and I could clearly see the love shining out of them. I couldn't help myself.

"When did you break up with her?"

"What?"

"When did you break *up* with her?"

"Months ago. Back in March, I think. And it wasn't so much a breakup as a drifting apart. I just wasn't into her, and I decided it wasn't fair to act as if that might change. I knew it never would. Even before I saw you again, I knew it never would change. I love you, Becca. I always will." He reached around to slide his hand into my hair at the back of my neck, then covered his mouth with mine, his kiss both gentle and demanding, his teeth playing against my bottom lip. When he sucked gently, the vibration brought on a matching vibration in my belly. I couldn't help it...I moaned softly.

He murmured against my mouth, "So can we get out of here? Can we go back to your place? Then we can talk about this as much as you feel you need to." I nodded. He pulled me to my feet, tossed some bills on the table, and slid his arm around my waist, pulling me close for another kiss. "I love knowing you're my woman," he said against my ear. But when I glanced back at Savannah, she didn't seem happy about it at all.

***

As it turned out, we didn't talk about Savannah any more that night, or anything else, for that matter. By the time we got to my house, I was dead on my feet and just wanted to sleep. I wasn't really worried about her, not after I'd gotten past that first spate of petty jealousy. Through a series of embarrassing yawns, I begged Mark to go so I could get to bed.

"Long as you're not really upset with me," he said, cradling my chin in his hand and lifting it so our eyes met. I pulled him down for what I hoped would be a reassuring kiss.

"I'm fine, I promise. I just didn't realize how all that time on the water exhausted me. But that's okay – you can invite me out on *Destiny* again anytime you're ready."

He grinned. "Ready for an all-day deep sea fishing cruise?"

"I don't know about that," I giggled. "I like the lazy days myself."

"I'll keep that in mind. 'Night, love. Sweet dreams."

Chapter 28

IT HAD BEEN FIVE DAYS SINCE my fiery fireworks date with Mark. I sat in the parking lot, willing my body to get out of the car and walk into Dr. Ferris's office. Lorelei had promised me I would like the way the doctor conducted her therapy sessions, but I still found it hard to even think about sharing private stuff with a stranger. After several minutes of procrastination, I forced myself to go inside.

The office seemed more like a spa than a therapist's office. Soothing Celtic music played, a small fountain burbled quietly in one corner, and seating in the waiting area looked soft and inviting. After checking in and taking care of paperwork, I settled into the chair nearest the fountain, hoping its sounds would distract me until my turn came. I heard my name not five minutes later. *Promptness – I like that.*

Dr. Ferris wasn't what I'd expected. Then again, I don't know what I *had* expected. She was maybe forty, no older, with soft blonde hair falling to her shoulders. One side was held behind her ear with a jeweled clip. Her handshake was firm and friendly. She smiled and motioned me to a sitting area with soft lighting. No overhead fluorescents in this doctor's office. I commented on her non-medicinal décor, and she laughed.

"Well, I try to make my clients comfortable."

That will be quite a feat, Doc.

I was uncomfortable for the first twenty minutes or so, but then I found myself relaxing enough to give her a condensed version of my life history. "I can't believe I just told you all of that, Dr. Ferris," I said, looking at my watch. Fifty minutes had passed, and I felt surprisingly relaxed.

"It's a good start. And call me Angie if you'd feel comfortable doing so. That is, if you want to continue our sessions." She raised one beautiful brow inquiringly.

"Yes, I do." I had just surprised myself. "Lorelei told me I would feel comfortable with you right away, and she was right."

"That's great. I'd suggest once a week for a while, until we see how things go." I nodded. "Get with my receptionist and set up a schedule before you leave." We rose and shook hands. "Rebecca, I look forward to working with you."

That wasn't so bad. In fact, I had a feeling of lightness as I walked back to the car. I picked up my phone to report to Lorelei.

***

At home later, I fixed a glass of lemonade and sat down in the cool living room with Richie's journal.

November 14, 2002: Just got back from a visit home. Mom and Dad are fine. Made it home in time to go to the OS football game. Saw a bunch of the old gang, since it was homecoming weekend. Greyhounds won 21 to 6. Great game. Becca came home with me, but she hung out with Lorelei most of the weekend. We got into an argument on the way back to school. She'd been kinda snippy with Mom and I tried to talk to her about it, but she wasn't ready to listen. I hope my baby sister grows up soon. She won't do too well out in the workplace if she can't control her mouth better than she does. I don't know how Mom puts up with some of the crap Becca says. I could see how much it hurt Mom, but Becca only wanted to tell me her side of things. No matter what, though, Mom doesn't deserve to be talked to that way.

I swallowed hard, blinking back tears. I wondered what I'd done and said that weekend. I remembered coming in for homecoming one year, but I had no memory of getting into it with Mom. Angie had suggested I make notes about anything I wanted to talk about, so I scrounged around in the old roll top desk and found a small spiral notebook and pen, jotting down a few words to help me remember. I padded barefoot into the kitchen, made a sandwich and refilled my lemonade. I took my dinner upstairs, where I ate watching TV, then took a shower and went to bed early, tired of talking, tired of thinking.

***

The afternoon was hot but a nice breeze was flowing over the waves, and when I reached the old pier down near where the National Seashore begins, I decided to walk out and cool off. I'd been sitting with my legs dangling off the side, for about ten minutes, I guess, when I suddenly had the feeling I wasn't alone. Unconcerned, I turned my head to greet a fellow jogger, I supposed.

But the man was no jogger.

Uh-oh, I thought, one of the panhandlers. He must be desperate, to be way over here instead of near the Biloxi beach. Much more opportunity there. Richie had taught me to defend myself, so I wasn't that concerned. Besides, he didn't look like he would have the strength to physically assault me.

Probably best to be on my way, just in case. As I jumped to my feet and began to walk back toward shore, the man began to walk directly toward me. Already close to the steps of the pier, he reached them before I could.

I wasn't really frightened until I got a closer look at him. Shaggy gray hair under a dirty Saints cap, week-old whiskers too scraggly to be called a beard, and a definite unsettled look in his brown eyes. Something about those eyes seemed familiar.

He touched his cap and nodded, and I gave him a brisk hello as I marched determinedly toward the safety of land. He didn't move. I halted.

"Don't mean to cause trouble, ma'am," he said, his gravelly voice giving evidence of too much alcohol, too much tobacco, or both.

"Okay…then you won't mind to let me pass."

"In a minute. Aren't you Rebecca McCallum?"

Startled, I said, "Do I know you?"

"No. We never met. But I think you know my son right well."

Who could he mean? Then I looked at the brown eyes again. No, it couldn't be. How would he know *me*? And why would he be here?

I'd reached him by now, and only a few feet separated us. I laid my hand on one of the rickety posts.

"Oh? And who's your son?"

"Paul Simmons. Deputy Paul Simmons." His mouth twisted on the word "deputy."

"You're Paul's father?" Hard to believe, but the eyes didn't lie.

"Yep. I'm his old man. Don't see much of the boy now that he's all grown up, though." He put one foot onto the first step and leaned an elbow on his knee.

"Yeah, that's what my parents say, too," I said, trying for casual.

"Your brother was that deputy that got killed a few weeks ago, right?" He spit off to the side and wiped his hand across his lips.

"Yes, he was my brother. Why are you asking?"

"I'm just wondering if your brother ever told you about the time the two of us met. See, I doubt he did."

I recalled Paul pacing in my living room and telling me about how Richard "saved" him from himself. I didn't let on that I knew anything.

"No, I don't think he did. But you know, Richie met lots of people."

"Not like the way he met me, I'll bet. You see..." He stopped suddenly, seeming to think twice before continuing. "You know, Ms. McCallum, you're probably not gonna believe me, anyway. But what the hell... Your brother drove up in his patrol car one night when my *son* was beating the hell out of me on the side of the road." He paused, as if waiting for a reaction from me.

I shook my head doggedly. "I don't know what this has to do with me, Mr. Simmons. Now if you'll excuse me..."

"Well, see that's the thing. Your brother covered for him, and don't nobody know it but me. He pulled Paul off of me, and he put me in his police car and took me to jail. Lied, too. Said I went crazy when he tried to arrest me, and he just defended himself. That's how I got all bruised up."

"What's your point?" I asked, suddenly scared. Did he plan a big exposé about Richie?

He leaned forward, his eyes boring into mine. "I'll tell you. See, I've been reading in the papers some stuff about my boy being investigated over charges of police brutality. And as I understand it, your sister-in-law has had a few things to say about how she thinks he might have had something to do with your brother's murder."

"I don't pay much attention to rumors. Maybe you shouldn't, either."

He clearly wasn't letting me by before he had his say.

"Oh, I don't have to listen to rumors, Miss. As I said, I have first-hand experience with Paul's temper." He rubbed his jaw, as if remembering a fist hitting it. I swallowed hard.

"Mr. Simmons…"

"You see, I thought you ought to know, straight from the horse's mouth, so to speak, that Paul ain't always as in control as he might want everybody to believe. He can be brutal when he wants to."

"I don't see what this has to do with me."

"Are you like the widow? You have some questions about what really happened to your brother?" His eyes held me mesmerized.. I blinked a few times, breaking the spell. "Yeah…I can see you do. I just want you to do one thing for me. You think about what I've said about Paul. And then you think about what might have happened out there that night. That's all I ask."

He pulled his foot off the pier and stepped back, his hands hanging at his sides.

"I don't know what to say to you. Obviously there's some trouble between you and your son, and I don't want to be in the middle of it. Paul has been a good friend to me. Now, I have to go."

I jumped onto the sand and began to jog away.

"Oh, I'm sure he has been," he called after me. "You might want to ask yourself why!"

I shook my head to clear it and ran all the way back to my car. I looked back once, and he was standing where I'd left him.

I can't listen to him. He clearly has it in for Paul from that night. But what is he up to at this late date? He's trying to cause Paul to lose his job, for one thing. And he thinks if he causes me to start asking questions, he won't even have to get involved.

What a lousy excuse for a father.

I drove home determined to put Simmons's words out of my mind. But that was easier said than done.

Chapter 29

"**P**LEASE, GOD, LET HER BE ALL RIGHT," I prayed, as I sat like a stone statue in a corner of the ER waiting room. Was it only six weeks ago that I'd been here, the night I lost my brother?

I'd brought my new friend Lucy in half an hour ago. Jake had brought her by to visit me this afternoon. I'd called him on our way to the hospital, getting only his voice mail, but he'd called back just after they got Lucy triaged and taken back to a private observation room. He said he'd call his Uncle Martin and would be at the hospital as soon as he could. I waited for him now, trying to convince myself to be supportive for Lucy's sake. I had to put aside my personal animosity toward the man who intended to take my brother's place with his family.

"Rebecca!" I heard the fear in his voice as he crossed the room toward me, his head of curls slightly mussed and his eyes wild. "Where is she? What happened?"

"Calm down, Jake. Your aunt is going to want to see you soon, and she doesn't need to see you this upset."

He ran a hand through his hair. "What happened? I just left her with you an hour ago. She was fine then."

"Yes, she seemed perfectly fine at first. We were sitting in the living room, when all at once she stiffened and laid her hand on the middle of her chest. She said, 'Becca, dear, I think maybe I'd better go to the emergency room, if you don't mind.'" I shook my head, remembering her incredible calm. "I asked if she was in pain, and she told me she'd been having a few episodes for the past couple of days, but the pains didn't really seem very different to ones she'd had before, so she didn't take much notice of them."

"Two days? She hasn't let on that she didn't feel well. Wonder if Uncle Martin knew."

"I doubt he had any idea. She said she didn't want to 'worry the menfolk unnecessarily,' I think that's how she put it. The triage nurse who checked her in said her pulse seemed irregular but her blood pressure was only slightly elevated. Lucy told her in no uncertain terms she wanted them to call her personal physician, and the nurse came and told me a few minutes ago he had arrived and was in examining her then."

"That's good. I called Uncle Martin, but it may be a while before he gets here. He had gone up to Jackson to visit his brother today, and I promised to take care of Aunt Lucy. Really good job I did there."

"You can't blame yourself for this. Lucy told me on the way over here she'd decided to come and visit me today so she'd be close to the hospital in case she needed it. She has a mind of her own, Jake, and she's a strong woman. She'll come through this just fine."

I saw a nurse coming and touched Jake's arm. "Maybe we'll get some news now."

He stood to meet the slim, blonde young woman who wore an air of authority and confidence as well as she wore her puppy- and kitten-patterned scrubs. She smiled at me and turned her baby blues on Jake. "Are you Mrs. Ledbetter's nephew?"

"Yeah, I'm Jake Coffee. How's my aunt?"

"Resting comfortably now. Dr. Gordon ordered a battery of tests, but he does think it's her heart. She'll be busy for the next hour or so, and then you can see her." She hurried back into the ER.

***

Jake and I settled into an uneasy silence after the nurse had gone. I didn't know what to say to him or how to say it, so I didn't say anything. *Play it by ear, Becca...get a feel for the situation.*

"I probably wouldn't be here today if it hadn't been for Aunt Lucy," Jake said suddenly, breaking into my thoughts. "She and my mother were sisters, you know. After Mama died, she and Uncle Martin came to Vicksburg and got me and my little brother. I was thirteen, Hal was nine.

They'd never had kids of their own, but you'd never have known it, the way they took us in and gave us a home – more of a home than we'd ever had, really."

He shifted on the stiff plastic sofa, trying to get comfortable. I sat in a chair, also uncomfortable. Finally he crossed one leg, ankle over knee, and splayed his arms along the back of the sofa.

He began to talk, in a monotone almost, about his early life. I don't quite know why he decided to share his history with me – we certainly weren't friends. Surely he knew that I wasn't happy about his relationship with Justine. Yet we were being drawn together by our concern for Lucy, about whom we both cared deeply.

"I was twelve when Daddy died," Jake said, as if reciting facts about someone he barely knew. "The old man was what I guess you'd call a functioning alcoholic. He worked at a body shop in downtown Vicksburg, kept the same job for years – I don't know how. Friday afternoons he headed straight to the liquor store or beer joint to stock up for the weekend. He'd be half gone by the time he got home. Weekends weren't much fun around our house. We lived in a rundown apartment house about three blocks from the river. I spent a lotta time hangin' out on the bluffs overlooking the river, wishing I could be on one of the barges goin' past every day – didn't care which direction, anywhere would'a done.

"But I couldn't leave Mama. She was a good woman. How she ended up with a louse like him…I never asked her…don't think I wanted to hear the ugly details."

I shifted in my seat, my bottom about to go to sleep, but Jake didn't notice. He kept talking. I watched the comings and goings of the ER: nurses and doctors always in a rush, would-be patients waiting "patiently" or demanding help in agitated shouts, police officers filling out reports. Police officers… Richie. .. murder… I jerked back to awareness as Jake said, "The gambling got him in the end. After he'd been kicked out of every casino in town, he started looking for other places to gamble, and that put him out on the highway going from one truck stop casino to another. I guess then it was just a matter of time before the gambling and the drinking led to a bad car wreck."

"One night just before I turned thirteen, cops came to the door and told Mama he wouldn't be coming home again. She went off the deep end after that. First she stopped eating, then sleeping. Until one day I got home from school a few minutes before Hal, like usual. The house felt real quiet. I knew before I went in something bad was inside."

Jake's eyes held a faraway look of pain and anguish. I wondered how Richie and I would have turned out if our situations had been reversed.

"Every room was empty, but her bedroom door was shut. I knocked but got no answer, so I went in. She looked more comfortable than she had in years. I saw the pile of empty bottles on the table beside her. I checked for a pulse, but she was already cold. She must have taken them all right after we left for school."

"Oh, Jake…"

He went on as if I hadn't spoken. "I went outside and waited for Hal, took him down the hall to Mrs. Mason. She was always good to us. I knew we were in trouble when the woman in the black suit arrived. They packed us off to Child Protective Services while they started looking for relatives. While we waited, they put us in separate foster homes. I could see Hal was scared – I was too – but I couldn't do a damn thing about it.

"They finally found out Mama had a sister down close to Biloxi. Next thing I knew, Aunt Lucy and Uncle Martin were there volunteering to take us in. They're real good people, loving and protective." Jake suddenly seemed aware of me again. "But you know that, don't you, Becca?"

He smiled, and I smiled back reluctantly.

"Aunt Lucy told me later she and Mama hadn't seen each other in ten years. I didn't remember ever having met her. She said she'd tried to get Mama to leave Daddy, but Mama refused. Finally Mama told her to go back home to Uncle Martin and forget about her.

"Aunt Lucy said she went home and cried for days, until finally Uncle Martin gave her an ultimatum: Either go back to Vicksburg and drag Mama and me out, or forget about us and not talk any more about saving her sister. She loved Uncle Martin too much to mess up her life with him, and besides, she didn't figure my mama would stay out even if she did get her to leave."

Part of me wanted to reach out to the young boy Jake had once been…but the other part of me recoiled at the thought that he might have murdered my beloved Richie. I settled on doing nothing.

Finally I couldn't take the silence anymore. I jumped up. "I'm going for a cup of coffee. You want one?"

Jake looked up distractedly. "What? Oh, yeah. That'd be great. But let me get it." He got to his feet.

"No, Jake. You wait here for the doctor and your uncle." I waved him off and headed toward the cafeteria. It was harder than I'd imagined it could be, sitting around the same ER where we'd lost Richie.

Coffee in hand, I wound my way back toward the waiting room. Just before I rounded the last corner I heard Jake's voice raised in anger. I stopped without thinking about it, still juggling the two cups of coffee.

"You've got a hell of a nerve bringing that up here," he said, his voice strangled.

"Now, now, I'm just checking up on your family," said a man's voice I didn't recognize.

"Dammit, I know what you're trying to do. You're probably the one that landed my aunt here in the first place."

What? Who was this person? What did Jake mean?

"I didn't say or do nothing to your aunt, buddy boy – just your kid brother. And I came by to make sure you don't get any funny ideas about spillin' the beans. If you don't want anything else happenin', to the kid up in Parchman, you'd best forget about that night. You're in too deep. You know your little woman wouldn't be at all happy with you if she knew…"

"Shut your damn mouth, and keep her out of this," Jake hissed. The man chuckled. "And get the hell out of this hospital."

"I'll see ya later at work, bud. Be sure you make it before closing time."

"Yes, sir, *Mister* Anders," Jake snarled.

I had to see the man's face. But how could I go back to Jake myself? Surely my face had drained of color. I looked at the foam cups I held – they were shaking enough to spill the coffee. I backed up and set them down on a magazine-filled table beside the wall. My breath came fast and shallow. The words I'd heard just now flitted through my mind again: "probably you that put her here...your kid brother...spillin' the beans...your little woman wouldn't be at all happy if she knew...see ya at work, bud." Work. The man worked with Jake. My God, what had all of that meant?

I struggled to gain control of my nerves. Could I lay my condition off on being worried for Lucy? And then...a reprieve.

"Jake, son, where's Lucy?" Good, Mr. Ledbetter had arrived. I dashed around the corner. His farmer's tan was missing, his face pale and drawn. Martin held out his hand to me. "Rebecca, you brought Lucy in?" He turned to Jake again, laying a gnarled hand on the younger man's shoulder. "I'm glad you're here, boy."

Jake put his arm around his uncle. "Sit down, Uncle Martin. I'll tell you what we know – it's not much, but..."

Before they had gotten seated, however, the ER doors opened. "Martin! Glad you're here! Lucy's been asking for you." I turned to see a man of about forty-five, looking more like a businessman than a doctor – gray slacks, pale blue golf shirt, navy sport coat. Not much taller than me, maybe five foot ten, slim and trim enough to be a good example to his patients.

"Hey, Doc, how's she doing?" Mr. Ledbetter's voice was husky.

"She's going to be fine. Nothing too serious. She's like you – she's no spring chicken, but she's strong." The doctor turned to me. "Are you the one who brought Lucy in today?" I nodded.

"You did well getting her here quickly. She was on the verge of a light heart attack, according to her enzyme tests."

Mr. Ledbetter stiffened beside me. "Heart attack! Is she really all right?"

The doctor smiled. "Listen to me, Martin. She's *fine*. Not happy I told her she's staying here tonight – but come see for yourself."

Thank God. Lucy will be leaving the hospital alive.

Jake exhaled heavily and flopped back onto the couch. "Man, Becca, I didn't realize just how scared I was until that doctor said she's gonna be okay."

I looked down at this big tough guy who seemed more like a lost little boy at heart and wondered what that conversation had been about. Did it mean Jake Coffee was a killer?

***

Sunday morning I dropped by to see Lucy. Martin decided to go to church since I'd be with her, so I pulled up a chair next to the bed. She looked much better, but seemed to have something on her mind. I didn't know if I should encourage her to talk or try to keep her from it.

I'm not sure how she brought the conversation around to what happened to Richie, but before I knew it she was saying, "I'll never forget that Friday afternoon. Jake had come home from work looking pale and feverish at the same time, and I was worried about him, but he almost snapped at me, telling me he was fine." She confided, "He does that once in a while. Has ever since he came to us. But he always apologizes right away. There's still a part of that hurt little boy in him, guess there always will be."

Was that all there was to it, or was he consumed by guilt?

"We'd settled down to watch the six o'clock news. Martin and I always eat right after. For once Jake was there to eat with us. I wondered if he and his girl had had a fight, but since he didn't feel well I decided not to tease him."

"Oh? Jake has a girlfriend?"

"Yes, but we've never met her. He's told us when he's ready to get married we'll meet the 'lucky lady,' as he puts it. We'll certainly care about any woman Jake cares for." She smiled, gazing out the window as if seeing not the hydrangeas and crape myrtles outside but the young couple she and Martin had once been. "Martin and I always wanted lots of children," she said, "but the Lord didn't see fit to send us any of our own. After Jake and Hal arrived, we figured that was best."

"Back to what I was talking about." She lowered her voice to barely above a whisper. "We were all together when the report about your brother came on. When they gave the location, Martin said, 'Why, that's right down the road from us. Sounds like the old Roberts place.' They didn't have many details, but they did report a deputy and a suspect had been killed. I remember thinking what a terrible waste.

"Jake had leaned forward with his elbows on his knees like he was very interested. When the report ended, he jumped up and made a beeline for the bathroom. I heard him being sick and knocked on the door to see if he needed anything, but he told me to go away. I could've sworn I heard him crying. I'd never known him to cry but once before, the day they sentenced Hal to prison."

"You're a good woman, Lucy." I held her frail hand, gently caressing its speckled, paper-thin skin, and she reached to cover my hand with her own.

"You're a special young woman, Becca. I cannot begin to imagine what those days must have been like for you. I admire you so for having come through all of that as well as you have, how you've accepted the situation."

I felt the red creeping up my throat toward my ears, in part because of her praise but mostly because she had no idea just how little I'd accepted anything. "Lucy, I don't deserve to have you say that about me." She held up a thin finger.

"I know what I see when I look at you. I see a young woman who's learning to live, and perhaps love, again, and who has a heart as open as a cloudless sky. Now, you go on and get out of here, before I start crying."

"No, we just need to change the subject. I'm staying till Martin gets back."

I'd brought a book, so I convinced her to settle back, not talk anymore, and just listen. I cleared my throat and began to read. "It is a truth universally acknowledged that a single man in possession of a good fortune must be in want of a wife." Lucy giggled.

Chapter 30

SITTING IN MY PICKUP ON THE D'IBERVILLE off-ramp on Monday morning, a week after Lucy left the hospital with a sweetly solicitous Martin, I scanned the sky and watched as the first wispy clouds far out ahead of Hurricane Charla began to stream inland. A caravan of cars, trucks, and RVs was heading north across the bridge leading to Interstate 10. From there people have three main choices in deciding how best to get away from approaching storms.

Straight north takes them toward Highway 49 and Hattiesburg. *If they go that way, let's hope they have family or friends to take them in.* Every hotel within a hundred miles was already booked. Some evacuees will head west toward Louisiana, while others will choose Florida or Alabama. Most people have their destinations plotted out way ahead of hurricane season, so MEMA and the DPS just have to make sure they can get out of Dodge expediently and safely.

According to weather reports, Charla *could* still turn toward New Orleans, or even farther west to the Texas coast. Since she still churned along in the middle of the Gulf, many were staying put until she got closer. The downside to waiting was not that you'd wait too long and get stuck, though that could happen, but that you'd get caught up in the flood of vehicles leaving at the last minute, with the resulting problems of gasoline shortages and traffic jams. Nobody wants to be on the highway when a hurricane hits.

Charla had looked to be a strong storm, but we weren't so sure now. Our last storm, Isaac, had hit the coast in 2012 as a Cat 1 hurricane and had been mostly a rainmaker, with a few tornadoes thrown in for good measure. Some people had been stuck inside their homes for a few days, but those who lived in areas prone to flooding knew the chances and stocked up before things got hairy.

No time to be thinking about the past though. I had to help things keep running smoothly here. Now, with the situation stable, I picked up my cellphone and called the office to tell Susan I was taking a break for lunch. In downtown D'Iberville I pulled in at Maggie's Drive-in, thinking about her fish tacos. By this time mid-week, I might be eating canned tuna.

As I bit into my second taco, someone rapped on the passenger window. Jake stood there grinning, motioning for me to unlock the door. I hesitated. Though it was against state policy to have civilians in our vehicles, my reticence came more from the fact that I didn't know if I could be civil to him. I was, after all, about seventy-five percent sure he'd helped murder my brother. But this might be a good opportunity to try to trip him up. I waved and unlocked the door, motioning him inside.

"How's it going, Jake?" I asked between bites. "Want to order something?" I motioned toward the speaker by my window.

"Hey, Rebecca. Going good. How about you? Ready for the storm?"

"Getting there," I said. "How are Lucy and Martin? I suppose they're staying put?"

"Sure are. Say they haven't left for a storm yet and don't intend to. Guess I'll hang out with them for a few days."

"Aw, Jake, that's nice. I'm sure you have friends where you could go to get away from all the mess and confusion."

Probably not with Justine, though. She was making plans to visit her folks in San Antonio if necessary.

"Hey, order me a Maggie's Special, would you?" He stretched his stocky frame to reach the wallet in his back pocket. After I ordered he asked, "Have you been anywhere near the Donut Place over close to the mall lately?"

I shook my head no, my mouth full. I tried to avoid the Donut Place.

"You need to come by as soon as things settle down after the storm," he said. His eyes were sparkling and he had a huge grin. Something sure had him excited.

"Why? What's going on?"

"I'm opening a fitness center next door." He laughed, "It'll be a couple of weeks till I get someone trained at Bert's, then I'm gone." My antennae went on alert at the mention of Bert's name.

"That's great. I'm sure you'll be good running a place like that. You obviously know the ropes when it comes to exercising." My stomach lurched at the words coming out of my mouth, but I had to keep him unaware of my suspicions.

His deltoids flexed and I realized he'd made the move unconsciously. Heavens, here was a man so caught up in his own body he didn't even realize he reacted visibly to compliments. *What a jerk. And probably a murderer, too, remember?*

As I ate he talked about his new business venture – Coastal Fitness. The name wasn't half bad, but I gushed about how effective I thought it would be. Jake continued to preen.

When his food arrived I motioned the attendant to his side of the truck and he paid, handing her a two dollar tip. *Not stingy. Wonder who financed him.* I decided to probe.

"So, Jake, it can't have been easy, financing all that expensive equipment."

"Yeah, but I have a friend who came into some money, and they helped me out. I didn't want to ask Aunt Lucy and Uncle Martin. I'm sure they have the money, but I knew if Mama was alive, she wouldn't be very happy about that."

"We do want our families to be proud of us, don't we?"

"Yeah, we sure do. Speaking of families, Aunt Lucy's beginning to think of you as family, especially after you took care of getting her to the hospital and all." He dropped his head and I strained to hear him. "I'm not good at this, Becca, but I want to thank you again for all you've done for her. I can't imagine Uncle Martin making it without her, or her without him."

"You don't have to thank me. I think you know how much they've come to mean to me." He nodded, and his next words startled me.

"We haven't talked about it in a while, but...are you satisfied about Richard's death, after you went out to where it happened?" He took another bite.

Be careful now. Don't stir up his suspicions.

"It's tough. They say Tommy Hollingshead acted alone, and I suppose I have to believe that, but there's a part of me that keeps remembering how strong and competent Richie was. That part of me, I suppose, will always have questions."

He'd been nodding his head while I spoke. Now he turned to meet my eyes. "I don't know if you knew this, but me and Tommy worked together."

"Really? I didn't know that." *I did, but he doesn't need to know.* "What do you do at the body shop?"

"Paint mostly. Sometimes prep work too. Hearing Tommy was involved came as a shock to all of us." *Oh, really?*

"Did you know he had a prison record?"

"Yeah, but he seemed like an okay guy. He kept his nose clean."

"You thought so, at least."

"Right. But I guess we don't always know what's really goin' on with other people."

I hated discussing this with him. "Since my brother's dead, and *his killer* (I emphasized these words) is also dead, what does it matter?"

He flushed. "Sorry, Becca. I shouldn't have brought it up."

"It's okay. I still don't like to talk about it. Richie was my only brother – but you maybe knew that already."

"Yeah, Justine mentioned it." I saw the burger pause for a second on its way to his mouth, but then he took another huge bite.

I strove to sound unconcerned as I asked, "How's Justine doing? Been so busy getting ready for this storm I haven't seen her this week." *Gonna bite?*

He hesitated, then said, "She's good, I guess, especially if you take into account all she's been through."

"Yeah, I know what you mean." My voice was dripping with sympathy. "Have you convinced her to join your fitness center? She's never been one for much exercising."

"I think I've got her talked into it," he enthused. *I'll bet you have.* "What about you, Becca? You're real fit and all, and I've seen you running the beach, but would you be interested in trying indoor exercise for a change? I've got a neat setup I think you'd enjoy." My flesh crawled.

"I'll think about it – might be a good place to work off stress."

"Tell you what. Why don't you drop by one day after all this craziness is over? I'll show you around, introduce you to my trainers, give you a complimentary month while you try things out. How about it?"

"Thanks, I'll do that. Maybe next week, depending on how things go."

"Great!"

"But now I'd better get back to work."

"Oh, sure." He moved quickly to get out of the truck. "Nice having lunch with you, Becca."

"Same here. Give my love to Justine and Owen when you see them, okay?"

"Will do." He nodded and shut the door. I started the motor, waved, and backed out of the space, giving him one last smile. *I bet you will.* I do hate being devious…but it'll be worth it to find out what really happened to Richie. Tommy Hollingshead wasn't solely responsible, and I intend to make everybody else involved pay, too.

***

"This was a good session, Rebecca." Angie closed her notebook and stood. "Tell me, how are the plans coming for Charla?" We discussed the storm as she walked me out, and she wished me luck. Stepping into the reception area, I glanced into my fountain corner, then glanced again. Paul Simmons sat, head buried in a magazine. *Should I say hello? Or should I pretend I don't see him?* As I debated, Paul looked up and our eyes met. Decision made, I smiled and walked over. He smiled, too, and stood to give me a hug. I whispered, "I'm so glad to see you here. How long have you been seeing Angie?"

He gave me an odd look. "This is my first time to come here."

I laughed. "Oh, well, it probably won't be your last. I really like her." I patted his arm. "I need to run. Good luck today." I started to walk away but turned back and met his brown-eyed gaze. "Richie would be so proud of you." Before my eyes misted I hurried out into the steamy afternoon.

***

By Wednesday I was beat, but things were looking up. Those who'd evacuated were long gone, and the rest of us were hunkering down. Most of us MEMA workers were sent home Wednesday afternoon and told to be on call for the duration. If they needed me, they'd send a truck for me. Sounded good to me.

Mark had offered to come over late this afternoon to help me with storm shutters, but I hadn't decided what to do. Latest reports from the Hurricane Hunters showed Charla losing intensity fast, and she might not even still be hurricane strength when she hit the coast. But we were for sure about to have a huge rainmaker. The system was widespread and rain had been falling since early morning, leaving several roads under water. Highway 90 had been closed since about two this afternoon. Winds had picked up, too.

I got this cozy feeling when Mark asked if he could stay with me until the threat passed. I hadn't looked forward to spending the next few days alone. I heard his car horn and opened the front door to meet him as he splashed his way across the yard. He jumped onto the porch, laughing and slinging water from his hair like a dog wet from his bath. God, he looked sexy.

"Where's your raincoat?" I opened the door wider and held out a towel.

"Don't have one." He kicked off his Tevas and left them lying in the hallway. He rubbed the towel over his face and then his thick hair, causing it to stand out wildly. His emerald eyes glittered as he whistled. "Crazy out there already!"

"Yep. Glad I'm in for the night...at least I hope I am. I guess if I got called to work your Escape would get me there?"

"No problem, but I don't want you going anywhere." He smiled down at me and kissed the top of my head. Dropping his backpack beside the sandals, he said, "Before I get dried off, what did you decide?"

"It's no to the shutters. The house gets stuffy without electricity, with all the windows boarded up. I could leave one window on each side of the house uncovered, but I don't think it's necessary."

"Then I'm gonna change into dry clothes. Be back down in a sec." He grabbed his pack and bounded up the stairs two at a time.

The man seems to feel very much at home here. Damn, that feels good.

I turned the TV back to the local weather report and went to the kitchen to check my pot of beef stew. I liked to have something cooked when the power might go off at any time. I checked the oven; cornbread was almost ready. I pulled butter and cheese from the fridge and lined it all up on the counter. I'd just taken the bread out when I felt Mark's arms come around my waist.

"Smells great in here." He nuzzled my neck. "Food smells good, too." I laughed. "Let me do the honors while you get the bowls." I watched as he began to slice and butter cornbread, whistling as he worked. *I could get used to having you around the kitchen…maybe a few other places, too.*

***

After dinner we cleared the kitchen while we still had electricity and ran water in some gallon jars I kept for that purpose. I also ran a bathtub full of water in my bathroom. Doing that has come in handy more than once during storms, most recently with Katrina, when we'd been without power for about ten days.

We met back in the living room to watch the latest weather reports. Local stations were breaking in frequently with updates, but we mainly left the TV on the Weather Channel, since we were most interested in the periodic reports from the Hurricane Hunters who flew out of Keesler AFB. I was fascinated that they would fly directly through storms to gather information to help local officials around the country decide what steps to take to protect the citizens.

We were amazed by the nine o'clock report – the Hurricane Hunters reported a significant rise in pressure and decrease in strength from the previous report, and the meteorologists were now suggesting Charla might be a weak category one, or even drop down to tropical storm strength.

"That figures," I groused, "after all that work we did getting ready, she'll probably fizzle out and not amount to anything!"

"That'd be fine with me. Don't tell me you're actually looking forward to a hurricane hitting Mississippi after what we went through a few years ago."

"Don't be silly. It's just that we've spent so much time the past few days making preparations – but I suppose it's like paying for insurance you hope you'll never have to use."

"Good way to look at it. Do you still want me to stay, since it's probably not gonna get bad?"

"Heck, yeah! You never know what'll come up during tropical storms. Besides, I might need a ride somewhere."

"It's so nice to be wanted for your companionship," he said, swinging his legs up onto the sofa and tickling me in the side with his toes.

I couldn't let that go unanswered. I shoved his feet off the couch and got on my knees to crawl down next to him. His arms came round me reflexively and I laid my head on his chest. "I *do* want your companionship. Don't you know that by now?"

"I do, but I sure like the way you show me."

For the first time in what seemed like forever, we had a nice, relaxing evening, with the wind howling and the rain beating down. Yes, it *was* relaxing. And I finally got Mark caught up on the latest information I'd learned about Jake – that he had been working at Bert's but was leaving to open his own fitness place – his own "body shop."

Mark warned me again to be careful.

We spent the next couple of days watching Charla continue to weaken, until by Friday she was nothing more than a tropical depression.

We watched a lot of television and ate a lot of popcorn while we listened to the unrelenting rain beating against the windows. The cities had some low-level flooding, but not much worse than we get from many of our weather systems. Mark and I both made it to work on Friday, and I was suddenly back in my big house alone.

Chapter 31

THE AFTERNOON SUN BLAZED WHITE-HOT, with low-level clouds in a holding pattern above the horizon. Off to the south, several miles out to sea, were thicker accumulations filled with moisture – smoky blue underneath and dark gray on top – a sure indication to sailors to keep a sharp lookout through the afternoon.

In the summertime we coastal residents often see an angry thunderstorm build up offshore with bright flashes of lightning that telegraph rumbling booms to those on shore, reminding me of the booms of muskets from Civil War reenactments. If the storm decides to move northward, which seldom happens, and you find yourself out enjoying the beach, you might be fortunate enough to witness an event seemingly designed with the nature photographer in mind; for as the clouds darken and creep closer, the sailboats afloat decide as one to head for safety, first one popping out of the mist, and then a couple more, until finally varicolored sails emerge from the low-lying rain clouds like so many oncoming cars appearing suddenly from a thick fog blanketing a highway.

I'd been running for half an hour, having parked my car at the foot of the bridge on the Ocean Springs side. I'd planned to run the bridge, but when I saw the clouds building I'd decided to stick to the beach. I ran for about a mile along the hot sand, grains flying up behind to sting the backs of my thighs. I turned back then, not wanting to be too far from the car in case of a downpour. I figured I could make another lap if the weather held.

I was thinking about this morning at work. Once again, I'd slept poorly and then overslept when I did drop off, making me more than an hour late for work. Cassandra had called me into her office – for the second time. She'd made it plain this time: If I can't get my shit together, I'll be out of a job. *So just how do I do that, Cassie?*

Turning back toward the bridge I scowled but stopped when I saw a dark figure coming toward me – a fellow runner. His face was in shadow but his build was familiar. Damian. We slowed to a stop as we neared each other.

"Becca, hi! Nice afternoon, huh?"

I bent at the waist and clasped my ankles, then raised my arms above my head for a good long stretch. I felt his eyes on me the entire time. "Hey, Damian. Yeah, it's nice out – may not be for long, though."

He glanced toward the approaching storm. "I worked over today and got a late start. We've been working a rash of car thefts, and our resources are stretched thin."

"Really? Well, they'd better not mess with Bernice. She bites."

He laughed out loud. "They'll probably leave her alone. She's not their type, anyway."

"Now I'm offended. What's wrong with Bernice?" We'd both started walking back toward the bridge by this time.

"Oh, she's a great little car, but there aren't enough VW bugs along the coast to make her a major target. SUVs, Hondas, Toyotas, Ford pickups. Those are the most likely targets for thieves involved with chop shops."

"Chop shops. I've heard of those, seen them in movies. Didn't know we had them here around Biloxi."

"It's beginning to be a major problem. Over the past year the number of stolen vehicles has more than tripled. The Biloxi P.D. has put together a special task force, aided by detectives from DPS, to try to get a handle on the situation, but now the thieves are spreading out through the county."

"Like Tommy Hollingshead, you mean."

He gave me a sharp look. "Yeah, but Tommy was one of the small fry. We'd really like to know who he was working for. Too bad he wasn't taken alive."

"You don't think Paul killed him unnecessarily, do you?" I knew what I believed but wanted Damian's take on things.

Damian stopped walking and rested his hands on his hips. "Hey, can we sit down here for a while and watch the storm? I haven't experienced many here yet. We can make a run for it if we need to."

I surveyed the beach and chose a flat space farther up the sand with sea oats waving in the breeze. "How about here?" We settled ourselves and were quiet for a minute, gazing across the whitecaps buffeting the beach in advance of the storm clouds.

"Now, about Paul," Damian picked up where we'd left off. "No, I believe things went down like he said. I'm sure Rich talked to you about our training, how we're taught to shoot."

"Yeah, that's one thing he hated most about cop shows on TV. 'They're always trying to take the guy alive so they can question him,' he'd say. "The hell with that. If a perp pulls a gun on me and shoots, I've been trained to stop him any way I can. And that's what I'd do.'"

"Damn straight," Damian nodded.

The rolling booms of thunder had grown louder as we talked, and now we felt the first spits of rain. I knew from experience what to expect. "Race you back to the cars," I said as I stood and brushed the sand off my behind.

"I could help you with that," he said with a dimple-filled smile.

"I'm good, thanks." I raced off down the beach, laughing, and heard him scrambling to his feet behind me. Well, I deserved a head start – his legs were longer. By the time I reached Bernice the rain was coming down in a heavy shower. Steam rose from the hot pavement, making the parking lot feel like a sauna gone berserk. Around me the few people who'd been out enjoying the sand were now scrambling for car keys, jumping into cars, and heading toward home and dry clothes.

Damian caught up and slouched against Bernice, and, as the rain stopped suddenly, the only other cars in the lot stopped, too, their owners wondering if this small shower might be all we'd get today. I shook my head. "They may as well leave. The bulk of the storm isn't even here yet." In support of this statement a lightning flash followed almost immediately by a clap of thunder struck somewhere in the nearby neighborhood.

"Okay, okay, we're going!" Damian yelled. "Good to see you, Becca. Stay out of trouble, okay?" With that admonition he loped off to his car, and I drove out of the lot behind him.

"Glad your seats are leather, huh Bernice?" I grabbed a couple of tissues and gingerly blotted the worst part of the rain from my face and arms. The rest could wait till I got home. I headed down Hwy. 90 and drove through a fast food chicken place. Twenty minutes later I parked in my driveway and hurried inside, for the rain had begun in earnest now.

I planned to spend the evening having a bite to eat and studying on the things Damian had said today about the car thefts. Something was nagging at me, something way out on the fringes of my consciousness, something I knew instinctively would have to come clear in my mind if I ever wanted to solve Richie's murder.

***

I woke in the middle of the night in a sweat and sat up, reaching to turn on my bedside lamp. The dream hovered on the fringes of my consciousness. *Another message from Richie? I need to remember. I know it was important.* I'd heard you remember a dream better if you don't try to push it but don't back away from it, either. I drew my knees up to my chest, clasped my arms around them, and rocked gently back and forth, taking slow, measured breaths.

"I'm worried about the Hollingshead kid," Richie said as we jogged our way across the bridge. "Who?" I asked. "Tommy Hollingshead. Do you remember me talking about the kid I thought got a raw deal a few years ago? He's just so childlike. I worry about some of these characters at the places he hangs out – I'm afraid they'll try to take advantage of him. I think he was used as the sacrificial lamb last time. Don't want to see that happen to him again," Richie said, shaking his head. "What kind of work does he do?" "Different things, odd jobs here and there. Heard he's got into a job at a body shop. Hope they're not up to anything illegal there. He doesn't need that kind of trouble."

This hadn't been simply a dream – it was a dream of a memory, brought back to me complete. This was another piece of the puzzle, I knew. If I could only figure out how I was supposed to use it. I glanced at the clock. After 3 a.m. *Might as well get up for a while – not gonna be able to get back to sleep.* I padded downstairs and picked up Richie's journal. *Let's see what he wrote about this time.*

An hour later I closed the journal and caressed the soft leather. Richie, did you write about anything else but me? So that's what he really thought of me back then. Spoiled. Selfish. Self-important. Temperamental. Oh, he still loved me as much as ever. In fact, that's what he'd said had him so worried. He said he kept waiting for me to "mature," and "grow out of it," but he was beginning to wonder if I ever would.

He'd written that in my senior year at USM, after one of our weekend trips home. He'd swung by to pick me up on his way down from Jackson, and I'd apparently done or said something during the weekend that got him stirred up. He didn't write many details, just used a bunch of mean, hurtful words about me.

I probably deserved them – but some of the fault had to be his. He'd always spoiled me, letting me tag around after him, always ready and willing to chauffeur me and my friends to the movies or to the mall before I got my license. He never turned me down for anything, never disappointed me.

Well, dammit, Richie, I promise I won't disappoint you this time. I will think this through, and tomorrow I'll do something about it. Not sure what...

I finally dropped off to sleep about six, about the time I should have been getting up to go to work. But I'd left my phone alarm upstairs, and I didn't have the energy to move from the sofa... I woke up and knew immediately I was in trouble. The clock showed nine-thirty. *Oh, shit.* I hit the number for work and gave Susan what I knew was a lame excuse about a water leak, but I don't think she believed me. I'd had too many days lately of not making it to work.

I poured a glass of orange juice and went out to sit in the swing and think about that dream-memory. I remembered the day well, now that the dream had refreshed my memory. It had been a late fall afternoon, probably a couple of years back. I'd met Richie at the parking lot on my side of the bridge. We'd made it about a third of the way across the bridge when he pulled up suddenly and turned to watch a car going toward Ocean Springs. "I think that was the Hollingshead kid. Wonder what he's doing over here."

"What's wrong with people coming over here?" I had asked, pretending to be offended.

He'd swatted at my face, managing like always to come within an inch of my nose. I never moved, and he never hit me. We had begun power walking then, and that's when he made the comment about Tommy, about worrying about him getting mixed up with a bad crowd, and Richie was afraid they'd make him their fall guy.

Well, I knew where Tommy was working when he was killed – Bert's Auto Body Shop – with Jake. I went to the kitchen and opened the junk drawer and fumbled around. Good, I still had a Yellow Pages book. I thumbed through and found it. Bert's Auto Body Shop, Bert Anders, Owner. The address was far out Hwy. 90 on the west of town. I wasn't sure but thought it would be somewhere close to Edgewater Mall. It *must* be the same place Richie took me last year, where we saw Tommy.

I'd soon find out. I headed upstairs to shower.

Later I drove into Biloxi to look for Bert's shop. I found it with no trouble – a large, open building with several vehicles in the good-sized parking lot. I was right – it *was* the same place. *That's way too much coincidence for me. While I'm here, maybe I should locate Jake's new place, too.* Coastal Fitness was easy to find, but I decided not to stop at either place today. I wanted plenty of time to plan my next move.

***

When I arrived at work on Thursday, Cassandra called me into her office. Her face was drawn into a pinched scowl, and she wasted no time in getting to the point.

"Rebecca, I hate to do this. You've come in late several times in the last few weeks, and you've missed work two days out of every week. I've tried to be supportive of you, because I know how much the loss of your brother has hurt you."

"I know, Cassandra, and I am doing better now. I think things are turning around for me."

"I'm afraid it's too late. We've talked about this too much already. I have to let you go. I'm sorry."

I shouldn't have been, but I was stunned. "When?" I asked.

"Immediately. Take your time about gathering your things. The end of the week will be fine. I really am sorry…" Her voice trailed off.

"No, I understand. I'm sorry, too. I'm surprised you've kept me on this long." I turned and walked out – straight out of the building and to my car.

I started the car, got the AC going, and called Mark. When I heard his voice I felt the tears begin. I had meant to keep from crying until after I'd talked to him. I didn't want him feeling sorry for me. In some ways I was okay with losing this job, but I hated I had brought it on myself. I wasn't proud of how I'd been slacking off at work.

"Becca? What's wrong, hon?"

"I just got fired." Deadly silence.

"Why?"

"Why do you think? Coming in late, not coming in at all. I brought it on myself."

"Hey, you've been through a lot this summer…"

"I know, but people lose people they love all the time. They take their three days of funeral leave and then they get back to work. I should have done that, too."

"Listen, don't worry. You'll find something else. Will you be okay till tonight?"

"Yeah, sure. And I have something else to talk to you about."

***

Part of me had been afraid Mark would be angry because I'd screwed up my job, but I needn't have worried. He brought dinner, gave me a hug, and then suggested we talk about something else.

"Someday, maybe, I'll get used to having your full support. It's nice."

"I expect the same from you. I'd like to think in forty years we'll be like the Ledbetters."

I thought about Lucy and Martin, smiling as I remembered the way they would touch each other, or share a private glance I didn't understand, and I couldn't help smiling.

"I hope that smile means you're hoping the same thing." He stepped onto the back porch and stood for a few seconds, then came back inside. "Nope. Just too damn hot for the swing tonight." His disappointment was so endearing. I put my arms around him and led him into the cool living room.

"Never mind, baby. We'll get to use your swing sometime soon, I'm sure."

"Promise?" He feigned a reaction like Owen might have had.

"I've been thinking about changing careers," I said, as soon as we were seated on the sofa. Mark sat back and whistled softly.

"How long? Just since you lost your job, or…"

"No, it's been on my mind for a while now. I'm thinking about going into law enforcement."

If I'd said I wanted to be a stripper, I don't think he would have been more surprised.

"Why? I've never heard you talk about that before. Is it because of Richard?"

I shrugged. "I'm sure that's a part of it, but not all. I've learned a lot about what goes on around here, from hanging out with Richie, and now with Damian." He gave me a dark look but I ignored him. "With my MEMA background, I think I have something to contribute. I'm feeling compelled to do something along those lines, at least to check it out a bit further."

Leaning back and folding his arms, he shook his head. "You just need to be sure you're not doing this for the wrong reasons. You need to take more time…at least that's what I think. Besides, I would worry about you every time you went out on patrol."

"I agree I need to take more time. But while I'm job hunting, I'm also going to check into what the requirements would be. Might need classes, and I know I'd have to go to the training academy at some point. I'm planning to talk to the Chief about it."

"Maybe he'll be able to talk you out of it." Mark grinned, but the darkening in his eyes told me he was dead serious. We'd have to work on this.

Chapter 32

WITH TIME ON MY HANDS, I DECIDED to buckle down and really try to figure out just what I knew about That Night, what I thought I knew, and what I didn't know at all. I pulled out my trusty notebook and began a new summation.

So who are the main suspects, and why?

1. Jake Coffee. He's having an affair with Justine, seems to really love her. He lives with the Ledbetters, where the 911 call came in from. At least that's the way it appears. He's involved in something most likely illegal with his boss, Bert Anders. Bert owns a body shop. Tommy Hollingshead, the apparent shooter, also worked at Bert's.

2. Because both Jake and Tommy worked at Bert's, Bert is also a suspect. As the owner, he has to know what's going on. And I heard him at the hospital with Jake, apparently threatening him, and talking about something they were involved in together. He suggested he had something to do with Jake's brother being beat up in prison, and Jake was incensed, but a bit cowed. Damian told me there's been a rash of auto thefts and there's a task force looking into that. Also authorities know some chop shops are involved. Bert's would be ideal for that.

How would Bert know about the money? Could he have heard Jake bragging? Bet nothing goes on in that shop he doesn't know about.

3. Paul Simmons. He was there. He'd had issues with anger on the job and Richie had covered for him. Richie was pushing him to see a therapist and Paul worried it would cost him his job and his career. But Richie had always been a mentor to Paul and they were friends. Could Paul have

managed to set the situation up with the plan of killing Richie? He passed a polygraph test that said he didn't do anything more than what he said he did that night. But some people manage to fool those tests, and, again, he was there.

4. Damian Wentworth. Old friend of Richie's from Jackson. He had a girlfriend involved in the drug trade and he turned her in. Then she offered to tell about him being involved, in exchange for leniency. Richie knew all about that. Could he have known something else, something that proved Damian *was* involved? I do not believe that, and there's nothing to tie him to the scene of the crime. For the time being, he has my trust.

5. Justine, the merry widow. She was having an affair with Jake, and she may have wanted to be with him enough to have Richie killed, especially since she would have been terrified of losing custody of Owen if they split. She loves spending money, and there was a large policy on Richie that she would get control of. I *know* she couldn't have planned and carried this out, and there's nothing that says she wasn't at home with Owen that night. That's where she was when they came to tell her about Richie. Could she have helped plan it, though? Very possibly.

Who is the most likely suspect? Jake had been, hands down – until his boss Bert entered the picture. I've seen Jake look at Justine, and I believe he would have done *anything* to be with her. Could Bert have been working with him? Jake has come into some money recently. And I don't think I like Bert. He sounded mean.

I needed more information, something else to support my suppositions before I could take this to the police. But I'd decided I would by-pass Sheriff Bixby and go straight to the DPS facility out on Hwy. 67, to the crime lab. Maybe they'd listen. But first I needed to go to the library or the *Sun-Herald* offices. Between now and then I needed to get the exact date Tommy was arrested and a copy of his police report.

Maybe it was a blessing in disguise that I'd just lost my job, all things considered. Now I had time during business hours to get to the places I needed to. My first step would be to pull out the small stack of newspapers Mark had saved for me...I hadn't yet had the heart to look at them, but I had a reason to now. I opened the top drawer of the desk and lifted out the small stack, looking for one that mentioned Tommy by name.

Here: "Slain Officer's Alleged Killer Identified." I skimmed the article until I found what I'd hoped for. The reporter had done her job. According to the paper, Tommy had been arrested in 2009 for armed robbery, along with two other people. Since he hadn't been in trouble before, his sentence was eighteen months, and he won release early for good behavior. Okay, now time to hit the library and delve into the newspaper's archives for his specific arrest date.

***

Thus my first stop the next day was at the Biloxi Public Library on Howard Avenue. After a couple of hours, I found what I was looking for.

I hated microfilm, but it was worth the frustration. I now had that date: March 18, 2009, a liquor store hold-up. Nobody was hurt. Police arrested the guys later that day and recovered most of the money. I didn't recognize the names of the other two men, but I wrote down their information all the same. I skimmed ahead until I found the next mention of the case. In May, Tommy had pled no contest and been sentenced to eighteen months, as indicated by my earlier information. Okay, now I needed the police report. It might or might not give me more information, but I would check anyway.

I had no idea where to begin trying to get my hands on that report, so I walked the few blocks from the library to the building where I knew police headquarters was located. I had just begun to tell the receptionist what I needed when I heard a familiar voice.

"Becca, what are you doing here?" Damian asked, and I turned to see him standing with his hands on his hips.

He wasn't in uniform, so I retorted, "I could ask you the same thing," and gave him a wicked grin.

"I'll tell you if you'll tell me," he said, holding out his hand. I glanced back at the clerk.

"I'll be back," I said, and she winked as if to say she'd be leaving with him if she could, too.

"C'mon, let me buy you a cup of coffee."

We left the building and looked up and down the street. "There's a great donut place a couple of blocks from here," I teased.

"Lead on, MacDuff."

Once we had our pastries and coffee, Damian said, "You first." He looked so serious I decided not to argue with him. I told him how I had spent my day, and what I hoped to find at the police station.

As I talked, the furrow between his thick brows grew more pronounced, until finally I said in exasperation, "What is wrong with you? You're acting like I'm the one doing something illegal. I'm just looking for information, and I think that's acceptable under the Freedom of Information Act."

I'd meant that last as a joke, but he looked like he was giving it serious consideration.

He leaned in and folded his arms on the table. After glancing around the nearly empty shop, he seemed to come to a decision. "Becca, I'm gonna have to ask you to trust me on something, just for a couple of days. I need you to do something for me."

"Sure, if I can."

"You can, and for all our sakes I hope you will."

"What do you need me to do?"

"I need you to go home and forget about investigating this any further until you hear from me."

If I'd had coffee in my mouth it would have spewed all over him. "What!" I spluttered. "I'm just now making some headway!"

"I know, it sounds like you really are. And I'm not asking you to quit, just to give me time to talk to some people. Then I think I might be able to help you with what you're looking for."

"Are you serious?" I said, grabbing both his hands. "How can you help?"

"I'm not free to say right now. Again, I'm asking you trust me for a day or two, and I'll get in touch with you as soon as I know anything."

"How long do I have to wait?" I asked, wondering if I was making a mistake to trust him.

"Not more than two days, really," he said, looking at his watch. "That is, if we can get out of here right now. I need to see somebody this afternoon to get the ball rolling."

"What are we waiting for?" I grabbed my purse and beat him to the door. Still, he insisted on walking me back to my car. With his promise to keep in touch with me often, I decided to trust him. I drove back home to figure out whether there was anything else I could be doing while I waited.

***

"Sorry to keep you waiting, Rebecca," Chief Sikes said as he ushered me into his office. "Come in and have a seat." It was two days after I'd run into Damian, and I had come downtown to meet with the Chief, at his request.

"No problem, Chief," I said, stopping just inside the door in confusion, looking around the crowded room. I hadn't expected to see anybody except maybe Damian, but there were three other people in the small room. I took the only empty chair and shot Damian a puzzled look. He gave me a wink and a reassuring nod.

The Chief introduced me to the two men and one woman and said, "They're here because they're part of the task force we've put together to work these auto thefts and related cases. Wentworth says he's mentioned it to you."

"Yes, sir, I hope that's not a problem. You know you can trust me to…"

"No, that's fine. The existence of the task force is not a secret or anything, but we do need to keep what's going on with it under wraps. We've decided, though, that we need to make an exception in your case, at least with a certain amount of information we feel comfortable sharing. I trust we can still rely on your discretion, and your cooperation."

"Cooperation? I'm not sure I understand."

"Here's the thing, Miss McCallum," the man seated nearest to me, Sam Fields, said. "We have come to believe that our investigation into illegal activities in our three counties and the murder of your brother are connected."

I stared at him in shock. "Are you trying to say Richie was involved in something illegal? Because…"

"Oh, no, nothing like that. I'm sorry if I upset you. I guess I didn't start off very well, did I? I've been told by several people how devoted you were to your brother, and that you have been sort of investigating on your own because you believe there's more to the story of his death than meets the eye. Would you say that's correct?"

"Absolutely. It's just that I've gotten no cooperation from the authorities at all, so I guess I'm a bit surprised that you're suddenly talking to me." I looked at Chief Sikes, who had the grace to duck his head.

The woman, Angela something or other, spoke up. "I suppose you can guess that we need something from you now, am I right?" I looked around and gave her what I call my Jennifer Grey Look. If you saw *Dirty Dancing*, you know the look I'm talking about.

"Rebecca, we have made a good bit of progress here recently, and things are beginning to come together for our investigation. We just need a little more time. We fear that if you keep up with your unofficial enquiries, you may spook the people we're looking at. So we are requesting that you put a halt on your activities and give us a chance to take care of both our investigation and your situation at the same time," the Chief said.

"How do I know I can trust you people? You haven't seemed concerned about Richie up to this point."

"I think we all believed things were just as they appeared," Mr. Fields spoke up. "But recent discoveries have made us re-think that situation. I think I speak for everyone here when I say we're fairly confident we can apprehend your brother's killer, or killers, in a short time – if, that is, you agree to back off and stop stirring the waters."

I looked pleadingly at the Chief. "I just don't know if I can agree to do that."

Angela said, "I know it's a difficult thing to ask. We can't give you any names, no specific information – both for the element of surprise and for your safety – and we're asking you to have faith that we're being up front with you."

"And they really are, Becca," Damian said. "I hope by now you trust me to tell you the truth. I can't give you details, but they are on the right track, I'm sure of it."

I stared at him, trying to read the truth in his eyes, while everyone else waited for my answer and a battle raged in my head. In the end, Richie tipped the scales. My by-the-book brother would expect me to give them a chance.

I sighed. "Fine. I'll back off. But you'd better not take too long. I don't know how much patience I have."

That was what they wanted to hear, apparently, because they all stood as one and let out a collective sigh of relief. Fields held out his hand. "You won't regret this, Miss McCallum. We won't let you down."

"You'd better not," I warned him, and I heard a few chuckles.

"We want the truth as much as you do, hon," Chief Sikes said.

"Just don't take too long to get it done. I don't know how much more I can take."

A week later I had kept my bargain, but I wasn't sure they were keeping theirs. Someone should have let me know the status of the investigation, I thought. They hadn't, so I decided to ask the Chief about it. But when I got him on the phone he wasn't forthcoming at all. I hung up more frustrated than before. *So much for cooperation. So, Becca, what do you do now? Okay, back to square one.*

Chapter 33

I SHOULD HAVE BEEN IN MY THERAPIST'S OFFICE this afternoon, but things were beginning to come together in my head, and I needed to know about that body shop. So here I was, parked outside Bert's, psyching myself up to go in. The place was impressive. The building consisted of three bays in the main garage, an office at the far left end of the building, and a couple of paint booths at the rear of the open bays.

One guy near my age was working on a late-model Mustang apparently being primed for a new paint job. Water stood all around on the floor near the car, and he was using soft cloths to smooth the surface. The car looked like it had been sanded down and then washed. *Sort of like refinishing furniture.*

I stepped inside the shop and waited for him to notice me. No sense sneaking up on him and startling him right off the bat. As I watched, someone wearing what looked like a Haz-Mat suit emerged from a door at the back of the shop. A painter, I guessed. He peeled off his head gear as he walked toward the front, and streaks of sweat ran out of his hair and into his face. He pulled a clean cloth from an inside pocket and wiped the sweat away.

"Can I help you?" he asked as he came nearer.

Hearing the painter, the guy working on the Mustang also turned in my direction. "I'm sorry, ma'am. I didn't see you there. What can we do for you?" He glanced outside and I saw his eyes light on Bernice; I suppose she was the only unfamiliar car on the grounds.

"Wow, you guys must stay busy here," I gushed, trying out my feminine wiles on the Mustang guy. "So what is it you're doing to this car? Getting it ready to paint?"

"Yes, ma'am. I've about got it primed for Lance, here. He's our head painter now. He does a really good job. Do you need something done to your car? Is that your little bug out there?"

I laughed at his eagerness. "Well, no, Bernice is in good shape. I was hoping I could talk to you guys who have been here for a while. Somebody I knew used to work here, up until a couple of months ago." I frowned and gave a deep sigh. "Tommy Hollingshead. Did you know him?"

I saw a quick look pass between the two men before Mustang guy said, "Well, I knew Tommy, sort of, from hanging out down at the Rib Shack on the beach. I didn't go to work here until after he...you know..."

Here the painter stepped forward and nodded. "Lance Varner, ma'am. This is Joshua Freeman." He nodded toward Mustang guy, who grinned at me.

"Rebecca." I nodded, purposely not giving my last name. "I was hoping to find out a bit more about Tommy's work place, what he liked to do after work, that sort of thing."

"You some kind of reporter?" Joshua asked.

"Oh, no, nothing like that. I just..."

"I'll tell you what she 'just,'" I heard a gruff voice say off to my left. I recognized that voice. It was the voice I'd first heard at the hospital. I looked up to see an older man who had come from the office. He wore a white set of coveralls that looked like he hadn't done a speck of work all day. This would be Bert, the owner, I surmised. *Good, seems I have the whole gang here.*

"Excuse me?" I asked in a slightly offended tone, one I thought might possibly hit the right notes. I was new at this skullduggery stuff, after all.

"Miss Rebecca McCallum," Bert said, stepping briskly across the open space between us. He either had a very keen memory, or a reason to remember my face after all these weeks.

I heard a grunt from Lance, and the painter wandered off toward the far corner of the garage. I took it he didn't want to get involved. Well, we'd see about that after I finished with these two.

"Yes, that's right," I said, flashing another smile, but not an overly friendly one, since I was first and foremost the grieving sister. "How did you know?"

"Remember you from the news when your brother was killed."

Joshua turned back and said, "That was your brother? That deputy?" I nodded. "I'm sure sorry, ma'am. That was some bad stuff. But at least they got the guy who did it. Hey, Bert, she was asking about Tommy."

"We didn't know he was involved in any illegal activities like it seems he must have been," Bert said.

"You did know he'd been in prison for a while?"

"Well, yeah. He had a parole officer comin' around once in a while. But he seemed to have decided to turn his life around, and we all deserve a second chance in life, don't you think?" Bert puffed out his chest.

"I guess so, but then it doesn't seem to have been such a good idea in Tommy's case, does it? He took my brother away from me." I glanced at Joshua, who was now standing with his mouth hanging open, and said in his direction, "Do you know, my brother tried to help Tommy get straightened out when he was first arrested? And he kept in touch with him for a while after he got released. But Tommy didn't seem to want anything to do with him more recently."

"Miss McCallum, I am very sorry for your loss. But I've got a business to run here. We don't have time to stand around and have a pity party for you. So if you don't have any problems with a vehicle we can help you with, I'd appreciate it if you'd move along. My guys have lots of work to take care of before closing time." He turned his back, saying to Joshua, "This car ready to go to the paint booth? Tell Lance when it is. Where is he anyway? Lance!"

I saw Lance raise his head from down beside a pickup on the far side. "Yes, sir? I was checking the frame repair work on the truck."

"Come inside and talk to Mr. Harris. He's getting antsy about his quote."

Lance nodded and hurried toward the office door, glancing at me as he passed. Bert spun around and frowned at me, his beady eyes almost disappearing into his bushy eyebrows. "You still here, Missy? Best be on your way now." He stood with his feet braced apart, hands on hips. I saw no alternative but to do as he said.

"Nice to have met you." I waved to Joshua on my way out.

I'd learned one thing – a place Tommy had liked to hang out – the Rib Shack. Maybe Joshua still hung out there. I knew what my next stop would be, right after their quitting time.

I felt eyes boring into my back as I left, but I refused to turn back. I was sure it was the owner, Bert; he was the only one who'd shown me animosity. *I won't let you scare me off. And I* will *be back.* I unlocked Bernice's door. "C'mon, Bernice. Let's get out of here where we can think."

Well, that went well, even better than expected. I'd seen the lay of the land, so to speak, and met the major players there at the body shop. Now if I could figure out who's who. Maybe after I check out the Rib Shack. Joshua might be there. Maybe he'd tell me something more, maybe something he doesn't even know he knows. Isn't that how the detective stories work?

Mark called as I was waiting to pull onto the highway. "Hey, guy, how're ya doin'?"

"Becca? What's gotten into you today?" he laughed, his voice warm as sand on a sunny day and smooth as the bay on a windless afternoon. I gulped, realizing how much I loved hearing from him.

"Why? What do I sound like?" I really didn't want to talk to Mark about this yet – I much preferred to stop by the Rib Shack by myself. I figured guys there would rather talk to a woman alone than one with a bodyguard.

"Ah…let's see. I'd say you sound like the cat that swallowed the canary, but I don't remember the cat having a voice. Just a purely self-satisfied smile."

"Maybe a bit. What's up with you today?"

"Just calling to see if you're free for dinner tonight."

I thought fast and said, "Dinner sounds great. But I don't really feel like going out. Why don't you come over to the house?"

When he offered to get dinner, I told him I'd heard about this great barbecue place down on the beach I wanted to try. "I'm in Biloxi, so I'll pick supper up for us before I leave town. I just have a couple more errands to run. Is eight okay?"

He agreed, and I spent the next hour strolling the beach and thinking about what kind of questions I'd need to ask if I found anybody to talk to at the Rib Shack.

***

A car, two trucks, and two motorcycles were parked in front of the barbecue joint when I drove into the caliche parking lot. The smoke-filled air coming from the building smelled heavenly. Nothing compares to the aroma of wood-fired smokers filled with slabs of beef and chunks of pork. I realized suddenly I hadn't eaten anything since breakfast – and my stomach was definitely letting me know. I pushed open the door and stepped inside.

A young woman of about twenty worked behind the counter, and people were in different stages of devouring plates of barbecue at several of the tables. I breathed in deeply, and I saw the counter clerk smiling.

"I guess you get that a lot," I said as I crossed the room. "Do you ever get to where you don't notice how good it smells in here?"

"Not really. But sometimes when I go home at night I have to wash my hair before I can go to bed. Otherwise I'll be dreamin' of choppin' meat all night," she grinned. "What can I get you?"

I pulled out my prepared list – I remembered how Mark liked his barbecue. "Let's see, I need about half a dozen ribs, a pound of beef brisket sliced, and a pound of pulled pork."

"Hungry, are we?" she laughed. I knew she must say that a lot, because when we Southerners order take-out barbecue, we plan on having plenty – and plenty for leftovers.

"Well, there *will* be two of us eating," I said, making a face. She threw her head back and laughed.

"I think I like you," she said. I watched her work; her motions were fluid and unhurried, but there seemed to be no extraneous movements. She was one of those people who could get a lot done while looking like they weren't doing anything at all. I hated people like that. But I thought I could like her.

Glenda, her name tag read. I figured she'd probably looked all grown up at the age of twelve and would probably still look as youthful at forty as she did today. She had a figure guys gravitated toward, but I didn't feel jealous. *Might be a first for me.*

Or have I changed that much? A year ago I would have looked on any young, attractive woman as competition. I'd always found it hard to make friends with other women. Lorelei said it was a good thing we met before she got her "full growth" on her, or I wouldn't have given her the time of day. Sadly, she was probably right.

I used to blame it on growing up with only an older brother – there were always guys at the house, after all. But it was other guys, guys my own age – guys I met hanging out at the skating rink, or at the movies, playing video games – I always felt more comfortable with them than with my girlfriends. I usually got most of the attention when I was with a group of girls. Lorelei said it was because I demanded that attention. I used to think she was just kidding around.

"Now for sides, I need a large coleslaw, a small baked beans, two corn on the cob, large potato salad, and two, no make it four rolls." She nodded, taking down my requests.

"And could I get a large unsweet tea to go?"

"Sure, miss. Help yourself to pickles, peppers and stuff over on the sideboard. To-go containers are there, too. What about dessert? Cherry pie or banana pudding?"

"Banana pudding, I think. I haven't had that in a while." I frowned, thinking back to the days before Richie's funeral, when we'd had every dessert known to man thrust at us.

"You okay?" she asked, sliding the foam container of tea across to me and setting out a small bowl of lemon slices.

"Yeah, I'm fine, thanks. But it's hot out this afternoon, and I've been rushing around town."

I pulled out my wallet and waited as she figured my bill, and when I'd paid she suggested I have a seat, saying they'd just had a large order called in and it would be a few minutes before they could get to mine.

"No problem." I plopped down on one of the four stools at the short eating counter, where I'd usually be uncomfortable, and surreptitiously surveyed the room. I gave a start when my gaze met that of Lance, the painter from Bert's shop. *Coincidence he's here? I hope not.*

Nobody came in for the next few minutes, so we chatted away, Glenda stopping once in a while to get a refill for a customer, me gathering odds and ends of condiments. I kept feeling Lance's stare on me but wouldn't let myself look around. I looked up at the sound of a bell from the kitchen. "This is your order," Glenda said. She took a minute to check the packages against the order slip and then packed it all into two large plastic bags. "I'll help you carry these out," she offered, moving to come around the end of the counter.

"Here, let me," said a voice behind me. I turned to see the painter, looking a bit uncomfortable but determined. "I'm leaving anyway, Glenda. I can help the lady."

Glenda looked from him to me and nodded, saying, "It's okay, I know this guy. He won't try anything with you. If he does he'll answer to me. Now, don't be a stranger. You come back soon, and let me know how your little dinner goes tonight."

"You get the door and I'll get the bags," he said, as Glenda handed him my food.

"Come back soon, hon."

I waved as I hurried to the door to hold it for Lance, then went ahead to unlock the car. I held open the passenger door and lifted one bag at a time from him to get them settled for the ride home.

When I turned back to thank him, he had his thumbs hooked in the belt loops of his jeans and was rocking back and forth nervously. "I kind of wanted to talk to you for a minute, Miss," he said in his soft drawl. He didn't sound like what I thought a painter from a body shop should sound like. *Well, isn't that a snotty thing to say.*

"Oh?" I asked, trying to sound only casually interested.

"Yeah, my name's Lance Varner. Don't know if you recognized me, but I'm the painter at Bert's Body Shop. I'd just come out of the paint booth this afternoon when you were there."

"Oh, right!" I said in acknowledgment.

He glanced from side to side. "Listen, I can't be seen hanging around with you, but I heard what you were asking about and I wanted to tell you something."

My mouth grew suddenly dry and my throat tightened. "What's that, Lance? Something about Tommy?"

"Yeah, Tommy and some other people. I know who you are, and I know what happened to your brother, and there's stuff I think you oughta know." He ran his words together as if he was afraid he wouldn't get them out unless he said them fast. Would you meet me down at the marina? I work part time for a guy who's got a boat down there, *The Seasoned Wench,* and he's out of town so I'm staying there."

"Oh, I don't know, Lance. Why should I trust you?"

"I can't explain that now, but..." He glanced furtively around the parking lot, "I can't stand around here talking to you. Don't need anybody to see me. Listen, I dropped a napkin with my phone number into your bag. If you decide you want to meet, give me a call. Hope you do." He nodded and loped off toward his motorcycle.

Chapter 34

WHEN SATURDAY CAME, I CALLED JUSTINE to ask if Owen could have a sleepover at my house. She hemmed and hawed, but I figured in time she'd give in, since it was the weekend and she'd probably want to go out. So I was a bit surprised when she finally said no.

"I think it would be better for all of us if Owen stayed closer to home for a while. He hasn't been sleeping all that well, and I want to have him with me for now."

"Is he all right? He's not having nightmares, is he?"

"No, of course not!" She sounded as if I had questioned her abilities as a mother. "It's just taking him time to get adjusted to not having his daddy to tuck him in. He'll be okay; it'll just take time."

"Guess I'll have to swallow my disappointment and wait it out until he's feeling better. Think I might come by this afternoon and take him out for a snow cone?"

A slight hesitation. *Come on, Justine.* "Maybe. Text me later and we'll see what's going on with us."

I had no choice but to let it go – but if she thought she was going to wean Owen away from me she had another think coming.

***

Since I couldn't see Owen now, I decided I should drive out to see Lucy. I had intended to go see her earlier in the week, but my investigations had kept me busy.

As I dressed I thought about the things Jake had confided to me that day at the hospital. I had a vivid picture in my mind of two little lost boys being carted from the river town of Vicksburg half the length of the state to a new home on a farm with people they'd never known existed a month before. I could just hear Lucy making small talk in the front seat while the boys munched on her lemon cookies in the back seat and Martin drove sedately down Highway 49. They must have felt a bit hemmed in as the car began to move through the pine forests dotting that part of the state. River rats, that's what they were. What a frightening time it must have been for them.

I shook my head in annoyance at myself for getting caught up in such thoughts again. I glanced at the clock on my cell phone. 1:10 p.m. *I should be at Lucy's in twenty minutes.* No way was I going to make it. I picked up the phone to let her know I'd be a bit late.

The heat slapped me in the face like a handful of wet noodles when I stepped outside, and I sucked in a heavy breath. In the middle of July there wasn't much to be done about the high humidity, that weighty, soggy feeling that made us southerners want to crawl under one of our live oaks and wait for Christmas. I was glad I'd decided to wear my lime green sundress with the pink hibiscus blossoms dotted across the skirt. The dress gave me a psychological boost, making me feel a couple of degrees cooler – and drier. I'd take whatever help I could get at this point.

"C'mon, lady, let's go see Miss Lucy," I said, opening Bernice's door. "Whew! Or let's not just yet." I eased into the seat and stuck the key in the ignition, trying not to touch the car's metal parts. I used the hem of my dress to protect my fingers as I pushed buttons to roll down the windows. I never think to go outside ahead of time to get the car cooled off before I get in. Leaving the driver's door open, I stepped down the driveway to get my mail and pick up the paper. Seeing Mrs. Goodson wave from her front porch, I waved back but then hurried to the car and jumped inside, in no mood to stand outside in this heat and fend off questions about Damian and Mark.

I turned the AC full blast, plugged my phone into the car's USB port and found my favorite driving playlist. Traffic headed north out of town was light today, with most people off work and the weather so unaccommodating. The beaches would have plenty of tourists, but even they usually stayed inside until later in the afternoon. I was alone with my thoughts – and the music of Three Doors Down.

I hoped Lucy would volunteer a bit more information about Jake, and I hoped he wouldn't be there. With his new fitness center having just opened, I figured he'd be out of the picture today. I was almost certain Jake was involved in Richie's murder, especially since he had a strong motive: Anyone with eyes and a brain could look at him with Justine and see how he adored her. And, according to Owen, Jake had done *something* to really upset Justine, something she wasn't happy about. I wondered if it had anything to do with what Bert was holding over him. And I wondered just what Bert's role had been. I wouldn't put anything past that man.

I'd been driving almost on auto-pilot, letting Bernice lead the way, when the message got through to my brain – a pickup behind me had been back there for a while. I was on a four-lane divided highway, so there was no reason for it to be close behind me and not pass. Unless… I decided to check the way they do in the movies – I dropped my speed to about forty-five; the pickup slowed down, too. I sped up to seventy-five; the truck sped up, too. I slowed to about forty, and the truck following me (for I was sure now it was following me) did, too. *What is this? Is it something random, or is someone after me? Does it have something to do with my asking questions?*

My palms were damp where I held the steering wheel in a death grip. Suddenly the truck pulled into the inside lane and made as if to pass me. *Finally!* But instead of passing, the driver pulled the truck up even with me. When I glanced over, I couldn't see into the darkened passenger window. They could see me, though, I thought. They could see my scared face.

As I watched, the truck swerved directly toward me and I instinctively jerked the wheel. Bernice's right wheels bounced off the edge of the shoulder. By exerting all the strength I had, I managed to cling to the shoulder and fight my way back into the right lane. I was shaking all over, barely able to control the car. I was scared witless now.

Where had the pickup gone? Was he ahead of or behind me? I saw nothing on the road ahead, and when I checked the rear view mirror at first I saw nothing there, either. But then I saw it – a dark speck growing larger by the second. My heart was again in my throat. A short bridge lay directly ahead of me; I couldn't let him catch me there. But I also didn't fancy the idea of what might happen afterwards. The embankment was steep all along this stretch of road, and Bernice and I probably wouldn't survive a ride to the bottom.

I had only seconds to decide what to do. *Richie, I sure could use some of your fancy driving maneuvers right here!* The turnoff to Lucy's was about a mile past the bridge. If I can only make this work...

I slammed on my brakes and the truck did, too, then I floored the gas pedal and shot away from the truck and crossed the bridge well ahead of it. I slowed slightly when I came off the bridge and I could see the driver planned to repeat his earlier maneuver. But this time I was ready. I had to be. Bernice weighed about half as much as the monster behind me. I saw the steep 'Y' of the Ledbetter's road approaching on my right. Waiting until the last second, I kept up my speed, even as the truck caught up with me again, and again drew around to my left side. He was determined, I'd give him that.

Watching both the truck and the turn-off, I hit the brakes and skidded as I lost speed quickly. At the last second I spun the wheel and dove for the side road. The green pickup shot past – but when I glanced in the mirror I saw his brake lights come on.

Fishtailing madly, like I hadn't since I was in high school running the roads, I fought to maintain control of Bernice on the much smaller road. We swung from one side of the road to the other, coming so close to a mailbox that I felt sure I could have read the addresses on the letters inside. I only had to make it another mile. Glancing into the mirror, I saw the green blob turn onto the road behind me, and I prayed I'd have enough time. I pushed on the gas pedal again.

There. Lucy's driveway. Now could I do again what I'd done turning onto this road? I had to try. *I think I can make it. Here we go, Bernice. Hold on.* Making the turn was much easier this time. My speed wasn't so great, and somehow I felt confident it would work.

I rattled onto the driveway and bumped up the gravel drive lined with crape myrtles, their white blooms a blur as I shot by. I laid my hand on the horn and my foot on the brake and didn't stop until I'd driven almost to Lucy's front steps. I'd worry about the flowerbed later.

Lucy had appeared on the porch almost as soon as I turned in. She stood wringing her hands as I jumped out and ran for the porch steps, my foot slipping on the first one. I fell to my knees but scrambled back to my feet.

"Inside!" I screamed at her, and with a look of shock on her face she began backing into the house, with me right behind her. I looked up to see Martin coming through the door from the kitchen.

"Call 911!" I said and threw my arms around Lucy. "There's somebody after me!" To his credit, Martin said not a word but picked up the phone and dialed. When he had the dispatcher on the line, he simply told her he had an emergency and held out the phone. I took a deep breath to steady my breathing and took the receiver from him.

"Whoever it is, they probably won't try coming in here after you. Sounds like somebody thought it'd be a good idea to put a scare into you." He headed toward their bedroom. "But on the off-chance…" He came back moments later carrying a double-barreled shotgun and loading a handful of shells into it. Seeing his calm movements brought me a sense of safety for the first time in the last…what had it been? Ten minutes? I had no idea how long the ordeal had lasted.

"Dispatch said they'll have someone here soon," I reported when I hung up.

"Becca, what in the world is…?" Lucy began but she faltered, reaching out her hands to both me and her husband. "Martin?" She took one step toward me and then tilted to one side, her eyes going glassy.

"Lucy!" Martin and I both cried at the same time. I managed to latch onto her arm while Martin gently placed the gun in the corner. Then he grabbed her other arm and we steered her to her chair. I'd never forgive myself if I caused something to happen to this sweet lady. *I should never have come here.*

"Nonsense, girl," Martin said, and only then did I realize I'd spoken aloud.

Lucy stirred a bit. "Becca, are you all right?"

I choked, torn between laughing and crying. "Me? Are *you* all right?"

"Me?" she parroted. "I'm fine. Just got a bit dizzy for a minute. Are the cops on the way?"

"The cops? I don't think I've ever heard you use a slang term before."

I looked over her head at Martin, to find him laughing with relief. "I'm not sure I have either, not in all our years."

"Well, are they?"

"Yes, ma'am. They'll be right here."

"What happened to you, anyway?"

"I'm not sure. Can I wait until the police get here?"

She nodded. "Martin, I don't know about Becca, but I could sure use a cool drink."

As he returned with two glasses, I heard a distant siren. "Good, they're almost here. I'm sure we're fine now." I walked to the front door and looked out through the single small pane. The yard was empty, except for Chester, who had come around the house barking, at the siren I supposed.

Martin opened the door a couple of inches and yelled at Chester to cease and desist. I stifled a nervous giggle. Apparently I wasn't far from hysteria at that moment. The siren grew louder and I could tell the car had turned into the drive. Martin stepped onto the porch and I saw him lift his hand in a welcoming wave. Then he stepped out of my line of vision.

"Are you sure you're okay, Lucy? I'm so sorry about this." I knelt in front of her chair and held her hands.

She poo-pooed my concern. "I'm fine. I just got a bit excited when you came wheeling in here with your horn blowing."

"I'm so sorry about your flowers. I'll buy you some more to replace the ones I squashed."

She was telling me I'd do no such thing when Martin came in followed by Damian. *My Lord, I can't get away from him.*

"Damian, how did you get stuck with this callout?" I asked, rising to go across and give him a hug. His arms felt strong and comforting, his body sturdy beneath his blue uniform. I couldn't help but think of Richie. He held on to me a few seconds longer than necessary. I saw the Ledbetters looking at each other in surprise, and Lucy had a saucy smile on her face.

"What happened to you, Becca? Your car's almost on the porch. And what happened to the side of it? Looks like paint scrapings on the driver's side."

"It's green paint, I'm sure. That's the color of the pickup trying to run me off the road a little while ago." I saw professionalism and personal feelings warring in those blue eyes, and I knew by their deepening shade how upset Damian was – but the professionalism won out, as I'd expected it to.

"Sir, is there a place where we could sit so I can take Becca's statement?"

"Not until I get all of you introduced to each other," I said.

***

Formalities dispensed with, we were soon all seated around the kitchen table and I began to describe my harrowing drive earlier. When I happened to look over at Lucy and Martin, they were holding hands, shoulder to shoulder, visibly upset.

As soon as he had what little description I could give of the pickup, Damian excused himself to go out to his car to call in the report.

"My, Rebecca," Lucy said, and I heard the smile in her voice. "If you're going to find yourself in need of rescuing, that's a nice looking knight you've found there."

"I can't believe you're teasing me at a time like this," I complained. "I was scared to death out there."

"I know, honey, I'm sorry," she patted my arm. When Martin left the room to put his shotgun away, she added with a twinkle in her eyes, "But doesn't he have the cutest dimples you ever saw?"

"You're incorrigible!" I giggled, coloring as Damian walked back into the kitchen.

"Well, I'm glad to see you're over the worst of your upset," he smiled, causing the dimples to make another appearance and Lucy to titter behind her hand.

"Watch it, Lucy," I warned her.

"I think we missed something," Damian said to Martin, who shrugged.

"Women," was all he said.

***

Damian insisted on following me all the way home and checking the entire place when we got there. Backing down from his inspection of the treehouse, he said, "Okay, I think you're clear." I didn't want him to see how nervous the attack had made me. As it turned out, it didn't matter – he was determined not to leave me alone.

"I'm going back to the sheriff's office and file my report, but then I'm taking the rest of the day off and I'm coming back here."

"Damian, you don't need to do that," I protested. We'd reached the back porch now and I plopped down in the swing.

"And you don't need to be sitting out here alone," he retorted. "Becca, this is serious. Can't you see that?"

"I get what you're saying. But I can't stop living my life. I have Owen, friends, my running."

"Well consider me your constant companion for running until we get this situation under control. We have to find out who was behind this attack." He gave me a speculative look, cocking his head and raising an eyebrow, one foot perched on the bottom step. Damn, he looked good all in black. "Do you have any ideas about who this might have been?"

"Not specifically. But I'm sure it had something to do with what happened to Richie, and the people working at that body shop where Hollingshead worked."

"How can you be sure it's related to Richard?"

"We've talked about this, Damian. You know I believe somebody planned and carried out Richie's murder that night. Your own task force is even investigating. How can it not be?"

He looked off into the distance for a long moment, then turned to me.

"Listen, I've gotta run. I'll be back as soon as I can. I've never noticed – do you have an alarm system?"

"No, never thought about one before. I think I'd like one now."

"I'll ask around at the office and see who folks there use."

"No need. Lorelei and I went to school with a guy who went into the security business. He's a good guy. I'll give him a call."

"Even better. I'm going to go now and let you go in and make that call." He held out his hand as if to help me out of the swing.

"You go on. I think I'll stay out here a bit. This place always calms me down."

"Nope, sorry. You're going to have to calm down inside today, and maybe for a few days. You have to give us time to get a handle on this situation and find out what happened today and who was responsible."

"But Damian..."

"No buts. I don't like the idea of giving you orders...I know how independent you are, and how stubborn. But Becca, this is the same thing I'd be doing if you were a woman I'd never met before. I am a public *safety* officer, you know."

He smiled, and I gave in. "You're working those dimples, Wentworth. Not fair." But I smiled, too. "Are you trying to take Richie's place in taking care of me?"

Helping me to my feet he slipped his arms around my waist and pulled me to him. "No ma'am, I'm definitely not trying to replace your brother. My feelings toward you aren't brotherly at all." Intent on making sure I understood where he was coming from, he kissed me lingeringly, then released me and stepped back.

I touched my finger to my lips and stared at him, with his self-satisfied grin. My lips tingled from his kiss, and I couldn't decide if I wanted him to stop or kiss me again. He decided for me. He led me into the kitchen and watched as I double- locked the back door, and for once I didn't protest his giving orders. When we got to the front door, he gave the locks a once over and said, "Lock these, too, as soon as I'm outside."

Then I was alone...to relive the harrowing few minutes I'd lived through earlier. If I'd had doubts before, which wasn't the case, now I knew for sure Richie had been murdered. And now I had become the killer's next target because that unknown person thought *I* knew something. *Well, I do...just not enough. But that's about to change.*

Chapter 35

AFTER DAMIAN LEFT I PACED THE FLOOR, unsure about what to do next. I still had way too much drama in my life. I appreciated Damian's support, and I knew he cared about me; I cared about him, too. But then, I *knew* I loved Mark, and our relationship had just reached a new level during the hurricane. He and I had a history together, while I had only met Damian recently. *Then how could you respond to Damian as you did? Are you serious about Mark or not?*

How could I trust what I was feeling about either one of them right now? All I wanted to do was bring Richie's killer to justice. I had the rest of my life to get my own house in order. Right now, the police were on the verge of getting enough evidence against Bert and Jake to bring them in – at least that's what I was hoping for.

I found myself jumping at each little sound, creeping around the house like a mouse in search of cheese and trying to avoid the family cat, afraid to make a noise that might prevent me from hearing any unusual sounds.

Damian called back, sounding disgusted. "Hey, I can't take off. Johnson called in sick and we're short-handed."

"That's okay, I'll be fine here."

"Just stay inside," he said as I was hanging up.

***

I should have been fine, I know. I'd been through hell today, but it was over. I was back at home, safe and sound. So why was I still so unnerved? It finally dawned on me that Mark knew nothing of my latest adventure. He would want to know. *So call him.*

I checked the time…close enough to five. I hit speed dial. He showed up forty-five minutes later.

"So, what have you done now?" he asked, one side of his mouth lifted in a lazy grin.

"Don't start with me, Mark, or I'll send you right back where you came from."

"Fine, I was just teasing you."

"This isn't a good day for that. I'm fine now, but I had a rough encounter earlier this afternoon. Do you want to hear about it?" I turned toward the living room.

He sobered instantly. He grabbed my arm and stopped me in my tracks, almost making me spill the glass of wine I was holding. His hold on me was both gentle and firm.

"Becca, I don't know how many of these episodes I can take." I heard the anguish in his voice, but what he said rubbed me the wrong way. I pulled out of his grasp.

"*You* don't know how much *you* can take? Funny, I think these things keep happening to *me*." I drained my glass, sat down at the far end of the sofa, and poured myself a healthy second glass. *Slow down, or you know you'll do something stupid.*

Mark snorted and ran a hand through his hair, making him look even more attractive. I did love that habit he had of tousling his hair. *Wait you're mad at him, remember?*

"I'm sorry. I'm just…worried." He sat down near enough for me to breathe in his clean familiar scent and to see his sexy five o'clock shadow. My hand itched to reach out and stroke his square jaw and trace his lips with my fingers – but I didn't. His face was pinched, and I hated I'd put those worries on him.

"It's okay," I breathed, looking into his eyes and thinking how intriguing they were, the way they could transform in an instant from a sea green to jade or emerald based on his moods. They reminded me of the mood rings I wore when I was a kid. Right now they were smoldering, and I couldn't come up with a word to describe the shade, but it was having a major effect on me. I dropped my gaze to my hands.

I did reach out then, laying my hand on the side of his face and tracing an eyebrow with my thumb. He'd always liked that. He relaxed and laid his head back against the sofa, sighing with what might have been pleasure…or contentment…or resignation.

"How're you feeling?" I asked.

I saw a lazy smile beginning to spread across his face. "Come here, you, and I'll show you." He opened one eye and squinted at me. "Or are you afraid to?"

For an answer I leaned over and planted an unrestrained kiss on his lips. When I drew back he sighed. "Does that feel like I'm afraid?" I murmured.

He opened both eyes then and I watched them turning shades once more, this time to an almost black emerald green that spoke of love and passion held tightly in check. He gave a slight shake of his head and folded me into his arms. I laid my cheek against his chest, feeling the steady, if rapid, beat of his heart.

Mark cleared his throat. "Now, how about telling me what happened today?"

To his credit, he interrupted my recitation a scant two times, once to ask if I'd seen the face of the driver, and the other to mutter a curse. When I'd finished, up to and including Damian following me home and insisting I get an alarm system installed as soon as possible, he sat there wagging his head from side to side as if to clear his thoughts, which I suppose he might have been. I don't know what I'd expected from him, but based on our earlier confrontations I guess I'd been waiting for some kind of explosion.

So it came as a surprise when he only said, "Thank God you're okay. I couldn't take it if anything happened to you, McCallum."

I tried to make light of that sentiment, I'm not sure why, but he flat out rejected my teasing comment about how his life would probably be a lot simpler then. "I think we've had this conversation before, Becca. This isn't a joke to me. I understand you wanting to laugh and tease your way through it, but I can't. Besides, *you* didn't want me teasing just a couple of minutes ago. I don't want to think about what could have happened to you today."

"But I'm okay, babe. Really, I'm okay."

"No thanks to whoever was after you in that pickup. I swear, if the police don't start to put two and two together soon, I may come over to your side and help you figure this out without them."

"You have no idea how much it means to me for you to believe me about the whole situation," I said, reaching for his hands. He squeezed and then lifted my fingers to his lips for a kiss – an endearing habit I'd already grown accustomed to and fond of. I was, in fact, crazy about it. Whenever my fingers touched any part of his body I felt a tingling deep inside my core. This was something new. When we were together before, I'd thought I was in love with him. We'd done our fair share of making out, and it had been pleasant but lighthearted.

This, though, this upwelling of emotion when we are together, this urge to hold him close and never let him go – this was new. I thought back to earlier today when Damian had kissed me and I had responded, and I realized I'd had a purely physical reaction. The man was special, and he treated me special. He cared for me and didn't mind to show it. He was handsome, smart, definitely sexy – and he couldn't hold a candle to Mark Barrington. *So much for my plans to postpone all decision making until later.*

Even if I'd had thoughts to the contrary earlier, I had no doubts at this moment about how I felt. Damian had been a dalliance, a distraction from the unbelievable loss I'd felt when I lost Richie. He may not have been wanting to take my brother's place, but all of a sudden it seemed clear to me – that was the role I hoped he would come to fill for me.

Mark stared at me, his brow furrowed and his head tilted to the side. A slow smile eased lazily into place on his sweet mouth, a smile that made it all the way into his gorgeous eyes and stayed there. I felt a warming glow settle over me and knew I was blushing.

"What?"

He laced his fingers with mine. "I'd give anything to be able to read your mind right this minute."

"Sometimes a woman's thoughts don't need to be shared, but that doesn't mean they're not about you."

"Good enough for me." He laughed, a comforting, comfortable laugh, and for some reason a picture of Lucy and Martin sitting side by side this morning flashed into my head. I smiled, and then my body betrayed me with a yawn.

"Okay, then. You look like you could use a long soak in a lavender scented bathtub. You do still like lavender, don't you?"

"Things like that don't change much," I sighed. "And yes, even with it ninety-five degrees outside, I would still enjoy a hot, soaking bath right now." As I said this, I realized my muscles were bunched into knots through my arms and shoulders, where I'd worked so hard to control the car this morning. I winced. "And maybe a bit of Epsom salt, too."

"Then you go upstairs and fix that bath and take all the time you need. I'm gonna have a look in your kitchen and see what I can find for supper."

"You're not joking, are you?" The promise of a hot bath with food at the end of it sounded heavenly. "My stomach hopes you're not."

He pulled me to my feet and steered me toward the stairs. "And don't come back down for at least an hour. No matter what noises you may hear," he added with a theatrical rumble in his voice. He gave me a playful swat on my rear as I left the room.

I was still giggling when I started my bath water.

***

I felt as relaxed as if I'd had one of Lorelei's all-day spa treatments at the casino – so relaxed I wanted to lie down across the bed for a minute after I'd toweled off.

My eyes flew open. How long had I been out? I scrambled off the bed to find my phone: 8:25. Good, only about fifteen minutes. All in all, though, I'd been up here for a little more than an hour. Mark would be looking for me soon.

I walked into the closet and stood contemplating possibilities. Capris – skirt – sundress – shorts – Nothing looked right. I pushed the hangers back and forth, not knowing what I hoped to find. Then I saw it. Yes, perfect.

Five minutes later I headed downstairs, my bare feet making no sound. I'd decided on a gauzy white peasant blouse over a floor-length skirt with a high slit that I had chosen because it matched Mark's eyes. I felt as if I were floating on air, the aftereffects of the wine and the long soak in the tub, so I held tight to the rail as I descended, to keep from tumbling headfirst down the stairs.

The blend of spices assaulted my nostrils before I reached the kitchen. Curry? Mark couldn't possibly be making curry. I saw him before he saw me and I stood gazing at this stranger in my kitchen. His tie was gone – so were his shoes. He stood barefoot in his grey slacks, the shirt sleeves of his grey and green plaid shirt rolled up, his shirttail loose.

He was whistling. I listened to the tune – something from one of the Bond films. *Skyfall*? *I should suggest we watch that next time we have movie night.*

I must have made a sound because he turned and smiled at me, and my heart flip-flopped. He'd gotten comfortable, all right. His shirt was open, showing the white tee underneath. God, he looked sexy.

"How're you feeling, sweet thing?" he asked, coming across to plant a boisterous kiss on the top of my head. "Mmm, even your hair smells of lavender." He reached one arm round my waist and swung me in a circle.

"You're in a good mood," I laughed.

"No, I'm in a great mood," he retorted. "And why not? I found all the stuff I needed to fix dinner, I've got my woman in my arms – well, arm," he gestured with the spatula in his other hand, "and you may not know it, but we had showers all evening and I think it's gonna be cool enough to sit in my swing later."

I laughed out loud when he did his Groucho Marx imitation, waggling his eyebrows at me as he danced across to the stove. I'd missed his Groucho face.

"Maybe, we'll see. So what are we having for dinner?"

"Have a seat and I'll dish it up."

Was this the same man I'd dated for more than two years, the one who once burned a grilled cheese sandwich? "Mark, when did you learn to cook?"

"You don't know yet that I have," he teased over his shoulder as he lifted lids off pots and pans and filled two plates, which he set gently on the table.

"Smells wonderful." I unfolded my napkin and laid it on my lap.

Mark poured our goblets full of ice water while I surveyed my plate. Fluffy rice topped with chunks of chicken in a curry sauce, asparagus spears curving gracefully around the side of the plate. I started to pick up my fork, but he stilled my hand.

"Allow me." He forked a small amount of rice and chicken. "Open up." He held my gaze as I did as instructed, up until the moment my eyes closed in delight. I felt a smile creep across my face and heard his pleased grunt.

How could I have thought the guy was sexy before? He was an adolescent then compared to his demeanor now. I opened my eyes to find him staring at me, his eyes crinkling at the corners. *He has a few more lines, and every single one adds to his appeal.*

"Okay, dig in," he said, handing me a fork and breaking the spell. I realized then – it had been another of those no lunch days and I was famished. I did as he suggested.

When I looked up at him once, he was leaned back in his chair and staring at me with a bemused expression. I had a feeling the night might be a long one.

Chapter 36

WE HAD FINISHED DINNER, loaded the dishwasher, and were relaxing with a bottle of wine. Somewhere in the darkness nearby droplets of leftover rainwater clanged as they hesitantly dripped from the roof onto something metal, and the tree frogs were in the middle of a lively concerto. The swing moved lazily as Mark guided it with his foot. His other foot was propped on the porch railing. Moonlight glistened on the leaves of the trees and shrubs, giving the backyard a fairy tale atmosphere and providing a perfect backdrop for the dozens of fireflies meandering across the yard.

"This is the way life is meant to be lived," he said.

"You mean me having long baths while you cook dinner? I'd agree with that."

"Doofus." He flicked me on the nose with a finger, and I made a stab at latching on to the offending digit with my teeth. "So that's how it is?" He turned in the swing and began to tickle me with both hands, but stopped as suddenly as he had begun. "Sorry, Becca. I forgot how crazy that used to make you."

"Some things are different now, Mark. I've changed in lots of ways over the past few weeks."

His hands had remained at my waist, and now I felt them kneading gently as they slid underneath my blouse and his mouth reached for mine in the moonlight, seeking.

I slid around to face him, swinging my legs up and across his thighs and moaning softly as his hand slid down to my hip. His teeth were nipping at my lips, my neck, my lips again.

I took his face in both my hands and opened my mouth to his, our tongues meeting tentatively at first, then beginning a sensuous dance with each other, testing, seeking, finding, finally melding into one.

"Mark, sweetie, I…"

His mouth closed over mine again, insistent, demanding. When we broke for air I twisted away from him and stood abruptly.

"Sorry, baby. I didn't mean to push you…"

I put my fingers across his lips and he kissed them, groaning in surprise when I ran my hand down his arm and took his hand.

C'mon, sweetie," I whispered. "Let's go inside."

He followed me without another word, and we left the swing to the creatures of the night.

***

I'd left a small lamp burning dimly in the living room, and I followed its glow to the chest where my stereo system sat waiting. I tuned to Pandora and thought about my stations. Did I want "Norah Jones Radio" or "Her Diamonds Radio?" I loved making my own stations. I finally chose Norah Jones – can't go far wrong with her music.

Soft music, soft lights, and the solid feel of the man I loved beside me. That's what I wanted. I turned from the stereo to find Mark holding out his arms; I moved into them without hesitation, and we began to move to the music.

One hand slid up my back to stroke my hair, and he eased my head onto his shoulder. "We fit together really well, don't we?" he asked huskily.

"Mm-hmm," I breathed, wrapping both my arms round his waist.

"Becca," he breathed against my hair. "Look at me, sweetheart." I raised my head, looked deep into his eyes, and felt myself drowning in the longing I saw there. When he bent his head to kiss me, I felt like I imagined it would feel if I'd been hit with a bolt of electricity.

"I like that sound," he chuckled, lips against my neck. "Oh, and that one, too." He drew me toward the sofa, kissing me all the while, and sank down against the cushions, pulling me onto his lap. I swung my legs onto the sofa and he did the same, and then I was lying crushed against his solid chest, my loose hair spread out around both of us.

I heard myself almost purring as he ran his hands over my back and ribcage, and when he cradled my breasts and drew lazy circles around my nipples, they responded by hardening into bullets. "Naughty girl," he whispered. *Is he teasing, or is he serious?*

I drew back, bracing my hands against his chest. "You don't want this?" I asked, sliding away from him and adjusting my skirt. I stood staring down at him, hands braced on my hips. Something just didn't feel right.

His eyes roved over me, pausing on my breasts. I looked down to see my nipples standing darkly erect through the gauze of my blouse. He shook his head slowly, smiling lazily. "I don't think that's what I said at all."

This wasn't going at all the way I'd expected. I thought Mark would have had me undressed by now. Maybe he didn't want this commitment as much as I did. Because he knew me well enough to know that for me it would be a total commitment. Suddenly I couldn't stand there with his eyes on me, my face flushing with frustration and embarrassment.

"I think I need a drink," I said, hurrying to the kitchen. I took the half empty wine bottle from the fridge, grabbed a mug, and poured it full.

Strong hands gripped my shoulders from behind and spun me around. "Hey, baby, what's the matter? What'd I do?"

"Nothing," I said, but the tears gathering in my eyes and spilling over gave the lie to my words. "It's just, I just thought...well, I thought you wanted to make love with me as much as I wanted to be with you, and you don't. I'm sorry – I'm just making a fool of myself."

He gave an exasperated grunt and ran both hands through his hair, leaving it tousled and more tempting than ever. "You think I don't want that? Don't want you?" I shrugged, my throat clogged with tears. "Come back and sit down. Come *on*," he said when I hesitated, and began to pull me along with him.

He sat on the sofa and patted the seat beside him. Sniffling, I sat, but I couldn't face him. "Look at me, Becca. Please," he said, taking one of my hands. I dabbed at my eyes with my other hand and finally turned my face toward him. The passion was still there in his eyes, tempered by something I didn't understand.

"Sweetheart, I think we need to slow down and take time to clear the air before we take this any further."

"Clear the air about what? Have I done something wrong? Well, besides looking for Richie's murderer when you asked me not to?"

"It's not that," he said, shaking his head for emphasis. "That *is* an issue that stands between us," he conceded, with a twist of his mouth, "or at least it's been an issue up to now. But, hon, there's something else we need to discuss…"

"Then what?"

He sighed. "I think we need to talk about Damian."

Chapter 37

DAMIAN! WHAT DID HE HAVE TO DO WITH what was happening – or not happening – between Mark and me? "I don't understand," I said as I crossed the room to turn off the music. Clearly this wasn't the time for "Come Away with Me." "What does Damian have to do with us?"

"Are you honestly asking me that, especially after telling me he was there for you today and made sure you got home safely?"

"Well, he did do that. He's a good friend." *A good friend. Was he being a friend when he kissed you all those times? Even today?* I felt myself blushing, which made me all the more embarrassed about the thoughts I'd had about Damian before.

"Hey, what's the matter? What are you thinking about?"

"Nothing," I said a bit too quickly, probably. "It's just, you seem to think there's something more than friendship between Damian and me. I have told you he's a friend. He was one of Richie's best friends. He's been supportive of me and I've tried to be supportive of him."

"Is that really all?"

Mark came to stand looking down at me. I knew I had to meet his gaze or he'd be more suspicious, but he had hit upon just enough truth that I hardly knew how to answer. I couldn't lie to this man I loved so much. "That's all there is now," I finally said.

"I guess we'd better sit down after all." I settled back onto the sofa, this time in one corner so Mark could stay as far away from me as he wanted to. He sat down at the far end and stretched his legs out. I watched as one foot began to tap out a tattoo on the side of the coffee table, a sure sign he was still upset.

Lord, please give me the right words to say to make him understand.

"Baby, you're right, at least partly right. When I first met Damian, you know I was feeling vulnerable. I wouldn't have gotten through that awful time without *you*. You held me together and gave me a shoulder to cry on, and you were there when I needed you. I kept telling myself to always remember how kind you were being and to never forget how much I owed you for being there for me."

"But…I was just the old boyfriend, and Wentworth blew into town and knocked you off your feet. Is that it?"

"What? No! That's not it at all. He hasn't 'knocked me off my feet.'" I sat forward, trying to make him see how earnest I was being. "You are the one who's knocked me off my feet. Can you not see that? Can't you feel it, in how I responded to you tonight?"

"I thought I could." He shook his head as if trying to deter a gnat from flying into his eye or his nose, something at least that unpleasant. "But then when I brought up Damian's name, I saw your reaction. You can't tell me I didn't. That tells me there's something between the two of you."

"But there isn't, not really," I protested. He continued as if I hadn't interrupted at all.

"I'm not saying I think you're in love with him. I believe you when you say you love me, I really do. But it's not impossible for a person to be in love with two people at the same time. And that's one thing I can't do, Becca. I can't share you, not with him, not with anyone."

My head was in a spin. How was I supposed to convince him he was wrong, when I had to admit to myself I'd had feelings for Damian? I had to figure out the right words to use, and fast.

"You're right. I absolutely owe you complete honesty, and that's what I'm about to give you. We can't have anything but honesty between us if we want this to work, not now and not ever." He nodded encouragingly, and I pressed on. "At the time I met Damian and began to get to know him, you were spending time with me, but you were acting more like a big brother than anything else. I thought – I truly believed – you were just being nice, being supportive because of what I was going through. I had no idea you still had feelings for me."

"Becca, come on. I pretty much laid my heart in your lap from that first morning at the hospital. How could you not see how I felt?"

"How? Because the way I remember it, you didn't say a word to me to give me a reason to believe you'd forgiven me, not really. I thought you were just doing the right thing because you still had a few nice memories of our time together, and I'd just lost Richie, and you felt really sorry for me, and..." My voice trailed off. I wasn't sure what to say next.

"My God, woman, I did feel sorry for you! I knew as well as anybody in the world how much you loved your brother and what losing him was sure to do to you. I wanted to do anything I could. I didn't think it was any time to be putting moves on you."

"Are you saying you knew right then you still had feelings for me?"

"Rebecca Irene McCallum, I knew as soon as I walked away from you last year I'd made a stupid decision. I should have stayed and fought it out with you, should have made you see reason."

"You mean you should have made me see how horrible I was behaving, how wrong I was treating you. And you're right, you should have. We both should have done some things differently. But we're back together now, and it feels so right. It is right, Mark. I love you. I never stopped loving you, and I'll love you always."

"But?" He leaned forward, searching my face for something, a sign, I suppose, that I didn't have more to tell. I knew I had to lay it all out for him or I would lose him, for good this time. And I couldn't bear that.

"But, as I said, I really thought you were just being the best friend in the world and nothing more, and when things got settled down, I expected you to sort of go back to the way things were before, I mean with you not having anything to do with me."

He snorted. "You must not have a very good opinion of me, then."

"No, that's not it. I don't have a very good opinion of myself. I know the things I did were selfish and self-centered and immature. I wasn't good enough for you when we were together before, and I don't blame you for walking away. And by the time I realized there might be a chance, if a slim one, for us to maybe get back together, well, I'd met Damian, and we'd spent time together talking about Richie, sharing memories." I shrugged. "It made me feel really close to him, you know?"

"How close?"

"Okay, we kissed – a few times. He held me – a few times. Once after I'd gone through a bad time with Justine, he happened to see me in an anxiety attack, when I felt like I was going crazy. I don't know what I'd have done if he hadn't followed me to the beach that day."

Mark gave me a sharp look. "When was this? What happened at the beach?"

"A few weeks ago. I saw a scene between Justine and Jake that made me sick to my stomach. I went to the beach to try to shake it off, but it wasn't working." My voice dropped to a whisper, as I said, "I was in the middle of an anxiety attack when Damian found me."

"You never told me about that. Why not? I told you I wanted to be there for you whenever you needed someone." I heard pain mixed with anger in his voice, and in the way he kicked at the coffee table with his foot. The old Becca would have enjoyed his show of jealousy and gone into a fit of giggles over the way he looked, but this was no laughing matter and I knew it. *I must be a bit more mature than I used to be. About time!*

"Well, I had to go back to Justine's to pick up Owen – he was coming to spend the night. Damian and I walked on the beach for a while. By the time we went our separate ways, I felt much better, could even joke about having to go face the Wicked Witch. And then Owen said some things that pushed that day out of my mind. By the time I saw you again, it had become not so important to talk about any more."

"So, is that all?" I was blushing and he saw it.

"Becca?"

"I have to tell you this – after we got back here this morning – Damian kissed me." I jumped when Mark kicked at the coffee table and cursed.

"Did you kiss him back?"

I snorted in exasperation, but didn't answer immediately.

"So Damian was there for you when you needed him – twice – and the two of you have shared things you didn't think important enough to share with me."

I was losing patience with him. "Mark, come on! I've told you we had a few encounters. But as time passed, I realized they didn't mean anything to me. Because I never stopped loving you. I couldn't ever love anyone else." *Please let that be the truth.* I reached out a hand, but he clasped both hands behind his head and looked away, and I let my hand fall into my lap. "Fine. If that's the way you want it, I guess there's not really anything I can say to make a difference. Maybe you should leave."

"No, dammit, I don't want to leave! I want us to talk this out. But it's really hard for me to listen to you tell me about another guy holding you and kissing you. Is that all there was to it?"

"Didn't I say that? I don't like having to repeat things like that. Do you believe me or don't you?"

His fingers ruffled his hair, making it stand out in all directions. *Lord, the man's so clueless about his own sexiness.* Still he didn't answer me.

"Okay, that's enough. If you can't even answer me…" I jumped up and headed to the kitchen. "You know the way out."

I hadn't taken three steps when I felt his hands on my shoulders, and he spun me around to face him. I clenched my hands into fists at my side, determined not to let him know how hurt I was, but he slowly slid his hands down my arms again.

"I'm not going anywhere. Neither are you."

"Let me go, Mark." I tilted my chin and looked up at him – which was a mistake. His green eyes, as hard and sharp as emeralds, bored into mine, and I felt a trembling begin in the pit of my stomach and spread outward. Damn, but I loved the man. I waited. Finally, after an eternity, I saw the melting begin, and I saw him begin to accept what I'd been saying. I saw the love come spilling out in his tears, and I felt my own begin as well. "Oh, sweetie, I love you so much. I only thought I loved you before. I didn't really know what love was about. It's you – it's always been you. And it'll always be you. And you believe me, don't you?"

"God help me, Becca, I do. I believe all you've been saying. Come here." He pulled me to him, holding me so tightly I could barely take a breath – and it felt wonderful. I was crying in earnest now, great shuddering sobs I couldn't control. "Hey, hey, I said I believe you. Please stop crying. You're tearing my heart out."

But I couldn't stop. I felt the soft touch of his hand caressing my hair while he whispered words I couldn't understand – and didn't need to. The nicer he was to me, the more I cried. Somewhere in my brain was a synapse trying to tell the tear glands it didn't make sense to keep the waterworks going, but the message wasn't getting through.

"Ahh, hell," he said finally in exasperation, scooping me up in his arms and marching through the kitchen and out the back door. He kicked the screen to behind him and maneuvered us into the swing. "If we can't fix things here, they can't be fixed," he said matter-of-factly.

For some reason this struck me as funny – hilarious, in fact. A small giggle escaped my lips. "Are you laughing? After all the tears, you're honestly laughing now?" The giggle escalated into peals of hysterical laughter, and after a minute I felt Mark's body begin to shake as well.

The tears combined with the wild laughter brought an exhilarating release, and when, minutes later, we were able to pull ourselves together, I nuzzled the side of his neck, just beneath his ear, and moved until my lips were touching his earlobe. "Mom's always told me I should find a man who was willing to laugh with me *and* cry with me. I'm so glad I found him."

"Me too, sweetheart, me too," Mark said, turning his face so our lips met. "We have to take really good care of this swing," he said after a moment, his voice still husky from tears.

What a strange thing to say. "Well, I agree, but what makes you say that right now?" I asked.

"Because this is where we're going to come every time we have a fight. I'm telling you, it's magic. I can't stay mad when I'm sitting here holding you. Don't you feel the same way?"

"You know I've always loved this old swing. Almost as much as I love you. Now kiss me again."

I could feel him smiling in the dark. "With pleasure, woman." He brushed his lips across mine, nipping at my bottom lip and setting my nerve endings aflame. He ran his hand up my back to tangle his fingers in my hair, and I savored the sweet roughness in his kiss.

"Touch me?"

"Like this?" he murmured against my ear before covering my mouth again. His hand kneaded my waist before sliding up to caress my breast.

"Um-hmm," I whimpered.

He breathed in deeply and exhaled. "I love you, Becca – love you with all my heart and soul. I want to show you how much. I want to make love to you."

"Yes, love. Take me upstairs." He stood, holding me as I slid off his retreating lap, and we shared one more earth-shaking kiss before heading indoors. I turned off lights as we went, but when we reached my bedroom I left a lamp burning, not wanting to miss a moment of the rest of this night.

***

I woke the next morning to sunlight streaming across my face and stretched, smiling as the memories from last night came flooding back. I turned my head on the pillow, expecting to see the man I loved – but the other pillow was empty. Maybe Mark was in the shower, but listening I could hear no sound at all.

What if he'd had second thoughts about us? What if he'd slipped out quietly so he wouldn't have to face me and tell me it had all been a mistake? I sat up in bed to get my bearings and my eyes fell on the plaid shirt draped across my reading chair. So he hadn't walked out on me after all. I picked up my phone to check the time: 9:30. Gosh, I hadn't slept this late in weeks.

Guess that's what love will do for you, I thought, slipping out of bed and padding into the bathroom. When I came out of the shower my eyes lit on the shirt again and I couldn't resist. I slipped it on and hugged it tightly around me, breathing in Mark's unique scent of sandalwood and mountain streams. I turned this way and that in front of the mirror to admire how I looked wearing it, smiling to myself as I did up the buttons and rolled up the sleeves. I brushed my dark hair out in long languorous strokes and pulled it forward over both shoulders.

Then I headed downstairs to find my man.

The aromas coming from the kitchen were heavenly. How did I get so lucky? And when did Mark learn to cook?

The doorbell rang just as I reached the top of the stairs and I hurried on down. Mark, however, beat me to the door, and I arrived just in time to see Damian stepping inside. Great, just great. The looks on their faces were priceless though, and I was so happy I couldn't even worry about them all that much. Besides, I had to worry about not bursting into giggles, which would have been entirely inappropriate.

The two men circled each other as if I were some sort of prize...irritating, but still funny. Mark behaved perfectly, though. He was polite, inviting Damian in for coffee. I was uncomfortable in just Mark's shirt and my underwear, even if the shirt did cover more than a pair of shorts would have. It didn't *feel* like more. But it didn't matter, because no way would I leave these two alone to go up to change.

In the kitchen we had coffee and juice and discussed my case. Very professional. The police had no leads on the pickup, as I'd expected. I had a feeling I knew where it was, but I decided not even to mention that idea right now.

About ten minutes later Damian took his leave, and I knew he and I needed to have a talk soon. I'd seen the glances he'd sneaked at Mark and me, had seen the narrowing of those spectacular blue eyes. And I had to admit, the blue eyes combined with the dimples still gave me a tingly feeling deep down inside. But then I'd look over at Mark and there was no contest. I decided I must be just experiencing the residual effects of my infatuation with Damian. Whatever the case, though, he deserved to hear directly from me what was going on. Just as soon as I figured out what *was* going on.

Alone again, Mark and I had breakfast in relative quiet, both of us a bit shy with each other this morning. We didn't discuss Damian at all, for which I gave thanks. Picking up our plates and carrying them to the sink, I felt Mark's eyes following my every move.

"I'll never be able to wear that shirt again without thinking of you, here, this morning." I felt myself blushing, but I was also happy he liked me wearing it. "I'll get those, babe," Mark said, getting up from the table.

"Nope, I have to pay for my breakfast."

He slipped his arms around my waist from behind and pulled me in close against him, splaying his fingers across my belly, and my knees went weak. "I can think of more fun ways for you to pay off your debts."

I dried my hands and turned to give him a kiss. "Then what are we waiting for?"

"Who's waiting?" he laughed, pulling me toward the door. "Race you upstairs!"

Chapter 38

I SHOULD HAVE BEEN GIDDY FROM ALL the love I'd been experiencing over the past few days. And I was. Except for the fact that I didn't hear anything at all from anybody at police headquarters. Most people would have accepted the situation and been able to wait it out. But I wasn't most people.

I called the Chief first thing Monday morning.

"Rebecca, I understand how anxious you must be. All I can tell you is this. That old saying about the wheels of justice grinding exceedingly slow, something along those lines, well it's true. I wish things were moving faster. Just give us a little more time, all right? I promise I'll let you know something just as soon as I can."

I hung up, at least as frustrated as I had been before I called him.

I thought through my options, but kept coming round to the realization I only had one. I went to the junk drawer and found the napkin with Lance Varner's number.

"I'm really glad you called," he said in that soft drawl.

We discussed our situation and hashed over possible meeting places. In the end, we decided to meet at the Vietnam Memorial just in front of the small craft harbor, next to the Hard Rock casino. I considered it a decent compromise…close to *The Seasoned Wench*, the boat Lance was tending, yet in a fairly busy public place. Sort of like hiding in plain sight, I thought. We agreed to meet the following Saturday morning at ten.

***

Next I set about taking care of the alarm system. Only after the installer arrived would Mark consent to going off to work. I did a bit of cleaning, but it was no use. Staying inside drove me crazy. I decided to visit the tree house, hoping for some inspiration, something to lead me in the right direction. Things were coming to a head – I could feel it in the air.

I thought of how different my situation was to Richie's. Clearly a great deal of planning had gone into his attack. They were getting sloppy with me, though, almost as if the murderer had decided that if the police labeled whatever might happen to me an accident, that'd be great, but if they called it murder, the perpetrator still felt safe from discovery.

I'm not nearly so sure they can't be found out.

With nothing better to do, I hunted up my notebook and began to sift through things I'd written at different times. I worked a good two hours, then stood and stretched, trying to get the kinks out of my back and shoulders. I'd been so caught up in my thoughts I hadn't realized how long I'd been hunched over my notebook. Feeling more relaxed, but excited at the same time, I sat back down and began to read over my notes. Things had finally come into focus for me, at least I thought so. Right now I needed to look at the big picture one more time, to be sure I'd reached the right conclusion. I couldn't afford to make accusations until I was completely certain – and some aspects of this case almost defied me.

I'd written a summary about two pages long, and now I began to pore over it.

What are my main reasons for not believing the official report has it right?

1. Richie was shot in the back of the head, from the side. Sounds like execution. How could one person do that? Besides, Richie was too smart to fall for some charade, too strong for Tommy H. to take his gun from him, too good at his job to get caught off-guard.

2. Several people would have benefited from him being dead. Justine would have gotten her freedom, Owen, lots of money, and Jake. Jake would have gotten Justine, along with part of the money. He does have a backer for his fitness center. Paul would have benefited because he would have had

Richie off his back. Not a good enough reason. I'd already removed Damian from the list.

***

I glanced at my phone's clock: four-fifteen. I planned to cook for Mark tonight, and it was too late to go investigating – businesses would be closing soon. I closed the notebook and took it with me as I headed back across the backyard. I paused a second on the porch to smile down at the swing, remembering last night.

Well, Richie, people are always telling us something good can come out of something really terrible. With your death, it's clear – for me that was bringing Mark back to me.

I went inside to get my keys and purse and had almost made it out the door when my phone rang.

"Hey, babe, everything okay with you?" Mark's voice, silky-smooth like warm honey, turned my insides into a quivering mess. How could one little question do that to me?

"I'm fine, how about you? What time do you think you'll be home?" *Did I ask him when he was coming home?*

A slight hesitation told me yes, I had asked him that. "About seven, I think, if nothing else happens around here. Need me to pick up anything for dinner?"

"Thanks, but I'm headed out now to shop."

"Oh, your turn tonight?"

"You bet. Mark?"

"Hmm?"

"I love you."

"Love you too, sweetheart."

I stood for a moment in the front hall, thinking about our exchange, which had sounded so normal, so ordinary. How great it would be if we could get this situation sorted out and live like normal people. I could almost hear Richie saying, "Now you're talking, Sis."

***

I enjoyed making dinner for Mark. *Wonder how long that'll last?* I'd boiled fresh shrimp from the pier and fixed lots of sides to go with them. We ate until most of the shrimp were gone and we could barely move.

"Think we might try the swing for a while?" Mark asked, nuzzling my neck as I scraped our plates.

"If you keep that up, we can sit anywhere you want."

"I'll have to keep that in mind," he said with a leer as he spun me around for a prolonged kiss. "C'mon woman, leave these. I'll do 'em later."

With that offer, I dropped the dishtowel and we headed out back.

After a few minutes of cuddling and kissing, which tended to distract me from what I'd intended, I decided I'd better stop putting off telling Mark what I'd been up to today.

"Can I talk to you about something?"

"Always, and anything," he said against my ear before he began to nibble. He knew I couldn't help giggling when he did that.

"I'm serious," I said, twisting away from him. "And I think we need to go back in the house."

Over his noisy protests I dragged him through to the living room where I'd left my notebook earlier. He tried to pull me down on the couch beside him but I held my ground, and finally he sat, feigning anger but his eyes sparkling. I picked up my notebook and sat down at the far end of the couch facing him, one leg tucked under me.

"What'cha got there?"

"My notebook about Richie's murder." I struggled to keep my voice level. He sat up straight and leaned forward, giving out a long, low whistle.

"Sorry, baby. I didn't know this was what you wanted to talk about. But what do you mean, your notebook about his murder? What's in it?"

So I told him all of it. How I'd been obsessing over the situation ever since he'd gone with me out to the barn. How I hadn't been sleeping much. About my suspicions of almost everybody, and how and why I'd discounted first one and then another.

"Let me get this straight. You have discounted both Paul Simmons and our friend Damian. You suspected Justine, but now you think her being involved is unlikely. Jake, you thought about him longest, then almost discounted him, but now you're almost convinced he's involved, along with his boss. You thought about Justine and Jake together, but you're willing to give Justine the benefit of the doubt, because of your suspicions about Jake's boss. And you still have Paul Simmons on the list because of all these allegations, and the fact that Richard knew about them. Does that about cover it?"

"Pretty much." His raised eyebrows and half smile told he was still skeptical. He ran a finger across his top lip and tilted his head to the side.

"You don't think I'm on the right track, do you? Why not?" I sounded defensive, but dammit, I'd put hours and days and weeks into thinking about this. "I get the feeling you've just been playing along with me when we talk about this. Do you think I've imagined the whole thing about someone trying to kill me, too?" I leapt off the couch and stood looking out the front window into the darkness, arms folded across my chest. I understood Mark about as well as I could see from here into Mrs. Goodson's living room – through her heavy brocade drapes.

"Becca, you know better than that – don't you?" He came to stand beside me, but I pulled away from him and sat down in the first chair I came to. He knelt in front of me and placed his hands on my knees. "Sweetie, look at me." With one hand he tilted my chin so I was looking straight into those green eyes – smoky and full of fire. "Now, listen…are you listening?" His hands moved to my thighs and he kneaded gently, making it kind of hard for me to listen at all. *Sorry Richie. He's just so darned attractive, you know?*

"I'm listening," I said, more for my benefit than for his.

"It was just a few days ago somebody tried to kill you. Haven't I been completely supportive of you since then? Do you doubt that I believe what you say happened, happened? Because I do believe you. Why else do you think I've been going crazy whenever I have to leave you alone? It was hell being at work all day today and fighting the urge to call you every half hour to make sure you were okay. But I knew you wouldn't appreciate that." He gave me a wry grin and I couldn't help smiling myself.

"So do you want to hear my theory about what happened?"

"Sure thing – if you'll come back over here with me. I don't like you being halfway across the room." He stood and held out his hands and I took them, letting him lead me to the couch and settle me back where I'd been. "Okay, I'm listening. Lay it on me."

So I began to talk, and the more I talked out loud about things, the clearer they became even to me. After a while I could see Mark's face change and I realized he was no longer humoring me but had come to believe the scenario I'd laid out was more plausible than the one we'd been given by the police.

"Simmons would still be high on my suspect list. Do you have any other reasons to suspect him?"

"Only that he seems to be protesting his innocence a bit too loudly."

"I'm with you, Beck. But I can't see Jake being innocent here – he's just too involved at too many levels."

"I know this Bert guy is involved as much as Tommy was. Could Jake have been helping? Very likely. But how do I prove it?"

"How do *we* prove it, you mean. I do not want you to do any more investigating by yourself. I've gotta make you believe me. I can't live without you, Becca. I tried it for more than a year, and it just didn't work. You've got to stop putting yourself in the line of fire. I promise I'll help you, but you've got to give me a chance, instead of always going off on your own." He stretched his legs out on the sofa between us, nudging my hip with his toes.

"I see you lost your shoes again."

"Don't try to change the subject. I'm serious."

"Okay, fine. I won't 'investigate' alone, or without you knowing where I am and what I'm doing. Is that agreeable?"

"I don't know – seems you gave yourself some wiggle room there. But we'll hash that out later. Come here, woman." He swung his legs down and held out his arms, and I crawled down the couch; I laid my head in his lap to look up at him.

"I don't want to fight about this," I said and reached up to drag his face down to mine. When our lips didn't quite meet, I giggled. I wormed my way backward until I was sitting propped up against the arm of the sofa, and we tried again. This time we got it right.

***

I thought we would discuss my upcoming meeting with Lance later that night, but somehow the time never seemed right. Part of me, I had to admit, dreaded getting into another argument with Mark when we were getting along so well. I put off telling him until Thursday, when I knew I could no longer delay. As I'd expected, he hit the roof.

"I've been waiting for you to tell me about your day," Mark said, "but I guess you're going to make me beg."

We'd tried sitting out in the swing, but it was too hot for me. So we were cozily ensconced back inside where the air was nice and cold, lounging on the sofa. We faced each other, each with a glass of wine, my feet propped comfortably across his stretched out legs.

He set his wine aside. "Ooh, that feels great," I sighed, as his hands began to knead the soles of my feet. "I'd forgotten how good you were at that."

I took a deep breath and said, "I'm planning to meet Lance Varner down by the harbor on Saturday morning." He stopped massaging my foot, his hands and his face both absolutely still. I wiggled my foot to remind him of what he was supposed to be doing, but he still stared at me.

"My God, Becca, are you crazy? Going off alone to a place like that, meeting up with some guy you don't even know? You're liable to get yourself killed, or worse, if you keep doing crap like that." He removed my feet from his lap and sat up straight.

"I'm being careful, Mark. I'm sure he can help me find out what really happened with Richie. I know it's tied to Bert's body shop."

"Exactly!" he exploded. He ran his hands through his neatly arranged brown hair I'd decided was the color of English walnuts. "You're right…it does seem like there must be a tie to what happened to Richie. But that's even more reason why you don't need to be asking questions and making people suspicious. You sure as hell don't need to be thinking about meeting this guy."

Now it was my turn to explode. "What? I will if I think there's a chance to help me, and I do," I said, swinging my feet to the floor. "If he has information I need, why wouldn't I go?"

"Why wouldn't... Well, I can give you a few reasons. One, you don't know anything about this guy. He could be trying to lure you down there for his own reasons. Two, you don't know if he really has useful information. Three, he could be the murderer himself – or did you even think about that?" He briskly paced figure eights around the room.

I had to admit I hadn't thought about that last point. But I shrugged my shoulders in what I hoped was a casual manner. "I'll only meet him in a public place. I'm not worried he'd try anything. Besides, Glenda at the Rib Shack said he was a good guy."

He stopped pacing and looked at me incredulously. "And you're taking the word of someone you just met? Who's Glenda, anyway?"

"The waitress and cashier at the Rib Shack. She seemed like a really nice girl."

"Unbelievable. You waltz into a place you heard about from somebody you don't know, who you met while you were asking weird questions at a body shop where the guy who's supposed to have killed your brother used to work, and you don't think there's anything dangerous about that?"

"The Rib Shack is a nice barbecue place," I protested.

"I'm not talking about the damn Rib Shack! I'm talking about your actions taken all together. Rebecca, you don't seem to understand this is serious business, and you really have no idea who all the players may be."

Rebecca. Uh-oh, not a good sign.

I crossed the room to wrap my arms around his waist. His body was stiff and unyielding. "Mark, it's you who doesn't seem to understand. No, wait..." This as he tried to pull away from me. "Listen. I lost my brother less than two months ago, and except for you, nobody seems concerned we may not know the whole truth about that night. I have to know, can't you see that?"

I leaned back to see if he was listening; his jaw muscles flexed as he struggled to control his anger.

"I know, Becca, believe me, I do understand. But if we're right – if you're right – then somebody made some extremely elaborate plans to get to Richard that night. Who's to say they aren't making similar plans for you this minute?" He placed his hands gently on my shoulders. "I couldn't make it if something happened to you." His voice broke on that last word and he hugged me close.

I felt a vibration between us, unsure whether it came from Mark or from me. In truth, it must have been coming from both of us. We were strung as tight as mistuned strings on a Fender guitar.

"I want to do this," I said, my voice muffled against his chest. "I just need to, that's all."

"I know you do. But I don't have to like it. Now, I think I'd better go." He started toward the door.

"Mark, don't leave here mad, please."

"I need time to think. Maybe we've been moving a little too fast. I'm not sure either one of us is ready to get back into a deep relationship." He stared into my eyes for a long moment, then said, "God, Becca, you're a special woman, but I can't take this craziness."

"But I just…"

He held up a hand to stop me. "I know you think you have to do this. But I want you to think about something. I've been here for you as much as I possibly could be, and I'd do it over again. What we had before was something special, and I'd begun to think we were onto something even better this time. But if you can't understand I'm worrying myself sick about you, then maybe you haven't changed as much as I thought you had. I just need time to think."

I put a hand on his arm. "Mark, don't go."

He looked at the ceiling, sighed, and then slowly shook his head. His eyebrows, those perfect brows my fingers itched to trace, were drawn together into a deep scowl. "G'night, Becca. Be careful, whatever you do. And let me know if you find out anything." He kissed the top of my head, turned, and walked out the door.

Please don't walk out of my life again.

I turned out the lights and went up to bed, determined to show Mark I could take care of myself. I would meet with Lance on Saturday, then I'd re-evaluate my way of doing things.

Chapter 39

THE CLOCK ON THE CITIZEN'S BANK read 9:45 when I headed to the marina on Saturday morning. My stomach was in knots but I was determined to see this through. I'd tried to forget about the argument with Mark until after this meeting. Thing was, I'd never been involved in anything remotely clandestine and I really didn't know what I was doing. Would Lance expect payment for what he had to tell me? Would he want the payment up front? And what *was* the going rate for snitches these days?

Technically, I thought, he wouldn't be classified as a snitch. Don't snitches get that name by providing information to the police? With me he'd only be sharing information – sort of like gossip. I was still thinking about the terms I needed to use when I made the light and turned into the parking lot in front of the marina.

As we had arranged, I chose a bench under the Vietnam Memorial's spreading oak and parked nearby. I rolled down my windows about an inch to keep Bernice from exploding. The temperature wasn't so bad; after all, it was only mid-morning. By this afternoon temps would be in the high nineties with the humidity almost the same. *Best get this meeting over with so I can get back home under the AC for the rest of my Saturday.* Grabbing my keys and cell phone, I tucked them in my pocket and settled myself on the bench, leaning an elbow over the back of the seat so I could keep watch on both the parking lot and the boats at anchor behind me.

By ten fifteen I'd begun to think Lance might not show up. I walked back to the car for a sip of water and stared at the two motorcycles in the parking lot, wondering if either belonged to Lance. *Some detective you'd make. Rebecca my girl, you'd better brush up on your skills of observation if you want to be successful at this.* Where did that thought come from? I didn't necessarily *want* to be a detective – I simply wanted to find out who'd murdered my brother. For the first time I felt like I was making progress, but I wished Lance would show up so we could get this over with.

By ten thirty, I couldn't sit still another minute. What if Lance had changed his mind, decided it was too dangerous to talk to me? What if someone had gotten to him? What if he'd become too afraid of losing his job? But if that were the case, it would lend credence to my growing conviction that Bert's Auto Body Shop was at the epicenter of the mystery surrounding Richie's death. *We're so close, Richie – I can feel it. I just need a few more days, a few more pieces of the puzzle.* I willed Lance to appear in front of me. When that didn't work, I decided to check out the boat he'd told me about.

I stepped out onto the wooden pier and began to check the boats moored there. I'd gone almost to the end of the first row when I saw it – saw *her*, I mean – *The Seasoned Wench.* The boat appeared to be deserted. I stood for a moment admiring the sleek craft, which looked to be somewhere between thirty and forty feet long. The boat was well-maintained. It gleamed from one end to the other. The rigging appeared to be neatly and correctly stowed – to my untrained eye at least – and both the name and the stripes along the side of the boat had been recently painted – Lance's work, probably.

Well, so much for this little foray; I should have stayed in bed this morning. As I turned away, intending to give up the chase, I glimpsed something large in the water, bobbing almost underneath the pier, which might explain why I hadn't noticed it before now. A chill completely at odds with the heat of the morning shook me; I had a sinking feeling I knew what I'd find if I stepped closer. I didn't want to see but something compelled to look all the same. I edged closer to the open-sided dock, grabbed onto a piling and slowly leaned forward.

A strangled cry erupted from my throat and I stepped back so quickly and violently I came near to going off the other side of the pier backward. I grabbed another piling just in time – out of reflex, to be sure, because I wasn't making rational decisions at that point. I clung to the piling a few seconds, shaking all over, looking to see if anyone was nearby, but all looked deserted. I hurried back onto dry land, away from the nightmare behind me.

My knees sank onto the scorching sand. It burned my skin but I couldn't get farther away, because just then my stomach clenched and emptied itself of its contents. When I finished, I spat once and wiped my mouth on the hem of my blouse, willing away the bitter taste. With my eyes closed, I could not will away what I'd just seen. The scene played over and over: the shirt billowing loosely away from the already bloated body, the hair I thought I recognized from last week, the large gash on the back of the head.

Shuddering, I looked across the marina, searching for someone, anyone, who might be around the boats. I didn't see a soul – but then I heard the sound of an engine trying to start. Someone *was* out here, somewhere. I waited until the traffic quieted once more and then yelled, "Hello! Anybody there? I need help! Please, anybody!" I could hear panic setting into my voice, and I could feel the raw edges of an anxiety attack twining around the back side of my brain. I yelled once more for help, and then I heard it…an answering shout.

I saw him then, a gray-bearded man with a balding head leaning out of one of the boats on the other side. "What's up?" he yelled in a friendly voice.

"Help! I need the police! There's…there's been…" but there my voice trailed off and I began to cry, my body shaking there in the sand. I didn't see him come off his boat, but the next thing I knew he was kneeling beside me, making grandfatherly sounds, trying to comfort me while asking what was wrong at the same time.

All I could do was point down the walkway, my finger shaking so badly I lowered it again quickly and clasped both hands in my lap.

"It's a person, a body," I choked out. "He's in the water. Down there."

"You don't mean it!" he said, but then looked at me closely and answered himself: "Of course you do, poor girl."

I watched him scurry down the walkway, looking from one side to the other as he went along. I didn't have the strength to yell again; besides, I think I hoped I'd imagined the whole thing. Then I saw his body jerk, and he backed up and leaned over, beside *The Seasoned Wench*, and I knew. This was no dream; it was real…all too real.

After a moment of staring over the side, the man hurried back to me. "Have you got a phone?" he asked. I nodded, pulling my cell from the pocket of my shorts. I held it out to him.

"I don't think I can call." My tears started again, and I said, "I'm about to be sick again." I scooted a few feet from my last mess and started my breathing exercises. In through the nose, count four, hold four, breathe out through the mouth to the count of four, repeat. Thinking through the exercise did help a bit. I felt the queasiness begin to abate, and I finally stopped bawling. I wiped away the tears with the back of my hand and looked over at the man, who had his back turned to me and was speaking quietly but clearly into the phone.

"Yes, that's right. We're at the Biloxi Small Craft Harbor. There's a body in the water out next to one of the boats. No, I don't see anyone else around. Yes, we'll do that. Yes, we'll be right here. Hurry, please."

He came over to where I'd settled myself and squatted beside me, looking me over without saying anything for a minute. "I believe you'll be all right now. I know this was a shock for a young woman such as yourself. Tell the truth, it shocked me, too." He laid a tentative hand on my shoulder and patted softly.

"Thank you," I said shakily. "I don't know what I'd have done if you hadn't been here. I've never been through anything like this before."

"Me neither," he said with a nervous chuckle. "Hope we never do again, don't you?"

I looked up into watery blue eyes that, even though we were in the midst of this horrible nightmare, still held a touch of humor. "Ah, it's probably somebody that's had a heart attack," he said.

"But what about the big gash on his head?"

"Could have hit it on something and then fell off into the water. Just have to wait and see what the experts have to say."

"Yeah, if we can trust them to get it right," I muttered.

The man gave me a strange look. "What's that?"

"Nothing. Never mind. I'm sort of rambling I guess."

Within minutes, sirens sounded from all directions. The first to arrive were two white city vehicles. Seeing the man waving, the officer in the lead car drove onto the lot and straight over to the edge of the pavement. The other car blocked the entrance to the marina, I supposed to keep anyone else from driving in.

Suddenly, out of nowhere, Mark was there, pushing and shoving, trying to get to me, a police officer holding him back.

"Becca, are you okay? What's going on?" he yelled. He had stopped fighting against the officer, but his eyes were still wild and he looked like he might take a swing at any moment.

"I'm all right, Mark. Stay there. I'll come to you." I got up and began to walk toward them. "Is that okay, officer?"

"And who are you, ma'am?"

"My name's Rebecca McCallum. I think I was the first person to find the body...over there." I gestured toward the slips. "That man can show you."

"Sure thing." He smiled, tipping his cap to me. *He knows I'm Richie's sister.* He moved off to consult with the man who'd helped me.

"Becca," Mark said, grabbing my hands. "You're cold as ice!" He gathered me into his arms and held me tight, chafing my arms briskly. After a minute he held me away from him to look into my face, as if only then would he really know whether or not I was okay.

"It was horrible. It made me sick. I know I smell terrible, but..."

"Don't worry about that. But what were you doing here, anyway?"

"Me? What are *you* doing here?"

"I was meeting with one of our suppliers across the street, and I noticed your car out by the road, didn't see you anywhere. Thought I'd better come see if you were all right. As I started across the street, these two cops showed up, and then I really freaked out. I took off over the fence and then I saw you over here, and, well, here I am."

"You're weird, Mark Barrington, you know that? How did you manage to be here when I need you?"

"I hope I always will be," he said huskily.

I turned to watch the scene on the pier, and again Mark wrapped his arms around me; I felt warm and safe. Then I remembered.

"Mark?"

"Hmm?"

"You knew I was supposed to meet Lance this morning…"

I felt his arms around me stiffen slightly. "Yeah, so?"

I whirled to search his face, suddenly suspicious. "Did you really have a meeting, or were you spying on me?"

"I was *not* 'spying' on you! I just wanted to make sure you were safe. Didn't do a very good job of that, now did I?" He gave me a sheepish grin.

"Well, I'm glad you're here…but I am still mad at you," I said. "You didn't trust me to handle myself here alone."

"Didn't do such a good job, did you?" he muttered against my hair.

I pulled away from him. "I think I did fine, except for losing my breakfast."

"You know what I mean, don't you?" he asked.

"Oh, I guess so. Yes, as it turns out, it wasn't such a good idea after all."

"There may be hope for you after all, Ms. McCallum," he said, hugging me close once again.

"Becca!" Damian, looking sweaty but yummy in shorts, a tank top, and running shoes, was jogging toward us. "You all right? What's happened?"

"She's fine," Mark answered for me. "Or she will be, as soon as I can get her away from here."

"What's going on? Gotta be something major."

"I found a man floating in the water. Dead." My voice still shook, and Mark hugged me tighter. "Over there."

"Wentworth, is that you?" It was Chief Sikes's voice. He strode up to where we were all standing. "Rebecca? What are you doing here? Are you all right?"

I gave a shaky laugh, thinking I might be near hysteria.

"What's funny about this?" Mark growled.

"Nothing." I sobered. "But you all keep asking me the same questions."

"That's because we're all worried about you, Becca," Damian said grumpily.

"Excuse me, but I'd better get this taken care of. See you folks in a bit." He tipped his Stetson and stalked off, like a tugboat plowing its way across the bay.

"I wish we could get out of here. Why do you need to stay?" Mark asked.

"Because I found the body, I expect."

"Where was this?" Damian asked.

"Out there." I jerked my head toward the far end of the dock where several people had congregated to confer. "Close to the *Seasoned Wench.* About fifteen minutes before you got here."

Mark led me across the parking lot to a shady bench within the stilts of the Harbor Master's Building and Damian followed. They were acting like two schoolboys circling each other, preparing to duke it out. *Over me? Interesting. Have to think about this later… Rebecca, that thought is beneath you.*

"What were you doing here, Becca?" This from Damian.

"What concern is it of yours?" This from Mark.

"Would both of you stop it? I just discovered a dead body, nasty and bloated from the water. I lost my breakfast, I'm hot and sweaty, and I have lots on my mind. So cool it, okay?"

"Sorry, babe," Mark said, taking my hand.

Damian stood a few feet away, legs spread, arms folded across his muscled chest, scowling. "I'm sorry too, Becca. That has got to be hard on you. Have you given them your statement yet?"

"No, they haven't really even talked to me. I wish they'd hurry up. I'm ready to get out of these clothes."

As I said this, I heard a grunt from Damian and looked up to see him looking toward the dock. Following his gaze I saw Chief Sikes striding across the lot toward us. Maybe we were about to get this show on the road.

Chapter 40

"REBECCA, I THINK YOU AND I NEED TO TALK. What say we go inside the harbor master's office?" The Chief had a notebook and pen in one hand, so I stood up from my bench.

"Sure, whatever you say. Let's get this over with."

"You two guys stay out of these folks' way. I don't know how long this is going to take us." I had the feeling he thought both men were being nuisances, but personally I was glad they'd been here. I gave them both a weak smile and went with the Chief.

As we climbed the stairs to the office, I saw the Medical Examiner's van pull into the lot, followed by another van, this one black, with the words "Crime Scene Unit" in gold on its side.

The office was empty, and it was nice and cool, with a desk and chair and a couple of comfortable looking green leather visitors' chairs. The Chief motioned me into one of these and took the other himself.

I laid both arms out along the chair's cool arms. "This feels wonderful! I was about to melt out there."

"Oh, I don't know," the Chief drawled. "It felt kind of frosty to me." His eyebrows were arched and I knew he wanted to ask a question, but he was too old school for that. I couldn't believe he was trying to joke at a time like this.

"Let's get down to business, what do you say?" I nodded, trying to hold in another shiver. "What brought you down to the marina this morning?"

I told him I was supposed to meet a guy named Lance Varner, somebody who worked at Bert's.

He grunted. Prompted by the Chief, I described Lance the best I could. I told him about Lance not showing up, and my getting nervous, and of going down to the boats to look for him. When I got to the point of describing the body I said, "I've never seen anything like that before."

"I'm sorry you had to see it at all."

"How do you guys handle this kind of call? You must see things like this, and worse, all the time. I don't see how you do it."

"If anybody ever tells you it gets easier with time, they're not being honest."

"Richie said something like that to me once. But he said the worst part, no matter what kind of shape a body had been in, was still notifying the next of kin. But I don't see how that could be worse than seeing and smelling the things y'all must."

"Well, Rebecca, he may have been right, but this part is plenty hard enough. Now, I need to ask you some more specific questions. How long have you known Lance Varner?"

"I don't really know him. I saw him for the first time last week when I went to Bert's, and then again at the Rib Shack. He offered to carry my bags to the car."

"Did he work there?"

"No, he was eating, I think – I didn't really notice. I'd been talking to the girl at the counter, waiting for my order, and when it was ready he was leaving, too. She told me he was an okay guy, so I let him help me."

"And did anything else happen, other than him carrying your bags out? Did he say anything unusual to you?"

I'd been dreading this part. "Yes, he did. He told me he knew who I was and what I was doing, and said he had some information I needed to know. He seemed worried someone would see us talking there, and he asked if I'd meet him somewhere. He gave me his number and I called him a few days ago."

"What did he mean, he knew what you were doing?"

"Chief, don't get upset with me. I went to Bert's hoping to find someone who would talk to me about Tommy."

Sikes snorted. "Rebecca, I told you to let us handle all of that. Now see what it's got you into?"

I gulped audibly. "So you're saying it *was* Lance I found?"

"I shouldn't say anything about that," he hedged, but then nodded. "There has been a tentative I.D."

"I won't say anything until you say it's okay."

"That includes to those two out there." He jerked his head and gave me a stern look. "Don't let them push you into talking about this case. The fewer people involved right now, and the less they know, the better."

"I understand. But I don't know much myself." I was getting a bit testy...it had been a long morning. "You don't need to treat me like a child, Chief!"

He stared at me for a long moment, then gave an exasperated sigh. "Don't I? You're out there snooping around town, trying to find out if somebody planned to kill your brother. I've told you my people are checking all that out. You need to let us do our jobs, and you need to stay out of it. Your dad will never forgive me if I let something happen to you."

"I'm trying to be careful. I just asked general questions, and I didn't get anywhere with those guys anyway. Except maybe Lance."

"But you don't know who you might have antagonized. You're in over your head and you need to stop. I need you to promise me you *will* stop."

"I would say I think you're overreacting, if it weren't for that body out there."

"Good girl. Now, let's finish this up and get you out of here."

Half an hour later Chief Sikes was satisfied he knew all that I knew, and we walked out of the office together. The steamy heat blasted my face as soon as I stepped out of the building. I could feel my lips drying out and my skin starting to wrinkle. I reached for my bag to get lip balm, then remembered it was in the car.

Mark and Damian sat at opposite ends of the bench I'd vacated almost an hour earlier. Both men jumped to their feet when they saw us. I looked from one to the other, not sure how to approach them. Mark made the decision for me.

"Beck, are you free to go? I think we need to be getting you home."

The Chief nodded his approval. "I'll be in touch, Rebecca, if I need anything else from you. Just remember what we talked about." With a nod, he turned back toward the dock.

"So what's been going on while I was inside?"

"The CSU brought a tent and set up a place to work from out of the sun. They took the body away a few minutes ago. But the CSIs will probably be here a few more hours," Damian said.

"You ready to go?" Mark asked again, impatiently this time.

I nodded. "Damian, thanks for being here, and for being concerned about me. I'll call you later, okay?"

He dimpled at this, cocking an eyebrow at Mark as if to say, "Back to you." *Guys.*

Mark draped an arm over my shoulder (*Protectively or possessively? Not sure*), and we walked toward the street. I nodded toward Bernice, sitting forlornly under her tree.

"Think she'll be okay there for a while? I don't really feel like driving by myself right now."

"She'll be fine. We'll come back later if you're up to it."

"Okay, just let me get my purse."

He waited while I did so. "Now let's get you home, and you can tell me about your talk with Chief Sikes."

"About that..." He stopped walking and gave me a questioning look. "He told me not to discuss it with anybody yet." He frowned but didn't say anything else.

How hard are the next few days going to be?

Chapter 41

MARK INSISTED ON STAYING WITH ME after we got back to the house, and I confess I was glad he did. Rattling around that big house all alone for the rest of the weekend wasn't something I looked forward to. I finally got my appetite back by the afternoon, after I had about a two hour nap, and we decided to go out for dinner.

"What did you do while I slept?" I asked, coming downstairs about three that afternoon.

"Well, let's see. I replaced the light bulb in your utility room, oiled the chain on the swing, and watched a movie."

I giggled. "I should find a body every weekend."

"Bite your tongue, woman!" He shook me by the shoulders, but he was wearing a wry grin.

I heard "Jackson" playing somewhere and went looking for my cell phone. I finally found it on the kitchen counter. "Hey, Damian," I said breathlessly.

He didn't say anything right away, and when he did I thought I could hear a strain in his voice. "Becca, how are you? Am I interrupting something? I can call back."

No, that's fine. I just couldn't find my phone," I laughed.

He chuckled too, and I realized he might have jumped to the wrong conclusion.

"I'd just thought about calling you. I know I promised I would. But we sat and talked for a while, and then I went up to take a nap. I don't know how, but I slept for almost two hours."

"You had a shock this morning, after all."

"It's good of you to call. I'm feeling much better now. In fact, we were making plans to go out to find a bite to eat." I hesitated, but then plunged ahead. "Why don't you join us?"

"Umm, I don't think that would be such a good idea. I'd love to see you, don't get me wrong. But I think three would definitely be a crowd tonight. Y'all go on and have a good time. Can I call you tomorrow?"

"I'd like that. Thanks again for today."

"Anytime, lady. Good night."

I hit the off button and laid the phone back on the counter. When I turned around Mark was standing inside the door looking at me like I was the Rosetta Stone and he was trying to decipher my language.

***

We ate at the Paradise, and as I'd hoped, Lorelei and Bob joined us. When Bob and Mark got into an involved conversation about work, I managed to give Lorelei an abbreviated version of the morning's adventure.

She took sides with everybody else, telling me to lay off the investigating.

"You're not Miss Marple, and this is not a 'cozy mystery,' you know. This is real life, and it could well be life or death. Don't want anything to happen to you, kiddo."

My entire list of acquaintances seemed to know what was best for me better than I did. I decided to give it a rest. "Okay, okay. I don't want anything to happen to me, either. Now let's relax and forget about it. I promise to behave."

"Good girl. Hey guys, let's have a toast: To Becca's decision to behave!"

We all clinked glasses, and Mark's green eyes smoldered as he stared into mine over his glass. I smiled, holding his gaze for what seemed an eternity.

Back at home I swallowed my pride and asked Mark if he'd spend the night, even though I didn't want him looking on me as a helpless female.

"I'm going to make cocoa," I said, once we'd gotten settled in. "I know it's hot outside, but I've felt chilled all day long. Want to come with me?"

"Right behind you."

***

Shortly, we were settled on the sofa with our mugs and a bowl of popcorn, flipping through movie choices on Netflix. I pushed for a love story and Mark held out for a comedy, so we compromised and loaded *Love, Actually*.

"It's still a love story," he groused, and I slapped him on the shoulder.

"But hilarious, too," I protested. "Hey, sweetie, I was talking to Damian the other day. Guess what he told me?"

"He's moving back to Jackson?" I made a face at him.

"No, silly. He went to Ole Miss, too. Y'all share the same alma mater."

"That better be all we share." His voice was like velvet, but his words, I knew, were like steel.

"I'm going to ignore that remark."

An hour or so into the movie I scooted down to Mark's end of the sofa. Wise or not, I needed to be held, and I knew how strong his arms could feel.

He opened his arms and I slid inside, nestling back close against his ribcage. I could feel the steady beat of his heart against my spine. He shifted a bit, kicked off his loafers, and rested his feet on the coffee table.

"Feels like old times," he murmured against my hair, and I felt his hand gently smoothing a few stray tendrils.

"Thank you," I said, sighing with the relief that this awful day was almost done.

"Anytime, Becca," he whispered. "You should know that by now."

I breathed in his familiar scent – a mix of sandalwood, spices, and mountain streams – and sighed contentedly.

I think I dozed for a bit, because I jerked when I felt Mark's body shift, though I realized he was trying not to disturb me. "It's okay, I'm awake," I mumbled. "Is the movie over?"

He laughed and I could feel the rumble in his chest – a pleasant sensation. I sat upright, swinging my legs off the sofa. "Sorry, hon, but my arm's gone to sleep." He stood and unfolded himself from his cramped position, stretching his arms overhead. His shirttail was untucked, his hair tousled, his eyelids drooping. He looked sexy as hell.

I yawned in sympathy with him. "It's getting late. Think it's time we turned in. Need anything before we go up?"

"Just this," he said, putting his hands on my waist and pulling me to him. I expected a kiss – I wanted it, but I hadn't been prepared for the vehemence of my response. I couldn't get close enough to him, couldn't taste him enough, couldn't stand the thought of his mouth separating from mine. He pulled away before I did, holding me at arm's length to smile down at me, emerald eyes dancing.

"God, I love you, woman." He drew me close again. I felt his body shaking and knew mine was doing the same.

"I love you, too," I said, gently extricating myself from his embrace. "I just want this to all be over. I want to live just an ordinary life, no excitement at all. And I'm exhausted."

He brought my hands to his lips. I felt like a heroine in a Jane Austen novel – and immediately felt ashamed of making light of this moment.

"I get what you're saying," he said. "This has been a helluva summer for you, and now it's getting dangerous, too. I'm staying with you tonight to make you feel safe, not so we can make love. It's just..." He ran a hand through his hair and sighed. "You feel so damn good in my arms I want to hold you there forever. But you're right – you need rest."

I nodded. "I probably shouldn't have asked you to stay. I'll be fine now if you want to go on home."

"No, I'm here and I'm staying. But I do think it's time to call it a night. Let's get you to bed." I didn't know whether I was glad or disappointed that all we did was sleep.

By Sunday the local paper and TV stations were all over the story of the man found dead at the marina. They weren't privy to a name yet, but they speculated nonetheless. I almost found it funny. One station thought it might have something to do with the local drug trade, and another that it had the signature of a mob hit. *If they only knew.*

***

It was a few days later that I finally got the call I'd been waiting for. Chief Sikes phoned to tell me Lance's death had officially been ruled a homicide. Hearing the words, I shivered so hard I almost dropped my phone.

"Rebecca, I want to caution you to be extra careful while we work on finding out who was responsible for Varner's murder. Don't you go around asking any more questions, you hear?"

"I'll try not to."

"Don't *try* not to, just don't do it. You're gonna get yourself into a fix you can't get yourself out of. And there's not always going to be somebody there to help you when you get into trouble."

I heard what he was saying, but I couldn't stop myself from asking, "So, what's your office doing about all of this, Lance's murder, the car thefts, everything? Don't you think there's got to be some kind of connection here?"

There was silence for a minute, and I wondered if Sikes was about to give me one of his fatherly lectures.

"Let's just say that we are aware of many connections at varying levels. But we have to have more evidence than we have now, or we won't be able to get a judge to issue any search warrants."

"Search warrants – what are you looking for?" I felt more excited than I had in weeks. The police seemed finally about ready to start earning their pay.

"Forget I just said that," he muttered. "Just be sure you do as I say and don't put yourself into dangerous situations. Just try to be patient. We *will* get to the bottom of this."

I prayed he was right.

Chapter 42

TWO MONTHS. HARD TO BELIEVE. I got out of the car carrying my tote bag and walked out to Richie's grave. *Hey, big brother, I've been missing you.* I sat down on the thick grass beside his tombstone. *Today's an anniversary, you know. I guess something like that doesn't mean much to you now, but it does to me. So I brought you something.* I pulled two bottles out of my bag. *Your favorite…Southern Hospitality. Yeah, brought me something too – just a cider.* I opened both bottles, took a drink from mine, and poured a bit of the beer out of Richie's bottle onto the ground where his head should be.

A chill went over me suddenly, as if someone were watching me. The sun was still high in the sky, and I'd never felt nervous here before. But I had already had a few twinges today – now I realized it was another of those Brighton women things. I tried to shake it off.

I'm getting close, Richie. I have all these things tumbling around in my head, and I know at least some of them are important. Wish you could help me figure it out.

But he couldn't, and in the deadly silence I found that I couldn't stay there even a minute longer.

Back at home, I stepped out of the car and hurried to the street to empty my overflowing mailbox. When had I last checked it? Last Friday, I think. Things had been a little crazy lately and I hadn't been that concerned about things like mail. Once inside, I punched in the numbers to turn off my new alarm system and tossed all the mail onto the hall table.

Mark had been going home to stay in his apartment, and that situation suited me fine. I didn't want us to overdo the familiarity thing. Last night, though, I'd fallen asleep during a movie and didn't stir until he had me halfway up the stairs. When he laid me gently on the bed and pulled a blanket over me I said, "Stay with me tonight, babe. I don't want to be alone."

He'd kissed me and whispered, "You know I will." He lay down beside me and pulled me up against him. I fell asleep "spooning" with him, his arm wrapped securely around me. We didn't make love, yet I'd never felt closer to him than in that moment.

I showered and dressed in a flower-sprigged sundress and flip flops decorated with silk roses. Then I headed downstairs to figure out something for dinner. I made a gigantic salad and found breadsticks to pop in the oven when Mark got here. After setting the table I picked up the mail and sat down on the sofa to get it sorted. Magazines, bills, flyers, credit card offers, odds and ends. I thought about attacking the bills but couldn't face them yet.

I'd just finished an article on how to organize your pantry when I heard a key in the lock. "Surprise!" Mark called as he came in.

"And a good one." I got up to give him a warm kiss.

He pulled me close and we stood in the hallway swaying as if to an unheard song. "Man, I could get used to coming home like this."

"Dinner's almost ready. Hungry?"

"Not so much – too hot outside."

"Good."

"Why good? Is your fridge empty? I'll take you somewhere if you need real food."

"No, we're good. I've made a salad with everything in it but the kitchen sink and have breadsticks ready to heat."

"Fantastic. Let's do it."

We sat in the swing and talked for hours after dinner, more relaxed than we'd been in ages. Since that first night together, we had by tacit agreement not discussed the future at all. I'd been thinking about my job future, but I decided I'd rather make out with my guy than argue with him about my decision.

After Mark left I wandered the house restlessly. Glancing at the coffee table I saw that huge stack of mail and decided to dive in. I pay most of my bills online, so the stack contained mostly junk. *What's this? Plain white envelope, addressed by hand.* I turned it over. No return address. *That's strange.* I picked up my heavy silver letter opener and slid it under the flap, and my doorbell rang. I sighed. Laying the letter aside, I opened the door to see Damian standing there, thumbs tucked into his jeans pockets.

***

He began fidgeting soon after we got settled on the sofa. He started out with just small talk – almost an hour passed before we got around to talking about the Elephant in the Room.

"I'm not sure why I'm here." He shifted sideways to face me, and I shrugged my shoulders. *Hell, I sure don't know.* But when he reached for my hand and slid a bit closer, I had a good idea. "You look beautiful tonight – but you always do."

"Thanks." I felt color flood my face. I had a decent tan – maybe he wouldn't notice.

"I didn't mean to embarrass you." *Guess he did notice.* Still holding my hand he caressed my fingers sensuously, using his thumb to trace the length of each one.

I felt myself responding. How on earth could this be happening? I loved Mark wholeheartedly. I couldn't understand. Damian was a friend, and a good one, but that's all he was – wasn't it?

No time like the present to find out. I knew it was wrong, knew I was playing with fire, but I couldn't seem to help myself.

"No, it's okay. I'm glad we're friends, Damian."

"But that's all – isn't it?" His eyes darkened noticeably, and as his gaze bored into mine, some part of me, deep down in my core, responded. He could see it. He slid down next to me on the sofa. "Isn't it, Becca?" He cupped my face in the palms of his hands and those gorgeous eyes came closer, so close I only saw them as a deep blue blur. His nose rubbed across mine, Eskimo-style, we used to say as kids, and my stomach flip-flopped.

"Oh, God." I leaned into him and he covered my mouth with his, first soft, then hard and insistent. He clamped down on my bottom lip and groaned. The moment he released my lip I struggled with him, and our tongues met.

He began to nip at my lips, my eyes, my ears. He trailed his lips down my throat and I moaned as he brought his hands to the front of my waist. His lips captured mine and he slid his hands under my blouse, kneading my sides before sliding toward my breasts. Now it was his turn to moan, as he buried his face between them.

"God, Becca, you smell so good – good enough to eat. You smell of lavender, and vanilla." He kissed at one breast through my clothes and I arched my back, willing him to continue. I opened my eyes and saw the raw hunger in his. "I want you, Becca. I want you so much it hurts. Hurts my body, my heart, my soul. I see you in my dreams, I dream of you awake. I need you. I didn't plan to fall in love ever again – but sweetheart, you've got me. I do love you!"

It was that word – "love" – that caught me up short. I could hear myself swearing my love to Mark. Did I *love* this man driving me crazy right now? No. I wanted him, for sure, but that was all. For lots of people, I knew, that would be enough. But not for me. And not for Damian.

I pulled back from him, shaking but determined. "I'm sorry. I'm sorry, but I can't. I just…" I held my hands up in front of me. I knew I'd gone too far. "I'm so ashamed, Damian. You don't deserve this."

"Deserve what, sweetheart? What's wrong? What'd I do? I pushed you too fast?"

"It's not you, it's me." I got up from the sofa and moved to my least comfortable chair. I stared at my hands twisting in my lap. "I can't deny I want you – I'd be silly to try." My entire body was still on alert and it wasn't easy to concentrate, especially with Damian's eyes, now the color of smoky sapphires, devouring my face.

"Yeah, I was pretty sure you wanted me. So, I didn't read you wrong, then?"

I shook my head and looked away from his gaze, finally. "No, and I feel like a slut, but you're not wrong."

"Dammit, Becca, don't talk that way. Just tell me what's wrong. I'll fix it, whatever it is."

"You can't fix it, Damian. There is nothing to fix. Listen, if I come back over there, will you promise not to touch me?"

He hesitated, then said, "Whatever you want, lady. I promise not to touch you…unless you ask me to." He settled back into his corner of the couch and waited, and I took the other corner.

"I have all kinds of phrases running through my head right now, words I've read in romance novels over the years, like 'I've played you false,' and 'used you.'"

He made a dismissive sound, somewhere between a grunt and a laugh. But he wasn't laughing.

"I have to confess something to you. It's killing me having to say it, because it's shameful, but if you'll please listen I'll try to explain." He crossed his arms and nodded, saying nothing – just staring into my eyes. I took a deep breath, trying to decide where to begin.

"That day at Justine's, the afternoon after Richie was killed, I answered the door and you stood there. My brother had just died, and I looked at you, looked into your eyes. And do you know what I said to myself? Well, it was that next day that I said, 'A girl could get lost in those eyes and never find her way out.'" I saw a flash of his dimples.

"I was ashamed of it then, because of Richie. I'm not ashamed of it now – you've got the sexiest blue eyes I've ever seen. There was a popular song I loved back in high school that said, 'You've got the most unbelievable blue eyes I've ever seen.' Remember it? Well, that's you…but you know that, don't you?" I smiled.

"I've been told a time or two." Dimples flashed again.

"And the dimples make you even more deadly. You've got a gorgeous body, and you're one of the sweetest guys I've ever known."

"I sense a 'but' coming." He frowned. The dimples disappeared.

"But I'm not in love with you, Damian. I'm in love with Mark. I've always loved him. I didn't mean to lead you on. It's just…"

"It's just you thought you'd have a little fun before you settled down to one man," he spat out. Flinging himself up from the sofa, he began to pace back and forth.

"What? No, no! It wasn't like that."

"Really? Then why don't you tell me what this is all about, Rebecca. Tell me you weren't ready to give yourself to me only a few minutes ago."

"I just had to know," I said miserably.

He stopped mid-stride. "You had to know what, exactly?"

"I had to know if what I feel for you is just a strong physical attraction, or if it's something more."

"And?"

"I care about you as a friend. I'd love to be able to keep you as a friend, but that's all it can ever be between us."

"Even though right now you're afraid to let me even touch you, because you want to make love with me so bad?"

"I want to have sex with you, I admit that. I don't understand this pull I feel toward you, but I know I can't act on it, not ever. I know sex with you would be earth-shaking. But I won't do it. I can't. And if you hate me for doing what I did just to see if my feelings were love or something else, I don't blame you."

His blue eyes were smoldering. "Oh, Becca, love. I told you. I'm in love with you. I can't help it. But I have to say…" He shot a dimpled smile at me and my toes curled. "I do appreciate you giving me a chance, checking out your feelings."

I looked up at him in surprise. "I don't understand."

He flopped back on the sofa and sat forward, his elbows on his knees. "I hope Mark appreciates what a special woman he has."

"How can you say that? I was almost ready to throw away all I have with him for…"

"Some awesome sex? The most earth-shattering experience you'd ever have?" he said with a devilish grin, and I blushed. "I said he's lucky because you care enough about him to put yourself out there and find out if your love for him is strong enough. God help me…it is."

"I do love him – love him with all that I am. And given time, I swear I will fight off this feeling."

He cocked an eyebrow at me and winked. "You don't know what you're missing. And you're always going to wonder."

"Maybe so, but if that's the way it turns out, so be it. And it's not like I'm choosing love over sex." I couldn't help my lips curling up at the corners. "With Mark I have both, and sex with him is pretty awesome, too."

He slapped a hand over his heart. "Ouch, that hurt." But he smiled then, a sad smile that flickered from his eyes.

"I think it would be best if you go now," I said, walking toward the front door.

He followed close behind me, and I could feel the heat radiating off him. At the door I said, "I hope someday you can forgive me for this and we can maybe be friends again."

His eyes were filled with pain, even as he nodded. He tweaked my nose with the tip of his finger. "Count on it, Becca McCallum. You call, I'll be here. No strings. Don't forget that. And if he ever hurts you, I'll be here. Don't forget that, either."

I shut the door behind him and leaned against it, still shaking from his touch on my nose.

Chapter 43

I WOKE EARLY THE NEXT MORNING, surprising myself after that late night tête-a-tête with Damian. Passing through the living room I glanced at the mail. The stack looked much more manageable today. I stopped and backtracked, looking down at the envelope and letter opener. I had forgotten all about that strange letter. I sat down and picked it up, turning it in my hands. The packet was thick, and the plain envelope crackled as I turned it. Impatient to see what was inside, I ripped it open and withdrew several sheets of lined paper folded together.

I laid them across my lap to try to smooth them out, glancing at the salutation:

"Dear Miss McCallum,

By the time you get this letter, one of two things will have happened. One, you will already have learned everything I'm about to write to you. Or two, if you don't yet know it, something will have happened to me."

What on earth? I flipped to the last page and looked at the signature: *Lance Varner.* A chill went up my spine and in my hands the letter began to shake. It was as if I'd received a message from the hereafter – maybe I had. I settled back into the corner of the couch, tucked my leg under me, and began to read.

***

The birds were chirping and singing in a raucous chorus this morning as I sat swinging and thinking. I'd moved to the swing with Lance's letter, which I'd read three times now. I still could scarcely believe the story he'd laid out. *But why would he bother to write this many detailed lies? How could someone make up that many lies? What reason would he have had?* He had lost his life, probably because he knew the things he'd told me in here. God bless him, he'd tried to do the right thing, and it cost him everything.

The question now was what to do about it. If the things in this letter were true, then Tommy, Bert, and Jake had all been involved in Richie's murder. I closed my eyes and said a prayer for Lance's soul. I had the facts, at least as he knew them. I could continue to investigate on my own and try to find more hard evidence. If I chose that path, I could probably forget about a future with Mark. Besides, I figured I'd done about all I could do on my own.

And if I take this letter to the police, to Chief Sikes or Sheriff Bixby? Can I trust the authorities to follow through? Maybe this would be the last piece of evidence the task force needed to accomplish what they needed to.

I made up my mind. I'd done all I could. Now it was time for the authorities to do what they were hired to do. I went inside to call the Chief at home.

"What's that? You say you have a letter from the dead man you found last week?"

"Yes, and it's filled with details of things he said he witnessed at Bert's Auto Body Shop. His words are very incriminating, Chief."

"You hold on to that letter and don't let anybody know you have it, and I mean anybody. You hear me? I've got a meeting with emergency people from the three counties all morning and won't be back in the office until about one. Can you come in then and bring the letter?"

"Sure, Chief. It's unbelievable, the things he wrote…"

"Rebecca, you hold on. You've been through worse things this summer. In fact, this might end up bringing you a sense of closure. But I won't know what our next step is until I see that letter. So I'll see you at one, okay? I'll have a few other people here, too."

I laid the phone down, refolded the letter and slid it into its envelope. I located my purse and placed it inside. It was all of eight-thirty now, four hours before I could head to Police Headquarters. I wanted to talk to Mark, but Sikes said tell nobody. If I called him he'd know something was up, so I shouldn't call. I didn't like keeping something from him, even for a few hours. I supposed I could understand Sikes's concerns. Still, it was shaping up to be a long morning.

***

At twelve-thirty, after I'd scrubbed all the kitchen cabinets to keep my mind occupied, I left for the drive to downtown Biloxi where the public offices are located. I arrived about fifteen minutes early and bounded up the curving staircase to the Police Department, avoiding the nervous-looking people in the downstairs lobby waiting for traffic court. I grew impatient waiting. I paced, drummed my fingers on the countertop, paced some more. I glanced up at the receptionist, who was glaring at me. Blushing, I retreated behind a magazine and willed myself to keep still.

Shortly after one, Chief Sikes blew through the door, nodded at me, and motioned for me to follow him back to his office. He hung his Stetson on the coat rack and greeted a tall, slender man of about forty, who had risen as we went in.

"James, good to see you."

"You too, Wayne. Rebecca, this is Wayne Cotton from the DPS Crime Lab." We shook hands, the Chief waved me to a chair, and the two men sat.

I looked up to see Sheriff Bixby coming in. "Bascom," the Chief greeted him. "Good, now we're all here. So let's see this letter."

I pulled Lance's letter from my purse and handed it over. All three men had donned latex gloves. The Chief did the same thing I'd done, opening the letter, reading a few lines, and flipping back to the signature on the last page. I watched expressions move across his face as he read. When he finished a page he handed it over to the Sheriff, who read and passed it to Mr. Cotton.

"When did you say you got this? And how?"

"It was in my mailbox when I emptied it yesterday. Last time I had emptied my box before that was last Friday or Saturday, so I don't really know when I got it."

"But it went through the post office, and the date and time show 5:30 p.m. on August 2, which was Friday," he said, glancing at his desk calendar. He glanced up when I made a startled sound. "What is it, Rebecca?"

"That means he mailed the letter two months to the day after Richie died," I said quietly.

"It's okay, hon. You are going to get through this, too," he said, gesturing to the letter.

"Sounds like he was afraid someone was coming after him and he wanted this story told," Bixby said, handing back the final page of the letter.

"It seems that way, but we have to get this checked out – see if this is his handwriting, things like that. Somebody could be trying to lead us off in the wrong direction. And we've had enough of that," said Mr. Cotton.

"So how long do you think it'll take to check out whatever you need to?" I asked.

"Could be a couple of days, could be a couple of hours. I'll get this to our Crime Lab. They work reasonably fast. I'll get right on it," Cotton said, standing. He nodded toward me and walked out.

I turned to the Chief. "So can I share this with Mark? I don't like keeping things from him."

The Chief gave me a fatherly smile. "You and that young man getting serious?"

I ducked my head, shy as I'd been when I was a little girl and he teased me. "Yes, sir. Seem to be."

"Thought for a while you and Wentworth might be seeing each other." Sheriff Bixby looked up sharply. The Chief had the hint of a question in his voice, but he couldn't make himself come out and ask directly. I decided to let him off the hook.

"Damian's been a good friend to me. He and Richie were big buddies, and he's been hurting a lot, too. We've leaned on each other a great deal."

"That's good to know. Your Mark seems like a fine man, too. Well. We'd better get to work on this." He stood.

"Great. I'll wait to hear from you. You will let me know as soon as you know something?"

"Sure thing. Now I want you to be real careful until we get this taken care of. We don't know who wrote this, and we don't know if there's still somebody out there who's got you in their sights. Don't go out running alone, in fact don't do anything alone."

"Don't worry. I've had enough excitement to last me a lifetime."

Little did I know how exciting things were about to become.

***

"Becca, where are you, babe?" I rushed down the stairs when I heard Mark calling. He hugged me close for a while and then I took his hand and led him to the sofa.

"I'm glad you could come over so quickly. I have lots to tell you! Let's get comfortable – this is gonna take a while." Mark settled on the seat beside me. "I opened a letter this morning, and the police have it now; so I'm going to have to tell you from memory what it said."

"A letter? Who from?"

"Lance Varner, the guy I went to meet last Saturday. The dead guy."

Mark whistled. "Where'd it come from? The mail?"

"Yeah, it was in the stack I brought in yesterday. I'd not emptied the box in a few days…I've been so busy." At this, Mark gave me a sexy smile and I felt my neck turning red. "Well. There's so much to tell. But if the letter is really from Lance, and if what he says is true, then we know who killed Richie."

Mark sat forward again in surprise. A hint of a smile played around his eyes and he blinked rapidly. I felt tears, too, and swallowed a couple of times.

"What's in the letter?"

"Here's his story. He'd been working at Bert's shop for about three years. He and Jake painted all the vehicles. Tommy had started out as a sort of gofer but finally started tinting windows. Bert mostly just ran the place. Lance said he began to notice about a year ago Bert, Tommy, and Jake having little conferences, making sure he didn't hear. He asked Jake about it but Jake waved him off. He asked Tommy, and Tommy seemed scared or upset, Lance didn't know which. For a while he tried to do his work and ignore them. But it started getting to him, so he decided to find out what was going on."

"He put all this in a letter?"

"That and lots more. Sometime in May, he said, he was in the paint booth finishing a job when he realized nobody had come back from lunch. He turned out the lights and opened the door, hoping they might talk if they thought he was gone. He was gonna pretend he'd been sleeping if someone caught on to him.

"The guy had guts, I'll give him that," Mark said.

"Sure enough, Bert and Jake came wandering in having an argument. Jake said he didn't want to be a part of something – Lance didn't know what – and Bert said it didn't matter how he felt because he already was a part of it. Bert reminded Jake he had access to Jake's brother in prison, and Jake started cussing him. Bert just laughed. Told him to come in the office a minute and go ahead and get one of the guns."

"Guns! Whoa. Wonder what that's about."

"Lance didn't know what guns, but he took the chance when they went inside to sneak out and pretend to come back a few minutes later. So then he wanted to know about these guns and waited for a chance to check them out. His chance came about a week later when all three guys went out to lunch together, and Bert told him to watch the shop.

"So Lance went into the office and looked around. All he saw was a locked storage cabinet in the corner – so he picked the lock. He found all kinds of guns inside. He got scared and closed the cabinet and locked it back. He didn't know what to do, so he didn't do anything. About a week later, he heard the news about…about…" But that was as far as I could go.

Mark had been holding my hands, rubbing his thumbs across my knuckles. He'd listened intently, surprising me by not asking questions. He had nodded once in a while but that was all.

"This is unbelievable. But if it is true, they'll have Richard's murderer – or rather, murderers, and this will all be over," he said.

"Not quite. They'll have to find and arrest them first. Then I suppose there will be a trial at some point, and that's gonna be hard to get through."

"But I will be here with you. Sweetheart, you don't have to worry about anything anymore. We're together, and we can get through anything." He gathered me into his arms as I started to cry. "Hey, what's this? This is good news, babe. This is the time to celebrate, not mourn. You've helped make sure your brother gets justice. Damn, I hate it turns out Jake was in on it. I'd hoped for Owen's sake he wasn't."

I sniffed, and Mark leaned over the end of the couch to grab a couple of tissues. "Me, too. I hate to think what this will do to the little kid. And Justine, too, as angry as I've been with her, I can't help feeling sorry for her."

"Once this is over, though, y'all can get stuff worked out. You'll see. It's gonna be okay." He hugged me tighter. "So what's our next move?"

"Just to wait and keep quiet. Chief Sikes said they would get the letter checked out, and if it is authentic they should have enough to convince a judge to give them a search warrant. If they can find some hard evidence, they'll be able to arrest both of them."

"Sounds good. Then I won't have to worry about you so much."

"It might be a couple of days, but we can handle that. I plan to stay off the roads and stick close to home. So you can go on to work for the rest of the week and not worry about me."

"No, I'll still worry. But if you promise to stay here I do need to go on back for a while to make sure the new equipment's gonna work all right. We had another big problem today."

"I promise. I won't leave the premises. I don't want another altercation."

I kept my word, and Mark found me asleep on the couch when he got home about nine.

"Man, I'm beat." He raised my legs and sat down, laying them back across his lap. "This has been one long day. We had to send over to New Orleans for a part and I thought it'd be there by the time I went back, but it finally arrived about an hour ago." He laughed, tickling the sole of my foot at the same time. I jerked my foot away and he stopped. "Damnedest thing though. The guys had the machine broken down waiting for it, so when it got there they slipped it in place, put it all back together, and things are running like a dream."

"That's good, isn't it?"

"Yeah, sure, but somehow I thought when I got to be the big boss," he scowled, and I laughed, "I didn't think I would be doing grunt work anymore."

"Poor baby…is there anything Becca can do to make it all better?"

He bared his teeth and gave me his Groucho face again. "As a matter of fact…"

***

I woke sometime in the night and reached across in the dark. The bed was empty. "Mark?" I called, "are you here?"

"Over here, angel," he said, rising from my reading chair by the window. He padded back across to the bed and slid under the sheet next to me, pulling my body in next to his, his arms holding me safe and secure. He had on silky boxer shorts, and the hairs on his legs tickled as he wrapped them around mine. "I like your lingerie," he said, running his hand through my hair and pulling it to the side so he could murmur into the back of my neck.

"But I'm not…oh. Oh!"

"'Night, sweet thing," he murmured a few minutes later.

"Night, Mark. I love you." But his breathing had become even and he didn't answer. I snuggled a bit closer and closed my eyes. *Thank you God, thank you for bringing him back to me. And thank you for helping me learn the truth.*

Chapter 44

MARK SLEPT LATER THAN USUAL the next morning and I fixed breakfast for him for a change. Bacon and spinach omelet, a huge bowl of cut fruit, coffee and juice. He ate with gusto and suggested that since I'd be home all day, I should try for a hearty supper tonight as well, saying he didn't have much energy today.

"Some sexy woman woke me in the middle of the night."

"Umm, no. You were awake when I woke up. Why were you awake, anyway?"

"I don't know. I couldn't stop thinking about what you had told me. This all seems unreal. But we can talk about it later. I've gotta run. Thanks for breakfast." He gave me a lingering kiss and then another. "Later. You staying in today?"

"Unless I hear something more from Chief Sikes. I'll call you if I do."

"Do that. I'm sure glad it sounds as if this will be over in a few days." He leaned in for a lingering kiss that took my breath away. "Doors locked and alarm set," he reminded me. I made a face at him as he left the kitchen, but I was sure thankful he'd be coming back. I smiled as I wondered what my neighbor Mrs. Goodson had been thinking these mornings.

***

I puttered around the house all morning, vacuuming and dusting, going through the rest of the mail, trying to decide what I wanted for dinner. About one o'clock I went upstairs and fell asleep, and when I woke I lay staring at my pale blue ceiling, remembering when Richie had painted it for me. I smiled and stretched, rolling onto my stomach.

Richie, it's all turning out okay. The people who took you from us are going to pay for what they did. And I have Mark back. You knew it all along, didn't you?. I have another chance. I only wish you had another chance, too.

I wandered downstairs and picked a book off the shelf, settling on the couch and opening it to the first page. Twenty minutes later I was on page three and had no idea what I'd read, if anything.

The heck with this. I tossed the book aside and checked my pocket to make sure I had my phone. Then I slipped out the back door and headed across the yard to the treehouse. I wanted to get it straightened up for the next time Owen came over. He would need my support now more than ever, and I hoped Justine would allow us time together. I worked for about half an hour and was about to head back into the house when my phone rang.

"Rebecca, it's James Sikes. Where are you? At home?" He was speaking faster than I'd ever heard him and sounded out of breath.

"Yeah, I'm home. Why? Has something happened? Oh, Chief, is it over?" I felt butterflies flitting about in my stomach.

"Calm down and I'll tell you what's going on. But is Mark there with you?"

"No...Chief, you're scaring me."

"I want you to make sure your doors are locked and don't open for anybody unless you can see it's someone you trust."

"Okay."

"Here's what's happened so far. Our people verified the Varner boy's letter and Judge Wilson granted us a search warrant for three places: Bert's shop and his home, and Jake Coffee's home."

Oh, no...Lucy and Martin!

"We found what we were looking for at Bert's shop, in that cabinet Varner wrote about. Over two dozen weapons stolen from Harvey's Pawn Shop back in March. That's about half the amount that was stolen. Anders had probably already unloaded the rest."

"But did you get Bert?"

I felt his hesitation. "Not yet, but it's only a matter of time. We've got an APB out for his vehicle. Would you believe he has a green pickup registered to him?"

I gave a shaky laugh. "Not surprised at all. But it's the middle of the afternoon. He wasn't at the shop?"

"No. One of the guys there said he got a phone call about half an hour before we got there and took off out the door, didn't say where he was going."

"Could somebody have tipped him off that you were coming?" It seemed suspicious to me.

"Yeah, well, we're going to figure that out, believe you me. But for now the main thing is for you to stay in the house with the doors locked."

"Umm…"

"You said you were home. You *are* in the house, right?"

"Um, not exactly. I'm out in the treehouse."

"Dammit, girl. Excuse my language. Git in that house this minute. And stay on the phone till you see the situation is stable and you're safe."

"Yes, sir. I'm putting my phone in my pocket while I climb down." I snatched it back out as soon as my feet hit the ground. "Okay, I'm on my way in," I said as I ran across the yard, looking from side to side, fearing what I might see…or who.

"Be careful, girl. Let me know if you see signs of anybody. I'm worried he's gonna come after you."

"Gee, Thanks, Chief. Way to reassure a girl."

"Well, it's the truth. And once you get inside, you call Mark and tell him to get over there right now. I don't want you alone. I'm sending an officer over there as well."

"Will do, Chief. And Chief?"

"Yes?"

"You be careful, too. Okay?"

"Yes, ma'am."

"Okay, I'm inside now," I said, shutting the door behind me and locking it. "Everything looks okay. I just activated the alarm."

"All right. Then I'd better get back out in the field. Be sure you call Mark."

***

I hung up the phone and slipped it in my pocket, then went to peer out the living room window. I double checked to be sure the front door was locked and then hit Mark's number on speed dial.

"You might want to put that phone down, little lady." I whirled around to see Bert Anders standing in the doorway to my kitchen with a gun pointed at me. I suppose I froze for a few seconds. My mind struggled to process what I was seeing. I hardly recognized him. He was scruffy and his eyes were wild and bloodshot.

"Where did you come from?" I demanded, trying to take a few steps away from him. I don't know why I thought that would help – I really had nowhere to go. "And what do you want?" I tried to put force into my questions, but the quiver in my voice gave me away.

"What do I want? I want my life back like it was before you wandered into it," he snarled. His face was contorted into an ugly grimace. His clothes were disheveled, and it looked like he hadn't shaved in about a week. "Interfering little bitch. If it wasn't for you I'd be out of this, free and clear. But you had to go sticking your nose in where it didn't belong."

It was a stupid thing to do, I know, making him even angrier, but I couldn't help it. "What do you mean where it didn't belong? You killed my brother, you bastard!"

"Everything was going along just fine," he said, leaning against the door jamb and punctuating his words by jabbing the gun toward me. "Jake got me the money, and I let him out of the business so he could open his place. We were all happy till you started meddling."

If I only knew the best way to approach the situation… In movies the person with the gun trained on them always seems to be able to talk their way through without getting shot. *I should be so lucky.*

"Now give me that phone, and don't try anything."

I eased my way toward him, holding out the phone. "You're the one with the gun. I'd really like it if *you* don't try anything."

"Trying to be funny?" His eyes flicked toward my hand and he held his out, palm up. "Give it here. That's a good girl." He held the phone up so he could see both it and me. "What the...? Who did you call?"

I shook my head violently. "Nobody. Really, nobody. I was going to call my boyfriend, but you scared me so bad I couldn't punch in the number."

He held the phone to his ear. "Who's there?"

I could hear Mark's voice through the phone as far away from Bert as I was standing. "You son of a bitch, you'd better not touch her. I swear I'll kill you if you try anything."

"You and who else? Who is this, anyway? You the boyfriend?"

"Dammit, you'd better be gone before I get there, if you know what's good for you."

"Yeah, and where am I supposed to go? The cops are gonna get me no matter what. But I'm going to make your little woman pay before they get to me. You should have kept her at home where she belonged, instead of letting her run all over the county making trouble."

"I'm not the one making trouble! You started this when you killed my brother, you sorry lowlife." I'd been watching him while he talked to Mark. I thought he might not be that far from going over the edge. "Mark! Don't try to come in here! He's crazy!" I screamed.

"Becca? Becca! I swear, Anders, you touch a hair on her head..."

"And you'll what? Gonna come busting in here like gangbusters and save her at the last minute? Don't count on it. I'll be finished and long gone by the time you get here." With that he held the phone out and with a flourish hit the red button, tossing the phone up against the wall, where it shattered.

"Why did you do it? You didn't even know him. He was a good man, and you killed him! Why?"

"Doesn't matter why, does it? He's dead. Now that the cat's out of the bag, so to speak, they'll be coming after me, and I'm not going to prison." He wiped a bit of spittle from the side of his mouth with the back of his hand.

"So, what then? Are you going to kill me, too? If you are, won't you please at least let me hear it from your own mouth, just once? I've tried so hard to understand why someone would have killed Richie." I'd started to cry now. I wasn't expecting sympathy, but I did think it might buy me a bit of time. "Please?"

"We don't have time. Let's just say it all had to do with the money. Jake said your brother was worth more dead than alive, so me and Tommy just helped him work that all out."

"But how did you manage to get Richie's gun away from him? Frankly, I just don't think you're smart enough."

His face turned an ugly, mottled red, and he shoved me by the shoulder so hard I spun half around.

"You shouldn't underestimate old Bert. I planned it all. Used the kid as a patsy, found a house for sale across the pasture so I had a way to escape, got the goods on Jake's brother so he had to help." He spat out the side of his mouth. "It was all going fine till you started poking around."

"What did you expect me to do – just let my brother's killers go free? You're all going to pay for what you did. The police know it was you."

"Only because you wouldn't leave it alone. Now you're gonna be sorry you didn't."

"I'll never be sorry about that! You're really a sick bastard. And you *will* pay."

"Just shut the hell up! Get over there on the couch. Don't fight me, and I might let you live afterward." He had begun to hitch at his belt with his left hand, but the gun stayed trained on my face. My eyes darted around the room, looking for something, anything, to create a distraction. Nothing.

I was still standing and he shoved me again, so that I fell, hard, onto the couch, scraping my leg on the coffee table on my way down. He came down over me on one knee, keeping his other foot on the floor. He rammed the gun against the side of my head.

"I'm going to die just like Richie," I thought. "I'll never get to have a life with Mark. I won't be here for Owen. Mom, Dad, I'm sorry. You'll have to bury your other kid, too."

"How does it feel, little girl?" His voice was gravelly and his breath stank as he spat out the words. "That's right where I put the gun on your brother's head, you know that? Same exact spot."

The knowledge of how Richie must have spent his last minute on earth tore at my heart, even as I lay there expecting the same thing to happen to me any second. But no, I wouldn't get off that easy.

"Put your hands above your head," he whispered. "Be a good little girl and it won't be so bad." I raised my arms slowly, like he said, turning my face to my left to try to escape his fetid breath. "Don't turn away from me, darlin', you don't want to make old Bert madder do you?"

I turned my face back toward him, and he lunged and grabbed both my hands in his one greasy one. *Greasy. His hands are greasy.* I might be able to jerk one hand out of his grasp, but I'd have to time it perfectly for it to work. Because I knew what I had to do. I had seen it when I turned my face away to escape his breath.

On the coffee table – not two feet away – next to that irritating stack of mail my beautiful, heavy, silver letter opener.

"You're gonna pay, you little bitch. My life might as well be over. But before that, you're gonna be sorry you ever messed with me." He stuck out his tongue grotesquely wide, covered with saliva, and began to lick the side of my face. I struggled to make myself lie still and not retch.

Please, Richie. Please, God. Help me. Give me strength, and please let my arm be long enough.

I groaned, sliding my head toward the edge of the couch, hoping he'd think I was just trying to avoid him. I blinked madly, fighting to get the tears out of my eyes so I could see what I was looking for.

"You like that? Sounds to me like you enjoyed it a little bit. Let's try that again." His tongue came out again, flat and wet, slavering on me. I could feel the slimy wetness oozing down into my ear. Just then he bit down on my earlobe and I screamed. I began to struggle in earnest then, hoping to make it hard for him to keep his balance. If he shot me in the head, well, he was probably going to do that anyway. So what did I have to lose?

"Be still, dammit." He backhanded me across the side of the face with the hand holding the gun and my vision blurred. *No, not now. I'm so close.* I blinked madly trying to clear the film from my eyes.

At that moment he landed all his weight on me, probably trying to knock the breath out of me. He very nearly succeeded. I could feel him moving against me, and when I could finally see again I looked straight into his eyes and yanked my left hand downward with all my strength.

My hand slipped out of his grasp and he cursed. I calculated I had maybe two seconds. I slung my arm outward, hitting the table, grasping. *No, it's not there. Where did it go? Did I knock it off? No! There!*

I closed my hand round the handle of the letter opener and gripped it with all my might. Twisting my wrist so the point was turned toward me, toward us, I brought my arm across and up, aiming for his side but hoping for any contact at all.

The blade struck and stuck, and my whole arm went numb. He gave a grunt and lost his balance, falling, crashing into the coffee table on his way down, landing with the letter opener somewhere beneath him. The gun hit the coffee table and bounced away. I didn't know where I'd caught him, didn't know if it would be enough. I didn't wait around to find out.

I scrambled up off my back, sobbing, and crawled to the end of the couch away from his body. I looked back once, fearing to see him coming toward me, but he lay without moving. I crawled over the arm of the couch to avoid his body and ran for the back door.

Chapter 45

MY FINGERS SHOOK SO THAT IT TOOK WHAT SEEMED an interminable time to undo the lock on the kitchen door. But at last the door opened, and accompanied by the screeching siren from the alarm I hadn't taken time to shut off, I was out, and running – running for the side of the house. I heard sirens in the distance, and I kept running, out into the street. Brakes squealed nearby and I came to a sudden stop, looking around wildly.

And then I saw him. Mark was here. He had come for me, and I was going to be all right. I stumbled toward him.

"Becca! My God, Becca. Are you okay? Did he hurt you?" And his warm arms were around me, pulling me safe and sound against his heart. I could feel it pounding against my cheek as if he'd run a marathon. I clung to him with all my might, which at that point I don't think amounted to much.

He held me away from him, his eyes searching my face, my body, looking, I supposed, to see if he could find any damage.

"I'm okay, baby, I'm okay." And I clung to him again, my body now wracked with sobs – now that I was safe.

"Thank God," Mark whispered. "Thank you, Sweet Jesus."

"Amen," I whispered back. And then my legs buckled. The next thing I knew, we were on the lawn, I was leaning against Mark's shoulder, and Mrs. G. was kneeling beside me, fanning me madly with one of her catalogs.

Sirens descended on us from all over, it seemed. Officers were yelling, pointing, running.

"Miss, are you all right?" one asked, and I nodded.

"He's in there." I gestured toward the house with my head.

"Babe, you're bleeding," Mark said, turning my head to the side. "Good, it's only a scrape. I thought he might have hit you."

"He did once, with the back of his hand," I said, feeling the hysteria coursing through my veins and trying to break out.

"I'll kill him," Mark said, adding an obscenity.

"I think I already did." I began to sob quietly against him.

Mrs. G. gasped. Funny, she hadn't said a word so far.

"You what? Never mind. You can tell us later. You need to get someplace safe and you need to get out of this yard before it turns into more of a circus here."

"Becca? Mark?" The Chief was there. "Come over to my car and have a seat." He led us over to the Crown Vic and opened a back door. I slid gratefully inside and he removed his Stetson so he could lean into the car.

"Girl, you gave me a real scare. Thank the Lord you're okay. My men have the house surrounded. Do you think Anders is still inside?"

I nodded without looking at him. "Most likely," I said between sobs. "since I stabbed him."

"You don't mean it!" He yelled to someone, "He's likely still inside, and he's been stabbed. Move in, but cautiously. You know the drill. And get these civilians out of here."

Mark was dabbing at my face with a damp cloth.

"Where'd you get that?" I asked in surprise. The cool felt wonderful.

"From that woman who was fanning you, whoever she is."

I smiled. "Mrs. Goodson, bless her. I need to introduce the two of you one of these days."

The Chief put his head back inside. "You sit right here and try to relax. We'll have somebody here to take care of you soon." In fact, I could hear more sirens as he said this. Then he was gone and Mark was gathering me into his arms.

"You're okay. Everything's going to be okay now. You're okay, and that's all that matters." I nodded weakly and slumped against him, happy now, just waiting for it all to be over.

***

For the second time in two days I found myself walking into a police station, this time in my hometown. A detective met us at the front desk.

"Ms. McCallum, I'm Detective Connor Yates." He escorted us back to a bare bones office with a wide wooden table and several mismatched chairs. Mark followed, but Yates had him wait outside.

"Okay, Ms. McCallum, if you're ready we'll get started," Yates said, unbuttoning his jacket and sitting down across from me with a legal pad and pen.

With a bit of guidance from the detective about where best to start, I began to talk. I heard my voice not sounding like me, but rather a low monotone. Yates had to ask me to repeat words occasionally. As time went on, though, I began to relax and talk both louder and faster. That is, until I got to the part about Bert attacking me. My throat tightened and my head began to pound as I described things he'd said and done. When I broke down at one point, the detective said a break was in order and motioned Mark in. I stood and backed away from the table, and he held out his arms.

"I'm sorry. I should have gotten there sooner. I'm so sorry, sweetheart." Startled by the anguish in his voice, I leaned away so I could see his face and was surprised to see his eyes glistening. As I watched, those eyes brimmed over and tears spilled down his cheeks.

I laid my hands on his face and gently wiped them away. "Please don't cry for me, not about this. I survived. And he didn't hurt me, not really." My words seemed to have no effect. "Hey, it could have been worse. I could be dead."

He stared into my eyes for several seconds while the tears continued to spill out. "You're right. You're alive – that's all that matters." He blinked.

"Sorry I don't have a hanky. I don't have anything. My purse is at home." I stood in front of him and used the hem of my shirt to dry his face. "Now, no blowing," I said in my sternest voice. "That's good – at least you can grin. That's my Mark. Hey, how come I'm comforting you? I'm the one who…" I broke off, not wanting to say those words even one more time. Instead I kissed him.

Detective Yates cleared his throat as he came back in, and from that point on things went much easier. Another two hours, and I'd finished reliving the afternoon; then we waited while someone typed up my statement. After I read and signed it, Sheriff Bixby stuck his head in and said, "Y'all come back here to my office for a minute."

***

"Rebecca, I hate you had to go through this today, and I know going over it again for us was probably almost as bad, but it had to be done."

"It's okay, Sheriff. It was worth it. Now you know for sure who killed Richie."

He nodded. "I thought you might like an update. Bert Anders has about a four inch puncture wound in his side, a bruised kidney, and a knot on the side of his head, I guess from hitting the coffee table. Is that right?"

"I don't know if he hit it, but I didn't hit him – I only stabbed him." I giggled, and the sheriff narrowed his eyes and looked down his broad nose at me.

"He will be taken into custody as soon as the doctors say it's okay. Probably tomorrow."

I shuddered as if I'd had a chill.

"You sure you're all right?" the Chief asked. He looked from me to Mark. "What do you think?"

"Well, sir, I think she needs to get out of here. Would that be okay now?"

He sighed heavily. "I guess so. C'mon, I'll walk y'all out." He strode out of the room first, with Mark and me trailing behind like two little kids. We got a few sympathetic looks as we were leaving, but there was no celebrating going on here. Most people appeared stunned by the sudden turn of events this afternoon.

One of the officers, a blonde woman, stepped forward to open the door for us. "Good job, Ms. McCallum," she whispered as we reached her.

It felt surreal to be congratulated for stabbing someone.

I smiled shakily at her as I slipped through the door ahead of Mark.

I shielded my eyes from the late afternoon sun as we emerged from the building. News trucks filled the street, WLOX front and center, but Mark cleared a path through all the reporters, not slowing down once.

316

"Becca! Here, girl!" It couldn't be.

I turned to Mark. "Lorelei? How did she find out about this?"

"Are you kidding? Nothing happens in this town she doesn't know about." He was right.

We hurried through the throng to where she waited, standing beside her silver Mercedes in a matching silver linen pant suit, and for a minute we stared at each other without talking. I could read the emotions on her face: the love, the sadness, the relief. I knew my face showed much the same thing. I ran to her and flung my arms around her. "Oh, Loree, it was awful," I blubbered.

"Well, sure it was, Beck. But it's over now, and you're safe. Let me take y'all away from here, okay?"

I realized we were sort of stranded, since Mark and I had ridden in with the Chief. "I'm a mess. I need to go home and get cleaned up."

"Oh, you can't get in there. I went by before I drove over here. There's yellow crime scene tape over half the neighborhood. Girl, you sure know how to get attention."

"Well where am I going to go? I can't even get my clothes?"

"Nope. I already asked. Not till at least tomorrow, they told me. But don't you worry. Lorelei's got it covered."

"We can go to my place," Mark said, and I could tell he was feeling overwhelmed by Lorelei's enthusiasm for her project of taking care of us.

"Is my shirt clean?" I asked straight-faced, opening my eyes wide to feign innocence. "I'll be fine if I just have my shirt." Bless his heart, Mark blushed.

Lorelei looked from one to the other of us, head tilted and brow furrowed – for a second. Then she caught herself in the frown and relaxed her facial muscles until her brow was perfectly smooth. "Well, I'll be damned." I fell into a fit of giggles as we got into the car.

"Girlfriend, you are the biggest news to hit this town since Katrina!"

"You mean since Richie," I corrected her.

"Now I loved that brother of yours, but I swear the entire coast is in a buzz over *you*."

"Great." I scooted down in the seat.

"Do you know how proud I am of you, Rebecca McCallum? Don't you dare slink around like you're the one who did something wrong." She glanced at me frequently as she navigated her way down Washington, then onto Government and across the bridge into Biloxi. "You're going to be fine. Especially with this guy," she jerked her head at Mark in the back seat, "looking out for you. But right now I'm going to look out for both of you. So, Mark, want to swing by your place and pick up a few things?"

Thirty minutes later we pulled up to valet parking at the Paradise and a young uniformed woman loped toward us. "Hey, Mrs. Steggemann, how are you?"

"Fine, Julie. Tell you what I need. Get one of the guys over here to take this gentleman's bag, and then we're all going in through the valet entrance with you."

The girl threw a quick, curious look into the car but lost no time in following her boss's wife's instructions. Ten minutes later we were being whisked to the top of the hotel. Bob had joined us at the private elevator, and we were all quiet as the car ascended smoothly, the chimes at each floor sounding closer and closer together as if we were gaining speed. At twenty-nine, the car eased to a stop and the doors slid open soundlessly. Bob stepped out and motioned us to follow.

He walked down the thickly carpeted hall and stopped at a set of double solid oak doors. "Here we are," he said, inserting a key card and swinging the door open for us.

"Oh, my gosh!" I said as I stepped into a living room twice as large as my own. The furniture was all modern but comfortable looking, with lots of chrome but lots of plush pillows as well.

A large circular table, as large as my dining table at home, stood front and center in the entry. Bob dropped two key cards on the table. "Just in case you *need* two," he said.

"Okay, let me show you around," Lorelei said. "Here's the kitchen and dining area" – I gaped at a table set for twelve.

"Are we expecting company?" I asked in a small voice, never knowing what to expect from my best friend.

"What? Oh, that! No, course not. Just for looks. C'mon, let me show you the bedrooms." She whispered as she pulled me into the hall, "Now you don't have to mess up both of them. The maids are discreet." She winked at me and giggled. "So this is the master bedroom. And your bath." I gawked like a schoolgirl. Looking at the gold fixtures and the hot tub sized bathtub, I couldn't decide if they were gaudy or beautiful.

"I ordered up a few toiletries from Soiree downstairs, but if y'all need anything different pick up the phone and tell the Concierge. She's expecting to hear from you. Here's your closet. I ordered a few things in your size, but let me know if you need anything else." She stopped her frantic tour and put her hands on her hips. "Come here, Becca." She held out her arms and I fell into them.

"Oh, Loree, I thought I was dead," I sobbed. "And then I thought he was going to rape me before he killed me, just so I'd suffer more. And his tongue, he licked me all over my face. I don't know how I kept from throwing up all over him."

"You're a strong woman, that's how. Now you listen to me. You sure you're okay?" I sniffled but nodded. She pulled me down to sit next to her on the bed, whipped out a tissue, and dabbed at my face.

"I said listen to me. You accomplished something today three law enforcement agencies have not managed to get done in two months. You've got the man of your dreams out there, and he's so crazy about you it's not even funny. I thank God you're okay – at least you're going to be okay."

"Yeah, I know you're right. I'm going to be okay now. I don't know how to thank you for rescuing us."

"Oh, honey, it was kinda fun." Her laugh was so infectious I couldn't help joining in.

"Now that's the Becca I know and love. Come on, we'd better check on our menfolks." Bob and Mark were talking quietly by the solid wall of windows overlooking the Gulf. The reddish gold rays of the setting sun streamed weakly through the tinted glass, reflected in my guy's eyes, which took on a new shade, a fascinating mixture of greens and golds.

"C'mon, Bob, we've done all we can here," Lorelei said with a dramatic flourish. "Y'all get some rest. Food will be up in about an hour. I'll call you tomorrow! I love you, girl!"

I blew her a kiss across the huge room. "I love you, too." Bob waved, saluted Mark, and then they were gone. I turned to Mark and raised my eyebrows. "Are you okay with this?"

He shook his head, laughing, and held out his hand. "I'm okay with anything, as long as you're here with me. Lorelei's something, isn't she?"

"She's the best. Best friend, that is. You're the best overall." I leaned in for a kiss. "Is it okay if I go try out that gigantic bathtub?"

"Only if I can come with you."

***

We stayed at the Paradise for two restful days and nights. We refused to watch the news during the entire time. Room service became our best friend. I felt bad taking all of the things Lorelei and Bob were providing for us, until she pointed out it wasn't any more than the "whales" got when they came to town, and not as much as some of the high rollers.

I called Mom and Dad first thing the next morning. I should have called them right away, but I needed to put a bit more distance between myself and Friday's events.

Mom answered the phone. "Hello sweet daughter of mine! How are you?"

I swallowed hard at the lump in my throat. Yesterday I didn't think I'd ever hear her voice again.

"Hi Mom. I'm good. Hey is Dad around? I kind of wanted to talk to him, then I'll talk to you again, okay?"

So it was that I could say to our father, "Daddy, I know the truth about Richie's murder. It's all over now." Since I hadn't confided anything at all to them, it required a great deal of explaining. We talked for about half an hour, with me giving them as few details as I could get by with.

Mom got back on the phone last. "Becca, I need to know one thing more. Have you and that sweet Mark worked things out?"

I looked across the room to where he lay propped up on about half a dozen pillows. When he smiled at me, my heart just about melted. "Yes, Mom, we have," I said, laughing through my tears.

"Good. Then all is right with my world. 'Bye sweetie." I held the phone away and looked at the screen.

"Huh! She hung up on me." I crawled onto the bed and sprawled across Mark's chest. "Right after she found out you and I were back together. She said 'Then all is right with my world.'"

He wrapped his arms around me and rolled so I was under him, and tenderly covered my mouth with his. "With mine, too," he said huskily.

Chapter 46

I SLEPT SOUNDLY IN MY OWN BED Sunday night and rose early, feeling refreshed. I smiled at the memory of last night's dream – I was at the beach hearing Richie's voice again. This time he sounded pleased. *"Thanks, Sis. I knew you could do it. I'm very proud of you. It's time to say goodbye. I'll love you always and forever."* His voice had faded away, and I thought it just might be the last time I'd dream of him.

Blackberry tea in hand, I stepped out onto the back porch and breathed in the freshest air I'd felt since last spring. A cool front had passed through in the night, depositing an inch of rain and taking with it the humidity that would normally be plaguing us, even early in the morning, in August. I took it as a good sign.

"Hotel California" interrupted my reverie, and I rushed to the kitchen to try to catch whoever was calling, but the line was dead. I checked my missed calls and was surprised to see it had been Justine. I thought about it long and hard, but in the end there was only one thing to be done. I took a deep breath and hit the call back button. The phone rang three times in my ear before Justine picked up, and there was a long pause before I heard her tiny "Hello? Rebecca?"

"Justine, sorry – I was on the back porch. How are you? How's my nephew?"

"We're okay, I guess, considering everything that's happened. Owen doesn't really know what's going on yet. I don't know how to talk to him about these latest developments."

"I know he's gotten really attached to…to Jake, in the last few weeks…" I broke off, not sure if I could talk about these things with her.

"Rebecca, I want you to know how very sorry I am about how everything has turned out. I never meant…" Her voice caught on a sob, and I felt tears sting my eyes, too.

"Justine, I don't know if I can talk to you about this right now."

"I know," she said, her voice so small I could barely understand her words. "I don't blame you. I'm just hoping that, for Owen's sake, you will see fit to let me try to make things right between us."

"How do you hope to do that, Justine? Nothing you can say or do will bring Richie back." I knew I sounded spiteful, but her actions had made losing Richie so much harder.

"I want to start later this morning," she said. "I spoke with Sheriff Bixby, and he told me Judge Wilson has agreed to allow Richard's family to be in court for the arraignments. I'd like to sit with you there, if that's all right."

I'm not sure what I'd been expecting, but it certainly wasn't that.

"I don't know what to say. I'd have thought you wouldn't want anything to do with me, after how hard I've been working to bring Richie's killers to justice."

"I want justice for him, too, Rebecca, no matter what you might think of me," she said, her voice cracking. "I never intended… I never thought…" She was sobbing in earnest now, and so was I.

"Please, Rebecca? I want to be there, too, and I do not think I have the strength to walk in alone."

***

And so…

At 9:30 sharp, Mark drove his Escape up to the Harrison County Detention Center and we were waved through, the gates closing solidly behind us. Justine was already there, and she stepped out of her car, alone, as soon as we had parked. She seemed even tinier today, her face drawn, her brown eyes huge pools of misery.

We met at the end of the sidewalk and stood face to face for a moment before Sheriff Bixby walked out to meet us and escort us into the building. After several twists and turns, we arrived at the Justice Court courtroom, where we were admitted after having handbags examined and going through the metal detector.

When Mark had recovered the contents of his pockets, I said, "Let's do this."

Mark moved between Justine and me and escorted us down the center aisle. I don't know why I was surprised to see Damian at the front of the courtroom in uniform. After all, he seemed to turn up whenever anything having to do with Richie was involved. He pushed through the swinging gate separating participants and spectators and motioned us to the front row, just behind the area set aside for those facing arraignment.

The eyes of about a dozen reporters followed us, and I could feel their avid stares boring into my back. Mark sat between us, strong and solid, ready for anything. We sat without talking, each of us no doubt lost in our own contemplation of what was to come. Just before ten o'clock, I leaned over and whispered, "Sweetheart, thank you – for everything."

He squeezed my hand. "Always and anything, you know that."

"All rise!" the bailiff ordered, and there was a bustling as an attractive woman in her early fifties entered from her chambers. "The Justice Court of Harrison County, Mississippi, is now in session, Judge Emily Wilson presiding."

"Please be seated," the judge said, settling herself on the bench. And just that simply, the proceedings were underway.

I wasn't sure what to expect – I'd had almost no experience with the court system. The first few individuals brought in to face the judge arrived in a group of four. I speculated that the judge wanted all other cases heard before Jake's and Bert's, probably so she could dismiss court immediately after she finished hearing their cases.

We sat through several lengthy descriptions of charges, all of them answered with Not Guilty pleas. In other circumstances, I'd have found some of the cases hilarious, especially the one of the elderly man accused of being drunk and disorderly and urinating on the Biloxi Lighthouse early one morning. But today was not a day for laughter.

After the second set of four prisoners was escorted out, a flurry of activity signaled the main event was about to begin. Four additional armed deputies took up positions across the front of the courtroom. We heard them coming before we saw them. The sounds of their leg- and arm-irons echoed down the hallway, and all sounds inside the courtroom ceased as we all seemed to be holding a collective breath.

I heard Justine gasp as first Jake, then Bert, came into view. Two men I assumed to be their attorneys rose from their seats at a table in front of us, and they shook hands with their clients as the men were led to seats that were a bit too close to us for my comfort.

I began to take slow, deep breaths, determined to keep my anxiety at bay. I heard Justine sniffling on Mark's other side, and he reached into his coat pocket, withdrew a handkerchief, and handed it to her. *That's my man.*

Bert faced the judge first, responding Not Guilty to each of the many charges made against him, everything from robbery to assault to the murder of a peace officer. His arraignment took a full fifteen minutes.

I kept turning my gaze from him to Jake and back again. I was startled once to see Jake had shifted in his seat so he could look at Justine. When I glanced at her, I was shocked at the malevolence radiating from her. Jake seemed to feel her hatred as well, for he swiveled back to face the front and put his forehead down on the table.

What a sorry mess they had made of things.

Finally, Bert shuffled back to his chair, and just before he sat down, our eyes met. Not even on the day of his attack against me had I felt such hatred directed toward me. Mark put his arm around my shoulder, and I managed to meet the horrible man's gaze without flinching.

Then it was Jake's turn before the judge. He wasn't up there nearly as long, but the charges were as severe. I hazarded a quick scan of the courtroom behind us and breathed a sigh of relief when I didn't see the Ledbetters there.

As the deputy steered Jake away from the bench and back toward his seat, I realized he was being brought around behind the table, where only the wooden bannister would be between him and us...entirely too close.

Justine realized it, too. In an instant she had darted out of her seat and leaned against the rail, gripping it so hard her knuckles were white. Jake's head jerked up when he realized she was there, and something flitted across his face.

"He thinks she still wants to see him," I thought dazedly. "He just doesn't get it."

She had taken everyone by surprise, and the next moments went by as if in slow motion. She leaned as far toward him as her slight frame would allow.

"I hope you rot in hell," she spat, just before she drew back her arm and slapped him so hard she almost fell across the rail onto him. Mark lunged for her and pulled her back toward her seat as the deputy stepped between us and Jake, and then all was pandemonium.

The judge's gavel competed with the reporters' mass exodus as a phalanx of deputies, including Damian, surrounded the two prisoners and escorted them quickly from the room.

By this time, Justine was sobbing uncontrollably, bent almost double where she sat huddled against Mark. I didn't even know when court was adjourned. I moved to sit on Justine's other side, putting my arm around her and holding on. My tears splashed onto my forearms as I hugged her to me.

"I'm sorry, so sorry," she cried. "I deserve to rot in hell, too. But I didn't know – I swear I didn't know."

"It's going to be okay," I squeaked out, my cheek pressed to hers, our tears mingling. "You did just what I'd have liked to do. Come on, let's get out of here. Let's go home – home to Owen."

She looked up at me then, her eyes finally beginning to focus. I sucked in my breath and looked across her to Mark. "Take us home, baby?" I asked.

He stood and held out his hands. "You got it."

We looked around us at the almost empty courtroom, unsure which way would be best to exit. As if on cue, Damian was there, drawing Justine toward him and motioning for us to follow.

I couldn't help thinking, as we walked through the quiet halls and emerged from the building into the bright sunshine in its cloudless sky, that the four of us were the ones closest to Richie, the ones who, each in our own way, had loved him best.

Chapter 47

THE PLAINTIVE SOUNDS OF "AMAZING GRACE" filled the air, giving me a strong sense of déjà vu, as Mark and I walked hand in hand toward the bright blue awning set up next to the Hurricane Katrina Memorial on Hwy. 90. The mid-morning sun was already hot, suggesting we were in for another scorcher of a day, the norm in Biloxi in September. A blue-gray haze lay over the coast, dulling our view of the few wispy mare's tail clouds streaking the sky.

Mom and Dad walked in front of us, also holding hands. Ahead of them Justine and Owen led the brief procession to the tented area.

It was hard to believe we were here, three months to the day after we lost Richie, to dedicate a memorial stone to him. In homage to his ancestry, the monument was shaped like a Celtic burial cairn, and an oval frame on one side held a picture of a smiling Richie. A spray of red, white, and blue flowers stood to the side.

As I waited for the ceremony to start, I pondered how much my world had changed since June. Three months and one day ago, I had a job and a brother, but not the man I loved. Today I had no brother, no job, but I had the man I loved sitting next to me holding my hand in his two strong ones. I smiled up at him and he leaned over to whisper in my ear, "Love you, sweet thing. You're fine now." I nodded and blinked the first tears from my eyes.

Sheriff Bixby read the words carved on the memorial, praising Richie for his dedication to duty and devotion to the job to which he'd given his life. *I know you're up there watching, Richie. You didn't have as many years as a lawman as you had hoped, but I'm glad you had as many as you did.*

When Bixby finished, he called Justine and Owen forward to present them with a framed copy of the document and Richie's photo.

I was filled with conflicting emotions. Yes, Justine had played a role in Richie's death, with her cheating, but she'd also paid a heavy price for her actions. As she held the heavy frame, Bixby reached down and picked up Owen so he could see it better. The little guy was solemn, his blue eyes large and dark with some private emotion. When the sheriff set him back down they shook hands formally.

Then the sheriff presented Justine with the Medal of Valor, posthumously awarded to Captain Richard McCallum for heroism above and beyond the call of duty, laying down his life to defend the people of Mississippi. She walked over to my dad and said, "Ken, I think Richard would want you and Mom to have this." He stood, gave her a hug, and sat back down, holding the medal over so Mom could see. I could see it shaking from where I sat next to her.

I breathed a sigh of relief. The worst part of the ceremony was over. Chief Sikes took the podium last. Knowing his brevity, I smiled. We'd be away from here soon. He spoke with affection and admiration of his years knowing Richie. "These awards for law enforcement officers are very special. We have only had to give one other posthumous award in Harrison County in forty years. These aren't the only awards it's in our power to bestow. On behalf of both the Biloxi Police Department and the Harrison County Sheriff's Department, I would like to present an award to a special person."

I jerked to attention and felt Mark squeeze my hand as I heard the Chief say, "This person loved and respected her brother." He paused for a moment and I saw his shoulders shaking. But he sniffed, sighed, and raised his head to look directly at me. "She loved him so much she was convinced he was, as she told me, 'too smart, too strong, too careful,' to have died the way it appeared he had. She never let up, never let go. She was a bulldog, and she came close to losing her own life, but she believed it was worth the chances she took to bring her brother's murderers to justice."

"For her service to her brother and to her community, we'd like to present this Civilian Award for Meritorious Service to Miss Rebecca McCallum."

I sat, stunned, until Mark tugged me out of my seat. *But I don't want an award! Why didn't they tell me about this?* On the heels of that thought, I could hear Richie as clearly as if he were there: *Because you'd have ducked out of the ceremony, little sister. Now go up there and accept this with grace.*

Face flaming and tears beginning, I did so, accepting first a handshake and then a hug from the Chief. "God bless you, Rebecca."

"And you, Chief," I replied. Then, thankfully I could sit back down. I handed my plaque to Mark and he put his arm around me and gave me a little shake that said "Atta girl." A closing prayer, and we stood to accept handshakes from the officials.

The heat was stifling under the awning, and I pulled Mark over to stand under the ancient live oak that stood guard over the Katrina memorial – now over Richie's memorial, too. The thick, spreading branches hung with Spanish moss swayed in the timorous breeze sweeping over us. They seemed to envelop the entire scene, giving me a sense of security and safety.

Lorelei and Bob gave me a hug and a smile and moved on. I was grateful to them for that. When most people had left I went to Owen and told him how proud his daddy would be of him today. Justine and I clasped hands, and she moved me away from Owen and spoke softly.

"Thank you for forgiving me, Rebecca. I don't deserve it, but I'm grateful. I want to be on good terms with Richard's family. I want Owen to grow up knowing his heritage."

I hugged her quickly and walked away, unable to speak.

Mark stood to one side smiling at me. With a wink he said, "How about a walk on the beach later?"

"Deal," I said, if you take me home now." We walked to the edge of the grass near where the Escape was parked beside Bernice, which Mom and Dad had driven. I looked back at the scene, once more smiling through my tears.

***

The late afternoon sky blazed like a Monet canvas, with colors and shades of colors mixing and mingling in a glorious presentation I felt was meant just for the two of us. Mark sat beside me on a quilt taking in the scene, and even though it was hot enough to pop popcorn I was happy to be right here leaning against him. We had Front Beach almost to ourselves, with only one elderly couple wearing matching Hawaiian-print shirts down at the water's edge searching for shells.

"That'll be us one day." Mark nudged me in the side.

I snorted. "No way. I would never be caught dead in matching outfits, no matter how much I love you." He threw back his head and laughed with abandon, a wonderful thing to see and hear. "Hey, babe, would you mind to wait here while I walk the beach for a few minutes?"

His brilliant green eyes searched mine and I guess he decided I was okay, because he nodded and said, "Sure. I'll be right here waiting."

I kissed him and started walking, away from the sunset, thinking about my life and the people in it.

I had decisions to make, serious decisions. The problem was, I'd never been that serious a person. The last three months had done their best to change me into a person who couldn't laugh and enjoy life, but with Mark's love and help, I knew I had a chance to get at least parts of the old Becca back. True, there were parts of her I never wanted to see again. The selfish Becca. The whiney Becca. The self-centered Becca. I hoped those parts of me were gone for good.

What would I do, though, if Mark didn't want to wait around while I got my life in shape? He'd been making noises lately about things like "home" and "family," but I was not ready to commit to that. I'd done a lot of thinking and praying about going into law enforcement, maybe even with the Coast Guard. I did enjoy being out on the water.

Mark was making supportive noises, but I hadn't shared all my thoughts with him. I picked up a small chunk of driftwood and crumbled bits off of it as I walked, and I giggled, thinking about the sort of trust I had in Mark. Sure, I'd trust him with my life by now, but I didn't think I trusted him with my career.

I stood staring out across the lazy waves meandering up to the beach. No "crashing upon the shores" today – all was peaceful and calm. It was about time.

Thinking back over the past months, I knew there had been astounding changes in my life because of my losing Richie. And, I had to admit, not all the changes were bad.

I'd gained a greater appreciation for my old friends, Lorelei especially, and I'd met and come to love Lucy and Martin Ledbetter. It was sadly ironic that they had befriended me and then I'd been the one most responsible – besides Jake himself – for taking one of their only two nephews from them.

They've assured me they hold no animosity toward me – in fact, Lucy invited me out for tea and cookies last week. "He made his bed – he has to lie in it," she said. "But when he gets out – Hal, too – there'll be a place for them here. This is the only home they know." I wouldn't have expected less of them.

It remains to be seen if I'll be able to continue my relationship with them when that day comes. But it won't happen for years, despite Jake's turning state's evidence and helping the task force arrest about two dozen people involved in the car thefts and chop shop rings. Damian says only two vehicles have been stolen in the county since the arrests, and both of those involved teenagers wanting a joy ride.

Justine and I have made an uneasy peace for Owen's sake. I'm trying, and praying about it, but I don't know if I'll ever be able to forgive her completely for the things she's done that hurt Richie and led inevitably to his death. Owen is weathering the many changes in his life the way I think his daddy would have wanted him to, and I'm confident he'll grow into a fine man just like Richie.

I probably won't get to watch too much of that growing up, but I'm reconciled to the two of them moving to New Orleans to be near Justine's sister. I agree with Justine. They need a fresh start, and I don't think they'd ever get one here.

"Most important, though," she'd said last week when she told me about their new house right in her sister's neighborhood, "Owen will be with family close to his age. Francesca's children are teens and pre-teens, but they're good kids."

I get it. I'm happy they have a place to start over that won't be among strangers.

"And you and Mark are welcome anytime – the house is large with plenty of room for all of us. I'm sure Owen will want to come visit you, too, and we'll work out something during his longer vacations from school. I want him to know the wonderful aunt who brought his daddy's killers to justice. When he's older, I plan to tell him the whole story. I know it won't be easy, but I owe him that."

Maybe Justine's found a new maturity as well.

Paul Simmons is another who's been deeply affected by all of this. After months of being treated like a suspect and a pariah, he's back at work, and handling the whole situation much better than I probably would. At the memorial today when he stopped to congratulate me, he leaned in close to whisper, "I really like our therapist. How about you?"

"Love her," I said.

He nodded and ambled away.

As for my relationship with Damian, we're making progress. We've gone running a couple of times already and, by tacit agreement, have never again spoken of the day I almost ruined three lives. He's working hard to be one of the best deputies Harrison County has, but I wonder how long it'll be before he decides to leave. He has "state trooper" written all over him.

Last week when Mark and I were at Doc's for dinner, we met Damian there with a beautiful woman, a lithe blonde with blue eyes that rival his for intensity. I couldn't help thinking what exquisite babies they'd make.

Stopping by our table he'd introduced us to Sarah before their server took them across to their table. Holding her chair for her, he met my gaze across the room. He shrugged and cocked one eyebrow, and I had to look away.

***

I stopped and gazed at my surroundings, turning in a complete circle. I had covered a fair distance while I'd been thinking, so I turned back toward Mark. I could see him propped on one elbow gazing my way.

The sun had disappeared, leaving behind a kaleidoscope of colors that took my breath away. I was reminded of that afternoon I'd come here to wrestle with the premonition about Richie – the last day I still had my brother.

The premonition, and my guilt later about not stopping what had happened to him, flashed through my mind, but with a force of will I pushed it back. Richie wouldn't want me to wallow in self-pity and remorse. Not my big brother. Looking to the sky again, I noticed a large patch of sky surrounded by the majesty of the multi-hued and many shaped clouds. The sky there was the exact shade of Richie's eyes.

Love you, Big Brother – Love you too, Sis. I heard the words in the sea breeze swirling gently around me, and I smiled a smile that made it to the center of my heart.